The Loved and the Lost

Book #3 of
The Verona Trilogy

Lory S. Kaufman

**fiction
studio
books**

The Fiction Studio
P.O. Box 4613
Stamford, CT 06907

Cover design and graphics by G.M. Landis Marketing

Print ISBN-13: 978-1-936558-53-7
E-book ISBN-13: 978-1-936558-54-4

Visit our website at www.fictionstudiobooks.com

First Printing: February 2013

Printed in The United States of America

Dedication

For my children;
Jessica, Luke and Daniel

Acknowledgements

Once again, I'd like to thank my main editor, Lou Aronica, for his steady hand in guiding me through the first two books in **The Verona Trilogy, *The Lens and the Looker*** and ***The Bronze and the Brimstone***. His skills and experience was doubly important in the final book, helping make sure it kept the same intensity, making sure the characters remained fresh while maturing, and that it all ended in a satisfying way. It could have all been crazy-making, but Lou said just the right things at the right time and I thank him. Also, much gratitude and admiration is again due to my daughter, Jessica, for doing the first line editing, and also Virginia Bartley, for doing a great job on the copyediting on the final book. Also, my readers, Joanne Blais, author Tom Taylor and teacher Stephanie Taylor were invaluable in making sure I had a smooth-reading story.

BOOK ONE
A Butterfly's Wings

Chapter 1

Hansum had been watching his younger self for about an hour when Arimus said,

"See, my boy, it's not so hard,
and after a while it doesn't seem so odd."

The elder from the 31st-century was right. When Hansum arrived in his own past and saw his ten-year-old self playing in the commons of his 24th-century home village, he got the oddest sensation. He felt queasy and dizzy. But as Arimus predicted, those sensations were soon replaced with a growing sense of what had made Hansum the young adult he now was.

"Self-knowledge, my boy, self-knowledge," Arimus explained.
"You will go back in time and discover the whys and wherefores
that made your present therefores."

The first lecture Hansum attended at the new History Camp Time Travel University was about students going back to see themselves during key childhood events. The aim was to rid these time-travel candidates of unresolved childhood issues.

"After all," the visiting A.I. professor from the 31st-century said, "on your travels through time, you will see many disturbing things, things that just don't happen in our modern worlds. Only strong, centered individuals will be able to accept and navigate through the less-than-civilized cultures of the past."

"But I've experienced hard stuff," Hansum said to Arimus after the class. "I survived the black plague, medieval battles with cannons, fights with poleaxes and swords, poisoners, lying, cheating and beatings. Can't I skip this part of the course and just get on with going back and saving Guilietta?"

"Calm, Hansum, be composed," Arimus urged.
"You must be of calm and sound mind
in the new History Camp Time Travel Corps.
Your experiences in the past could be
an advantage to your advancement
or speed your exit out its door.
And there is no need for haste.
The past isn't going anyplace."

So, Hansum practiced patience. Or at least the appearance of it. He became a model student, both academically, which surprised his family and past teachers, as well as physically. Those who aspired to be agents of History Camp's newly-formed Time Travel Council were put through an incredibly tough physical regimen. And now here he was with Arimus, on his first *official* trip back in time, observing his younger self.

The two hovered, slightly out of time phase, and thus unseen by his younger self. They watched in amusement as the ten-year-old Hansum once again stole out of his home without the knowledge of Charlene, his A.I. nanny. The older Hansum then heard his mentor chuckle.

"Oh my, look, my boy.
Approaching is a favorite scene of you.
Let's watch your younger self respond,
and see how actions of one day, lead to habits far beyond."

"Oh, for Gia sakes!" Even Hansum had to smile.

The younger version of himself, already standing aloof and self-assured, was now puffing out his chest and assuming an even more affected posture. That's because two girls, thirteen-year-old Annadella and fourteen-year-old Darma, were walking up the path toward him. Hansum, at a mere decade, was tall for his age, as tall as these girls and, as soon as they got to him, each kissed him on opposite cheeks. The older Hansum chuckled at an episode he remembered, but was now seeing from a more mature perspective. The younger Hansum slid an arm around each slim, girlish waist and the three headed off to a stand of trees. The girls giggled and Hansum, like a peacock, strutted regally along.

The older Hansum stared at the girls, especially precocious Darma. Hansum remembered her through his ten-year-old eyes as so much more developed and womanly. But here she was, a long-legged and skinny child. But her eyes still looked the same, dangerous and potent.

Hansum remembered what happened next and looked up the path toward home. There she was. Charlene, Hansum's A.I. nanny, was steaming into view. He watched this memory-come-to-life, as the yellow orb caught up to his boyhood self and used her energy field to separate him from the girls.

Annadella and Darma giggled, but because Hansum didn't act embarrassed about being pulled away by his nanny, it made him even more worthy of pursuit. He watched his boyish self lock gazes with Darma, and saw how her piercing eyes seemed to say to him, 'later'. He smiled his agreement and the edges of her lips went up. Their eyes remained locked as he was ushered away up the slate walkway.

The older Hansum and Arimus, out of phase and unseen, used the technical abilities of Arimus's A.I. cloak and began floating five feet from Charlene and the boy.

"I don't like that Darma's eyes," they heard Charlene say to the younger Hansum.

The older Hansum remembered what his younger self thought about that comment.

'I **do** like her eyes, and I'll be looking at them again tonight.'

Hansum perceived Arimus looking at him, but couldn't take his eyes off this vision from his past.

"Once your family knew their praises for your looks and talents
had gone to your head in the wrong way,
they modified their indulgences.
But their influence had flown.
Time would have to smooth the sharp edges
you had grown.
Time and . . . History Camp."

Hansum started to say something. He opened his mouth, paused, and then closed it again. He continued watching Charlene cajole and push his younger self up the walkway.

"Once again it's time to fly,"

The elder placed his hand on Hansum's shoulder

"May I?"

Hansum nodded.

A moment later they were falling through a whirling vortex. They didn't have to jump into this one. Instead, a large cylinder of the Sands of Time streamed up from the ground and enveloped them. They fell in a controlled fashion through heavy air, moving their arms to keep balanced. As this was such a short trip through time it took only a few seconds before Hansum felt his feet touch solid ground. Looking around, he saw was back in the study of the home Arimus used when visiting the 24th-century. Before them was a Mists of Time viewer, upon which was the scene they just left.

"I was such a little brat," Hansum said, chuckling. "I can't remember if Charlene caught me later that night."

"To this you can be witness. Observe."

Arimus waved a hand in front of his Mists of Time viewer. The image broke up into a blur of tiny cubes and then reformed. It showed the scene later that night when ten-year-old Hansum quietly got off his levitation mattress and stole out of the house. The older Hansum shook his head as he watched the foolishness. The door to Arimus's study opened.

"Ah, look who's here," Arimus said.
"Lincoln, welcome.
But Hansum, do you wish to share
the sight of this childish affair?"

"What? Oh, sure. It's kinda funny."

"Though laughter is not what does grace your face."

Lincoln entered and, standing next to Hansum, looked up at the hollow in the wall which housed the three-dimensional image. The youthful Hansum was once again sneaking out of his house and running, a big smile on his face, across the village commons toward the woods.

"Hey, you were a cute kid," Lincoln said. "What were you there, twelve?"

"Nah, ten."

"Hmmph," the diminutive, though now well-muscled, Lincoln answered.

As young Hansum entered the woods, a girl's hand shot out from behind a tree and grabbed him. It was Darma.

"Holy Gia!" Lincoln said. "No way she's ten."

"Thirteen," Hansum said.

"Hey there, Hansum," Darma said, taking a step very close to the younger boy.

"Hey, Darma," the relaxed, self-assured ten-year-old Hansum answered. He didn't look anxious to start his petting session with Darma, who very obviously was. She looked at Hansum with her wicked and flirtatious smile. She stepped closer, her lips a whisper's breath from his. But Hansum didn't move. He just stood there, smiling and staring right back at the teenage girl. She then giggled and kissed him hard, quickly pulling back. They both laughed and Darma took the very young Hansum by the hand and pulled him further in the woods.

"Perchance we've seen enough," Arimus suggested.

"Hey, it's just getting good," Lincoln teased.

"Just puppy love," Hansum said, turning and facing his friend.

"Oh, I think it probably got a little sportier that that," Lincoln chuckled. Hansum shrugged, and there was a hint of embarrassment in his demeanor. "Don't sweat it, old buddy," Lincoln said. "Just yesterday I got a load of my own behavior from just over a year ago. That sure put things in perspective."

"I'm sure I don't have to mention,
This is the whole of the exercise's intention," Arimus said.

"Where's Shamira?" Hansum asked. "I thought she was coming with you."

"She's here, but someone followed her like a puppy dog. A very big puppy dog. Man, it's like those two are attached at the hip. They went to the community garden, saying they wanted to see the bee hives being brought out for pollination, but I think that was just a whatchama-callit, a euphemism."

"Ah, yes, the sculptor, Kingsley," Arimus recalled.
"I've heard the good word."

"Yep," Lincoln answered.

"Another artist?" Hansum asked. "I thought Shamira would have learned her lesson with Starini. Where'd she meet this one?"

"Kingsley Fine is a sculptor in
the same History Camp art historian course
as our Shamira," Arimus said.
"You'll not find him of the same low character as Master Starini.
He's talented and a gentleman of the first order."

"And he's hot," Lincoln added.

"You think he's hot?" Hansum laughed.

"Don't get me wrong, *muchacho*. He doesn't do it for me that way. But let's say he makes you look average. Taller, bigger, and besides an artist, a real athlete. Champion rugby player, planet-wide. And he's a nice guy."

"Planet-wide rugby star?" Hansum questioned. "I follow rugby. I've never heard of him."

"Oh, you wouldn't have," Arimus said.
"This fellow is from the 26th-century.
Apparently they've become quite . . . friendly?"

"Is that what they call it in the 31st-century?" Lincoln asked.

"Well, I'm happy for Shamira and this Kingsley," Hansum said.

"And Lincoln, how goes the first month's introduction
to your mind-delving instruction?" Arimus enquired.

"Yeah. Who would have thought you'd have that sort of talent?" Hansum mused. "Any sort of talent, for that matter. But an actual mind-delver?"

"I'm a deep well that hides many secrets," Lincoln jested.

"Back in school, and despite his jesting,
it was a talent uncovered by our clandestine testing."

Mind-delving was an A.I.-enhanced ability now being used during History Camp missions. If people were to learn from the past, they must properly understand what was going on — not just the historical facts, like dates of when things happened and what was invented when, but how people in the past perceived the world intellectually, emotionally and spiritually, as well as their feelings of justification for doing things that just seemed wrong now, like killing other people. To understand that, you had to truly be in someone's head.

"Have you tried doing it, yet?" Hansum asked. "And have you been paired with your mentor?"

"My whole class had a group experience, where we hooked up with an old A.I. teacher. It was pretty zippy. So much clearer than implants. You get to see what's really in a person's mind. And I have been paired up with a mentor, but haven't met him yet. We're supposed to meet here, so Arimus can determine if we're a good match."

"Ah yes," Arimus said,
reaching for a tiny hand-blown bottle of glass from his robe.
"Although, you are misinformed as to the gender.
Of that, your mentor is of the more tender.
Here is **her** tear vessel."

The bottle fit in his palm.

"Lincoln, please give your greetings to Medeea."

"Hello Medeea," Lincoln said to the bottle. "Sorry for the misunderstanding."

Mind-delving was performed by a person drinking a liquid full of nano bits. The collection of atom-sized particles from one bottle contained the A.I. personality of a single entity, like the neurons in a brain or the bytes in a memory chip. A human needed only to ingest a drop or two of the liquid and they could telepathically communicate with the A.I., as well as any other person who consumed some of the same potion.

"Lincoln, off with the cap and bottoms up."
Arimus urged.

Lincoln took the stopper out and carefully poured a single drop into the hollow cap. He held it up in salute.

"And yet another new adventure begins," he said, winking at Hansum. He downed the miniscule drink.

Hansum watched Lincoln's gaze quickly change focus to somewhere in empty space.

The nano-bit-laden drop had no sooner splashed against Lincoln's palate when he felt the glow of warm light behind his eyes. His first response was to grimace, for even though he knew of the super-quick integration of mind-delver nano bits into their host's nervous system, feeling another intellect overlay your own consciousness was disturbing.

On his first experience, within a few seconds of the light forming behind his eyes, the image of a wizened old professor appeared in front of him. It happened the same way now, except for one striking difference. As Lincoln's new mentor appeared, Lincoln's jaw dropped.

"Oh dear," a female voice in his mind said. *"I hope we're not going to have a problem."*

"Uhhh . . . ." Lincoln managed, then, "Oh no. Sorry. My first mind-delver was Professor Bix. You're . . . you're . . ."

"Who's he talking to?" Hansum asked Arimus.

"His mind-delving mentor, Medeea," Arimus answered.
"She's visible and audible
only to those who have taken of her waters."

"Lincoln, what's she look like?" Hansum asked.

Lincoln was still in a daze. "Oh, she's . . ."

"Please don't describe me," Medeea said in Lincoln's mind. *"It's part of my culture to be seen only by humans of the same sex, unless they are my students, mentors, or until I'm married."*

"Married?" Lincoln repeated dreamily. The image he was staring at was definitely not old, a professor or male. This was a beautiful young woman of maybe fifteen years of age, with cream-colored skin, raven hair and fine features. Her tiny frame, which could not have stood taller than five feet, was draped in a shimmering silk toga.

"Lincoln?" Hansum asked. "Are you all right?"

"Wha? Oh yeah," Lincoln began. "Medeea . . . Medeea? Yeah, Medeea seems a bit shy and doesn't want to be described."

"I am only for you," she said.

Lincoln's mouth opened a little wider as he stared into the apparition's eyes.

"Lincoln?" Hansum asked again. Lincoln turned to Hansum, definitely dazed.

"You're acting like you've never seen a girl before," Medeea remarked.

"You're . . . you're . . ." Lincoln fumbled.

"You can think it and I shall hear. Remember, I am in your mind . . . and body."

"You . . . are . . ." Lincoln began to think, and then he blushed.

"You think I'm beautiful and are attracted to me, even though I'm just a sensory image," Medeea said. *"Oh, and that too? Naughty boy."* Lincoln turned a deep vermillion. *"It's not just what you think to say to me,"* Medeea spoke in his head. *"I can see **everything** in your brain. Wasn't that made clear in Professor Bix's class?"*

"Yes, but . . . but . . ." Lincoln said out loud.

"But what?" Hansum asked. Lincoln shot him a confused glance.

"But . . ." Lincoln was too shocked to continue.

"Now you are embarrassed because I can read your most intimate thoughts. Even your . . . fantasies. You think I'm sexy."

Lincoln flushed brightly again. He turned to Arimus and spoke pleadingly.

"What should I do? She can . . ."

"Yes, I know what's going on," Arimus said.
"To judge if you two are a good match,
I too had a sip of Medeea.
Lincoln, you must gain the belief that
being open about your most inner contemplations
brings you closer to self-contentment.
As I said to Hansum, the quest is self-knowledge."

"What's going on?" Hansum asked.

"In the same way you have to confront your own self,
so you'll a time traveler be as your prize,
so must Lincoln.
He's just had . . . a little surprise."

"You okay, pal?" Lincoln heard Hansum ask, but he didn't look at him. He kept staring at Medeea, and she at him. Her smile softened.

"*Excuse my teasing,*" she said in his head. "*You're having a stronger reaction than expected. I tell you what. I can limit my reading of your mind to the thoughts you intend to share. Till you trust me.*"

"You can do that?" he asked.

"Do what?" Hansum asked, till Arimus put his hand on his arm to keep him quiet.

Medeea walked up to Lincoln and looked up to him.

"*Yes, I can limit what I read of your mind. But if this is going to work, and we are to become a team, we must have complete trust. Do you think that eventually you'll be able to handle that?*"

"*Well,*" Lincoln thought, "*like Arimus says, it's all about self-knowledge and growing out of why I feel embarrassed . . . it's a good thing, right?*"

"*A very good thing,*" Medeea replied.

"*Ya know what?*" Lincoln thought, "*The heck with it. Take it all, Medeea.*" And then he spoke out loud again, and with a flourish, "My mind is your mind. No restrictions."

"Bravo!" Arimus said.

"Yippee," Medeea trilled.
"What is going on, please?" Hansum asked.

"Again, like you, Lincoln is taking great strides quickly.
Such strides, in fact, I think I may return to Medeea
what is Medeea."

Arimus took the hand-crafted bottle and removed the stopper. He put the rounded lip of the vessel just below his eye.

"All right, my dear. It was nice communing with you.
To each I believe the other may be found valuable,
and for this I deem you both compatible."

"Farewell," bid Medeea.
Arimus blinked and a single shimmering tear formed in the corner of one of his eyes. It crawled along his cheek and found the bottle's lip, crept into the opening and plopped back with the rest of itself. The millions of Medeea bits were now reunited.

"Now it is just you and me," Medeea said, taking a step closer to Lincoln.

"You're a short, little thing, aren't you?" Lincoln thought. *"Even shorter than me."*

Medeea put a hand on the top of her head, like she was measuring herself against him, and touched the tip of his nose. To Lincoln's amazement, he could feel it. He jumped and Medeea giggled.

"It's all in humans' heads," Medeea laughed.

"I guess you're right, Medeea. I guess you're right," Lincoln said out loud and laughing.

"Am I going to have to watch Lincoln talking to himself from now on?" Hansum asked Arimus.

"Perhaps," Arimus answered. "Sometimes
a mind-delver and A.I. mentor's relationship casts
a special bond that a lifetime lasts."

"Oh, we're going to have a special bond, all right. I can feel that." Medeea said, and she touched Lincoln on the tip of his nose again.

"That tickles," Lincoln said out loud.

"See?" Hansum said.

Chapter 2

Shamira and Kingsley finally made it from the community garden to Arimus's front door. Hand in hand, Shamira beamed as she looked up at her boyfriend and saw how he was smiling down at her.

"Lean down," she told him.

"Again you're telling me what to do?" he teased.

"Now," she laughed.

The big man, well over two meters tall, sighed and bent over till he was face to face with Shamira.

"Do your worst," he said, and she wrapped her arms around his neck and kissed him. He laughed as he put his massive arms around her and stood up, lifting her clear off the ground, still kissing.

"Mmmm. You still taste of the honey from the hive."

"And I still smart from that sting."

"If you're going to steal the nectar, you've got to pay the price."

"All day long," he answered, and they kissed again.

"Ah, young love," Arimus's voice said.
"From whatever century,
it always finds its mark."

Shamira and Kingsley looked and saw Arimus, Lincoln and Hansum standing in the doorway.

"Arimus, Hansum, it's good to see you," she said as Kingsley gently put her down. She immediately went and gave Hansum a long, meaningful hug. "Oh, Hansum, I really missed you."

"I see you two are still up to no good," Lincoln said to Kingsley. "Young love," he scoffed merrily. "Young lust, more like it."

"One day, young Lincoln," Kingsley said.

Lincoln focused into blank space and smiled. "You never know, Kingsley, old boy. You never know." And then he looked back at the much larger teen. "Kingsley, this is Arimus, our H.C. mentor. And this is Hansum."

"I've heard so much about both of you," Kingsley said, shaking hands with Arimus. "It's nice to finally meet, Elder."

"It's nice to meet you close up,
though I've seen you in action often,
live on the rugby pitch," Arimus said.
"And I've gazed upon your sculpture.
Sublime work of both the male and female forms
for one so young."

"You can't be an athlete your whole life and I just have to create. I love to chisel away at marble, exposing the form within."

"We're all so glad you and our Shamira found each other.
Two talents together entwined often invite
visits by inspiration to take each other to even greater heights."

"Thank you, Elder. And it's so fantastic to meet you, Hansum," Kingsley said, extending a hand. Hansum wore a melancholy smile as he took the larger youth's hand. It was like Kingsley and Shamira's happiness made him sad somehow.

"I'm very pleased for both of you." Hansum offered.

Kingsley held on to Hansum's hand, staring into his eyes. His smile turned into a sympathetic frown. He reached over with his second hand and grasped Hansum's arm.

"Hansum," he began gently. "I'm so sorry about Guilietta. I hear she was an amazing person, and Sham says they loved each other like sisters."

"Thank you, Kingsley," Hansum answered. "We all loved her." Hansum's eyes looked soft, but showed little emotion.

"The greetings done,
I must again assume the role of tutor," Arimus said,
"and conclude Hansum's first time-travelling day
with a test back in time,
for his progress to be weighed."

"Are you going back to Hansum's childhood again?" Lincoln asked.
"Apparently I found toilet training traumatic."
"Where are we going, Arimus?" Hansum asked.

"Again, this may be something you wish kept private,
for it is not a jest, but a serious test of
your mind's most vulnerable parts."

"Nah, that's fine. You can tell me here. They're family."

"Very good," Arimus replied.
"I am taking Hansum back to 14th-century Verona."

"What?" both Lincoln and Shamira said with surprise.
"Why?" Hansum asked.

"You are the one most affected by personal loss.
To assume a History Camp time traveler's mantle
we must immediately gauge the stresses
you can handle."

"You mean whether I can handle seeing Guilietta," Hansum said.

"Just so, my boy, of course.
Guilietta is the key as to whether we may set you free
to relive and, what's more,
possibly change what's gone before."

"Oh, dear Gia," Shamira said, wide-eyed. "You're going to see Guil."
"I wanna go," Lincoln blurted.
"Me too," Shamira added.

"But you have your own agendas.
Lincoln, you must practice your new art with Medeea
and Shamira, your studies of art."

Lincoln turned and talked to the empty space beside him.

"Could we practice mind-delving back then, Medeea? Medeea says yes."

"Who's he talking to?" Shamira asked.

"His mind-delving mentor," Hansum said. "Only he can see her."

"You're a mind-delver?" Kingsley asked. "Wow, you're not just a joker. I'm impressed."

"Arimus, can we come with you?" Lincoln asked seriously.

"It's not a problem logistically," Arimus told him.
"And all the souls there will seem unattended,
for out of phase we'll be suspended."

"Hansum, do you mind if we tag along?" Lincoln asked.

"No, not at all. It would be good to have you all there for support. I don't want to pretend it won't be a challenge for me."

"Then it's settled," Arimus replied.
"And of those last words I'm glad,
for none could but notice your attempts to hide
the broil of emotions that in you reside.
Well done, my son."

"Would it be all right if I came too?" Kingsley asked.

"I don't mind," Hansum said. "Elder Arimus?"

Arimus put up a finger to give him a minute, and then touched a sub-dermal node on his temple. He mumbled for a few seconds, pausing and tilting his head, as if receiving information. Then he nodded and smiled.

"Kingsley, your dean and A.I. have given permission.
I have no objection, if you accept my authority
as the only condition."

"Most assuredly, Elder Arimus," Kingsley said.

"My gosh, we're going to see everyone again," Shamira said. "I'm so excited. And Kingsley, we can go see all sorts of fantastic art and even watch some being made. I know every church and piece of art in Verona, and there's lots that hasn't survived that you'll see firsthand."

"An art historian's dream," Kingsley agreed. "That's why I joined."

"Very well, then," Arimus said.
"Some preparations first.
Give me a moment."

Arimus touched his temple again and closed his eyes, communicating with some unseen and possibly faraway person, maybe in a different time. The others continued chatting.

"I wonder who we can mind-delve back then," Lincoln thought aloud, and then he snapped his fingers. "Hey, how 'bout Ugilino?"

"Oh, dear Gia," Shamira laughed.

"I'm happy you guys are going to be there to help me through this," Hansum said softly.

"Your back's covered, pal," Lincoln replied, punching him playfully.

"Yes, we're all here for you, Hansum," Shamira agreed, giving him another hug.

"Okay, Medeea. I'll ask her," Lincoln said. "Shamira, Medeea wants me to ask you something privately," and he came close and whispered in her ear. Shamira's eyes lit up.

"Sure," Shamira said to the space near Lincoln. "Medeea, I'd love to be your friend."

Lincoln took out the small hand-crafted bottle from his pocket and carefully poured a drop into the stopper.

"Medeea says, as friends, there won't be any deep mind-delving. You two will be able to share only what you want to say. And guys, Med apologizes, but the only males allowed to see her are her students, her family and elders, until she is married." Kingsley gave Lincoln a wink. Shamira took the cap and downed the liquid.

"Wow," she said when Medeea came into her mind's eye. "You're beautiful."

"Thank you, Shamira. You too. You looked like a person I'd love as a friend. Guys are great, but ..."

"Very well," Arimus said, rejoining the conversation.
"The supplies have been sent to me. Gather round."

Arimus reached into his cloak and took out a bundle wrapped in a handkerchief. He unfolded it and revealed four biscuits.

"Now, there's something familiar," Lincoln observed.

"Besides giving back your ancient Italian speaking node,"
Arimus explained,
"these morsels of food are truly high tech.
They'll form two sub-dermals at the base of each neck.
The one on the left will whisk you back home to our base.
The one on the right will bring you in and out of phase.
These must only be used when a colleague is mired
in a situation where their circumstances are dire."

"So, left whisks us back home to the 24th-century and right brings us in and out of phase. But they're only to be used in emergencies," Hansum recapped.

"Exactly. But coming out of phase, this trip does not include,
so we shouldn't have a fear of something going rude."

Each took a biscuit and ate it. After a few seconds they could feel new implants developing at the bases of their necks.

"Now come and take a handful
of this cloak of mine.
It's about to call up a vortex of time."

Arimus raised a hand and a whirling vortex formed around the huddled group. Within seconds, thousands of bright yellow spheres, the Sands of Time, appeared out of nowhere. Larger, translucent spheres followed, careening off of each other and whizzing right through the people they encountered. The ground beneath them began to fade, the image below became like something you would see when standing on a frozen pond, peering down at a different world through clear, frozen ice. Except, instead of fish, there was the long tunnel of yellow spheres, a blur speeding off down to a single point, into infinity.

"All right, my children. Let us . . ."

And what they were standing on, disappeared.
They fell.

If Hansum was going to succeed and be allowed the chance of saving Guilietta and the della Cappas, there was so much he needed to
know about time travel. The other day he had asked Arimus a number
of questions; how their bodies knew to stay balanced in the vortex, if
they were going at the speed of light and, if they were traveling through
folded time/space, why did it seem that they were falling straight?
And how the heck could they stop so easily, alighting on the ground as
smoothly as you pleased?

> "All in due time.
> If you pass your initial tests,
> you will meet tutors from many futures.
> They will share such knowledge with you,
> although there is much they can't."

"If I pass my initial tests? You don't sound confident that I'll succeed," Hansum said, half joking.

> "My job is not to give false confidence and
> I would not be your mentor if I was not among your fans.
> For soon the time of your testing will come, and I say,
> if the whisper of a butterfly's wings unfurled
> can influence the winds and change the world,
> why not you?"

The image of the butterfly beating its wings and changing the
course of the winds, and thus history, stayed with Hansum. He thought
of it often.

'And my time of testing is here,' Hansum thought as they streaked
through the time tunnel, the deep rumble making crosstalk difficult.

Hansum looked around at the others, their arms out from their sides, all balancing themselves as they fell through time. Lincoln had a broad smile, like he was enjoying surfing a primo wave. Shamira was holding hands with the much larger Kingsley. The gentle giant was floating more gracefully than Hansum imagined someone his size could. Arimus too looked serene. Then he turned and looked straight at Hansum. He held a hand up, spreading all five fingers, then four, then three, then . . .

'I'm going to see Guilietta,' Hansum thought. Suddenly his mind literally could not form thoughts.

Two fingers, one finger.

Chapter 3

The last time Hansum saw the della Cappa home, it was an inferno. The Master, in his drunken grief over Guilietta's death, knocked over the brass oil lamp Hansum had given him, setting the straw floor, and then the house, on fire. Hansum and Lincoln tried to save the Master and Signora, but were dragged from the house by neighbors trying to arrest them. Within minutes the old structure was engulfed and flames were bursting through the second-floor bedroom window. This was where the dead Guilietta lay. In Hansum's last vision of the place, he and Lincoln were running for their lives. The butchers, Ugilino and Father Lurenzano were chasing them. Hansum had turned as he ran and had seen the pursuers silhouetted in the fireball of what had been his medieval family's home, now his wife's funeral pyre.

As Arimus's hand flashed one finger, Hansum closed his eyes. He had relived that terrible memory on a daily basis. And now, as he felt the quick deceleration, he feared what he would find when he opened them.

"We're here," he heard Arimus say.
"But remember, we're out of phase.
Insubstantial to everything but the ground,
including the residents' gaze."

Hansum opened his eyes, expecting to be standing in the street, but his first surprise was to find himself inside the house, not outside.

The interior of the della Cappa home was as it had been before being cleaned and aired — dull and dirty. It was also empty of people, except for the time travelers. The front door was ajar and a leaden light shone in through the crack. Yes, it had been a cloudy day when they first arrived. As Hansum's eyes adjusted to the dark, he could see the dust-covered table and the gray and black straw moldering on the ground. Looking up, he was surprised to see the ceiling lower than he remembered. He heard some chatter outside and then a shout from the second floor. The voices sounded familiar, but he couldn't make out what they were saying.

"Press your Italian implant node," Arimus reminded.

As soon as he understood what was being said, Hansum knew exactly when they had arrived. It was Ugilino speaking.

"I had to swallow the coins you gave us, to hide them. I tell you, Father, if he did not have me, the devil would have him now."

The "he" Ugilino was referring to came stomping down the steps from the second floor. Hansum turned and there was the Master, alive and as irascible as ever. Agistino bounded right through the five "out-of-phase" travelers, grabbed a piece of firewood from the hearth and shoved the front door open.

"Hey, you tell stories of your benefactor?" Agistino bellowed. Thwack!

"Come, let's to the outside," Arimus said.

The elder ushered everyone toward the door but, instead of opening it, they all just walked through the wall and into the street, one of the benefits of being suspended out of phase.

They were all now standing on the cobblestones, watching Agistino beat Ugilino on the head with the piece of wood. Ugilino was already down on all fours, bleeding profusely from his scalp.

"It's the Ug-miester!" Lincoln shouted joyfully. "Yikers, that was a lot of blood."

"Poor Ugi," Shamira said. She took a step right next to the Master, looking up at him and trying to touch his arm. Her hand went through. "I've missed my second father so."

"You three look different," Kingsley observed. "Younger, yes, and more . . . naïve. But you did go through a lot."

"You've no idea," Lincoln said.

"Actually, I do," Kingsley went on. "I watched your adventures on the Mists of Time Chronicles as a kid in school. It's still required viewing." The three 24th-century teens were surprised. "I had such a crush on Shamira as a ten-year-old."

"You *stupido*! You idiot!" Agistino was still shouting and beating Ugilino.

The Arimus from the past, in the guise of Father Aaron, grabbed the Master's arm. "Peace, my son. Peace. He is only answering what . . ."

The older teens listened and watched their younger selves experiencing their first taste of the 14th-century. The bleeding Ugilino crawled a safe distance and then got to his feet, a sheepish smile on his face. The Master was embarrassed and afraid the neighbors would learn how he had brought his family to such lowered circumstances. And then he exploded at Ugilino again when he suggested he was to become Agistino's son-in-law. Finally, to defuse the situation, Father Aaron sent Ugi to town to have his wound tended by the herbalist, Signora Baroni.

As their younger selves were being led into the house for the first time, Lincoln made an observation.

"Wow, I hadn't realized how sad the Master must have been to be so violent."

"Your new maturity has taken you out of yourself.
Now you can feel for others and
put your childhood on the shelf."

"Oh, Kingsley, I'm so excited," Shamira said. "We're going to see the Signora and Guil . . ." Shamira stopped and looked at Hansum. He looked apprehensive and hadn't said a word since they arrived. She took his hand. "Come on, Hansum. We'll do this together."

As they re-entered the house through the walls, the Master was speaking.

"See how the mighty master has fallen," he said to the man he knew as Father Aaron. "Behold what I have brought my family to."

'. . . again,' Hansum thought.

"Fallen, only to rise again," Arimus, as Father Aaron, answered. "How can one appreciate joy if he does not know misery?"

"Then I shall be a connoisseur of joy when God . . ."

Hansum and the others continued to watch as the familiar scene played out, Agistino finally trudging upstairs to fetch the Signora and Guilietta. Their younger selves then started the familiar conversation of why Ugilino stayed when the Master beat him all the time and how he expected to marry the Master's daughter. Hansum watched his younger self snicker, while replying, "This daughter must be a real dog too." It was all ironic now.

Then, the expected shouting and arguing started upstairs. The Signora screamed and cried about how she rued the day she married the Master, the Master shouted back, there was the crashing of something hitting the floor . . . and then Hansum heard it. Even though he knew it was coming, it pierced his heart and surprised him. It was Guilietta's gentle voice. "Hush mother, I beg you." He strained to hear what she whispered and found himself stepping closer to the steps. He was still holding hands with Shamira and looked over to see her smiling.

The bed creaked and there were heavy footsteps. Everybody downstairs, both in and out of phase, looked up. As before, the Signora's fat, slippered foot appeared, followed by the rest of her lumbering bulk. The stairs shook and the pudgy, grimacing face that challenged the world came into view. But this time, the older Hansum no longer saw an anonymous crazy woman. This was his loving and fragile mother-in-law, a woman who had the misfortune to be born in a time when science couldn't help her. The Master followed, frustrated by having to wait for his wife to slowly navigate the steps, just like Hansum had to wait . . . wait. He involuntarily caught his breath and squeezed Shamira's hand.

And then it appeared . . . Guilietta's slipper, and then her skirt, moving over light, lithe legs, her steps graceful and delicate. Then that hand appeared on the banister. The hand that had held his, wiped his tears, embraced him. And then, that face, shyly looking down to take each step, Guilietta looked only briefly at the others in the room. Her gaze passed right over to where her future husband stood out of phase. It was as if, momentarily, her warm brown eyes looked right at him. The older Hansum felt his free hand rise over his heart, to keep it from pounding out of his chest.

As the dialogue of greeting and then the talk of the Signora's hallucinatory illness began, Hansum finally pulled his gaze away to steal a look at the older Lincoln and Shamira. They too were now equally enthralled at seeing their former family. The older Lincoln's joking attitude had disappeared and his eyes were darting about, trying to drink it all in. He took a step toward the Signora and reached out his hand to touch her sleeve, but his hand moved right through her. He then turned and stared with surprise and disappointment at the sour look on his younger self's face.

Shamira was wide-eyed and held a hand to her mouth. There was a glistening in her eyes and, each time she blinked, a long tear ran down her face. Kingsley reached out a large hand and wiped one away with his thumb. Shamira turned to him, smiled, and then looked back at the tableau.

Hansum had learned during his grief counseling that once you've allowed your initial emotions to run their course, you have to decide what to do with them for the rest of your life. He had decided to smile when he wanted to, laugh when it just happened and cry when he needed. But now they all happened at once.

"Yes, they are alive!" he laughed, happy tears streaming down his face. He looked at Shamira and Lincoln, both in a similar state. "And we have a chance to keep them that way."

That's when Guilietta's soft pink lips moved to speak. Hansum watched his younger self staring at her, his mouth gaping, a ready home for flies. He smiled again, wiping away his now copious and joyful tears.

"Holy Father," Guilietta was saying, "my mother thinks she speaks with the Archangel Michael."

'That blessed voice,' Hansum thought, falling back into 14th-century mind think.

"Don't be daft!" the mother began to retort, and then Arimus, the one not dressed as a priest, held up a finger. He spun it in a circle and a ring of the Sands of Time appeared up from the floor. Then the floor itself disappeared and the time travelers were falling again. The first reunion with their family was over.

Chapter 4

Hansum and the others now found themselves gently landing in the middle of an almost empty Piazza Bra square. It was morning and the market was just being set up, men and women of all trades putting out their wares. A large cart, pulled by a behemoth of an ox, trudged straight toward them. Everyone but Arimus reflexively jumped out of its way. It walked right through him, as if he were a ghost.

"Why did you take us away from the della Cappas?" Hansum asked. "And why here?"

"Oh, I'd seen enough," Arimus said.
You passed the first test."

"Even though I cried?"

"Tears do not mean weakness.
You responded properly to an emotional scene.
The question is, when you are in a situation
that some cruel fate will allow,
will you act properly then, and hence,
that is why I have brought you to now."

"What market situation is that?" Hansum asked, peering about.

"Not where but when is your question, and why,
We're a month and a bit from when you arrived
to a situation that happened on the morning we've roamed.
So the others must leave us, we continue alone."

"I've spent a lot of time in this market," Shamira said to Kingsley. "Oh look, it's Master Spagnolli, the butcher," she said as their old neighbor passed by. Lincoln snarled.

"The last time I saw Master Spagnolli," Lincoln said smoldering, "he was chasing Hansum and me for a reward. Dead or alive."

"Young Lincoln,
view the people you find without judgment.
That is the way to learn,
if a delver's role is what you wish to earn."

Lincoln's face had an uncharacteristically serious grimace on it as he watched the butcher walk down the market. He turned and focused on the blank air.

"Yeah, I know he's right, Medeea," he said. "Don't worry. I'll be cool."

"This place is amazing," Kingsley said. "It's so different standing in the middle of something than watching it over a Mists of Time viewer. Oh, what spire does that church belong to?"

"That's Saint Fermo. Wait till you seen the wooden ceiling and all the statues in the cloisters."

"I just realized something," Lincoln chimed in. "A bit more than a month after we got here . . ."

"Oh, that's when . . ." Shamira began, when Arimus cut her off.

"Tut! I'll introduce it to Hansum in the manner I planned.
You others keep busy with your own business at hand.
But whether it's delving or art that gives you delight
Remember to follow protocol and keep out of sight."

"Ya know, I really do want to delve Ugilino," Lincoln said. "Arimus, can you tell us where to find him?"

Arimus put two fingers to his temple, tapping twice with two fingers and once with one.

"Ugilino's location?" he enquired. Then he chuckled.
"You'll find our old friend at the
Pesci Di Fetore tavern this morning."

"The Stinking Fish Tavern?" Lincoln laughed. "That hole in the wall?"

"Be non-judgmental and learn," Arimus repeated.
"Hansum, touch my cloak, please.
We shall not be moving through time,
But merely site transport."

Hansum, his face showing an almost successful imitation of confidence, reached out and grasped the fabric of Arimus's A.I. cloak.

"Everything will be fine," Shamira said supportively.

"Ciao, Brother," Lincoln said, pointing a finger at Hansum and winking. "Catch ya on the flip side."

"Where the heck do you get all these sayings?" Kingsley laughed.

"An elective I'm taking at school. Twentieth-century slang. I don't have a clue what 'flip side' refers to. It's just sounds funny."

"Great," said Shamira, playfully. "I can't wait to hear what else comes out of your mouth."

But Hansum wasn't in the frame of mind to laugh at this jest. To what situation was Arimus about to take him? He felt his mentor's hand on his arm. Since they were site transporting, there would be no vortex or Sands of Time. Hansum smiled weakly at his friends and then just winked out of sight.

Everything turned dark and Hansum's feet suddenly found themselves on an uneven surface. And it was quiet. The quiet of the dead. Then, in the distance, he heard the echoing clicks of footsteps on stone.

"Where are we?" Hansum asked. "Why is it so dark?"

"Take three steps forward and turn left," Arimus instructed.

Hansum did so and, as he turned, he saw the dim, flickering of torch lights approaching. As the lights brightened, he finally saw the walls on either side of him. He gasped. It was the honor guard of San Zeno's crypt, the skulls of hundreds of priests and monks, their hollow eye sockets staring out from their places of repose. He saw row upon row of them, all neatly worked into a wall of thigh and leg bones, stacked almost to shoulder height.

As the torches came closer he saw the bishop of San Zeno. In his vestments and holding his shepherd's crook, he led a double phalanx of priests who carried a stone ossuary. Behind them Hansum could see the mourners.

"This is your funeral," Hansum whispered to Arimus. "Father Aaron's funeral. There's me and the others at the end."

"Quite correct," Arimus said.

They stood watching as the procession came towards them.

"There's nothing from this event that will stress me," Hansum said, as his younger self went by. "I look really freaked . . ." Guilietta passed him and he paused. ". . . really freaked out. But that's because I was confused at the time. We thought you were dead and that we were stuck here for the rest of our lives."

"Patience," Arimus advised.

When the ceremony came to an end, they followed the procession out of the catacombs. As before, they came up to a cloudy day and, when Shamira started weeping, Hansum watched the other teens gather around to support her. Lincoln took her hand and the younger Hansum and Guilietta put their arms around her. The older Hansum could almost feel Guilietta's hand as it fell on top of his counterpart's.

As they walked along the side of the cathedral, on their way to the plaza at the front of the building, Hansum broke his silence.

"Arimus, if this situation is supposed to test whether I can control my emotions when I am back with Guilietta, I think I've passed that test twice now. Like you said before, it's all about self-knowledge. We were upset because we thought you dead, leaving us marooned. But now there's nothing here that . . ." Hansum stopped speaking as the procession came around to the front of San Zeno. He caught his breath and stared wide-eyed. Anger shot through his brain.

"What's that you're saying?"
Arimus enquired nonchalantly.

Hansum felt his ire rise and his eyes narrow. "Feltrino!" he growled.

Chapter 5

Shamira and Kingsley laughed as they watched Lincoln walk away through the market. He was sauntering, swaggering, as he chatted with his unseen companion.

"Young Lincoln seems to have a crush on his new friend," Kingsley said.

"Ya think?" Shamira answered. "Too bad it's all in his head."

"Really? How provincial. My mother warned me about 24th-century girls," he teased.

"I suppose it's common for humans and A.I.s to have relations in the 26th-century?"

"Well, it's not uncom . . . actually, I can't tell you about that right now."

Shamira knew there were things people from the future couldn't reveal and the rule was, when they said as much, you weren't supposed to ask further. "But as far as Lincoln is concerned, do you really think he's smitten?"

"He's got all the signs of young love."

"And you're an expert?" Shamira asked.

"Oh, I'm the doctor on that subject," he said good-naturedly.

Shamira stared at him, deciding how to respond. She chose to turn her nose up and began to stroll into the market. Kingsley smiled and stepped quickly to catch up to her. After a dozen steps, he finally brought Shamira's haughty charade to an end by sweeping her off her feet and kissing her hard. She kissed him back and, as they stood invisible to everyone in the market, three laughing ragamuffins ran right through them.

The two young lovers looked surprised, and then Kingsley's laugh boomed. "I like 24th-century girls, no matter what my mother says," he said, eye to eye with Shamira.

"I could be your great, great, great, great . . ." she paused, counting in her head. "Well, you know. Your grandmother."

"Wow. Another provincial attitude to put up with." Still smiling, he put her down. "Hey, do you mind if we go to Signori Square? I'd like to see the Scalari Tombs when there was only the one for Can Grande. I took a virtual 14th-century tour through there on my family's Mists of Time viewer, but you can't get the feeling of the actual size unless you stand right by it."

"Sure. It's this way," Shamira said. "So, you like the 14th-century so far?"

"Absolutely. I mean, look at all this," he said spreading his arms. Just then, the three rambunctious urchins screamed back past them again. "Look at all the joy and energy everybody has. It's so colorful and inspiring."

The three children then ran right into a man and knocked him to the ground. They fell on him, laughing and wiggling around.

"Scusa Signor, scusa," one of the boys giggled. The boys and man got up. The children disappeared into the crowd and the man dusted himself off, all the while chuckling. As his hand passed over his belt he looked up startled.

"You little thieves. You stole my purse. Hey, they stole my purse!" he shouted, though nobody in the market gave him any notice. He ran off in the direction the children had disappeared.

"Happens all the time," Shamira said.

"The little rapscallions," Kingsley laughed. They started walking, hand in hand. "Shamira, you're so lucky to have lived here for, what, six whole months? All the art and colorful characters. It must really show up in your painting. That's what I'm hoping time travel will do for me. Inspire my sculpture."

"Thinking I was trapped here for the rest of my life did change my perception, and therefore my art, I guess," Shamira said. "But it's not as romantic as you think. Those kids, for instance. Probably three out of five of their brothers and sisters didn't make it till age five. They're all illiterate and dirty. Much of the time they're hungry."

"But since that's the only life they know," Kingsley answered, "they don't know they're missing anything."

A wry smile came to her lips. "And you think *my* attitude is provincial?"

"What do you mean?" Kingsley asked.

Shamira looked at him through veiled eyes, a small smile on her face. "No," she finally said. "If I have to learn some things on my own, so can you."

"How cruel," he replied playfully. "How delightfully callous. But seriously, don't you think the worlds we live in are so safe that they're actually boring?"

"Oh, finding your life boring lately, are you?"

"A bit. Till you came along. But you know what I mean. Is there anything about this place you miss?"

They were passing a butcher's stall. There was one of Master Spagnoli's sons beheading and gutting chickens. Shamira smiled deviously to herself and stopped. She pulled up the sleeve of her blouse.

"See the scar here? I wasn't here a day when, right in this market, I was robbed and stabbed. So, it's not all the fun you think." She was setting him up but good. "But, yes," she said, looking around, "I actually do miss some things. Coming to the market everyday with Guilietta and shopping. And the people and these surroundings are colorful. I'll grant you that. I even miss the smell of the place."

"That's my point. Our worlds are so sanitized and homogenous," Kingsley said.

"Yeah. I guess you're right. You know, seeing all this makes me want to . . . get the smell of the place in my nose. They say the sense of smell evokes memories the most."

"But smell is one of the things we can't sense when we're out of phase."

"That is too bad. Hey, maybe I'll push my node and go native . . . just for a few moments."

"But Arimus said we couldn't, except for emergencies."

"You're right. Darn. Well, how about if I just open up a hole, a small opening that nobody here will see?"

Kingsley searched his mind for the "how-to memory" that came with any new node. "Oh, yeah, I have it. But Arimus said not to."

Shamira looked mockingly at Kingsley. "And here I thought you were adventurous. Don't you know that girls find boys who act a little dangerous, attractive? Twenty-fourth century girls, anyway."

"Really?"

"Well, you might be chicken to do this, but I say, what the heck." And with that she pressed one of the nodes at the base of her neck gently, four times quickly in succession. She held up her index finger and the tip of it began radiating a soft, pink glow. Then she drew a small circle in the air, which glowed pink for a second. There was a popping sound, like air rushing into a vacuum. The apprentice butcher seemed to hear it and looked over. Shamira quickly withdrew her hand and he went back to his work. He took the bowl of chicken guts he had just filled and dumped it into the barrel where Shamira was standing. Hundreds of flies rose and buzzed around. Shamira looked mischievously at Kingsley, raised her eyebrows and stuck her nose into the hole. As the tip of it came fully into the 14th-century, it too glowed pink for a second.

"Ah, Verona," Shamira pronounced as she took a deep breath. "I'd almost forgotten your sweet smells." The butcher looked over again, like he heard something odd, and Shamira pulled back. The man shrugged and went back to cutting off the head of another chicken and threw it in the barrel. "You going to try?" Shamira asked Kingsley.

"That fellow almost saw you."

"Well, okay then," she said. "If you're . . . chicken. I thought you really wanted to experience everything . . . to help your art." She stared challengingly at him, in the way only a young woman can challenge a young man. "I'll close up the portal . . ."

"No, wait a minute. I'll give it a try."

"You don't have to if you don't . . ."

"I want to."

"Well, okay then." She stood back and watched, poker-faced. She saw Kingsley tentatively come close to the portal, stare down at the barrel of guts, heads, wriggling maggots and buzzing flies, and at the butcher, who was now fiercely plucking feathers off the newly gutted bird. "Take a really deep breath," Shamira encouraged.

Kingsley stuck his nose and mouth through the hole. They shimmered pink and he sucked in a mighty breath. He froze, mid-inhalation. His eyes bulged and his look froze with surprise as the unfamiliar and exceeding foul smell of the butcher's stall blasted into his nose, lungs and eyes. He then involuntarily gasped another noxious inhalation. His eyes began watering, he wheezed and a 14th-century fly flew in his mouth. He gagged and spit the thing out.

Shamira doubled over laughing.

"Why you little . . ." Kingsley managed to choke out.

The butcher looked over just as Shamira snapped her fingers and the hole closed.

"Maybe that will inspire your sculpture," and she took off running down the square.

Kingsley chased after her, still gagging but laughing too.

Chapter 6

Lincoln continued to saunter through the town, walking slowly and staring at Medeea beside him. The shimmering blue corona around her body lit up her sharp, fine features and glistened off her jet black hair, while her light blue toga, draped over her shoulders, small breasts and hips, outlined a perfect young body. And as she walked, her legs caused the knee-length draping to billow forward and fall back against her thighs. This gave the intermittent suggestion of a limber form underneath.

"You remember I know what you're looking at and thinking, don't you?" Medeea asked.

"Yes, and I guess I really don't care anymore," Lincoln said, "or that, at least, it doesn't bother me."

"That's good. You've adapted quickly. But you also realize I'm not really walking beside you. I'm in your head and in that bottle in your pocket."

"Yes, I know that too."

"And you still don't care?"

"Nah. I figure I'll just go with it. And don't forget, I can read what you're thinking too. You like flirting and playing. And what's the harm? The worst case scenario is I'll learn something about girls."

"But I'm not a girl," she laughed, *"or at least, not a flesh and blood one."*

"You want to be."

"Wow, you really are a born mind-delver. There are not many who could straight off move around in another delver's consciousness without them knowing it, or cope with having another personality over-layered in their brain. Often, beginners get the two personalities mixed up and lose themselves."

"Who would have thought that my stubbornness would become an asset? I'm so happy I'm good at this."

"On the other hand, don't get ahead of yourself. This isn't hard mind-delving, Lincoln. This is just me, who can help keep our psyches

separate. But when you have someone else in your mind, someone who doesn't know you're in their head, their ego will instinctively try to take yours over."

"Yeah, that was part of one of the lectures I was at. But I hadn't appreciated the implications."

"That's what field excursions are for."

"Have you ever had a student who you thought would do well, but didn't?"

"Oh yes. Often. But it's not worth worrying about. You'll either be able to do it or you won't."

"Hmmm. Bummer. Do you think Ugilino is a good first choice to try this on?"

"From what I saw of, what did you call him, the Ug-miester? It looks like he's been through the wars. I scanned his eyes and he's living with multiple, long-term concussions and even survived a bout of meningitis. He must have one incredibly strong immune system. If you can delve him, you'll be able to delve anybody. But be prepared to feel what he feels physically as well as emotionally. Ah, we're almost there. It's just around this corner. Ready?"

"How'd you know where to find The Stinking Fish Tavern?"

"Hey, I can move around in your head without you knowing it too. I can access anything in that cute little noggin of yours. Boy, oh boy. This place really is a dump," she said as they arrived at their destination.

To call The Stinking Fish a "tavern" would be overstating it, even by 14th-century standards. It was really just a narrow space between two buildings, with a thatched roof and rotten wood walls at each end. The door was a single plank with leather hinges and no latch. There wasn't even a sign with words. Some previous owner had just painted a crude drawing of a fish skeleton above the door, and that must have been years earlier as it was mostly faded.

"I've never been inside," Lincoln said. "But why would he be there now? By this time of day, we'd all be working."

"It doesn't look like a Sabbath or feast day," Medeea said. *"And we're not sure of the new date Arimus just took us to. But he said this is where our boy is. Come on. Let's pay him a visit."*

Now Lincoln experienced another odd sensation. Medeea reached out and took his hand. Although he knew it was all in his head, he felt his fingers entwining with a girl's warm, smooth ones. It gave his whole body a thrill. He felt the warm dampness of her palm and, before he knew it, he felt his arm, and the rest of him, being pulled through the wall of the makeshift pub.

As Lincoln went from a bright summer day to the dark recesses of The Stinking Fish, it took time for his eyes to adjust. Then he heard a familiar snore, and then a fart.

"Ugilino," he announced. He squinted and finally saw him. Ugilino was passed out, sitting on the dirt floor, his back against the wall. His whole body was tilted precariously toward the floor, his head and neck stretched, his mouth agape. Drool had dried and crusted against his cheek. This made the only clean place on his face.

"I always wondered where Ugilino went at night," Lincoln commented. "But he'd always show up fresh at sunrise."

"It's well past sunrise now," Medeea said.

"And you've no idea what day we've been brought to?" Lincoln asked. Medeea shrugged.

The rough wooden door to the tavern opened and light flooded in. Lincoln squinted and so did Ugilino, though he only stopped snoring momentarily. He shuffled his body against the wall, a sleeper trying to get comfortable. He managed only to fall the rest of the way to the floor, his face now resting on his arm as a pillow.

"Oh, sweet Jesus, he's still here," a rough female voice said. She was a tall, buxom woman, square and strong-looking. She lifted her skirt and picked her way across a floor strewn with tankards, discarded ceramic bottles and the remnants of food. "Look at all this garbage to throw on the heap," she said to no one in particular. Then, standing over and peering down at Ugilino, she added, "And here's the biggest bit to toss. C'mon, my ugly amore, wake up." Ugilino just lay there, snoring. "Mio amore, wake up," she said more forcefully. The woman didn't look malevolent, but neither did she look like one to be pushed around. She nudged Ugilino with her foot. He stirred, but only managed another long, whining fart. The tavern keeper's face wrinkled. "Hey!" she shouted, giving the sleeper's head a nudge with her foot. "Go somewhere else and do that! Hey! Get up!" Now she kicked the arm out from under his head and his cheek fell into the dirt. "UGILINO," she shouted, "TIME TO GO!"

"Wha?" he groaned, struggling to lift his head and open his eyes.

"You drank too much. Time to go. Now! Rapidamente!"

"Gimme another drink," he croaked, holding his head with one hand while trying to lift himself with the other.

"I said leave, you asino," she said loudly. "You've got no more credit. You drank all I gave you for the goods you brung . . ." and then she spoke softly, in case someone would hear. "I just came from pawning it. Didn't get as much as . . ."

Just then Ugilino's bloodshot eyes went wide, darting about. "It's day?"

"Way past sunup. You're usually back home by now. Your master . . ."

That really got Ugilino moving, or at least trying to. "The Master, the Father . . ." He struggled to his knees and grimaced in excruciating pain. His body folded into a kneeling fetal position. "Ohi! I need a drink. Per favore, Signora, per favore." He began rocking back and forth, his head buried in his arms.

"If it will get you outta here." The tavern keeper went to a table and peered into a jumble of ceramic and wooden mugs, and then poured the grim and varied remnants of each into one large cup. She went to pick it up when Ugilino suddenly started to weep in an uncharacteristically high, pathetic voice.

"Oh, the Father, the Father, the Father. The Holy Father," he lamented, continuing to rock.

Incensed, the woman forgot the cup and stepped back toward Ugilino, scolding him.

"I wouldn't be worryin' about forgiveness from God right now, my boy. Worry that your master forgives you."

"No, not God," Ugilino whined in a high, tremulous cry. "Father Aaron. He's dead! He's dead!"

"Oh, mercy, I heard about that in the market today," the woman said, crossing herself. "Robbed, killed and eaten by wolves. He's being buried today."

"Dear Gia," Lincoln said. "That's what day it is. I always wondered why Ugilino didn't make it to the funeral. He was here, drunk."

"He never wanted nothin' from me," Ugi wailed. "He said he loved me," and he rocked and moaned and rocked, his snot-smeared face buried in the dirt.

"Lincoln, I don't know if mind-delving Ugi in this state is a good idea for a beginner," Medeea said. *"It could be dangerous."*

Lincoln watched Ugilino weep, his body wracked with heaving sobs.

"No, I want to," Lincoln answered. "Like you said, I'll either be able to do it or won't. No use wasting time not knowing."

"There's the impulsiveness that got you into so much trouble," Medeea said. Then she laughed. *"But if it's bad, I guess I can break your link with him."*

"But not right away," Lincoln insisted. "I survived a battle where men were blown to bits with cannons and hacked to death. Even if it's hard, give me a chance to deal with it. How can we get into him?"

"Quickly. Put some of me in that wine glass."

"I saw his poor body in the cathedral last night," Ugilino moaned from his prone position. "What was left, it was all maggoty." Now tears squirted from his eyes and it seemed his words had to squeeze past his blubbering lips. "They fit his leavings in a little stone box and they're buryin' it at San Zeno . . . an I'm missin' it," he wailed, and covered his head with his hands.

"Oh, my poor little duck," the woman said with uncommon sympathy. "Here, I'll get your drink." Ugilino grabbed her leg and held tight.

"He said he loved me," he cried pitifully.

"Hurry," Medeea urged.

The knowledge Lincoln needed instantly flooded from his implant to his consciousness. He tapped his node four times, thought what he wanted and his index finger started to glow pink. He bent over the cup, looked to make sure the woman or Ugi wasn't looking, and drew a circle over the mug. It glowed for a second, subsided, and a portal into the 14th-century was established.

"Let go of my leg and I'll get your drink," the woman scolded.

"Quickly. Pour me in," Medeea urged.

Lincoln fumbled for the vessel of tears, pulled off the stopper and quickly tipped the small bottle as he put it through the portal. Half a dozen drops, more than needed, splashed into the cup. He pulled his hand back just as the woman turned to see what made the sound. He snapped his fingers and the portal vanished.

There were still ripples in the cup when the tavern keeper peered in. She frowned and looked up to see if a bird or bat had defecated from the ceiling, a not-uncommon occurrence.

"Dear Gia, this wine is foul" Medeea winced. *"Five different types, saliva and mucus. Blachhhh!"*

The tavern keeper brought Ugi the cup.

"Here ya go, mio amore. Drink to the good friar. He's among the priests I've not heard a single bad word about."

Ugilino could barely force himself to sit up. When he seemed to find his balance he took the mug and stared at the woman with soulful eyes. "He . . ." Ugilino's hand quivered uncontrollably. Liquid flew from the vessel.

"There goes some of me," Medeea said.

The woman grabbed the cup and steadied it. "Drink up, mio amore. A nail to drive out a nail," she quoted local wisdom.

Ugilino brought the cup to his lips and slurped it down, some of it slopping onto his cheeks.

"Is that you too?" Lincoln asked with concern.

"The liquid on the cheeks is okay. My nano bits are just a few atoms big. I can make my way through his skin."

"How about the stuff on the floor?"

"Just like a person is made up of trillions of cells, I'm made up of trillions of nano bits. I can stand to lose a few million. I automatically reproduce replacements."

Lincoln blinked. Medeea's nano bits were now in their new host and sharing what they found. The first visions from Ugilino's mind came flashing into his. It was Lincoln's turn to wince and then grimace . . . hard.

"Iyee!" he said, closing his eyes and clenching his teeth.

"I'll turn it down," Medeea said.

"No," Lincoln said emphatically. "Give me a minute." He forced his eyes open, though he couldn't get rid of the scowl. "My Gia, the poor guy," he said. "The pain he's feeling. Is it all his hangover?"

"No, much of it is from the concussions he's had over the years," Medeea said. *"He doesn't even notice it anymore."*

Ugilino tried to stand but stumbled. He fell to his knees again. Lincoln had to fight for his own balance too.

"Ya can't stay here," the woman repeated.

"Gotta go to funeral," Ugilino managed to say, trying, but failing to stand. When a streak of pain screamed through his brain and he winced again, so did Lincoln.

"The professor said it's possible to separate a subject's pain from their thoughts," Lincoln managed to say. "I can see how it's possible . . ." He paused, breathing hard. "I mean, I can see how to do it. I just don't know if I can . . . now."

"You certainly are a natural," Medeea said. *"You'll pick this up quickly. If you still don't want me to turn off your connection to him, can I at least lessen **his** pain?"*

"You can do that?" Lincoln asked.

"Yes I can. Time travel rules, and my programming, don't allow me to cure him of his afflictions but, because you are involved, I can ease his discomfort."

"Okay," Lincoln said. "Do it."

Medeea smiled and cocked her head. Instantly Lincoln felt clarity coming over the part of his consciousness that was Ugilino. It was like an ocean wave washing debris off a sandy beach.

"Oh, that's better," Ugilino sighed. "That nail did drive out the other." He thought his morning drink had cured his previous night's indulgences. Now he could stand. "Can I have another? I've got my eye on some candlesticks an old Jew lady is keeping close to a window. She's forgettin' to lock the shutters at night."

"Well, okay. For the good priest's sake. But still bring me the candlesticks."

"I'll put a healthy thought in his head," Medeea thought.

"Professor Bix said thought transplantation of natives isn't allowed," Lincoln noted. Medeea shrugged, and then spun her finger in a circle a few times.

"Wait, Signora," Ugilino croaked. "Maybe acqua instead." The tavern woman looked a bit shocked. "For the Father's sake. He'd want me to. A big cup, per favore." Ugilino drank down the large cup of water and Medeea spun her finger again. "Another, per favore."

"He should hydrate," Medeea thought.

As Ugilino left the tavern, Lincoln got a double dose of bright sun light, his own and Ugilino's. Lincoln and Medeea strode quickly beside Ugilino, who was in a hurry to get to the funeral. Lincoln was finding it hard to mind-delve and walk quickly at the same time, and was thankful when Ugilino pulled into an alley to relieve himself. As the big oaf pulled down his braise and squatted, Lincoln peered at him, trying to follow his thoughts. Medeea was being quiet, although he could sense her in his mind. When Ugilino closed his eyes and frowned, Lincoln closed his too. That's when he dove fully into a very troubled medieval psyche.

Ugilino's mind was collage of visions, sounds, thoughts and emotions. Images were jumping in and out of his awareness, one causing another to pop up and then be superseded by another. The stream of consciousness flickered by so quickly that Lincoln had trouble processing it all. He took a deep breath and squeezed his eyes shut, steeling his focus and determined to sort the hodge-podge of information flooding into him.

He saw an image of a smiling Father Aaron, his eyes soft, and Ugilino's inner voice saying, "The Father never frowned when he spoke to me." Then Father Aaron was laughing and touching Ugilino's cheek. "God loves you, Ugilino, and I love you too."

'Why didn't I tell him I loved him too?' Ugilino thought. 'Why was I afraid? Now he's dead!' and the image of the maggot-filled ossuary flashed in his mind, the memory of the smell making both Ugilino and Lincoln want to retch.

Ugilino's mind went blank for a moment, and then Lincoln could feel Ugi trying to soothe himself by recalling a pleasant memory. Lincoln felt a small smile come to Ugilino's lips and an incredible fantasy emerged. It was Ugilino and Guilietta in an intimate embrace, her stroking his scarred face. But it didn't look quite like Ugilino. The nose was much less broken, there were fewer scars and even his teeth were white. This was how Ugilino saw himself. "I love you, Ugilino," Guilietta was saying, leaning forward to kiss his lips. Their bed covers drifted upward in the fantasy, as if angels had beat their wings and caused a breeze to make them float up to heaven, revealing their two naked bodies. Lincoln could feel Ugilino's face flush and his respiration increase.

'I must not think of these things on Father's Aaron's death day,' Ugilino thought, but he wanted, needed to think of something fine. Lincoln sensed a smile come to Ugi's face and saw an even more improved Ugilino standing next to a very jovial Master della Cappa, both of them standing with other tradesmen. He saw the Master with his large arm around Ugilino's shoulder, introducing him to the members of the Crystal Guild of Florence.

"He's a better lens maker than me," the Master bragged.

"Oh, you taught me everything I know, Master," Ugilino said modestly.

"I have a daughter to marry this fine young man," a guild member told Agistino.

"This one's already taken," the Master retorted with good humor. "Holy Cristo, this boy can polish lenses."

Suddenly Ugilino saw himself tumbling down the stairs at the house in Verona. This was a real memory. He had been carrying the lathe and tripped. As the image of him crashing to the floor flashed in both minds, Lincoln could feel the severe pain that had exploded in Ugi's back. Then the Master was looking down at him with disgust and another wave of shame spewed up from Ugilino's stomach, deluging his brain. The echoing sound of one of the orphans laughing at him added to the tumult. Now it was Lincoln who felt ashamed. The orphan who laughed hysterically was none other than himself.

Lincoln opened his eyes to see what Ugilino was doing. He was just squatting there, eyes open, a sad, blank look on his face.

Ugilino was now remembering the last time he saw Father Aaron. It was in the market and Signora Baroni had cleaned and salved the big cut the Master had given him. She told him to go wash the rest of himself at the fountain before going home and Ugilino, now scrubbed and still wet, was starting off home when he saw Father Aaron talking to the herbalist.

'The Father has come to pay Signora Baroni for fixin' my head,' he thought. 'The Father does not lie and cheat like everybody else. He does what he says he will do.' Ugilino remembered walking up to the Father and herbalist, catching them by surprise. Father Aaron was talking to the Signora, and when he got close, he could hear they were talking in some odd language. He remembered only one strange word from the conversation. ". . . Australia . . ."

Lincoln looked at Medeea. She raised her eyebrows, like she was asking Lincoln, "So, do you know what to do now?" Lincoln closed his eyes and went back into Ugi's mind. Remembering what he was told to do in a case like this at one of the lectures, he dove deeper into Ugilino's memory. Ugi might not be able to recall the conversation he had overheard, but it was there, buried. The neuron degradation might not make it possible for complete recovery, but it would be close.

'Ah, here it is.'

"So, Catherine. Have you been home to Australia lately?" Arimus had said in Earth Common.

"Yes, I was home a month with my family," Signora Baroni answered. "I just got back a few days ago."

Lincoln's eyes popped open again.

"Signora Baroni is a History Camp elder?" he asked Medeea.

Again, she shrugged. *"We'll talk of that later. Get back in there."*

Lincoln put a hand to his head and leapt back into Ugi's mind. Ugilino remembered the Father being surprised to see him as he turned. Then the priest smiled. Ugi, and thus Lincoln, watched Father Aaron looking at the different, freshly washed parts of Ugilino, touching his wet hair in a friendly fashion.

"What language was that you and the Signora spoke?" Ugilino asked.

"Oh, Herbalist Baroni and I are old friends," Arimus replied evasively, but still smiling.

"That's what I . . . like . . . about you Father. You are friends with everybody. You have no enemies," Ugilino had said, but now he cursed himself. 'Why did I say 'like'? I wanted to say 'love'. Why, why, why?'

That's when Father Aaron had given him the satchel of herbs to take home for his mistress. He told Ugi to tell everybody he would be back in a month. Then he put his arm around Ugilino and walked with him a bit. Lincoln felt the warm feeling Ugilino got from knowing that someone was not afraid to touch his ugly body.

"I'm going on a journey through the mountains, Ugilino," the Father had said. "Pray for me as I shall pray for you. Remember, in this world where we don't know when God will call us to him, believe in yourself and remember always, God loves you and . . . I love you."

Lincoln now knew Arimus was telling Ugilino this because he was going to fake his own death, and this would be the last time he could ever talk to the youth. Now that Lincoln could see into the mind of the boy, he felt sorry for him.

Lincoln felt a break in his subject's thoughts and opened his eyes again. Ugilino had finished his business and was standing up. A church bell began to peal in the distance. It rang eight times.

'I still might be able to get to the funeral,' Ugilino thought as he pulled up his braise and quickly tied the cord. He began to run, remembering Father Arimus asking him, "Pray for me," and tears began to run from Ugilino's eyes again. 'I didn't pray for the Father. If he had my prayers added to the others, maybe God would have kept him safe. It's my stupid fault he's dead!'

Lincoln again found it hard to walk and mind-delve simultaneously.

"You don't have to walk when you're out of phase," Medeea advised him, and she pointed a finger in the air. Immediately, Lincoln's feet rose a few inches off the ground and he began floating close to the weeping Ugilino. Ugilino ran and ran, all the while berating himself for being the murderer of the only person who had acted consistently kind to him. Lincoln even felt Ugilino's toes being stubbed on loose cobblestones and the burning of his lungs from pushing himself to get to the funeral. Finally, Lincoln couldn't take any more of the turmoil which was Ugilino's life. He was just about to disengage the delve when his mind went silent. He blinked and looked at Medeea who, despite speeding along, smiled at him like they were alone on a picnic.

"I disconnected you, sweetie," the A.I. said. "You did incredibly well for your first time." She reached up to Lincoln's face. He felt her caress it, and put a hand to his own face. His cheeks were wet with tears.

One hundred paces from Basilica San Zeno, Ugilino spied the funeral procession coming onto the concourse from the direction of the crypts. Ugi was indeed too late and Lincoln watched Ugilino collapse in the roadway and begin weeping. While not in his mind anymore, Lincoln could now empathize with this person he had previously considered as only a joke.

Standing around the steps of San Zeno, Lincoln saw his younger self with the rest of the family, as well as priests and monks. The Master and Guilietta were standing by the bishop, but there was also someone else there, someone the older Lincoln had very sour feelings about.

"Feltrino!"

The younger Lincoln, Hansum and Shamira were standing a few paces away with Father Lurenzano. Feltrino was bowing to the bishop, then the Master — and now Guilietta.

Chapter 7

Hansum couldn't help it. When he said Feltrino's name, he actually growled, and this in the middle of saying how he had his anger under control. While one part of his mind seethed with rage, another was frantically exhorting itself to cool down. Getting the History Camp Time Travel Council's permission to become a time traveler and help save Guilietta was at stake.

So, Hansum bit his lip and said nothing more. He watched Feltrino standing haughtily on the steps as the funeral procession finished its walk from the catacombs.

"I'm . . . I'm okay," Hansum said to Arimus, but when he followed his mentor's gaze and looked down at his own hands, he saw himself gripping and re-gripping them into fists.

"Yes, I see your level of self-control
is certainly something for you to extol."

Hansum didn't respond to the sarcasm. Instead, he looked straight ahead, trying to see the good things about the scene in front of him. The Master was being seen chatting in public with the bishop of San Zeno. That was good for business. He and Guilietta had just touched hands for the first time. That was a nice memory. He felt under more control.

Forcing a smile, Hansum watched Feltrino step forward and bow to the bishop and then the Master. As he knew he would, Feltrino turned his gaze on Guilietta, who lowered her eyes. The older Hansum watched his younger self step forward to intervene, only to be jerked back by Father Lurenzano. The older Hansum's fists began clenching and unclenching again.

"Relax, my boy, relax," Arimus said.

Hansum forced a counterfeit smile again. He saw Feltrino and the younger Hansum lock gazes, Feltrino reflexively putting a hand to his sword. Feltrino smirked, as if to say to an unworthy rival, "Watch this," and he leaned forward and whispered something in Guilietta's ear. Later, Guilietta doggedly refused to tell him what was said, maintaining girls had to bear the rude suggestions men made, and that it was to no good purpose to tell their male relatives. This could only cause yet more trouble. The older Hansum could now satisfy his curiosity. He stepped forward, his hands still clenched, to eavesdrop.

"When death is all around, it is beauty such as yours that whets my appetite for life," Feltrino whispered.

'Nothing so bad there,' Hansum thought. His fists relaxed.

Feltrino added, "Maybe later I shall borrow the key to the crypt and you and I can revisit your Father Aaron." Hansum had to lean in even closer, as the next bit was said even more quietly. "Have you ever made love in a crypt, or on a tomb? I should like to be the shroud covering your pretty body."

Hansum's hands instantly curled into claws, flying to wrap themselves around Feltrino's neck. "I'LL KILL YOU!" Hansum screamed. "I'LL KILL YOU!"

Hansum felt Arimus's hand on his shoulder.

"Detachment has flown, supplanted by hot prejudice.
An adjournment is in order."

Arimus snapped his fingers and they site transported away.

In a flash, Hansum felt a quiet, cool breeze blowing through his still-grasping fingers. He looked around and Arimus was still by his side, clutching his shoulder. Hansum looked out and there, spread beneath him, was the medieval city of Verona. Arimus had transported them to the walkway of the city wall. Hansum recognized where they were, just west of the San Zeno city gate. From this vantage point he could see the Basilica of San Zeno in the distance with people, very tiny now, in front of it.

"Yes, that's our younger selves still there," Arimus said.
"I thought you needed some physical distance to
enhance your objectivity."

Arimus let go of Hansum's shoulder and reached down, gently touching one of Hansum's wrists. Hansum looked down and found his hands were still like claws.

"Allow a balm of calm to sooth your mind.
It's yours to give."

Hansum forced his hands to relax and watched as they started shaking.

"Wow. I'm . . . I'm surprised how I'm responding," Hansum said. He frowned. "Maybe I won't be able to control . . . no. No, I can. I can do this. I must."

"I believe you can too."

"Arimus, do I . . ."

"Do you what?"

"Do I save Guil? Or if you won't tell me that, will I at least be able to control myself without blowing up at Feltrino or the Podesta or, or any of the others I know try to sabotage us?"

Arimus laughed.

"You've had enough lessons about time travel
to know I cannot tell you this.
Come, let us take in this beautiful day.
For although faux-death has placed sadness in the many hearts below,
the joyful sound of songbirds still trills to give us a show.
We shall walk and talk?"

Arimus began strolling down the raised walkway. Hansum bit his lip and caught up.

"Okay, I understand you can't tell me exactly what happens in my future. But wouldn't you be curious if you met yourself? Wouldn't you want to know things too?"

"Oh, but I have met my older self often,
and in the beginning I was the same.
But then I've seen too much go awry,
so I don't ask a future self
who, what, when or why."

Hansum's brow knit in concentration. "So, I haven't blown it yet? I won't be disqualified from my apprenticeship because I'm having a hard time controlling my emotions?"

"Not just yet," Arimus said with a smile.
"Understanding your feelings is part of the course.
So don't be afraid of feeling worse."

They were out of sight of San Zeno when Hansum looked around. The place seemed familiar.
"Okay. So, where will you take me now?"

Sometimes we move through time and space,
And sometimes only place.
This time I've saved you some stairs to climb,
so we've only to move through time."

"Man, usually I understand what you're saying, but . . ." Before Hansum could finish his sentence, the Sands of Time rushed up from the stone walkway, a cylindrical wall obliterating the scene in front of them. Just as fast, the vortex vanished, and high above him, the sun was replaced by the moon.

"It amazes me how the same scene can look
so different under Luna's candle
instead of Sol's beacon. *Bella*,"
Arimus said, admiring the view.

"We're still at the same place," Hansum observed, "but it's night." He looked out over the now moon-drenched countryside beyond the city walls. He leaned between two parapets, his eyes widening as he realized why he was here. He looked at Arimus again. "Is this the time I came here with . . ." He heard footsteps and turned to see his younger self and Guilietta strolling along the walkway toward them. They were holding hands, chatting animatedly, and then they'd steal looks at each other and giggle. As they walked by the two time travelers, Guilietta actually walked through Hansum. He felt a shiver as the two shared the same place in the universe again.

The newly-minted couple stopped and looked out over the city-side wall, pointing to the different buildings — Castle Vecchio, San Zeno, the Arena — and Hansum saw how, when he pointed to where their house should be, Guilietta leaned toward him, pressing her arm to his. Then Guilietta turned and moved to the other side of walkway, leaning on the wall between two parapets, gazing out over the countryside and up at the moon. Hansum watched his younger self move behind her, put his hands on her arms and gently, very gently, lean against her back.

"It's a beautiful view," Guilietta said.

"*Si*, and I have an especially beautiful view," both Hansums replied. He watched Guilietta smile, as if she now knew for sure she'd won this young man's attention. The older Hansum took a long breath, anticipating what he knew was to happen. A breeze came up and Guilietta shivered. "It's getting cold. We should get going . . ." his younger self said, then . . . the older Hansum watched as the one girl he'd truly loved spun around and kissed him. He watched himself startle in surprise and then rise to the happy task. And then the older Hansum did something that really surprised him. He looked down, so as not to intrude on his former self's intimacy, looking up only fleetingly, with great embarrassment. He felt a sadness in his chest. He looked over at Arimus, who was not looking at the first kisses either, but at his student.

"You're playing with me," Hansum said. "You're doing this on purpose."

"For sure on purpose, but not to play.
If it's a Time Traveler you're to be,
this is the only way."

"I always thought love was just an emotion, part evolutionary imperative, mixed in with cultural conditioning. And because I could do it, chase girls, I did it . . . for fun. But," Hansum looked up at the embracing couple, their bodies pressed together, "when I met Guilietta, I knew love was real, and that loving could be an expression of that, not just some biological act." He watched the two stop kissing and look into the other's eyes.

"We'd better get going," the younger Hansum said. "Your father is going to wonder," and the older and wiser Hansum watched the two walk hand in hand into the darkness.

"You bastard," he said very softly to Arimus. "Where now?" Arimus motioned toward the two, now a way down the wall. "But that's when . . . No. We don't have to . . ." Arimus raised his eyebrows, and then motioned again to follow them.

Hansum began walking slowly behind the couple, letting the distance between them grow. They were now visible only as silhouettes in the moonlight. He heard them giggling and saw them stop to kiss and pet. He wouldn't let himself be hurried by Arimus, insisting on keeping a discreet distance.

"I must remind you,
We cannot be detected."

"We're close enough," Hansum insisted. That's when they lost sight of them and Hansum knew they had come to the empty guard room. Hansum stopped.

"It's all right to see this tenderness."

"It's not necessary," Hansum said somewhat sternly, but Arimus just raised a finger, rotated it once in the air and they were instantly site transported in front of the open garderoom door. Hansum was positioned so he could not help but see inside. His eyes widened, filled with tears and he pulled himself away and stood, back against the cold brick wall of the guardhouse. "I . . . I've had enough," he said to Arimus.

"Perhaps one more event, to complete the test.
And when that's done, successful or not,
I'll let you rest."

And with that, Arimus took hold of Hansum's arm. He felt a slight tremble as the huge golden Sands of Time streaked up from the stone floor. Hansum closed his eyes and felt the walkway disappear under his feet as the roar of the vortex filled his ears.

Quiet. Birds chirping. Then the familiar distant sound of the busy market. Hansum felt Arimus let go of his sleeve and opened his eyes. They were standing on a quiet Verona street just off the Grande Urbe market. There was only one person visible, a man standing about twenty paces away with his back to them. He was peering around the corner of a building. Beside him was a common wagon, like a farmer from the market would use. There were two horses harnessed to it. A large wagon horse and a slighter, leaner horse. Hansum froze. Those animals looked familiar. He saw the sword at the person's waist.

> "Steady my boy, don't be queasy.
> Nobody said this would be easy."

"Feltrino!" Hansum hissed.

Chapter 8

Lincoln looked down at Ugilino weeping on the ground, despondent about missing Father Aaron's funeral. Having mind-delved Ugi, Lincoln truly knew how badly the fellow was hurting. He looked at a chipper Medeea.

"It's not that I don't feel sorry for the poor creature," she said. *"I maintain a professional detachment from my subjects, a skill that you must acquire."*

The crowd for Father Aaron's funeral began to dispurse and Lincoln watched his younger self, along with the rest of his Verona family, begin walking home. They would have to pass right by. Ugilino made to scuttle away, but then remained put, sitting dejectedly in their path.

"Ugi thinks the Master is going to scream at him," Medeea told Lincoln.

The family stopped when they got to Ugilino and Lincoln saw how his younger self, Shamira and Hansum were holding onto each other for dear life.

"We were confused and frightened," he told Medeea. "We didn't know if this was for real or what. Man, look at us. We're really freaked. I hardly remember stopping for Ugi."

Master della Cappa was standing over a visibly shaking Ugilino. Finally Ugi crawled over to the big man and lay prostrate at his feet, embracing one of his master's boots. Agistino reached down, his hand clenched in a fist. As it reached Ugilino's head, he hesitated, and then opened it up. He patted the prone youth. Ugilino raised his head, eyes full of tears.

"I got drunk, Master. I'm so sad."

"Get up," Agistino commanded, his stony face impossible to read. Ugilino rose, but lowered his eyes. "You saw where my drinking brought the family, Ugi," the Master said. Ugilino looked up at the Master. "You do not want to go down that path." He paused. "Come. Let us go to our home and pray for our benefactor. All of us."

The smallest of smiles came to Ugilino's face and the group continued to trudge home.

"Why did God take Father Aaron?" Ugi asked.

"I don't know," Agistino replied. "I guess it's as the priests say. It's a mystery."

"It's not a mystery," the Signora said out loud. "Archangel Michael said it's a test for us. Especially the orphans."

"That Archangel can kiss my. . ." Agistino began angrily, and then he stopped. They were almost out of earshot, but Lincoln heard the Master add, "Maybe he's right."

So, how did you enjoy your first serious mind-delving?" Medeea asked Lincoln.

"I don't know if the word enjoy is the right way to describe it."

"You did fabulously," Medeea assured him. *"I'm so proud of my new lov. . . lovely student. So, shall we follow Ugi and, after you've had a wee rest, try him again?"*

"Honestly? I learned a lot from being in his head, but I don't know if I can take any . . ."

Medeea put up a hand for silence. *"I'm getting a message from Arimus. He's moving Hansum a bit forward in time and wants us to stay in the same day as them. He's sending a vortex for us and we can continue to mind-delve there. Ready?"*

"I guess," Lincoln said.

"Hey," Medeea said brightly. *"We can check on Ugi there."*

"I told you . . ." Lincoln started, but Medeea was already throwing her arms and legs around Lincoln. He felt himself toppling backwards. He would have hit the cobblestones, but the ground disappeared and a rush of the Sands of Time zoomed up. Like two people falling through the sky without a parachute, Medeea and Lincoln tumbled backwards in slow summersaults, Lincoln's arms pinioned at his sides by the insubstantial Medeea.

"Yippee!" she shouted like a cowgirl, and then she broke out into uncontrolled giggles.

Lincoln felt himself stop abruptly. He was now lying on his back, his backside smarting. Medeea was on top of him, all cuddled up. She raised her head and looked at him.

"I thought you knew how to land on your feet, but this is more fun."

"You, you caught me by surprise," he said. "Ow, my butt." Then he looked around and saw he was in an alley he recognized. "Hey, we're just down the street by the Master's house. Who are they?" There were two men standing with their backs to them, peering around the corner towards the della Cappa house. Lincoln worked his way onto an elbow and stared. "Is that . . ." and then one of them pulled back into the alley and spoke.

"That girl has swift legs," Feltrino Gonzaga said, and he pulled on his companion's ear hard, yanking him back into the alley. It was Ugilino. *"Andiamo!"* Feltrino ordered, and the two quickly got on a wagon with two horses. "We'll get ahead of her at Piazza Bra," Feltrino said, snapping the reins. "You'll run and snatch the looker from her." Then they were out of earshot.

"Holy jumpin'," Lincoln said. "This is when Feltrino kidnapped Guilietta and stole a looker." Then he looked doubly shocked. "Jeepers. We didn't know Ugilino helped him. He came back to the house like nothin' happened."

"Well, do you want to see what else went on or just lie here with me on top of you?" She looked like she could agree to either proposition.

"But they're so far ahead," Lincoln said. Medeea looked up with a mischievous grin and pointed a finger. "Oh, you're going to transport us?" he said.

"Yes," she said roguishly. *"But in a different way. I call it . . . the magic carpet, without the carpet."*

"Do I have a choi . . ." Medeea spun her finger once and zip, still lying prone, they rose off the ground and streaked down the alley at a blurring speed, as if on a magic carpet.

After some dizzying twists and turns, even though they could go through objects and people without trouble, they finally came to a screeching halt in Piazza Bra. There was Ugilino, already out of the wagon and jumping up and down among a throng of shoulder-to-shoulder people, trying to get a glimpse of Guilietta in the crowd. Lincoln managed to stagger to his feet and look around. Medeea just levitated, fairy-like, landing on her feet and then snapped her fingers like maracas.

"Ole! The magic carpet."

"There she is," Ugilino said to himself and took off running through the crowd.

"Here we go again," Medeea thought. Lincoln lifted a few inches off the ground, thankfully standing this time, and started to zip alongside Ugilino. Ugi's face was at once frantic, scared and determined. He bounded forward, pushing people out of the way. Lincoln craned his neck to catch a glimpse of Guilietta. Medeea read his thoughts, smiled and levitated them higher. There was Guilietta, weaving in and out through the crowd, smiling and apologizing as she bumped into people. And there was the looker, slung over her shoulder in its fancy leather case. She thought she was bringing it to the palace, supposedly because of a note from Hansum, but really the note was from Feltrino and this was a trap.

When they entered the Urbe Market, Guilietta was only about 20 paces in front of Ugi. The crowd became so thick that everything came to a halt.

"It's the Bishop with a relic of San Zeno," Lincoln heard a man in the crowd say. Soldiers and monks had formed a barrier for a religious procession to make its way through public space, blocking further progress towards the palace. He saw Guilietta work her way to the front of the crowd, but then stop while the procession passed. Meanwhile, right next to Lincoln, Ugilino's panicky eyes darted about. He was trying to figure something out. Lincoln levitated down and stared hard at him.

"How could you do this?" he asked an unhearing Ugilino. "You grew up with her. She's your family. If I find out it was you that hurt her . . ." Then he saw that, although Ugilino looked determined, there was also something else on his face.

"Connect me to him," Lincoln said to Medeea. Medeea smiled and then blinked at Lincoln. The teen felt Ugilino's mind drop into his, again with the same tumult of pain, confusion and even the physical feeling of being out of breath. "Filter out everything but his linear thoughts," Lincoln demanded brusquely.

Medeeas eyebrows went up in mock surprise. *"Yes . . . Master,"* she replied. *"I like a man who can give orders."*

"Just do it . . . please."

'Oh, dear baby Jesus,' Ugilino was thinking, *'I don't like this at all. Merda, why did I agree to help? Feltrino better take me to Mantua as his squire when I get the looker. I hope Guilietta doesn't see me. C'mon you stupid, ugly bastardo! Just sneak up and yank the case and run.'*

Ugilino took a dirty blanket he was carrying and draped it over his head. He began pushing and sneaking through the crowd, each step bringing him closer to Guilietta. Soon he was only a few feet away. The priests holding the wood and leather trunk with religious relics were just passing Guil.

"The bones of San Zeno," a priest cried, "The bones of San Zeno," and the crowd cheered loudly.

'NOW, YOU UGLY! GRAB IT NOW!' Lincoln heard Ugilino think.

He snatched the looker case and pulled as hard as he could. Lincoln experienced Ugilino feeling Guilietta trying to hold on to the case's strap, pulling back and starting to scream. The scream turned into a shriek as she was yanked off her feet, forcing her to let go as she hit the ground. Lincoln stayed by Guilietta, watching Ugilino as he began to run. He saw him punch a man in the throat and stomp on another's foot. Guilietta continued shouting as she got to her feet and began chasing him, Lincoln and Medeea following close by.

'Don't follow me, Guil. Sweet baby Jesus, don't let her follow me.' Lincoln heard Ugi think as he ran.

Guilietta was now at the edge of the crowd and broke into an open run.

"Please, Guilietta, please don't," Lincoln urged, speaking close to her ear. He turned to Medeea. "Can't we stop her? If we stop her, won't that action cascade down to where . . ."

"Arimus tried to intervene at different places," Medeea replied, still calm. *"We A.I.s ran many simulations in an effort to help, including this, but it didn't work."*

"I'm sorry, Guil," Lincoln whispered to the running girl.

Ugilino disappeared around a corner and Guilietta followed.

Chapter 9

"Feltrino!" Hansum hissed. Seeing the same horses he remembered from his fight at the river, Hansum realized this must be when Feltrino kidnapped Guilietta. He looked over at Arimus. "You're making me watch **this** now? After all I've seen?"

"Do you wish to leave? The History Camp Time Travel Council may grant an extension for your testing or they may not. I cannot guarantee it."

"I suppose I can . . ." Hansum stopped when Ugilino came steaming around the corner, right into Feltrino's arms.

"What the . . ." Hansum blurted.

"Guilietta's chasing me," Ugilino gasped.

"Yes, I saw her," Feltrino smiled. "Stand back here."

And then everything seemed to move in slow motion for Hansum. Ugilino stepped behind Feltrino. Feltrino, still smiling, brought back his arm and clenched his fist. Then, even more slowly, Guilietta appeared from around the edge of the building. She was running, her hands grasping the fabric of her dress, lifting it from the ground. Her expression, a mix of determination and anger, couldn't hide her inherent beauty. And then . . .

"Guilietta! NO!" Hansum screamed.

The slow motion stopped and, with blinding speed, the moving mass of Guilietta's head slammed into the oppositely moving cannon blow of Feltrino's gloved fist. Guilietta crumpled to the ground.

Hansum felt himself lunging forward, "I'LL KILL YOU!" but Arimus grabbed him.

"Control yourself, Hansum," Arimus urged.
"Remember that Guilietta survives all this."

"I'LL KILL YOU, I'LL KILL YOU!" Hansum screamed. He was totally out of control and tearing himself away from his teacher. Arimus had hold of him only by the fabric of his sleeve.

Just then, Lincoln came skidding around the corner. He stopped right by Feltrino and Ugilino, staring down incredulously at the unconscious Guilietta. Lincoln turned as Arimus shouted his name.

"Lincoln, help me hold Hansum back. Quickly!"

Lincoln ran and grabbed Hansum around the chest, blocking his way.

"I've got to save Guil!" Hansum cried. Arimus got a better hold on the frantic youth and brought his mouth close to his student's ear.

"No, you mustn't," Arimus said forcefully.
"If you try, you'll most likely be forbidden from continuing your time travel training."

"I've got to save her now!" Hansum cried, moving his free arm to his neck.

"Lincoln," Medeea shouted urgently, "he's trying to touch his emergency node. If he gets to it, he'll slip into the 14th-century and you won't be able to stop..."

"Arimus, his emergency node!" Lincoln shouted, grabbing his friend's free arm as well as twisting his leg around Hansum's knee, as he had learned in his self-defense training. He pushed Hansum as hard as he could, bringing the bigger boy, and Arimus, to the ground.

"Hansum, you must not do this!"
Arimus shouted as they fell.

Lincoln now lay with his entire weight on Hansum's arm and chest, stopping him from reaching the emergency node.

"If we save her now," Hansum cried with frustration, "it changes everything."

"But she survives, she survives,"
Arimus pleaded in the boy's ear.
"Think of the long game. Control yourself. Learn."

"Ya," Lincoln added, trying to sound calm. "Remember, right now Shamira and I are running to the palace. Your younger self will be hunting Feltrino down with the Podesta's men soon." Hansum stopped struggling. He closed his eyes and took a deep breath.

"*Oh, well done, Lincoln,*" Medeea said proudly. She jumped on the pile of people and Lincoln felt her throw her arms around him and give him a big kiss, right on the mouth.

"Lincoln's words are wise," Arimus said.
"And by their tomorrow, Guilietta and you will be
in the bosom of the della Cappa family."

"Including us," Lincoln added.
Hansum opened his eyes and tried to look at the scene.
"Let me up," Hansum said, exhausted.

"Learn your control, as I know you can.
Accept the pain, it's part of the plan.
And know by accepting it, you may find a way
to save your wife on another day."

By now Feltrino had dumped the unconscious Guilietta into the back of the wagon and tossed a blanket over her.

"You didn't say nothin' about hurting her," Ugilino argued, grabbing Feltrino's shoulder. But for his trouble, Ugilino got Feltrino's sword stuck in his arm. Blood poured out. Then Feltrino started screaming and swearing at Ugilino, telling him to get lost.

"But I'm your squire. You said . . ." Feltrino slashed Ugilino's face with his dagger. The astonished Ugilino ran several steps away. Feltrino laughed and berated him.

"You, my squire? A filthy peasant like you? And such a fool? Oh, I might as well kill you now," he said, taking a menacing step forward. At that, Ugilino turned and ran. Feltrino did not follow, but laughed wildly and re-sheathed his weapons.

There was a stirring in the wagon. Feltrino turned around.

"What's this?" he said. A groggy Guilietta was pulling herself to a sitting position.

"Now Hansum, observe," Arimus said.
"You must not turn away."

Feltrino walked casually to the wagon and leaned an elbow on it, looking into Guilietta's bruised face. "You are made of more stout stuff than I supposed," Feltrino said in a complimentary fashion. "That punch has felled many men for much longer." It didn't look like Guilietta was aware of her surroundings yet. Feltrino put a hand on her chin and faced her toward him. "You're getting a pretty bruise, my little toy," he said, admiring the raised welt on her cheek.

Guilietta blinked several times and appeared to be gaining awareness. Finally, she recognized her captor and her eyes and mouth sprang open. Feltrino smiled and reached for her.

"Please, no!" she screamed, but the bully's strong hand grabbed her neck and squeezed. A pitiful gurgling came from Guilietta's throat.

"Steady, my boy, steady," Arimus warned.

Hansum closed his eyes, so as not to look.

"Open your eyes."

Hansum did.

Chapter 10

As Kingsley and Shamira dropped out of the whirling vortex, they stopped kissing. Their faces were bright and flushed.

"Now we can say we did it in a vortex," Kingsley laughed.

"Kissing, at least," Shamira smiled. "I wonder where everybody is?"

"Arimus said he was taking Hansum forward in time and wanted everyone to stay in the same timeframe. I guess he'll call when they're done. Do you think Hansum will have any problems? He was pretty emotional back at the house."

"It's perfectly natural for him to cry after seeing Guilietta close up again. Arimus said so. I'm sure he's standing tall and passing any test Arimus throws at him."

They were on one of the many winding narrow streets of medieval Verona.

"Do you recognize where we are?" Kingsley asked.

"I think we're just off the big market." She looked around, and then pointed to a church spire. "There's where we were a few minutes ago, San Fermo. How'd you enjoy that?"

"Immensely. Seeing all the art that didn't survive to our times and the workmen working on the ceiling . . . incredible." Then he looked around the street. "But one thing I hadn't appreciated was just how much trash there would be lying around. It's so dirty."

"There was little sanitation and no understanding of germs or microbes back then. It's lucky we're back out of phase, so you can't . . . smell anymore," she teased.

"You got me really good with that butcher's barrel."

"Sometimes people gotta learn the hard way," she smiled.

"Your point is taken," and Kingsley bent forward and kissed Shamira again. She kissed back.

"Kissing in the vortex is one thing," Shamira teased again. "But to kiss an unmarried woman in public is frowned upon here . . . if she's a respectable girl."

"But when we're out of phase, are we really technically kissing in the 14th-century?"

"That's rather a philosophical question."

"I've got an idea," Kingsley said, looking around. They were alone on the cobblestone streets. "I learned this from a very kissable girl." He took his finger and lightly tapped his right emergency node. The air around his finger crackled and blue sparks flew. He drew a circle in the air and a portal, the size of his face, appeared. "You now. C'mon. Just for a second. What's the harm?"

"Oh, you are a naughty boy," Shamira teased.

"Well, this girl was very naughty too, and from the 24th-century. They're the naughtiest."

Shamira touched her node and drew a circle. The air cracked and a portal opened. The hot, fetid air of the city rushed in. They both crinkled their noses and put their faces through the opening. They kissed again, giggling.

"I don't mind the smell, if it's to kiss you," Kingsley said.

Just then, the pounding of feet coming around the corner caused them to turn their heads. A stocky man tore towards them. His cheek was sliced and blood was streaming from it. He was holding his shoulder and his tunic was covered in red.

"Ugilino!" Shamira gasped.

He ran right through Kingsley and came screeching to a halt, like he just realized he saw something. He turned towards Shamira and Kingsley and his eyes bulged even more. From his perspective, all he could have seen were two faces suspended in air, staring straight at him. Shamira and Kingsley pulled back at the same instant. A blue spark snapped in the air and they were gone. Ugilino turned and kept running.

"Please, no!" a girl's voice screamed from the direction Ugilino had just come.

"That's Guilietta!" Shamira said. They didn't have long to run until they came around the corner and stopped quickly. There was the wagon with Feltrino, his hand on Guilietta's throat. Arimus and Lincoln were clutching at Hansum, not far away.

"Why aren't Arimus and the guys doing anything? DO SOMETHING!" Kingsley shouted. Arimus's head snapped around.

Feltrino laughed as he raised the arm holding Guilietta's neck, hoisting her up and almost strangling her.

"I must put you to sleep again, pretty one, until later," and Feltrino drew back his other arm, clenching his gloved fist. Guilietta winced and closed her eyes.

"My sister! Guilietta, no!" Shamira screamed in terror. Neither Feltrino nor her sister could hear, but Shamira could see the reaction her fear had on Kingsley. He looked at Shamira and, without hesitation, pushed hard on his emergency node. The air crackled with blue flames and, pop, he was totally in the 14th-century.

"No!" Arimus shouted.
"The time is wrong!
The girl is strong!"

Hansum looked around when he heard the change of tone in Arimus's voice. There was Kingsley, charging toward Feltrino. It was obvious he had come into phase with the 14th-century and couldn't hear Arimus.

Kingsley was big and he was fast. His participation in the ultra-physical sport of rugby had taught him how to run into a man with force and determination. He smashed into Feltrino and Guilietta flew back into the wagon as the two warriors crashed to the ground.

"Holy Gia, no!" Arimus exclaimed, the first look of panic Hansum had ever seen on his mentor's face. He spoke quickly to Hansum and Lincoln, even foregoing verse. "You must both help me. We grab Kingsley, keep Feltrino from getting his weapons, push Kingsley's and our emergency nodes, then retreat. No speaking, no fighting, no helping the girl. No matter what," Arimus ordered, a finger pointing right into Hansum's face. Then the finger went to Hansum's neck, pressing his emergency node and then pressing his own. "Lincoln, now." The air around the three cracked with a blue aura and sparks.

As they ran forward, Hansum could see Feltrino struggling ferociously under Kingsley's weight. The bigger man had the Gonzaga's arms clamped tight to his side, but Feltrino twisted unrelentingly. He was struggling to get one arm toward the dagger on his leg and the other to his sword. Hansum knew only too well of Feltrino's skill and lack of compunction to use either. The experienced Gonzaga knight bucked and elbowed under Kingsley's great bulk. He even twisted his neck and snapped his teeth, trying to find flesh.

"Get your hands off me, peasant!" Feltrino spat. "I'll kill you . . ."

When Arimus, Hansum and Lincoln reached the struggling men, Arimus clamped a hand on Kingsley's neck and put the other to his own. Hansum and Lincoln jumped with their full weight upon Kingsley, to keep Feltrino pinned.

"NOW BOYS! YOUR NODES! TOGETHER!" Arimus shouted.

Hansum was pushing his emergency node when he heard her voice.

"Romero?" It was Guilietta. He looked up and there she was, bruised and bloody, peering over the side of the wagon. He felt the electrical tingle of the others disappearing into the future, and saw the reflection of the blue sparks in Guilietta's eyes. His impossible dream of Guilietta once again looking into his eyes was happening. Then he felt Kingsley's bulk disappear.

"Guil . . ." Hansum began, when an elbow smashed into jaw and a fist hit his eye. He staggered back and fell to his hands and knees as Feltrino jumped to his feet, a dagger in one hand, a sword in the other. Static electricity was still arching off the cobblestones and the wagon.

"What the . . ." Feltrino began, looking around for his other assailants. His look of momentary confusion was replaced by a wry smile. "It's you, apprentice?" he asked. "All that fight from you? She must be good indeed to make you want to lose your life for her." He slashed the air twice with his sword. "But I cannot stay and chat. I have a looker to deliver."

Hansum surreptitiously reached down and grabbed a loose cobblestone in one hand and a handful of dry horse dung in the other. As Feltrino stepped toward him, Hansum flung the dung into his face, which made Feltrino wince and pause, and then Hansum lifted the heavy brick to attack. Screaming, he lunged at his enemy, but Feltrino whirled around, swinging his sword. The weapon's sharp edge met the brick, but first sliced clear through Hansum's thumb.

Hansum's battle cry transformed to one of intense pain. He crashed to one knee, and then quickly bounced up and ran several steps away, so as not to be an easy target. Feltrino whipped his sword through the air again.

"Run or die . . ." he began. That's when Guilietta flew out of the wagon and fell upon the Gonzaga prince. He deftly twisted his body, throwing her off. Guilietta's head and back slammed hard onto the street.

"Guilietta!" Hansum screamed, pulling her off the ground and holding her close. Blood poured out of him and over the half-conscious girl. Holding her face to his breast while he faced the menacing Feltrino, he began running clumsily backwards. "Just take the looker and go, Feltrino. Please!"

"Apprentice, you know I cannot leave you to tell," a jovial Feltrino chided. "But how gallant of you to sacrifice a digit for your master's child. Now you both shall sacrifice all," he said raising his sword and stepping forward.

"No, not Guil . . ." Hansum swung Guilietta around to protect her. He started to run, awkwardly lifting her off the ground. She looked up at him, a look of recognition finally reappearing.

"Front or back, means naught to me," he heard Feltrino say casually.

"We must run . . ." Hansum began, when a stabbing pain exploded into his back. He felt the push of something terrible rip through his chest. A searing pain exploded in his lungs and shot up to his brain. His mouth gaped open . . . and then there was silence. He stopped and looked down at Guilietta . . . the same open-mouthed expression was on her face, her terrified eyes staring back at him. Then, her whole body shuddered and her eyes rolled up into her head. She began falling back, but Hansum could not find the strength to catch her. As she keeled over backward, away from her helpless husband, Hansum saw blood gush from her breast. Hansum's dimming eyes followed Guilietta's slow motion fall to the ground. That's when he saw the foot of blood-drenched steel protruding from his own chest. His and her blood. His sight began to fade and the scene darkened.

"Two with one," he heard an echoing voice laugh. He felt a boot on his back, pushing him away and forward. Hansum was flying through space and time.

BOOK TWO
Of Today and Tomorrow

Chapter 1

"Okay, here's a piece of his heart," the human surgeon, Dr. Elizabeth Barnard said, holding a centimeter cube of red tissue with tweezers. "What do you think, Dr. Ramma?"

The A.I. surgeon levitated close and analyzed what she held. He was a potato-shaped orb with two eyes, one with a monocle over it. He also had two piggy ears and a piggy nose with a fringe of bristly mustache underneath. Below that was a very serious mouth.

"Analyzing," he said, squinting his monocular eye. "Yes, cleanly done, my dear. This will do just fine. Put it in the growth medium."

A younger male human doctor brought a two liter container of liquid forward and Elder Dr. Barnard put the tissue in. It slowly drifted to the bottom.

"Please put the beaker into the time chamber and set it for ninety days," Dr. Barnard ordered.

"Yes, mother," the younger doctor replied. The time chamber was a solid box with a simple screen on one face. He touched the display. "Ninety days, Zat." The line-drawing of a face appeared and spoke.

"Okie dokie. See you then, Doc Stan. You too, Elder Dr. Barnard." Then the image looked at the A.I. doctor. "See you in three months, Dad."

"Just get going, Zat," the A.I. surgeon said. The face on the time chamber frowned, and then winked away into thin air. "He talks too much," the A.I. father added.

"Well, spending months by himself in a time vortex can be boring," the younger doctor suggested.

"You're too hard on him, Ramma," Dr. Barnard observed. "You were so patient with me, even when I was a bratty kid. And with Stan too. Why not with your own son?"

"You two wanted to become doctors and worked hard. My boy said he wanted to, but didn't put in the effort."

"Not everyone has it in them to be what they want to be, let alone what their parent wants," Dr. Stan said. "And now that we have time travel, he's found his place as a good time-travel tissue-minder. And he's always been a good friend to me, ever since we were young."

"But he talks too . . ."

Zat reappeared. He was yawning. "It's done three days early," the tissue-minder reported. "Strong heart."

Apprentice-surgeon Dr. Stan opened Zat's lid and took out the beaker, which now contained a healthy, fist-sized heart with long veins and arteries growing from it. The two human and one A.I. came in for a close inspection.

"Beautiful," they said in unison.

His vision was a blur of white and black static, like he'd seen on an ancient cathode ray tube at the museum of technology. A childish stick drawing of a devil danced against the static background, all the while poking a trident towards him. This was accompanied by a horrible pins-and-needles feeling that buzzed in his brain and bubbled throughout his whole body. It made him want to throw up. Finally a familiar sound entered his mind. Words.

"I think he's waking up," a girl's voice said. "Kingsley, get Lincoln. Hansum? Hansum, can you hear me? It's Shamira."

As Hansum's eyes quivered open, Shamira's worried face appeared above him. He squinted against the hard light, and then Lincoln appeared, causing a shadow to block it.

"Hey, pal, welcome back," Lincoln was saying. He still seemed far away. "Can you hear me?"

"Wha? Where?" A look of terror sprung to his eyes. "Feltrino! Guilietta!" Hansum tried to lunge forward, but a glowing red energy field held him back.

"You're not supposed to move, sweetheart," Shamira said. "You have to stay still for a few days, but you're going to be just fine."

Hansum didn't answer. He just looked up at the ceiling.

"She's, she's dead again. I got her killed even earlier."

"It wasn't your fault," another voice said. Kingsley came into view, a hard look on his face. "It was my stupid actions that caused it. I didn't understand . . ."

"Don't say that," Shamira exclaimed. "Arimus told you . . ."

"I don't need someone to tell me when I make a mistake."

Hansum started to cough in distress.

"Cool it you two," Lincoln broke in.

"Finally, he's awake," came Arimus's voice.

The room went silent. Hansum lifted his head a little and saw the elder standing in the doorway. Arimus walked over and stood next to Hansum, ignoring the others. His face was serious, not kindly and non-judgmental as usual.

"Guil . . ." Hansum managed to say.

"She's fine now."

"How?"

The teens could tell Arimus was extremely angry. He didn't even try to rhyme his words.

"As soon as we got you back to the future,
I took the best time travel emergency team available
and went back to fix things.
We even tried taking Guilietta forward with us, but still couldn't.
But, for some reason, we were able to put things back
to before my blunder occurred.
Time and events proceed as before."

Hansum closed his eyes and relaxed. It felt like the whole weight of world had just been lifted off his chest.

"Thank you, Elder," he whispered. "Thank you."

"Elder, it wasn't your blunder," Kingsley said resolutely. "I'm the one . . ." Arimus cut him off.

"Yes, you are the one whose gross actions precipitated this.
You broke the cardinal interference rule
and disobeyed my instructions."

"But it's really my fault," Shamira argued. "I'm the one who got Kingsley to go into the 14th-century, as a tease at first. And when he saw how upset I was when Guil was being hurt . . ."

"All are guilty and all are punished,"
Arimus shouted. Actually shouted.

"But they shouldn't have revoked your time travel license," Lincoln said. "That's not fair."

"The elder holds responsibility for all his charges.
It is proper. But it's only temporary, till an inquest is held."

"Still, I'm sorry," Kingsley said, his head down.
"Me too," Shamira added.
"What I don't understand," Lincoln said, "is why an inquest? Isn't that when somebody's dead? Hansum was, sure, but . . ."

"Never mind that death was defeated,
An inquest's held so the pain's not repeated!"
Arimus put a hand to his temple to take a message.
"This is Arimus. Has the Council . . .
What? Really? When?
So it happened the same way.
How is the Council reacting?
Any indication of its duration being different?
I shall see you directly." Arimus tapped his temple.
"That was Talos, my A.I.
There's news."

"What's up?" Lincoln asked.

"A blackout period.
Time travel has stopped."

"Like we learned about in the lectures?" Shamira asked.

"Yes," Arimus answered.
"It's the first time your 24th-century Council has to deal with this.
Some members are feeling overwhelmed,
since they must also deal with their first disciplinary inquiry."

As the teens had learned in their basic classes, blackout periods in time travel are not an uncommon phenomenon. Once in a while, the ability to travel through time stops completely and, on other occasions, traveling from one specific time on Earth to another specific time is affected. Even the lecturers from the future admitted the scientists from their eras hadn't figured out the exact causes. Their best theory involved the fact that the location of Earth in space is constantly changing, not only around the sun, but also as the radial arm of the galaxy spun around its center. Added to the computation, the Milky Way is also moving, expanding outward from the universe's "big bang" center, along with several billion other galaxies. Since the time vortices have to go from where the Earth is to where the Earth was, or will be, as it cuts through the fabric of time/space, they frequently pass by large singularities, stars, black holes, etc. It was postulated that it's the gravitational influences of these that stopped time vortexes from passing by them, so they can't remain coherent. The majority of blackout periods were usually only seconds or minutes, a few hours, and still fewer, a day to a month long. But some blackout periods had been known to last for a year or two, the longest having been ten years.

"I am called in front of the Council again."

Without saying goodbye, Arimus snapped his fingers and site transported away in a blink.

Hansum fidgeted under his energy restraints.

"Thank Gia, Guilietta is okay," he began, and lifted his arm. Then he remembered his thumb and looked. Though swollen and with a white line around where it had been severed, his thumb was there. It had been reattached. With effort, he moved it.

"I had the fun of picking that thing up," Lincoln said. "They say it will work as good as new in a few days. Hey, just about now you're cutting Feltrino's thumb off back at that river. What's that, Medeea?" Lincoln asked, looking to the empty space at his side. "Yeah, a thumb for a thumb, she says. It's kind of ironic. And Medeea says all your new scars look very manly."

"*All* my scars?"

Shamira's hand went to touch Hansum's bare chest. The bed's force field buzzed red again, keeping her away.

"Sorry."

Hansum bent his head and looked. The last time he had seen his chest, Feltrino's blood-drenched sword was sticking out of it. Now there was about a ten centimeter white cross welded into his flesh. It reminded him of the cross cut into the large loaves of medieval bread.

"Our patient is awake," another voice at the door said. Dr. Barnard walked in with Dr. Ramma floating by her side. "Let's take a look at him."

The other teens moved back, allowing the doctors to flank Hansum. Ramma floated right up close to Hansum's eye, his monocle only millimeters away.

"Open your eye wide, please. Very good. Very good. Now, bare your chest," he said cocking his head and aiming his piggy ear at the big scar. "Your new heart sounds just wonderful," he said. "Better than before."

"N . . . new heart?"

"That's when Feltrino . . ." Shamira began.

Hansum winced and closed his eyes, using the hand with the reattached thumb to cover his face. "Yeah, I remember."

"I watched your adventure on the Mists of Time Chronicles this morning, young man," Dr. Barnard said. "Half the planet has by now, I'm sure. You four young people certainly do get into interesting dilemmas."

Lincoln looked to his side. "Five," he said.

"Excuse me?" Dr. Barnard asked. "Oh yes. The delver girl. Okay then, let us finish with our patient. All of you out."

As the two doctors chatted, probed and admired their work, Hansum thought hard, remembering what had gone on less than a day ago for him. Once again he had been unable to protect his wife. And now, what was worse, his entry into the History Camp Time Travel Corps was at risk, along with all the others, including Arimus. He wanted to cry. He wanted to shout. But, as the doctors tapped and scanned him, he remained silent. After what happened, he couldn't see how the History Camp Time Travel Council could possibly believe he had the right stuff to go on with his training.

'If I ever get a chance to redeem myself,' he thought, 'I will never again overreact or let my emotions cloud my judgment.' He closed his eyes and repeated this to himself three times.

"I said, does this hurt?" Dr. Barnard's voice asked. Hansum opened his eyes and looked at her intently. "I turned off your pain block and asked you if it hurts when I touch your thumb."

"No," Hansum answered dryly.

"Good. That's good," Elder Dr. Barnard said. Hansum looked over at the A.I. doctor, who was staring at him. Hansum stared back, matching his inscrutable gaze. They studied each other. "And we can get rid of that scarring for you right now, on your hand and your chest," Dr. Barnard added. "Nobody will know there's been a problem. Soon, not even you."

"No," Hansum said again, still staring at the A.I.

"I beg your pardon?" Dr. Barnard asked. "No what?"

"Leave the scars," he said. "I don't ever want to forget what happened."

Chapter 2

A month later Hansum was sitting cross-legged in long grass, his razor-sharp rapier across his lap. He was watching two African warriors battle one another. The female, a Mino warrior of the ancient West African Dahomey Kingdom, had a grass skirt, a lion-skin top and a wicker helmet shielding her eyes. She held a single, long flint-tipped spear and had the much taller Zulu warrior well under control, even though he had a deadly bronze stabbing spear in one hand and a murderous-looking fighting club in the other. But then, Hansum knew she could take care of herself. She had beaten him nine of the twelve times they had fought.

As the fight went on, Hansum looked around. The others were either cheering the combatants on or watching in silence. There was the young man with an English bastard sword, eagerly yelling encouragement. As well, an Asian-looking girl with a Chinese Dao sword was whistling a shrill note through her teeth and pumping her arm up and down. Finally there was the quiet, serious looking middle-aged man with a Roman short sword. He was eyeing the fight with his customary shrewd assessment.

Hansum looked up at the sky. It was a bright, almost cloudless day. The sun was now half way down in the west.

Since the time travel blackout, every time Hansum looked at the sun or moon he thought how their solar system was speeding through the universe and wondered what far away object was affecting their ability to jump from era to era. He also wondered whether it would clear up by the time he had the accreditations to be allowed to present a plan for going back to save Guilietta.

All this made him very anxious, but he kept his vow. "I will never again overreact or let my emotions cloud my judgment." He repeated this to himself several times a day. Until he accomplished his goal, he would only show calm determination and excel in everything he undertook.

His vow was quickly tested. Two days after his heart replacement operation, Hansum went home to recuperate the required three extra days. That didn't work. His parents were bad enough, hovering over him and trying to anticipate his every need, but Charlene was worse. The sight of the scars on his chest and thumb horrified his A.I. and she cried and rebuked him for wanting to go back for more. Even when his parents said they respected his choices, his father saying it was Hansum's life and his adventure, they still tried to talk him into resting for a few months.

At the exact hour when his five assigned days of recuperation were over, and he started to do pull-ups on the tree branch outside their home, Charlene flew out of the house and loudly insisted he stop. He asked her to please quiet down and let him be, but she continued to hover around him, her eyes wide and her orb quivering. His mind made up, he kissed Charlene, then his parents, and he called for a transport back to the History Camp Time Travel campus. And here he was.

"Alma's got him now," he heard the youth with the bastard sword shout.

He looked over and the Mino female warrior had knocked the wooden war club out of the Zulu's hand. The big Zulu seemed unnerved as the shorter and quicker female pressed her attack. She continually lunged and swung the blade of her six-foot spear against his shorter stabbing weapon. The Zulu was being backed up against a tree, and you could see the desperation in his face and on his long, taught arm muscles as he desperately tried to find a way to stay the onslaught.

He grunted and made a desperate defensive lunge . . . and that was his end. The female warrior's deadly-sharp spear came under his blade and caught him full in the liver.

"Zzwitt!" came a sound from where the spear met the Zulu's leopard-skin cape. A large ring of red formed.

"*Bumanda!*" he swore and the woman pulled her spear back and thrust it again, "Zzwitt!," right into her opponent's chest, knocking him off his feet and onto his back. The animal skin clothing was now more red than leopard-spotted.

"Competition over," the man with the Roman sword called. The other two watchers cheered loudly, jumping up and down and waving their weapons in the air. Hansum remained sitting on the ground, offering only a perfunctory clap.

"Next fight, Hansum and Bill," the older man announced.

"Me?" the boy with the bastard sword asked. "Against Hansum? Ah, come on, Journeyman Marcon. No way." Journeyman Marcon, the man with the Roman sword, scowled. "But he'll kill me dead in a minute," Bill complained.

"Yours is not to question why," the Asian girl cried in a sing-song voice.

"Yeah, yeah, but it's my big butt that's gonna die!" Bill paraphrased as he plodded out to where the Zulu was lying face up. "Get up Larry," he said kicking the downed lad. "My turn to bleed."

The large Zulu opened one eye. "Did ya have to make me land so hard, Alba? It hurts," he said struggling to his feet. As he did, the large blood stains on his leopard-skin clothing faded. As well, the animal skin transmuted back to the tunic and shorts of a time travel student. "Why doesn't my A.I. uniform protect my butt from hitting the ground when it can stop a sharp blade from splitting me in two?"

"Because A.I.s have weird senses of humor," Bill replied, taking a few feeble practice swings with his large, sharp weapon.

Alba plopped down by Hansum, letting her shoulder knock into his. Her dark skin was glistening with sweat and, as she pulled off her wicker helmet, long golden hair streamed over her shoulders. She looked at him, blue eyes gleaming.

"Nice fight, Alba. You win . . . again."

"You're getting better," she replied. "You've beaten me a few times."

"C'mon," the Asian girl called. "Let's get this over with. I'm hot and want to shower."

"You're up," Alba said.

Hansum got up and walked slowly into the middle of the tromped-down grass, their makeshift arena. Standing at ease, he raised his sword and let the hilt flip over the back of his hand. It executed a back flip, the blade spinning in a large circle and ending up back where it started, gripped in Hansum's hand. Hansum took up an *en garde* stance, leaning slightly forward on the balls of his feet and staring at his opponent with hard, cool eyes. Bill swallowed perceptibly and assumed the position too, but Hansum could see trepidation in the other young man's eyes.

"Fight on," Marcon called.

Hansum cocked his head, just a little, and let his free hand go casually to the top of his tunic. He pulled down the fabric and seemed to scratch an itch, but his real intention was to expose the top of his ugly scar. His opponent's eyes widened at the sight and Hansum needed only to shift his weight, moving his weight to his front foot. This was enough to unnerve the youth, and he took a full step back. His apprehension was such that he stumbled over his own feet, and then he didn't have a chance. With one quick lunge, Hansum pushed his opponent's heavier sword down, making a parry impossible. Its blade came into contact with the fabric just below his opponent's breastbone, still aimed slightly up to pierce into his heart. "Zwwitt," came the sound from the A.I. tunic as it stiffened to protect the human flesh below. It created another animated circle of oozing blood where it was hit, but Hansum wasn't finished. He pulled his blade back and spun his whole body around. In one quick, fluid motion, the razor-sharp sword was now coming full force at his startled opponent's neck. Hansum showed no quarter and watched Bill's terrified eyes bulge out at the sight of a solid steel blade coming to decapitate him.

"Zzzwitt!" the electrical crackle came as the blade hit the A.I.'s invisible protection field an inch from Bill's skin. But although the suit protected him from the sharp edge, it did allow the transfer of kinetic energy. The overmatched opponent was thrown off his feet, his sword went flying, and he landed in a heap on his side.

"Ya okay, Bill?" Hansum asked, still holding his sword to his victim's neck, the tunic discoloring as the animated circle of red widened.

Bill, wide-eyed and pale, nodded. Hansum gave a little grin and bent down to retrieve the fallen sword. That's when Bill pulled his dagger from its leg sheath and, attempting to redeem himself, tried to stab Hansum in the back. But Hansum sidestepped and came around with a crosscut, "Zzwitt," into Bill's right kidney. Hansum fell back into a roll, to get away from any last-ditch revenge strike, coming up, again in the en garde position.

"Are we done?" Hansum asked.

Bill nodded once.

"Fight over," Marcon announced.

Hansum allowed himself a small smile, but still kept the very business-like attitude he was now known for.

"Gather round," Marcon called, motioning the students to him. Besides Bill, there was Larry, the tall black boy, all long legs, arms and enormous, beautiful hands. He again held the Zulu stabbing spear in one hand and the war club in the other. Larry's ambition was to become a History Camp time traveler and go back and study his Zulu ancestors before white settlers arrived. Luckily his mixed genetics didn't show the European blood he had in him. Then there was the chastened Bill. He had only been in class for a few weeks and had never touched a sword before. His interest was to study the bureaucracy of Rome at its height, but he had to take a physical elective. He had been heard to say that sword fighting "seemed like a good idea at the time." He was questioning that now. Marta was a tiny woman, just over five feet tall, who looked mostly Asian. But she was actually a second cousin to Larry, sharing a grandmother three generations back. She just liked to fight, she said. And then there was Alba, tall and athletic, with long blonde hair, dark skin and blue eyes. Only seventeen, she'd had a myriad of swords in her hand for a decade. And she had already been back to the very early 18th-century, to see what it would take to become a Mino, a female warrior. With her hair shorn and dyed, and her irises temporarily recolored, Hansum was amazed how she looked in the Mists of Time Chronicle recordings. And she could use a European sword as well as a fighting spear. Alba had invited Hansum to get-togethers at her family's home a few times, but he had declined, saying he had to study. But then, Hansum had begged off all of his class's social gatherings.

"All right then," Marcon said. "Bill, besides your fight with Hansum being a mismatch, why were you so nervous? You knew your suit would protect you."

"When I saw that sharp edge coming at my neck, I just had a visceral reaction, I guess." Bill said this, reliving the moment with a shudder. "But what really freaked me out was Hansum's scar. When he touched it, I saw the Mists of Time Chronicle replay in my head, when Feltrino just stuck his blade," he winced, "right through him . . . and laughed. And to see the results of that in person, it gives me the willies."

"Thanks for being so forthcoming, Bill," Journeyman Marcon said, and then turned to Hansum. "I've noticed how you use that little scar trick before each bout." Hansum gave a little smile. "Very effective . . . on a beginner. Do you think it would have any effect on . . . Feltrino say?" The smile on Hansum's mouth reversed for a second, and then it reappeared.

"Probably not, sir," Hansum said. "It doesn't with Alba either."

"Exactly," Marcon said. "And I'd lose that other little thing you do, flipping your sword around. This is not a sporting class. There's no point system. We teach real combat. It's only blood and severed limbs that count. If any of you ever meet an opponent for real, you can't be worrying about big ugly scars, or any other bluffs. A show of fierceness is not only to scare you, it's a distraction. Half way through making a face, opponents may lunge," he said jabbing his sword right at Larry, catching him off guard and stabbing him hard in the gut. "Zzwwitt!" He doubled over, a new red circle appearing. "And then sometimes they may act calm, so you don't know what skills they have." He said this taking a few nonchalant steps, and then swung his blade at Alba. Her wrist and arm moved effortlessly to parry or deflect the blow. "Very good," he complimented.

"Thanks," she answered, and then winked at Hansum.

"So train, be calm and don't do anything stupid," Marcon continued. "Because to do otherwise is to die or end up like this . . ." he said moving to Hansum and pulling down the neck of his tunic, "Or this," he added, holding up his arm. Just below his wrist, Marcon sported his own scar. It completely encircled his forearm, where his wrist and hand had been reattached. "Training is teaching the body to do things automatically in emergencies. Okay, day after tomorrow we're going to History Camp Castle Mamure. We'll review fighting on parapets and long stone steps, plus review castle and fort design. Meet here at 05:00 and we'll transport there together."

"Zippidy," Larry exclaimed. "They've got a great Mussulman night club there!"

"Yea! Party time!" Marta cried, waving her blade.

Then all the other teens but one shouted. "All for one!" and they hoisted their weapons into a circle.

"Excuse me, sir," Hansum said calmly. "I won't be able join you. I've got to make myself available for that Time Travel Council hearing . . . about the incident. I'm taking a transport to the capital in about an hour."

"Oh man, you don't come to any of our parties," Marta complained.

"Yeah, but good luck," Bill said, putting out his hand. "We'll all be watching."

"It's just a small meeting with Council elders. No big deal," Hansum said.

Hansum felt a hand on his arm. He looked and saw Alba's long, shapely fingers grasping his bicep firmly. "But you're coming back to class, aren't you? I have to give you a chance to get even."

"I'll be back," Hansum said plainly.

"Okay then, everyone go home," Marcon said. "Hansum, can you spare a moment?"

"Of course, sir."

The teens disbursed, all wishing Hansum well. He saw that Alba stopped and stood about fifty meters away, in the shade of a tree. She turned and stared patiently.

"So, Hansum," Marcon started. "Because of your situation, I've been keeping an eye on you."

"It seems everyone has, sir."

"Yes, you've become a bit of a celebrity. But also, you've been working extremely hard both physically and academically. After going through what you have, the new heart and all, most people would take a break."

"Have there been any problems with my performance or attitude, sir?"

Marcon shook his head slowly, continuing to stare intently at Hansum. "On the contrary, your physical recovery is excellent. As for your emotions, you are always very . . . controlled." Hansum looked at him, steadily. "One curious thing has been noted, though."

"What's that, sir?"

"Your family. Apparently you've been avoiding them. Any reason?"

'Darned History Camp,' Hansum thought. 'Everyone and every part of the system talks to the others.' He had hoped they wouldn't notice.

"No sir. I haven't been avoiding them. I contact them every other day."

"But you've not visited for three weeks, even though they've asked you to."

How could Hansum tell him this was the one chink in his armor? He could keep it together and be the brave soldier, staying hyper-focused on his mission, if he didn't go home. He knew if he saw his family, he might fall apart.

"Sir, I've been very busy and home's several thousand kilometers away. I admit I have an agenda. I'm not hiding that. I want to be ready to go back as soon as the time travel blackout is over. Arimus has submitted my proposal for a mission to the Council and I'm hoping to hear their initial reaction when I'm in the capital at the inquest for . . . this," he said, touching his chest.

"Yes, I read your proposal. That's what prompted me to have this talk."

"You read the proposal? But it hasn't been made public yet."

"All your instructors have seen it, my boy. We have to know what's in that head of yours." Marcon tapped Hansum on the head with one of his thick fingers. It reminded Hansum of the time Baron da Pontremoli did that to him in the 14th-century.

"But this, this head, we have only one like it in all the land," the long-dead noble had told him.

Hansum kept his frustration from showing and just nodded.

"It's a very — unique plan," Marcon went on. "You can't blame your instructors for being concerned we're training you to do something like that."

Now Hansum gave his instructor one of his famous smiles.

"There's truly nothing to be concerned about, Journeyman Marcon. If this plan is approved and I succeed, you'll still have a Hansum to train." Marcon didn't answer, but just stared at him coldly. "Now, if you will excuse me, sir, I have a transport to catch." Hansum raised his sword to his chest in salute. Marcon nodded and returned the salute, giving Hansum leave to spin around and walk away. He moved at a good clip, since he had things to get done before the transport to Lincoln's arrived. As he strode along, he saw Alba still watching him.

"Hi," she said as he approached. "Mind if I walk with you?"

"Not at all, Alba," Hansum replied. With her long, muscular limbs, she had no trouble keeping up. Hansum noticed, not for the first time, how her hands were feminine but large, wonderful to look at and perfect for holding a sword.

"You were different today," she said to Hansum as they walked. "When you and I were paired against each other, I could feel it. Your attack was much stronger and your footwork actually threw me off what your upper body was going to do."

"But not for long," Hansum laughed. "You got through that quick enough with a move I hadn't seen before."

"Yes, I did get through, but you had seen that move before." Hansum stopped and turned towards her. Alba stopped too.

"Really. When?" he asked, smiling.

"If you don't mind me saying, it's a move I learned watching you in that fight by the river with Feltrino. When he was playing with you."

The smile left Hansum's face, but he quickly forced it back on. "I didn't know enough at the time to recognize moves and remember them. It was lucky I had Pan that day."

"Anyway," Alba continued. "I just want to say I enjoy working out with you." And then the young woman lifted her hand and put it on Hansum's chest. Hansum looked down at her long, beautiful hands, the tip of one finger resting on the scar peeking above his tunic. Her hands were shapely, but their dark skin and size were so different from the last woman who touched him tenderly like that, Guilietta. But Alba's touch did spark something in him, and his pectoral muscles twitched. When he looked up, he saw her bright blue eyes staring at him.

"Listen, Alba," he said, a plaintive look on his face. "I'm not ready for that."

"I know," Alba said softly. Everyone knew the tragical tale of Romero and Guilietta. "I guess I am ready, is all. Bad timing," she added.

"Maybe another time?" The young woman was looking for Hansum's response. He stayed silent. She looked down for a second and then up again. She smiled. "So, see you when you get back?" Hansum gave a small, non-committal nod. Then Alba leaned in, gave Hansum a kiss on the cheek, turned and walked away.

As Hansum watched her go, she looked back and lifted her sword, touching the hilt to her breast. Hansum saluted back, and then raised his arm in a wave. Alba laughed and bounded off in a run.

'She'll make a great Amazon,' Hansum thought, and then he remembered. "Time," and the image of a clock and his schedule popped into his head. "Oh boy, and I haven't even packed yet."

Chapter 3

Not being able to time travel had affected the school curriculum for all time travel apprentices, including Lincoln. It meant they received a lot more home study. Today Lincoln was supposed to be watching recordings of The Battle of Hastings and then compose a report showing all the participants' points of view; nobles, military leaders, soldiers and civilians. Instead, he was spending the afternoon bouncing up and down on his levitation mattress while looking out the large window of his bedroom.

Bouncing on his anti-gravity bed was something he had done this since childhood, and to the uninitiated it looked like he was bouncing on air. He claimed it helped him think, and he had a lot to think about just then.

"Family!" he mumbled miserably, as he bounced up and down, up and down.

Lincoln was so fixated he didn't notice Medeea appear beside him, smiling and bouncing at the same rhythm. She bounced right around in front of him, to get his attention. Still no response.

"Excuse me, sweetie. Can we talk?" she finally asked in his mind.

"Wha?" Lincoln said, finally realizing he had company. They continued bouncing in unison.

"Hello my darling," Medeea continued. *"We may not be able to time travel right now, but you were definitely in another world. A small energy credit for your thoughts?"*

"Oh, sorry Med," Lincoln said, bending his knees to stop bouncing. Medeea slowed down too, in perfect synchronization.

"What were you thinking so seriously about, bonbon?" Medeea asked.

"What, you don't know?"

"I can read whatever is in that beautiful head of yours but, remember, we decided to keep a bit of the mystery up and . . . not be completely familiar."

"Oh. Right. That's right. Yeah, yeah," he laughed nervously. "Well, I guess I should tell ya before Hansum and Shamira get here, but . . . it's just . . . well ya know . . ."

"What, dear heart?"

"My, uh, family, my Mom and my Nan . . ."

Medeea's smile broadened. *"Your mother and grandmother? You told them about me? Wonderful. Go on."*

"It's just that, my Nan, well . . . Holy Gia, just delve me," he said dispirited.

Medeea, raising a finger to her temple, took in Lincoln's complete mind. Her smile disappeared as the truth sunk in.

"Your grandmother doesn't like me?" she said, hurt showing in her eyes and exuding through every part of her mind. Feeling her disappointment, Lincoln tried to minimize it.

"She doesn't even know you, Medeea."

"Well, you and I have known each other for over a month now and you've just told her about me?"

"Nan doesn't live near here and I haven't seen her much since going to History Camp last year. I told my mom though, and my dad."

Medeea put two fingers to her temples, a gesture of delving further.

"You told them about me, as your delving mentor . . . but not 'about' me. And you 'think' they guessed the other stuff? Some boyfriend you are."

"Medeea, c'mon now. Fight fair. We've only been, you know, for a week now. I can't tell them everything that happens in my life right when it happens. Let me get more . . . comfortable with things."

Medeea seemed to relax a bit and smiled. *"It has only been a week, hasn't it? Hmmm. Well, maybe we shouldn't do this,"* she said touching his chest lightly and walking her fingers suggestively across it, *"until you feel more comfortable about . . . things."*

Lincoln shivered involuntarily and laughed. "Medeea."

"And maybe, maybe I shouldn't do this." Suddenly, Medeea had an arm around Lincoln's waist and he could feel the curves and softness of a young female body being pressed against his.

"Ohhhhhhhhh," he sighed. "That's . . . that's definitely not fighting fair."

"Oh, well then I definitely shouldn't do this," and her other hand was behind his neck, pulling his face close to hers. She stopped, his lips only a micron from hers. *"Or . . ."* Lincoln felt Medeea's whispering breath on his lips and then the soft fullness of them pressing on his. He closed his eyes and felt their two bodies pressing hard together. He responded, embracing and kissing her back, nestling his mouth on hers. *"I want you,"* she murmured into his mouth, and a shiver sparkled in him, right from the tips of their touching tongues and down to his . . .

"Lincoln?" he heard a male voice say. "What are you . . ."

Lincoln froze and his eyes sprung open. Medeea was still in his embrace, but as he moved his eyes to the door, he saw Hansum standing with a look of confusion on his face. Lincoln realized how it must look. As only Lincoln could see Medeea, to Hansum, Lincoln was miming hugging and kissing someone. Another rush raced through Lincoln's body, this time one of embarrassment. Lincoln pushed away from Medeea and fell back onto the bed. He bounced to his feet and stood there, looking back and forth between Hansum and Medeea, a confused look on his face.

"Sorry pal," Hansum said. "Your Mom and Nan said to just come up. If you're going to do those things, you should lock the . . ."

"I wasn't . . ." Lincoln began, and then looked over at Medeea.

"Lincoln, are you embarrassed by me?" Medeea asked.

"I'm, I'm sorry," he mumbled to Medeea, and then turned to Hansum. "I was just, I was just . . . Medeea and I . . ."

"Medeea and you?" At first Hansum looked surprised, but then a smile came to his face. "Medeea . . . and you?"

"Yes . . . no, not like that. She and I . . . we were just . . . she and I were just, uh . . ."

"Kissing?" Hansum suggested.

"Well, yes . . . no. Well . . . maybe . . . kinda . . . But how could we, no, not real . . ."

*"You **are** embarrassed by me,"* Medeea said, putting her hands on her hips.

Hansum took another step toward Lincoln, continuing his tease. "Maybe? Kinda?"

"Well, we were, but . . . but . . ." He was staring at Medeea, a look of terror on his face.

"Whoa, buddy, it's okay," Hansum said in a conciliatory fashion. "Sorry to tease. And sorry to you too, Medeea," he said, nodding to where he thought she must be. "Hey, I've walked a bit on the wild side a time or two. A great diversion and all part of growing . . ."

"He thinks I'm some kind of diversion?"

"Hansum, stop trying to help me!" Lincoln said. "I'm doing poorly enough on my own." Instead of speaking, he thought what he had to say next. *"I'm sorry, Medeea. I'm really confused. I'm very close to my Nan and, if she is showing some old-fashioned prejudices, I can't help it."*

"You'd let your family say mean things about your girlfriend and not say anything back to them? And I have to find out about it by mind-delving, while you've been happy enough to do . . . what we've been doing."

"Medeea, this is all happening so fast," Lincoln thought, perplexed. He stepped toward her, but she moved back, which made Lincoln stop. He looked over at Hansum, whose look was of a man watching a very odd pantomime.

"Hey, listen, you two. I'll go down and visit with your mom and Nan."

"You can tell him to stay," Medeea said, miffed. *"I'm the one leaving,"* and with that, she disappeared in a way that reminded Lincoln of his old friend Pan, exiting in a puff of holographic smoke.

"Medeea!" he called out loud, but it was too late. "Hold up, Hansum. You might as well stay. She's gone."

Hansum turned around. "Gone? Where can she go? I thought she was . . ."

"She's not just in me. She has other friends and students she can go visit."

"And just what is going on between you two?" Lincoln made a face, like he didn't know quite how to explain it. "Okay. Is it just fun or are you serious?" Hansum asked.

"I think I'm serious, but when Mom told my Nan about Medeea . . . Nan kinda didn't like it."

"Your Nan? The one I just met downstairs? She doesn't look like a bigot. She looks really nice."

"She is . . ." Lincoln looked around, and then whispered, "But Nan just asked about an hour ago . . . what about grandchildren?"

"She's worried about grandchildren? Wow. That is pretty bigoted. Wow," Hansum repeated unbelievingly. A woman's voice called up from downstairs.

"Boys, the rest of the guests will be here soon. Make sure you're ready."

"Thanks Mom," Lincoln called back. Then, looking back at Hansum he said, "How's it feel to be the guest of honor?"

"What are you talking about?" Hansum asked. "Your Mom just invited me to dinner."

"You and all our family three generations back and forward . . . and most of the village. Everyone wants to meet the guy in the Mists of Time Chronicle."

"Oh great," Hansum said. "That's happening everywhere I go. But how about you? You were there too . . . and you saved my butt more than once."

"And you mine. But I'm not the one with the new heart, or the one who had the love affair in front of millions of people. Bro, you're a star."

"That's stupid, man. I just want to go back and save Guil." Then he looked serious. "Our notoriety could cause problems. The transport here was full of people all gawking at me and wanting to talk. And your mom and Nan, they fawned all over me."

"Well, maybe we shouldn't fight it, but find a way to use it."

"We?"

"Of course, bro. Wherever you go, I'll be there. Guil's my family too, ya know."

Hansum came and gave Lincoln a hug. "You and Shamira are the only ones I really trust." Lincoln hugged back.

"Isn't that sweet," a deep voice said at the door.

"Shamira! Kingsley!" Hansum and Lincoln shouted at the same time. Now everyone was hugging.

"Oh, Hansum, you look fantastic," Shamira said. "Let me hear," she said putting her ear to his chest.

"I'm better than ever," he said thumping his chest. Then he tapped Kingsley on his chest. "Maybe I can take you on now."

Kingsley laughed heartily. "We'll see, big guy, we'll see."

"Your Mom and Nan are nice," Shamira said to Lincoln. "Where's Medeea?"

Lincoln sucked in some air and made a face. "Well, Medeea and I . . ."

"Hello Shamira," Medeea's voice said.

Lincoln spun around and there she was, smiling. She walked over to Shamira and they embraced.

"It's so good to see you," Shamira said.

"And you too."

"Wish I could say the same," Hansum added. "Hello again, Medeea, wherever you are."

"Hi, Medeea," Kingsely said.

"Hello boys," Medeea replied.

"Medeea says hello," Shamira informed them.

Medeea came and took Lincoln's arm like nothing had happened.

"How was your trip?" Hansum asked Kingsley.

"We had a private transport booked, but that was cancelled and we ended up travelling with a bunch of other people."

"That happened to me too," Hansum said. "And when we landed here, there were other transports all full of people. Oh, excuse me. There's a call," he said clicking his communications node. "Hello? Hey, hello Elder Arimus."

"Hansum, the news is good,"
Arimus said, his previous anger long gone.
"We must contact the others quickly."

"I'm at Lincoln's, Elder. Shamira and Kingsley are here too. I'll connect them and you can tell everyone." He pointed around the room, a gesture that told his implant to share the call.

"Greetings, all," Arimus said.
"There has been a most positive development that couldn't be better.
The Council has agreed to hear Hansum's proposal
for going back and saving Guillietta."

"That is very good news," Hansum agreed, allowing himself a smile.

"Hansum, well done," Kingsley said.

"Zippy!" Lincoln added.

There was a look of concern on Shamira's face.

"Does that mean they like the plan?" Hansum asked.

> "Your plan has captured thoughts and hearts
> from Mongolia to Mars.
> It's so bold, it left many counselors cold.
> But even those opposed, you've captured their imagination.
> And to the public you've become a world-wide sensation.
> So many people wish to hear the proposal with their own ears,
> it has turned into the largest public meeting
> in the past hundred years."

"But the meeting's scheduled to be in a room at the Council building," Shamira said.

> "Oh ho, but within minutes of an announcement saying
> Hansum would a rescue mission proposal be making,
> not one seat in the regular meeting room's gallery
> was left for the taking.
> Within the hour, there were thousands of requests,
> and the new choice of a venue had to be addressed."

"So . . . if it's not going to be at the Council builiding," a nervous Shamira asked, "where will we be?"

Arimus's visage smiled in each of the teen's heads.

> "The Arena of Today and Tomorrow."

"Oh . . . good . . . Gia!" Shamira groaned.

"But that amphitheater is only used four times a year for the planet's district representative meetings," Hansum said. "It's about 30,000 seats."

> "Exactly that many," Arimus said.
> "And now even this venue is over-subscribed.
> The rest must listen from
> the plateau above the amphitheater."

"Hey, we're standing room only," Lincoln chimed.

"So that's why so many people are travelling," Kingsley realized.

"They're all coming . . . to see us," a wide-eyed Shamira said.

"I must go now, my children.
See you all the day after tomorrow at the amphitheater.
Never fear. The universe is unfolding
in the only way it must. Tra la,"
and he was gone.

The teens were beginning to see the many sides of Arimus, the mentor, the diplomat, the compassionate elder, but also the tough task-master with a mercurial temper.

"Fantastic news," Lincoln said.

"Yeah," Shamira said weakly, leaning in and hugging Kingsley's arm.

"Are you nervous, Sham?" Kingsley asked, putting an arm around her.

"I . . . I don't like being the center of attention in a big group," she said.

"You? You're one of the most outgoing people I know," Lincoln said.

"In a small group, sure. But public speaking? It terrifies me."

"I'll be there with you, Shamira," Kingsley said, giving her a squeeze. "I'm used to being in front of crowds."

Medeea came and took Shamira's arm. *"We'll all be there with you,"* she assured her. Then the delver turned and smiled at Lincoln.

"I'm glad you came back, Medeea," he thought.

"I'm not going anywhere," she answered, still stroking Shamira's arm. *"Obviously you aren't ready for something serious, so we'll just cool it with the . . . you know what."*

"Thank you." And then Lincoln realized. *"No more you know what? Darn!"*

Just then the sound of people shouting and laughing could be heard outside. Going to Lincoln's large glassless bedroom window, they all looked down at the scene spreading before them. The small village of some sixty people was now thronging with hundreds. Many carried picnic baskets and seemed to be making their way to Lincoln's home.

"There they are!" a voice in the crowd shouted.

Suddenly the teenagers in the window felt a thousand eyes upon them. Applause broke out and soon there was cheering. The teens looked at each other, wondering what to do.

"Smile," Kingsley said, and as they did the cheering got louder. When Hansum gave a small wave, the cheer turned into a roar.

"You were right," Hansum said to Lincoln, keeping a smile on his face. "We'll have to find a way to use this."

"And if it's like this here," Lincoln said, smiling and waving like crazy, "What's it going to be at the amphitheater?"

"Good Gia!" he heard Shamira moan.

Chapter 4

Shamira tried to keep her worries about being the center of attention in large crowds to herself, but her insecurity still showed through. She said little and didn't smile. Wisely, Kingsley didn't try to ease her discomfort by talking about it. Instead he was constantly by her side, just as he was now, holding her hand as Talos, Arimus's A.I. assistant, site transported them with the others to the Arena for Today and Tomorrow.

Talos was interesting in that his orb was like an old hammered-bronze mask, severe and emotionless. However, his green and gold-flecked eyes were most human-like, sympathetic and moist. It appeared as if a flesh and blood person was looking out from behind a metal mask.

The A.I. site transported them to one of the few open spaces on the huge concourse in front of the pillared entrance to the amphitheater. The place was bustling with people making their way to one of the thirty thousand seats.

"A public gathering this large hasn't happened on the planet for over a century," Talos reminded them. "The people's interest has definitely been piqued by time travel and each of your personal stories."

"Great," Shamira whispered sarcastically.

Talos looked over at Shamira. "Are you ready for this, Mistress Shamira?"

"I just want to get it over with," she said, squeezing Kingsley's hand.

"And you, Master Hansum?"

"Let's get on with it."

"Master Lincoln?"

Lincoln yawned. "I'll be awake by the time we get there," and he winked at Medeea.

"And he was teasing us," Kingsley said to Shamira, who finally gave the faintest of smiles.

"Let us proceed," and Talos led the way towards the entrance.

A century and a half earlier, designers made use of a natural bowl shape on the southern slope of a plateau to carve out the Arena for Today and Tomorrow. Its entrance at the top was flanked by a long row of varied building columns and arches, homage to the architectural ingenuity of humankind through the ages. The majority were ancient originals; Minoan, Greek, Doric, Ionic, Corinthian, Egyptian, Romanesque, Tuscan and even wooden palisades. But there were also poured cement columns with rusted rebar sticking out from their tops.

As the group walked toward the entrance, the eyes of many fell upon them, most smiling and nodding in recognition. Hansum, Lincoln and Kingsley seemed to take this in their stride, but poor Shamira, so bold in her private life, continued not to like it one small bit. As they passed through the towering pillars at the entrance, the amphitheater spread out before them, thirty thousand seats carved in a semi-circle, the whole theatre raked at an extreme angle, surrounding a small stage at the bottom.

The place was designed so that, by mid-morning, natural sunlight flooded the stage area for the rest of the day. As it was open to the elements, when inclement weather prevailed, an invisible energy dome would protect the space. As this day was hot and sunny, the field only kept out biting insects, while allowing in pollinating creatures and birds, all of whom flitted about the many plants artfully worked in around the pillars and concourses. The energy dome also screened out harmful rays and moderated the temperature, to keep everyone comfortable.

As the group began down the hundred and fifty steps to the stage, Hansum turned to Talos.

"Any hint of what the inquest verdicts will be?"

"The human elders guard their decision well and, as I am A.I. and not from this time, I may not comment," Talos answered.

"And changes about this new thing?" Lincoln asked. "About Arimus and that really old guy from the future? Is it still in kerfuffle mode?"

The world's communications web was abuzz about a new wrinkle that happened over the past twenty-four hours.

"Nothing has changed as to the kerfuffle, as you call it, although antipathy was expected when we reminded the Council of what it had agreed to," Talos explained. "We made contact with 24th-century History Camp officials when your scientists first achieved time travel. However, before agreeing to show ourselves to the public, we negotiated certain terms. The two most important at the time were that we would only give advice to your novice Council when we thought it was making a catastrophic decision. As well, we could veto any decision it made, again for the same reason. They liked the idea that their 24th-century Council would make all its own decisions and your scientists would invent their own breakthroughs."

"Sounded reasonable at the time," Hansum smiled.

"And now some on the Council have their knickers in a knot," Lincoln laughed.

"Precisely," Talos confirmed. "Over a line item that none of them thought important at the time. That was, a Council or inquest only has jurisdiction to sanction people from their own era."

"It makes sense to me," Hansum said. "But, besides the Council, apparently half the planet's population resent the fact that our Council won't be able to rule about what Arimus was brought in front of it for, and that your time's one counselor can veto any decision the twelve members of our Council make."

"I don't think people would object so much," Lincoln laughed, "if that old guy from your time wasn't so weird. He doesn't even seem to know what's going on."

"We shall soon see," Talos said. "We shall soon see. Are you sure you're all right, Mistress?"

They were almost to the bottom and Shamira hadn't said a word the whole walk down. She just trod ghostlike down the stairs, holding Kingsley's hand and staring straight ahead.

"Do we have to sit right on the stage?" she asked, seeing how the stage was arranged.

"I'm afraid so, Mistress," Talos replied.

The stage was simply set. There was a long wooden table and thirteen chairs for the Council members behind it. Five chairs for the council "guests" were situated on the other side, set back a distance from the table and exposing the people sitting in them to the gaze of everyone in the audience. The Council Elders were already seated, all but one with an A.I. hovering behind or beside them. This was the elder from the future, Cassian Olama. He was at the extreme right of the table and, although he sat ramrod straight in his chair, he looked asleep. There were conflicting rumors, one saying that he had left his A.I. at home in the future, but some saying that not everybody from the 31st-century had their own artificial intelligence. This was a very odd notion for the 24th-century mind.

Arimus was already onstage, his back to the crowd, talking to the two members seated next to the sleeping Cassian. One was Elder Cynthia Barnes, the chairwoman of the Council. She had also been the administrator the teens met when they first arrived at History Camp Verona 1347, about a year earlier. Next to her was Elder Parmatheon Olama, the vice-chair. Because of the perfect acoustics of the place, Elder Parmatheon's voice could be heard.

"Arimus, I am still angry that you're not subject to this Council's judgment," he was saying. "You were the one responsible on this botched foray to the past."

This seemed to cause the elder from the 31st-century to stir. He sat up and rasped, "Now, Great-grandfather Parmatheon," the voice of the much older man wheezed, "It has been said . . . many times . . . that we from the future cannot explain . . . our decisions. Be assured . . . it is a law made . . . from long experience . . . that people from specific times . . . must be judged . . . by their own . . . people. And your generation . . . must make . . . its own . . . decisions."

"And yet you can veto our judgments," Elder Parmatheon challenged. But it didn't register. Elder Cassian had already fallen back to sleep.

The situation was made more comical by the fact that the elder from the future, Cassian Olama, was a direct descendant of the 24th-century Council vice-chair, Parmatheon Olama. Cassian, however, looked like a light skinned Asian with limp white hair, while his progenitor had dark skin and short, curly black hair. To top that, the biologically much older Cassian insisted on calling the other "great-grandfather," which seemed to rankle his forbearer.

As the teens got to the bottom of the amphitheater steps, the members of the Council and their A.I.s noticed them. Arimus turned around, smiling and unaffected by the controversy. He was obviously in diplomatic mode. He came over, hugged each teen in turn and escorted them to their seats. Talos by his side, Arimus then smiled at the Council and tapped his temple, which seemed to reawaken Elder Cassian with a start.

"Come to order!" old Cassian blurted as his head shot up. "Must I veto something?" Some in the crowd laughed. Others shook their heads.

The energy field over the amphitheater darkened, except for a rectangular shape facing the sun. The clear opening caused a shaft of sunlight to form over the Council and guests. Elder Cynthia Barnes's A.I. levitated to center stage. He was an orb the shape of a comical scarecrow head, complete with a ragged bowler hat, two mismatched button eyes and a stitched five-o'clock shadow.

With the clear voice of a practiced orator, the A.I.'s speech echoed through the amphitheater. And as he spoke, a ten-meter high holographic image of him appeared above the stage so everyone in the audience, and everyone forced to listen from outside the amphitheater, could see him clearly.

"This Council is called to order," the A.I. began. "Please take your seats, adjust your levitation cushions and please be quiet throughout the proceeding. We ask that no heckling or commentary be made by the public. Many unique things are happening. Please accept them with dignity. Thank you." He then floated back to his place by Elder Barnes' shoulder. The holographic image of the A.I. was replaced by one of the chairwoman.

"Thank you, Demos," the woman with tight dark curls and warm brown skin said. "Let's make short work of the first part of this meeting. That is, what punishment, if any, should be given to Shamira and Kingsley for not following instructions and opening themselves to the 14th-century? Also, we need to decide whether any wrongdoing was done on the part of Hansum, Lincoln or Elder Arimus on that same day. We'll start with Shamira and Kingsley." Shamira fidgeted in her seat and lowered her head. Kingsley placed a large hand over hers and looked attentive.

"There can be no question that Shamira and Kingsley did contravene their instructions and made an opening directly to the 14th-century," Elder Barnes continued. As she said this, her holographic projection was replaced by the frozen image of Shamira and Kingsley just before Ugilino came running around the corner. Both their faces were peeking out of small blue-rimmed circles in the air. The image then animated and they kissed. The image froze again. A young female voice called from somewhere in the crowd.

"It was only for a kiss."

"Long live love," another shouted. Thousands muttered their approvals.

"Quiet, please," came Demos's voice.

The image of Shamira and Kingsley reanimated. It showed them turn as the bloodied Ugilino came into view and ran right through them. The image cross-dissolved into the frozen scene of the wagon, showing Feltrino holding up Guilietta by the neck and the hulking Kingsley, running, head down, arms out, ready to plow into the Gonzaga prince.

"Kingsley," Elder Barnes began. "Your transgression was greater. Not only did you disobey Elder Arimus's instruction by making a small temporal opening, you actually came full-bodied into the past and attacked a person from the 14th-century. This is a gross contravention of time travel protocol."

As Elder Barnes spoke, the frozen image started moving at quarter speed, turning the attack on Feltrino into a slow-motion ballet, with Kingsley's massive arms and legs pumping, his bent shoulder in perfect position to take Feltrino down. The crowd went eerily silent as Feltrino was slammed into. His arms slowly flailed outward, causing him to lose his grip on Guilietta. She seemed to float through the air and disappear into the wagon. Kingsley's arms wrapped around Feltrino, pinioning his arms, and then he fell upon him with all his weight. They bounced several times on the hard cobblestones. As the image faded, the silence was broken.

"He did it for love!" a woman's voice shouted from the crowd.

"Feltrino deserved it," another screamed, which was followed by the sound of tens of thousands of feet stomping in agreement.

"Please. Please. Please be quiet," Elder Cynthia Barnes shouted, but the crowd wouldn't listen. "May I remind you that people from the past are not fictional characters to be judged by us. They are creatures of their own times . . ."

"SCREW FELTRINO!" a man at the front of the audience screamed, to which a large part of the audience laughed and kept stomping their feet. Most of the people on the Council looked frustrated, except for Elder Cassian, who was snoring. The meeting had ground to a halt.

Hansum looked at Lincoln and winked. "It's time to use our popularity," he whispered. He stood and faced the crowd, raised his arms and gestured for everyone to quiet down. Amazingly, they complied. As the theatre went silent, Hansum put his hands together in thanks and gave a small bow.

"I love you, Hansum!" a female voice cried. Hansum ignored this and took his seat. He had not only received thousands of letters of support and condolences from all over the globe, but also proposals of marriage.

"To continue," Elder Barnes said. "The question is what, if any, punishment should be given for transgressing important rules, taking into consideration that you are novices who have not received your first licenses yet. Before we give our decision, do either of you wish to make a statement? Shamira?"

Shamira stood up. A large holographic image of her head appeared above the stage. She looked up and winced. "It, it was a mistake," she said quietly. "We were taking our visit too lightly. Now that I have more training, I can better understand the consequences of my actions. If I receive another chance, I assure you similar mistakes will not happen." Shamira sat down again.

"Thank you," Elder Barnes said. "I should add for full transparency, I was the elder who greeted Shamira and the others when they first met at History Camp Verona 1347, where the adventure that so many people have watched, started. I'd like to say that I am impressed how Shamira has matured and become a valuable member of society. Now, Kingsley." Kingsley stood. "While you are from the future, you have declined the option to be judged by elders of your own time and agreed to be bound by our decisions. Do you have anything to say?"

Kingsley stood tall and relaxed, but did not appear cocky. "Nothing to add, but I just want to reiterate that I take full responsibilities for my actions. Although, like Shamira, now that we have had more training, I can guarantee that something similar won't happen again. Also, I am accepting your judgment in hopes of not being sent back to my home when time travel begins again. I don't want to be separated from Shamira. I am deeply in love with her and it is my most fervent hope that we are not parted."

A sympathetic sigh was heard from thousands in the crowd and some began to shout.

"Long live love through time!" and "Kingsley!" and "Shamira!"

"Quiet please," Demos cried, coming center stage again. "Quiet! Quiet!"

"You may sit, Kingsley," Elder Barnes said. Kingsley bowed slightly, sat back down and took Shamira's hand, which brought another wave of "Ahhhhhs," from the crowd. Elder Barnes continued. "The decision of this Council was split, and therefore needed to be voted on by our A.I. advisors." You could see Elder Parmatheon Olama scowl and mutter something unintelligible. The A.I., Demos, floated forward to whisper something in Parmatheon's ear, but the human pushed him away.

"As for Shamira," Elder Barnes started. "It has been decided you did not have proper training before going back in time, but you did disobey the direct and simple instructions given to you. Your punishment is this; when time travel begins again, you will be prohibited from going on any missions to the past . . . for one month."

Half the crowd booed, thinking the sentence was too light, the other half cheered, seeing it as a light slap on the wrist. The teens on the stage smiled, Shamira looking relieved.

"As for Kingsley," Elder Barnes continued. The crowd became silent and Shamira looked anxious again. "The Council believes you too should have been better trained before being taken back. But you did attack a person from the past, and it was not in self-defense. For this you will not be allowed to travel back in time for the length of . . . three months after time travel begins again." Again, half the crowd complained and the other was happy.

"Quiet, quiet!" Demos shouted over the crowd, but they didn't seem to hear.

"Elder Barnes?" Shamira's voice barely carried across the stage.

"Yes, Shamira?" Shamira was looking at the elder with such pleading concern, her question was obvious. The elder smiled. "Don't worry,

Shamira. When time travel resumes, Kingsley will not be required to go home. He can stay and live, as will be the right of all people of modernity. The Council has confirmed a law that people of any time travel age can live wherever and whenever they choose."

With those words, Shamira and Kingsley leapt up and embraced. The crowd roared their approval.

"Quiet, quiet," Demos shouted. "Quiet, please. We haven't finished. We haven't finished the Council's rulings."

The arena slowly became quieter, though not silent.

"Thank you, citizens," Elder Barnes said. "I know everybody is reacting more enthusiastically these days as our society is going through a great change. But please, restrain yourselves. As for Hansum and Lincoln's part in what went on; Lincoln and his mind-delver mentor, Medeea . . . is Medeea here?" Lincoln nodded and looked over to his side, putting his hand out like he was touching something. "Good," the elder said. "Both of you acted in full accordance with your responsibilities and no fault was found with either of you. We wish you well on your training and hope you will find satisfaction in any time travel you experience in the future." Lincoln beamed at Medeea and nodded to the elders as applause and shouts resumed throughout the complex.

"Lincoln!" a few female voices shouted.

"Call me!" a lone girl called out. "I'm real!"

"Quiet please, quiet!" Demos cried.

"As for Hansum," Elder Barnes continued.

"Hansum, Hansum, Hansum!" many in the crowd chanted.

"Hansum was under much stress because of seeing his wife being attacked . . ." Elder Cynthia said with some compassion.

"Boo!" shouted the faction in the crowd who thought Hansum was being put through unnecessarily harsh situations. "I love you, Hansum!" shouted another lone female voice.

"Kick Feltrino's ass!" a male shouted.

"No fault was found with any of your actions. Since then, you have shown a most amazing recovery from your wounds, and I would like to add that you have scored highest in all your time travel classes. We wish you well in your pursuits."

"No thanks to Arimus!" someone cried.

"And as for Arimus . . ." Elder Barnes paused. The crowd, amazingly, went almost completely quiet. "For comment on his part in the matter, I pass the floor to my 31st-century colleague, Elder Cassian Ol-ama." The old man did not stir. "Elder Cassian Olama?" Finally Elder Barnes tapped him physically on the shoulder. He bounced awake and shouted.

"Come to order! Come to . . ." and then realized where he was. He looked at Arimus, who touched his own temple.

"Oh yes, our . . . my decision."

"No crosstalk!" said the younger 24th-century Parmatheon Ol-ama. "Arimus is secretly communicating with a Council member," he complained.

Old man Olama cleared his throat. "Thank you, Elder . . . Cynthia," he said slowly. "Charming . . . girl. Charming. I am . . . pleased . . . so pleased to . . . to be here. Anywhere, in fact. As for judgment, umm, on . . . Arimus . . . yes, Arimus . . . um, all is well. No fault found. Proceed, young man . . . carry on," he said waving his hand dismissively. "Was I to veto something?" and he fell back asleep.

A rumble of disapproving catcalls and crosstalk washed over the amphitheater, including from Elder Parmatheon. He stood up and shouted while pounding the table. Even his own A.I., an oversized soap bubble, came over and begged him to calm down, but Parmatheon poked it while continuing to yell along with the crowd. The bubbly A.I. popped, only to immediately reform itself and keep begging its human to sit. Finally, Elder Barnes spoke very loudly.

"And now for our decision on Hansum's controversial plan to change history and save Guilietta." Not surprisingly, the amphitheater went very quiet. "Thank you. Hansum, would you please stand? Thank you. First, let me say that over the past few days, the Council has received millions, millions of messages from all over the planet and beyond, offering comments and opinions on this controversial situation."

"Save Guilietta!" a lone voice cried from the crowd, followed by a rumble of assenting voices.

"Please, citizens," Elder Barnes begged. "Give us five minutes. I think most of you will be satisfied." The crowd relented. "As you know, the 24th-century Time Travel Council is charged with making decisions about what our time travelers can and can't do. But we are new to this and our associates from the future," she looked over at the Elder Cas-sian Olama, who was still gently snoring away, and then at Arimus, "they will not, apparently cannot, give us guidance. This makes our deliberations very difficult, but we press on.

"An application has been put to us by Hansum to go back and make changes to the past, the aim being to save his wife, Guilietta. This raises a great many questions, moral, legal, and practical. Morally, the young lady has been dead for a thousand years, so why is it a question? If we save her, she would still be dead in our time. Legally, though, she is the lawfully-wedded spouse of one of our citizens, and there is international and inter planetary law stating that governments must help a citizen save their legal family. Legal opinion suggests we must transfer this concept to time travel.

"Now, from a practical perspective, Elder Arimus has said his team has tried and failed to save Guilietta della Cappa several times. But Elder Arimus has also commented that Hansum's proposal has merit, though it also has a high degree chance of changing the future, our present, if it's not done perfectly. I would now ask Hansum to address this Council and tell us the details of his plan. When we hear it, we shall make our decision. Hansum?"

Hansum rose and faced the Council.

"Thank you Elder Barnes, and thank you to the entire Council for considering my application. I know the situation that my friends and I found ourselves in last year has drawn interest from around the globe, as well as from our settlements in space. We all understand that the true reason for us originally being taken back in time was to help youth everywhere appreciate the hard-won advantages of modernity, and to help society learn not to repeat the mistakes of the past. But there was some unexpected magic that happened when Shamira, Lincoln and I went back in time. We met people and we learned to love them. Me especially. I fell in love . . . with Guilietta." He said her name and paused, which caused it to resonate in the perfectly constructed amphitheater. Then, without a hint of quaver in his voice he added loudly, "I fell in love with Guilietta and I want to save her as soon as the blackout ends." You could hear a pin drop in the amphitheater. "So, this is how I propose to save my wife."

The thirty thousand humans in the amphitheater, over a quarter billion more in their homes, plus every A.I. on the planet, listened in rapt attention to Hansum's proposal. His unprecedented situation had captured the imagination of the whole of Earth's sentient population. His plan was a simple one, so didn't take long to tell.

At the heart of it was the goal of reclaiming lost love. The key was a sacrifice so great, so unselfish and so poignant that, when Hansum finished and took his seat, the crowd was left in shocked silence. The first sounds heard from the audience were a few sobs. Then applause started. Then more. Shouts of "Bravo" and "Brilliant" and "Yes" punctuated the growing din and soon the amphitheater was a roar of clapping, stomping and shouting. Demos came forward to try to calm the crowd. With no success in that regard imminent, Elder Barnes tried to call for a vote. She tapped her temple, trying to communicate with each Council member, but it was apparent that even that was impossible with the tumult around them. She literally couldn't hear herself think. Finally she got up to solicit each vote individually, which made Elder Parmatheon jump to his feet and dog her heels, making sure she didn't influence the votes he thought he held. Finally, at the far end of the table, Cynthia Barnes calculated the numbers in her mind, and then walked back to her chair. Parmatheon stomped his foot and scowled, especially at two of the members, and then sat down hard on his seat next to the Council chairwoman.

"The decision has been reached!" Demos shouted to the noisy crowd, and in a few seconds there was a brief oasis of quiet. Elder Barnes stood up.

"The motion for Hansum to execute his plan — has passed eight to four," she said simply, and then smiled. The crowd went wild again, exploding with a roar even louder than before. The story of Romero and Guilietta had truly captured the imagination of a whole civilization.

Hansum, Shamira, Lincoln and Kingsley jumped out of their chairs and hugged each other. Thousands from the crowds surged forward but were denied access to the stage by a force field. This did not dampen their enthusiasm. They just stood and continued cheering.

The face of each of the teens was projected above the crowd, each beaming with joy. Hansum directed his friends to hold hands and stand in a line across the stage, then raise their arms in collective victory. The crowd continued to roar and finally Demos gave up trying to quiet the frenzied citizens. Most of the Council members were smiling in amusement, but a few, especially Elder Parmatheon Olama, sat scowling.

Hansum pointed at Arimus, asking him to join them, but Arimus declined with a wave and just stood by Elder Barnes, his hands behind his back, smiling and rocking on his heels.

The applause went on for nearly twenty minutes. Finally, Elder Barnes shouted something into Arimus's ear and he came to the teens who were still taking in all the adulation.

> "I am requested to use my advanced technology
> and site transport you away from here.
> To Lincoln's home we'll disappear."

Hansum nodded, looked at his companions and smiled. He turned and waved to the crowd, putting his hand to his heart to say thank you, and then he bowed. The teens all put their hands on Arimus's A.I. robe, waved one last time and, with the roar of the crowd still in their ears, winked away.

The silence back in Lincoln's bedroom was deafening, especially since the teens still vibrated with the energy put out by the exultant throng.

"Now that's what I call zippy!" Lincoln laughed.

"And that's what I call understatement," Kingsley added.

"Congratulations, Hansum," Shamira said. "You did it."

Hansum just stood there, his eyes bright and steely, but reserved.

"That was just step one," he said with conviction. "Now the real work begins."

"We're with ya, pal," Lincoln said. "All the way."

"What's next?" Shamira asked.

"We continue training and studying the past recordings of what we went through, making sure our plan is perfect," Hansum answered. "We do that till the blackout's over and then we go."

"If you leave as soon as the blackout ends," Shamira said, "Kingsley and I won't be able to go. We've been restricted. I'm so sorry, Hansum."

"Hey, I'll still need your help training and working out the logistics, if you can make the time from your studies."

Shamira and Kingsley looked at each other and smiled broadly.

"I'm gonna train you so hard," Kingsley said, "you might even be in good enough shape to play rugby."

Chapter 5

Hansum flew through the air, but not for long. The sand greeted his back. Again. And his momentum kept him rolling till he was face down. He looked up, sand sticking to his sweaty face and hoots of laughter ringing in his ears.

"You're getting better, bro," Lincoln guffawed, "At landing!"

Hansum got to his knees, spitting out sand and brushing it off his shirtless torso. Kingsley's huge, outstretched hand was there to help him to his feet. Hansum took it but, as he pulled himself up, he immediately fell back and locked his legs around one of Kingsley's. He then rolled his body viciously forward. Kingsley's knee buckled and Hansum twisted himself even more, adding forward motion to Kingsley's fall. As the big man went down, Hansum continued rolling. He needed to keep Kingsley's leg bent and off the ground. When Kingsley's face and outstretched hands met the sand, Hansum sprang to his knees and lunged for Kingsley's feet and shins, bending one over the other in a leg lock. Hansum's face contorted with the strain of twisting tree trunk-sized calves together.

"He's got 'im now," Lincoln laughed.

"Do you yield?" Hansum shouted.

Kingsley playfully blew sand off his lips. He looked over to the girls, who were reclining on a thick, colorful blanket. He could only see his Shamira, but knew Medeea was there.

"Should I make him feel good and yield?" he asked Shamira.

Shamira giggled and looked over at Medeea. "What do you say, Med? Medeea and I say . . ." and she gave the thumbs down.

"Wha?" Hansum said, realizing he was, once again, in for it.

"Yield, Kingsley," Lincoln laughed, "before he brings out his big guns and tickles you."

"If he tickles me," Kingsley said, "then he really will be in trouble."

"Kingsley's so ticklish," Shamira said, looking over to Medeea.

"I can get Lincoln to do anything if I tickle him," Medeea replied.

"Don't I get sympathy from anyone?" Hansum cried.

"Nope," Kingsley said, and Hansum looked at the big man. He didn't like it when Kingsley grinned that way, and then he felt it. Kingsley's legs tensed. Hansum grimaced and tried to twist one of the massive ankles around the other, straining till his arms almost burst.

"If you put all the energy you're using to make that face into your arms," Lincoln jeered, "maybe you'd have a chance."

"No he wouldn't," Kingsley said, and before anyone could say more or laugh, Kingsley was on his feet, standing above a vanquished Hansum, who was now sprawled on his back. "I'm not helping you up again," Kingsley said, "but good try."

"Not good enough," Hansum said, puffing as he strained to his feet.

Lincoln came over, still laughing and helped brush sand off the opponents.

"At least you can still beat him with a sword," Lincoln said.

Suddenly everyone put their hands to their temples, grimacing like someone was screeching in their ears. Each was receiving a call. At the same time, they could see that someone was running toward them across the university campus, shouting at the top of his lungs. It was Arimus running, with Talos by his side.

"Now I've seen it all," Lincoln said. "Arimus has gone nuts, sending us a message and screaming like that."

It was extremely bad etiquette to shout when sending a message. They all double tapped, turning him off like they would a rude child.

By the time Arimus reached them, he was out of breath and even barefoot.

"It's . . . it's started again," he said puffing.
"Time travel."

Hansum grabbed Shamira and hugged her. Kingsley slapped Hansum's back. Lincoln hugged Medeea.

"Oh, I'm so happy for you," Shamira said to Hansum.

"But . . . but there's a problem,"
Arimus said, red-faced and doubled over.

The teens went quiet.

"What's wrong?" Kingsley asked.

Arimus was having trouble catching his breath, so Talos answered.

"A rare blackout condition still persists. We do not know the reason but just the symptom. It's called temporal bracketing."

"What's that?" Shamira asked.

"It's when people from one time in history can't travel to another particular one, if it's not their home location. It's very rare. We think it has something to do with the decay rate of the energy making up the atoms and molocules of animal tissue, but we're not sure. Technology isn't affected, only humans."

"And who's affected?" Hansum asked.

"Me and anyone from the 31st-century!"
Arimus answered, regaining his breath.
"We can't go back in time, I fear.
All seem to be stuck . . . here."

"Bummer," Lincoln said.

Hansum took a step toward Arimus. "But people from our time can travel back?"

"Yes, and I know what you must be thinking," Arimus said.
"But, without me along, I cannot give authorization
for such a dangerous operation."

Hansum looked at Arimus for several seconds, assessing the situation and the man.

"There's something else you're not telling me," he finally said. "You look scared, Arimus. I've never seen you scared. Why?"

"I . . . I . . . can't say."
Arimus was wide eyed.

"Can't or won't?" Lincoln asked. Arimus just stood there, silent. He always exhibited strong self-control, but not now.

"He's not allowed to say," Talos intervened. "It's information about the future. But in this instance, old friend, I think you may share it. The A.I.s give permission."

Arimus looked at Talos, his eyes showing true surprise, and then he nodded. Looking from teen to teen he, explained.

> "It's not supposed to happen like this.
> Coming from the future, we know your
> what, when, why, how and where.
> We're just not allowed to share.
> But now . . . but now . . ."
> Arimus' eyes went wide.
> "History is unfolding differently."

"Happening differently? How?"

> "In the known, established history,
> when time travel started again,
> I went back with you. . . but now I can't."

There was another prolonged silence as this sunk in.
"Did I succeed?" Hansum finally asked.

> "Succeed at what?"

"At saving Guilietta? In your established history, do I save her?"
"That he may not answer," Talos interrupted. "And if he could, it wouldn't mean anything now. As he said, history has somehow changed."

"Well then, I'm going back myself," Hansum announced immediately.
"And me with him," Lincoln added.

> "No," Arimus said. "This is not advisable.
> Remember, my people and I went back to save the della Cappas.
> But some force of time just wouldn't let us.
> You must not try by yourself."

"It would be impossible *with* you," Lincoln said. "You can't go. We can."

"With respect, Elder Arimus," Hansum added. "We've all learned much from you, but now it's time to make our own decisions. If we can go back and you can't, we should."

"You're not making any sense."

"It makes perfect sense," Hansum countered. "Consider this. You told me that when you couldn't save Guilietta, it was like time had a mind of its own. Well, maybe this same force is showing that you weren't the one to save her? Maybe it wants us to do the job?"

"Speculation. Anthropomorphism of nature's forces,"
Arimus argued. "And besides, your time's scientists
have so much they still don't know.
Their technology can only take you close to the times
you'll need to go.
You need our technology to complete your mission.
And of its use you won't get permission.
True, Talos?"

"No, my friend," Talos answered. The 31st-century Elder was stunned. "Arimus, the boy is correct and you are wrong. I have communed with the world-wide consciousness of all my A.I. brothers and sisters. They concur with Hansum's assessment. Some force is denying us and calling to him. All we may do now is lend our support and let him go."

Arimus looked at Talos, shocked. Then he took a deep breath, as if he were resigning himself to a new fate.

"You'll be needing my elder's cloak then,"
he said with equanimity.
"Sideways, show yourself to your new master."

"Who's Sideways?" Lincoln asked and, as everyone watched, a bass-relief face appeared on the breast of Arimus's cloak. He had a bold nose, fat lips and deep-set eyes.

"Greetings. I am Sideways. We have met many times, but never been introduced."

"One of the secrets from the future that
we can now reveal,"
Arimus said.

"And now we may be friends and colleagues," Sideways added.

"Why do they call you Sideways?" Lincoln asked.

"Because of the way I can move," and he blinked his eyes.

Without the hint of movement, Sideways disappeared off Arimus and was suddenly covering Hansum's bare torso. Arimus was left wearing what looked like boxer shorts and a plain tunic.

"How in the . . ." Hansum said with surprise.

"I site transported onto you," Sideways said. "Pretty good fit, but I think you need to look like this," and the cloak grew and changed color till it covered Hansum's body as an exact copy of the clothing he used to wear as a lens-grinding apprentice.

"Zippy," Lincoln exclaimed. "Just like old times."

"When should they go?" Shamira asked.

"Right now," Talos said.

"Good!" Hansum replied immediately. "Lincoln. Are you and Medeea ready?"

"You got it, boss man."

"Remember," Arimus warned.
"If things go wrong, your emergency return buttons press.
Sideways, where's the new piece of technology
Hansum's plan requires for success?"

Sideway face looked up at Hansum. "Please reach into your tunic, sir."

Hansum did so and pulled out a necklace with a simple silver medallion on it. It was a simple buffed disc, etched with the image of an hour glass.

"This is the modified temporal shielding you specified to complete your plan, sir," Sideways said. "It replaces the temporal time change protection built into your sub-dermal. Once you put it on, it will turn off and replace the protection the sub-dermal gives. However, if you take this new one off and the time line changes significantly, you will not be protected from disappearing from history."

Without hesitation, Hansum put the necklace on. Because of the sacrifice it symbolized and the fact it meant they might never see him again, everyone crowded near. Shamira threw her arms around him.

"It'll be okay, Sham," Hansum said.

"I don't want to lose you again."

"Hey, if this doesn't work, you'll still have me. And if it does, you'll just have to bring me back up to speed."

"But so much else can go wrong."

"Hey, that's what I'm there for," Lincoln said. "To look after this big galoot."

"And I'll look after Lincoln," Medeea thought to Shamira. The two girls hugged.

"It's been a privilege, Hansum," Kingsley said, putting out his hand. "Lincoln, my friend, travel well."

"Even in time travelling," Talos interrupted, "the phrase 'no time like the present', sometimes applies. We must take advantage of this opening."

"Very good," Sideways said. "Everyone stand back, please. Master Lincoln, take hold. Yet another adventure is to begin."

"I've heard that one before," Lincoln answered, grabbing the arm of Hansum's sleeve. "Ready, Med?"

Arimus stayed by Hansum as the others backed away. He grasped his student's hand and looked deep in his eyes.

"Your plan is a good one. Good luck."

"No luck," Hansum said. "Just success. Farewell, elder. Thank you. It's been a privilege." They hugged and Arimus stepped back.

"Master Hansum," Sideways said, "you must give the word. You are the lead on this mission."

"Take us to location one of the plan. Let's go!" Hansum said. The words were no sooner out of his mouth when the familiar whirlwind started to spin around them and the thousands of yellow spheres appeared.

"We love you," Shamira called.

"We'll be watching," Kingsley said.

The yellow Sands of Time sped up, followed by the larger translucent balls bouncing up from the solid earth.

"It's been a privilege," Hansum repeated, staring into Arimus's eyes, and the ground fell away.

Chapter 6

"It's like riding a bicycle," Lincoln shouted gleefully above the noise of the vortex. "Ya never forget." He was referring to keeping his balance while falling through time. His arms were extended and his eyes sparkled with anticipation.

Hansum held his arms out too, keeping himself what felt like upright. But his face was not animated like his friend's. He was surprisingly calm.

"Ya know what's weird?" Lincoln called. "I don't even feel nervous."

"That's what training is all about," Hansum answered. And it was true. They had been working extra hard the past month. Besides improving physically, Lincoln had mind-delved over one hundred people, and not once had he been detected. These skills and others were all part of the plan to rescue Guilietta.

"Okay, we should be there any moment," Hansum announced. "Ready?"

Lincoln looked at him with a broad smile, and then he turned to his side, winking to where Medeea was. "Things couldn't be better," he shouted gleefully. "I'm on an adventure with my best bud, Hansum, and my favorite girl, Med . . ."

Lincoln stopped mid-sentence. The vortex suddenly disappeared and they were not a few inches from the ground, like every other time they landed, but about six feet above terra firma. In the split second gravity allowed, they saw their surroundings, dark virgin forest, with trees towering above them and a tangle of underbrush coming up fast. Lincoln's broad smile changed to one of terror. They crash landed, Hansum falling on a narrow walking trail, while Lincoln hit the thicket. Hansum bent his knees and rolled to break his fall, but Lincoln had no such luck. He crashed into a tangle of bushes and, as his legs and arms hit, he became entangled in different parts of the shrubbery. One leg became ensnared, causing the rest of his body to twist violently as it continued downward. "Owooff!" The air was knocked out of him and his spine and free leg slammed onto massive tree roots.

"Lincoln!" the injured youth heard Medeea's voice shout in panic. *"My Lincoln!"* and he felt billions of nano bits streaming though his body, all thrumming around to assess the damage. Lincoln groaned and tried to move. *"Stay still, my darling,"* Medeea said with urgency. *"Don't move. Let me . . ."*

Of course, Lincoln tried to move, attempting to turn and push himself onto his elbows. "Owww!" he cried, falling back. "Frickin' frackin'!"

Hansum hurried over to Lincoln, but didn't touch him until his injury had been thoroughly assessed. Sideways's face looked quite worried.

"You've twisted one knee and torn the cartilage on the other," Medeea advised. "And badly bruised your back."

"I don't know what happened," Sideways said. "My calculations have never been off before, not in the thousands of site transports and hundreds of vortex navigations I've managed."

Lincoln felt a warm relaxation spread through his body. "Ah," he sighed. He looked up at Hansum. "Med says she's having my body create its own analgesic and anti-inflammatory. She's also creating micro splints to hold things together, so I can continue the mission." He looked up at Hansum. "Best laid plans, eh pal?"

"The first rule of executing a plan," Hansum replied, repeating a line from their field training, "is to be prepared that nothing goes to plan. Maybe we should abort."

"No way, man," Lincoln groaned. "What?" he said, turning to Medeea "She says I should lie still for ten minutes and then she'll be able to give a prognosis."

Then they heard it, a familiar voice shouting somewhere close by in the woods.

"Feltrino," the voice called. "I know you're hiding in the thicket with Guillietta. Feltrino."

It was the voice of the younger Hansum. They'd come back almost to the right time, just a bit early and a few feet too high. They were in the woods, some hours after Feltrino had stolen the looker and kidnapped Guilietta. The first part of the plan was to catch up with Hansum when he was pursuing Feltrino through the woods and before they got to the River Po.

"It must have been something about this past blackout," Sideways said. "It's thrown off my calculations a squig." His eyes glazed over for a second as he thought, his irises turning into quickly flipping numbers and symbols as he calculated. "Yikes," he said, finishing, "We're lucky we didn't materialize in space." Sideways closed his eyes for a second, and then opened them. "I've adjusted calculations. That won't happen again."

The voice of the younger Hansum cried out from somewhere in the forest again, just like the older Hansum remembered.

"Feltrino, can you hear me? There are many men close by. Leave Guilietta and the looker and just go. Feltrino, answer me!"

"We're early," the older Hansum said. "By about twenty minutes. I'm going to use the time to reconnoiter, to make sure there are no anomalies. When I come back, we'll see how you are and whether to press your emergency node and send you back home for help."

"You're not doing this without me, man," Lincoln said.

"Let's wait a few minutes to determine that," Hansum said, smiling reassuringly. Then he heard a voice that automatically made him get very serious. It was Feltrino, shouting back to the younger Hansum, as he had the first time.

"I won't talk to a damned apprentice. I'll only talk to an officer. And if anyone comes near, I'll slit the girl's throat. Do you hear me?"

"I'll be right back," the older Hansum said.

"Stay low," Lincoln whispered.

"No need," Hansum said. "Sideways, let's go out of phase." As he felt himself becoming invisible to the world around him, Lincoln and the surrounding area took on a slightly muted tone. He watched Lincoln turn to Medeea.

"Make me better. I need to help my friend."

"Feltrino," Hansum heard his younger self calling again. "Please, just leave Guilietta and the looker and we'll back off. Feltrino, please."

Hansum remembered how scared he was, his greatest fear being for the safety of Guilietta. Back then he had no plan but to stay safe and wait for an opportunity. At least the older Hansum had a plan, one that dozens of elders and A.I.s from the 24th-century had helped with. But that had already gone wrong. Hansum heard Feltrino start to shout the familiar exchange again, and he turned and started running toward the sound. When running out of phase, he didn't have to worry about running around objects, like trees and boulders. He ran right through them.

"You are by yourself, apprentice. Ha!" Hansum heard Feltrino call as he ran. Hansum also heard the sound of bushes snapping. That was Feltrino's horse starting to move from its hiding place. Hansum sprinted faster, running through several more trees and rock outcroppings. "I'm coming to kill you," Feltrino's voice rang through the forest. "Did you hear me, apprentice? You're going to die!"

Suddenly, in the distance Hansum could see the back end of a horse galloping away from him. The rider was Feltrino. Hansum slowed down, watching him recede. In a moment, one of Podesta Mastino della Scalla's men, the knight da Silva, would crash out of the forest above Feltrino and begin a fight to the death with him.

Hansum was still too early and couldn't interfere at this point. The A.I.s calculations were that if they saved da Silva, it could easily change history too much. Research showed how da Silva was an older brother who would inherit his father's small estate. When he died, his younger brother inherited and then had the resources to formulate some key inventions having to do with the olive oil business. The younger da Silva would also become a very good businessman, an international merchant, and a key player in helping make Italy a world leader in the lucrative olive oil trade. If they saved the older da Silva, the consequences of leaving the younger brother in poverty couldn't be predicted.

Hansum heard the soft nickering of another horse somewhere above him.

"Guilietta," Hansum said, and off he continued in that direction, again running through tree and rock alike. In a minute, there she was, sitting atop the large wagon horse, her arms tied to the old saddle and a gag in her mouth. Hansum walked very close to Guilietta, standing right by the horse and looking up. Guilietta had a concerned look on her face. She was trying to hear what was going on beyond her vision. Then she looked down at her bonds and started struggling to loosen them, but she was soon out of breath because of the gag. She stopped and sat there with a look of exhaustion and panic in her eyes. It brought Hansum's heart into his throat and he felt his hand going up to her restraints.

"Keep to plan, Master Hansum," Sideways warned.

Hansum paused. "I will," but he allowed his hand to move to Guilietta's cheek. As the tips of his fingers passed through her form like an apparition, she shivered.

Then came the huge, though expected, crashing sound. It was da Silva descending upon Feltrino, the horses colliding, armor banging, swords ringing. The horses screamed and Feltrino cursed. The cacophony spooked Guilietta's horse and it pulled back hard against its tether. The beast stumbled, almost unseating Guilietta. She struggled to stay on and Hansum reflexively reached to steady her, but his hands were insubstantial and disappeared inside the horse.

"Master Hansum," Sideways urged. "You must go check on this fight, to make sure there are no time anomalies." Hansum didn't move, but continued watching Guilietta struggle in her saddle till she was secure. "Now!" the A.I. commanded and Hansum took off without further hesitation.

By the time Hansum got to the fight, the two combatants were on foot and battling with swords. Feltrino's horse was about hundred feet away, calmly eating foliage. Da Silva's poor animal was down on its front legs, screaming in agony and with blood pumping from its chest. As before, even the armor da Silva wore was no protection against the far superior swordsman. Feltrino calmly defended himself and probed his opponent, patiently waiting for the right time. Because of his recent sword training, the older Hansum now appreciated that, in real swordplay, your opponent only had to make one mistake.

Then Feltrino noticed something and took a step backwards, disengaging from da Silva for a moment. Hansum turned to look where Feltrino was looking and saw . . . himself, his younger self, looking down from about a hundred paces up the hill.

Feltrino resumed his fight with da Silva, now going at him with earnest. Hansum had watched this sequence many times, often with Marcon. The instructor marveled at Feltrino's skill, although they always stopped the replay when Feltrino was delivering the coup de grace. But here he was watching the actual thing again. Feltrino reengaged da Silva and, with a few thrusts, parries, feints, moves to his right, and then left, he finally forced the della Scalla soldier to open himself up. Hansum was watching for it this time, how Feltrino quickly jabbed his sword, not at a vital area, but just between some leg armor, hobbling the man. He saw that, even though he quickly withdrew his sword, he twisted his wrist so the sword point would rip the muscle and tendon more. Da Silva tried to recover, but his knee buckled slightly, slowing him down a fraction. That's when Feltrino whirled his sword around, now two-handed, on the back of da Silva's neck. Even though he wore armor there, the power of the blow, along with the man's weakened knee, caused him to fall onto his face, a position from which he never recovered.

Hansum looked away as Feltrino drove his sword point between the helmet and back plate, looking up to see his younger self's reaction. All he saw was a frozen face, naïve and bewildered.

"You're next, apprentice," Feltrino shouted as he withdrew the sword from the dead man. The older Hansum could see his younger self sitting stoically upon his horse. At this time Pan, his trusted A.I. advisor, was shouting to turn and ride away, to force Feltrino to follow him till they ran into the Podesta's men.

"So, you are a coward, apprentice," Feltrino laughed. He picked up da Silva's sword and held it out to the younger Hansum, doing a slow pirouette to taunt him. Pan would be screaming at the younger Hansum now, ordering him to turn and run. Finally, he watched as his younger counterpart pulled on the large horse's reins, wheeled around, and galloped away.

Now Hansum got to watch Feltrino's reaction. He looked like he wanted to give chase, but the Gonzaga prince paused, obviously thinking. Then he shook his head slowly, buried da Silva's sword point-first into the ground and trotted back to his horse, not even looking at his latest victim.

Hansum was going to follow Feltrino and see how he treated Guilietta, but his communications mode turned on. It was Lincoln.

"Medeea's got me up and moving, old buddy," Lincoln said.

"How are you doing?"

"Still pretty shaky, but no reason to abort yet. Any anomalies?"

"Not that I can see. Okay, I'll be back in a few minutes and we'll move to the setup point." Hansum turned and began running back toward Lincoln. He heard Feltrino and Guilietta's voices, and had to check the impulse to go see what was happening.

"Ahem," came Sideways's voice. "Are you forgetting something?"

"What?" Hansum asked.

"You've got me. You don't have to run."

"Right. Site transport," Hansum acknowledged. As wearer of the A.I. cloak now, Hansum could instantly move anywhere on the planet. "Take me to Lincoln."

"That's my job," and before he could blink, Hansum's surroundings changed. Lincoln was standing before him, leaning against a large tree.

"Oh good," Lincoln said. "At least I won't have to limp over to the setup spot."

"But how about after that?"

Lincoln looked to his side, "Medeea says I'll be able to move well enough in about an hour. Those nano bits are amazing. I can feel my leg and back improving by the second."

Nothing's too good for my babes," Medeea said. Lincoln winked at her, but then winced.

"This is serious," Hansum interjected. "Will you be able to do your job?"

Lincoln grabbed Hansum's arm and pulled himself up. "No probs. Let's go!"

"Good. We have less than two minutes. We're in phase for the next bit," Hansum said and the two boys touched their temples. "Sideways. Now!"

In another blink they were in a different part of the forest, a well-trodden path on a downhill slope. The trees were much sparser, so it would be impossible for anyone approaching to miss them.

Hansum looked up the path. "I hear the horse. Get ready." Hansum spread his feet and put his hands on his hips. He motioned for Lincoln to stand off the path. "Just in case," he said.

The horse appeared suddenly, large and moving quickly towards them. The rider had a sword drawn and at the ready, his knees dug deep in his mount's sides. Hansum could see the other's eyes go wide with surprise as he recognized him. Hansum put up his arms, both to show he wanted him to stop and that he wasn't armed. The big horse was reined in hard and came sliding to a halt just in front of the two teens.

"What the . . ." the rider exclaimed.

"We've got to talk," Hansum said.

"Hey, pal," Lincoln said. "Just like I remember ya."

The rider didn't say anything, but the horse was acting very nervous. Then Sideways's face formed on Hansum's tunic.

"Greetings," he said.

"Where . . . when are you from?" the rider asked.

Just then, a meter high A.I. satyr appeared on the back of the horse's neck. It's hairy, hard face stared at the older Hansum on the ground, and then back to the rider on the horse.

"Master Hansum," Pan said to the rider. "There's another one of you." And then he looked back at the twin on the ground. "You're older."

"Hello Pan," Hansum said, holding back the emotions of meeting a friend he had previously seen killed. He could not in any way let this information get out, but Pan had an uncanny way of reading body language. "Please, both of you, don't ask too much. I'm restricted on what I can divulge."

"What are you, about a year older?" Pan asked, peering at him sharply. Hansum gave a small nod. Then Pan stared at Lincoln. "The same with you, young Master? Though now not as young?"

"Good to see you too, pally," Lincoln grinned. He looked at the Hansum on the horse. "He doesn't seem to be adjusting as fast as we hoped."

"Cut me . . . cut him some slack," the older Hansum ordered. "I was hyper-focused on catching up with Feltrino at the time."

"Cut the crap," the younger Hansum interjected. "Pan, who the hell are these guys?"

"Exactly who they look like, Master Hansum. You and Master Lincoln. From about a year in the future."

"No way. This can't . . ."

The older Hansum stepped forward and grabbed the horse's bit, steadying the nervous beast.

"Hansum," he said, looking at his younger self calmly. "Please get down. I'll explain everything."

"Tell me now."

"Come down. Please."

"No!" and he pulled the reins, making the horse back up. The older Hansum dug in his heels.

"I guess you forgot what a History Camp hard case you were," Lincoln laughed.

At the mention of History Camp, the younger Hansum relaxed.

"You're really from the future?"

"We're here to help," older Hansum said. "Please, get down and you'll know everything quickly enough."

"But Guilietta . . ."

"Trust me," Hansum said. The younger Hansum looked at Pan, who nodded, and the youth slid off the horse, coming face to face with himself. As the older Hansum put his second hand on the other's shoulder, the younger one noticed the scarring around the thumb. "It's a long story."

"Start explaining," young Hansum said. "All of it. Quickly."

"Okay then," Hansum began. "He looked down at his chest, where Sideways's face stood out, smiling.

"It's like this . . ." the older Hansum began, and a spark flew off his sleeve and into the young man's back. Young Hansum slid to the ground, unconscious.

"So, that's the plan," the more mature Hansum said to the A.I. centaur. Pan's holographic image was standing by his unconscious younger master, who was sitting propped up against a tree while Lincoln secured his hands around the back of the trunk. "If all goes well, Lincoln should be able to untie him by the middle of the night."

"I see," Pan said. He calmly watched the youth-turned-into-a-man walk over and retrieve da Silva's fallen sword. "So, this plan of yours. You're willing to make the sacrifice?"

"You know the answer without asking," Hansum said as he hefted the sword and slashed it through the air a few times. Satisfied, he slid the blade into his belt and put a foot into the saddle stirrup, preparing to mount. As he did, Pan jumped and grabbed Hansum's shoulder, hanging midway between Hansum's and Sideways's faces.

"Answer me this, older Master Hansum. What's he doing here?" he said nodding toward Sideways. "This is Arimus's guy. Why is **he** helping you? Why not me?"

Hansum paused, staring at Pan for a second.

"You're busy with Shamira. And Arimus . . . he couldn't come. I can't say more than that." Hansum pulled himself up onto the horse. "Anyway, I've got to get going. Sideways is going to help me and you're going to stay here with Lincoln."

"But if you're from the future, that means this didn't go . . ."

"Don't ask, Pan," Hansum said, pulling on the reins to turn the horse around.

"Ah, he's ready," Sideways announced.

"Who's ready?" Hansum asked.

"Reach into my cloak. Something's just been sent for you."

Hansum reached down the neck of his shirt and was surprised when his hand grasped something solid. He pulled it out slowly. It was a sword identical to da Silva's.

"What the . . ."

"It's a gift from the Association of A.I.s." Sideways said. "Release your fingers so it will drop," Hansum let go of the sword, but it didn't fall to the ground. It just hung in the air. "Gentlemen, let me introduce you to Pedang," Sideways continued. "He's less than an hour old, hatched especially for this mission." An image of a baby's face appeared on the wide end of the blade. It was like a reflection in a tarnished mirror.

"An A.I. sword!" Lincoln said, quite impressed.

"And isn't he cute," Pan added. "Happy birthday, little fellow."

"Thank you, Elder Pan," Pedang said in the squeaky voice of a toddler. "Hello, Journeyman Lincoln. Journeyman Hansum. I am at your service," he said, tipping his blade. "I am here to supplement your improved fighting skills."

"Zippy," Lincoln said. "Can you fight by yourself?"

"Yes, I can fight by myself or enhance a human's abilities." With that he whizzed through the air, slashing and thrusting.

"Okay, enough. We've got to get moving," Hansum said. "Welcome aboard, Pedang." He tossed da Silva's blade into the bushes and snapped his fingers. Pedang flew into Hansum's grip and was slid into place in his new master's belt.

Just then the younger Hansum woke up with a start and began shouting.

"What are you doing? Let me go! Pan, you traitor!" He pulled against his bonds, using every curse he knew.

"Here, take this," the older Hansum said, pulling off his time phase protection necklace. He tossed it to Lincoln. "Get that on him and make sure he understands why he's not supposed to remove it. I'll signal when to let him go." He started to wheel his horse back downhill.

"Hansum," Lincoln said.

"Yeah?" the older one answered.

"Goodbye, pal. It's been an honor."

Without another word or nod, Hansum kicked the horse with his heels and took off. Still hearing his younger self letting loose with a string of curses, he looked back briefly to see Lincoln fighting to put the necklace on the other youth.

"Come back, come back, you bastard," the tied-up Hansum shouted. "I've got to save Guilietta. Stop! Please."

"It's all right, Hansum," Lincoln pleaded. "That's what he's here to do."

The bound Hansum let himself fall to his side, facing away from Lincoln. "Leave me alone!" and then he struggled some more.

Lincoln looked at him with worried eyes and then over at Pan, who was staring at him curiously.

"You two sure have matured," Pan said.

"We couldn't have done it without you, buddy," Lincoln replied.

Chapter 7

The big horse thundered down the hill, carrying Hansum toward the Po River. They had been moving hard and fast for twenty minutes and the trees were thinning out, giving glimpses of the river below. That's when Sideways looked up at Hansum and shouted.

"Your younger self certainly was angry."

"What do you expect?" Hansum yelled back, continuing to urge the horse on. "He meets us and the first thing we do is lie to him and knock him out. Hopefully Lincoln and Pan can make him see reason, and if we're successful he'll appreciate . . ."

Hansum pulled back hard on the reins and came to a halt. There were Feltrino and Guilietta, stopped by the shoreline. Feltrino was desperately looking back and forth, like he was trying to recognize something. As before, the river was wide, too deep for a horse to wade across, and too fast for them to swim.

"I'll shout what I did the first time, to make sure he reacts the same," Hansum said. He stood up on his stirrups and called out, "Feltrino! Please don't take Guilietta into the water! It's too dangerous if she's tied up!"

Like the first time, Feltrino turned around and saw Hansum. He turned his horse and, pulling Guilietta's behind him, began galloping away along the shore.

"You're a little ahead of where you were before, Master Hansum," Sideways said. "You're a better rider now. Slow down a bit, so you don't spook him."

"Right," Hansum said, sitting back down on the saddle. He watched Feltrino feverishly whipping his horse. And poor Guilietta, with her wrists tied to the saddle, she appeared to be holding on to the draft animal's mane for dear life. Hansum tensed, forcing himself not to bolt to her aid. Then, just as the two horses disappeared into the tree line along the river, Hansum saw Guilietta turn and look directly at him. Hansum kicked his horse's flanks.

"Not yet," Sideways warned. "Steady, Master. Steady." Hansum waited for another half minute before Sideways said he could go. When Hansum's horse finally got to the place where Feltrino entered the woods, Sideways added, "Now trot. Just a bit faster. That's it. We need to time it so events happen as close as possible to the way they did before." After about three minutes, Sideways said, "Pedang at the ready." Hansum, keeping his eyes looking warily about, put out his hand. The A.I. sword extracted itself from his belt and floated into his hand. "Stop here," Sideways said. This is where the path split into two, one trail leading to the river. Hansum remembered how the heavily-leafed branches of the trees formed a dense canopy over this path, creating a tunnel of foliage until it opened up. "This is where Feltrino is trapped by a cliff over the river, with only this way out."

Hansum pulled the reins to turn his horse into the dark passageway. The bright light of the open river was about a hundred paces ahead. When he came along this path the first time, he found Feltrino well back from the opening, but couldn't assume it would happen similarly. A minute later, almost to the end of the tunnel, he felt Pedang rise a little higher.

"*En garde,*" he heard a babyish voice come from the sword.

With Pedang at the ready, Hansum walked the horse out cautiously. Inching into the light he found Feltrino staring at him. He was in the same place as before, on his horse, almost to the edge of the water. Guilietta's horse was beside him. That hadn't changed.

'Good,' Hansum thought.

"Romero!" Guilietta said, almost happily. This was like before. Then she said, "I thought it was you. Thank Cristo." That was different.

'Oh oh,' Hansum thought.

Feltrino stood up on his stirrups, trying to see if anyone was behind Hansum.

"Just let Guilietta go and you can leave," Hansum said as he had done before. "Captain Caesar and his men can't be more than ten minutes away."

"You're still alone?" Feltrino said, smiling. "That's enough time for me to kill a lowly apprentice."

"Please, there's no need." Guilietta said, begging. "I'll go with you willingly."

"You'll go with me willingly or otherwise," Feltrino said lightly. "I shall be back for you in a trice," and he dropped the reins for Guilietta's horse and pulled out his sword. "My blade is getting a good washing of blood today, apprentice. Ready?"

Without thinking, Hansum allowed the sword hilt to flip back over his palm, causing the blade to twirl around in a big circle, coming to rest again at the ready. Feltrino dug in his heels, pulling his horse up short and stared at the apprentice. Previously, Feltrino had kicked his horse into an attack.

"Mistake, Master Hansum," Pedang whispered.

'Fool!' Hansum cursed silently to himself, remembering Marcon telling him to lose that move. He had shown Feltrino he had better-than-beginner dexterity with a sword. 'From now, everything is going to be different.'

"Oh ho!" Feltrino called appreciatively. "Where did one such as you learn that?"

Hansum didn't care what chewed up time. Talk or fight, he was just trying to get Feltrino trapped here till the Podesta's men arrived.

"I taught myself," he answered, speaking as modestly as he could. "When I was a child, with a wooden sword."

"A wooden sword?" Feltrino repeated with amusement. Then he let his horse take a few steps forward. "Maybe," Feltrino added. "Maybe not." And with that he kicked his horse hard. As the horse bolted forward, Feltrino raised his sword point directly at Hansum's chest.

"You control the sword first, Master Hansum," Pedang said, "so I can see what you've got."

Feltrino's horse was next to Hansum in four powerful strides and Hansum saw the Gonzaga was going to make the same attack as before. At the last possible moment, Feltrino whirled his horse onto Hansum's flank, swinging his blade over his head in a big circle.

"Prima!" Pedang said loud enough for Feltrino to hear.

The blade came at Hansum's unarmored chest with the added energy of the horse's momentum. But Hansum's blade was there, in the "prima" defensive position. Then Hansum loosened his grip, to make the sword vibrate. He needed to feign a weak wrist, but the truth was, he had not only strengthened and conditioned his arms for the past months with training, the doctors had authorized Medeea to give him some nano bits to cause bone and tendon growth. Hansum's wrist and hand now had the extra mass and strength of a medieval soldier who had trained since childhood.

Feltrino had his horse step just out of range.

"You have a weak wrist, apprentice . . ." Feltrino said. "When I kill you, I will take your horse as well as your looker. And of course, I'll still have the girl." This dialogue was slightly different than before.

"Take the horse anyway," Hansum said, quickly sliding off of it, as he had done the first time. "Please, just leave Guilietta. I mean, you're right, Feltrino. I can't beat you in a sword fight. But killing me will take too long and I don't want us swinging swords around Guilietta."

Feltrino laughed. He leaned forward in the saddle. "Such gallantry for the girl, but no manly pride? You don't want to fight?"

Hansum stepped aside, clearing the path off the small spit of land, confident Feltrino wouldn't accept the easy way out. "Just take my horse and leave," he said. "And keep the looker."

"Perhaps you are right," Feltrino said. "My father would value me bringing a horse over a girl."

Feltrino peered at Hansum, squinting his eyes and cocking his head, and then he smiled again.

"Okay, here he comes," Pedang said.

"Oh, what the hell, I'll have it all," and, as before, the Gonzaga dropped off of his mount and rushed at Hansum, slashing his sword back and forth in a blur. The first time he lived this, Hansum just held his sword to center, but since he'd been able to study Feltrino's technique, he knew just when to sidestep and deflected the first three wild blows.

"Still want to do it on your own?" Pedang whispered.

"Yeah," Hansum grunted, as he repelled another blow and pushed Feltrino's sword away.

Feltrino stepped back and looked brightly at Hansum, giving another appreciative nod, and almost looking like he was about to say something. But, of course, that too was a feint. The Gonzaga quickly stepped in with three more blows to the right, a half feint further right, and then a back turn that took him onto the now exposed left side of Hansum. The wide arching blow would have sliced into the back of most opponents.

"*Seconda!*" Pedang's voice said, and Hansum's sword was there, blocking his opponent. This time Feltrino pushed off, stepping back out of range.

"Luck or skill?" Feltrino asked, this time not so lightly.

"We'll find out," Hansum answered under his breath, once again going to en garde.

Feltrino, now looking more cautious, returned the en garde, and took a small step forward.

"*Stretto passo,*" Pedang's voice came from nowhere, naming Feltrino's move. Feltrino took two more small steps. "Stretto passo, stretto passo," Pedang repeated, his infant voice sounding high and airy.

Feltrino looked right at Hansum, confused at not being able to connect the childish voice with Hansum. He took another half step forward.

"Stretto . . ." Pedang began, and Feltrino stepped back, confusion turning to frustration and anger. Hansum remained impassive.

Then, stealthily as a cat, Feltrino took a quick step forward and lunged, not trying to get to Hansum's flesh, but only giving a distracting smack to Hansum's blade.

"*Battuta,*" Pedang's voice chimed, labeling this move as well.

Hansum parried it easily, staring into Feltrino's eyes, as if to say, "I know you are trying to frustrate and trick me, but that will not happen."

"So, I was right to doubt you? Who was your teacher, pray tell?" Feltrino asked.

"He's monologuing, Master Hansum," Pedang whispered. "Another distraction. Don't answer."

Hansum said nothing, keeping his eyes and stance relaxed. That's when Feltrino's attitude changed. He scowled.

"You bore me now, apprentice," and then he screwed up his face and put his free hand to his mouth, biting his thumb. "I bite my thumb at you," he said, and spat.

Hansum felt his eyes foolishly follow the white blob and the blur of Feltrino's sword was suddenly coming at him. Feltrino's arms, legs and sword all moved constantly in a seemingly random manner. It took all Hansum had to keep up his defenses, but he was not able to find an opportunity to counter with his own initiatives.

"Now I have the measure of you," Feltrino said, and the Gonzaga prince picked up the pace. Blow after blow, thrust and counterthrust, Feltrino came on, moving Hansum left then right, forcing him to retreat and feinting only a few times to entice him closer in for the kill. Several times Hansum found the tip of Feltrino's sword close to his tunic, one time avoiding it only by stepping back towards the water. Hansum moved his feet to his right, trying to get back to open ground, but found Feltrino already blocking his way. Unbelievably, Feltrino increased his stroke tempo again. Now, Hansum could do nothing but keep his sword moving, desperately trying not to think, hoping the hours of conditioning would allow his reflexes to respond automatically. But as each of Feltrino's strokes fell, Hansum found himself closer to the cliff's edge.

"*Prima, Seconda, Terza, Quarta, Quinta, Sesta, Settima*," Pedang's tiny voice mewed, both commentating and giving advice as to which blocking guard to use, but the child-like speech no longer seemed to distract Feltrino.

Suddenly, Hansum's heel caught on a rock and he found himself tumbling backwards, his buttocks hitting the hard ground with a thump. He felt Pedang try to assert himself, but he held on to the sword too strongly and Feltrino took advantage by lunging at Hansum's chest. Hansum's eyes went wide with surprise as he felt the steel tip of his enemy's blade against his tunic. Hansum tried to roll, but it was too late. Feltrino thrust his sword even harder. The blade bent. Guilietta screamed, "ROMERO!" and Feltrino withdrew the sword, bringing it over his head in triumph and giving a mighty whoop to the sky. Then he went silent, his eyes puzzled. There was no fresh blood dripping from the blade. He looked down and there was Hansum, staring up at him, surprised, but not bloodied. His tunic was not even ripped.

"Good job, Sideways." Hansum panted, seemingly to the air.

"Thank you, sir," came a disembodied voice.

"Romero!" Guilietta cried with relief and joy, the fingers of her tied hands making a small sign of the cross. "Thank Cristo."

This seemed to enrage Feltrino anew. He turned and ran at his downed opponent, his sword coming straight for Hansum's head.

"My turn," Pedang said. "Just hold on, Master."

Hansum felt Pedang fly up and meet Feltrino's slash, and then twist, redirecting the strike into the ground. Feltrino grabbed his sword's hilt with two hands and brought it back the opposite way, in a large arc, again aimed at Hansum's head. Hansum felt his wrist turn as Pedang levitated one hundred and eighty degrees to deflect the blow in the other direction. Feltrino stepped back and lunged straight and, with Hansum still in the seated position, Pedang blocked a mighty thrust with what looked like an easy flick of the wrist. Feltrino lunged again and again, furiously attacking with unmeasured stabs, seemingly without any concern for defense. But each of his sword blows was easily turned away. There was no way Feltrino could keep up with Pedang's instantaneous A.I. reflexes.

The all-out attack went on for over a minute. Feltrino's chest was heaving with exhaustion. He backed up, at last something looking like fear showing in his eyes.

"Get up," Pedang said. "Quickly," and Hansum scrambled to his feet. "Do what I tell you," the A.I. sword said quietly. "En garde." Hansum put Pedang in front of him, tip slightly raised, right foot forward, left back. He was calm. Feltrino's chest was starting to settle, but there was still a worried look about him. "Circle right," Pedang said, and Hansum did so, just as he had learned in class. This robbed his opponent of some of his sword length when he thrust his weapon. Feltrino came to en garde, pivoting to keep Hansum square to him. It was Feltrino whose back was to the water now. "Step forward," Pedang squeaked, and Hansum felt Pedang shoot out like a missile. It was all he could do to hold on. Feltrino parried, but you could see he was surprised at the speed and took another step backward.

"Stocatta," Pedang's high voice called, and the blade thrust low under Feltrino's sword, touching his stomach. You could see Feltrino tighten, believing he was run through, but then Pedang backed up, as did Hansum. They couldn't kill Feltrino because they knew that, in his future history as a noble in Mantua, his calmer, mature self would influence many things.

"Mandritti tonda," Pedang said as he cut above Feltrino's sword, right to left, so quickly that the blade tip was in one position, and then immediately the next. *"Reversi tonda,"* as he cut the other way. The idea was now to just keep him here until the Podesta's men could arrest him.

Feltrino's eyes were now unmistakably wide with fear. He glanced behind him at the water.

"Don't let him jump," Hansum said, and Pedang flew in a circle around Feltrino, dragging Hansum with him and forcing him to forget his footwork. But amazingly, Feltrino did not counterattack. He just stepped back away from the water, confused.

"I hear the Podesta's men," Sideways broke in, his A.I. senses more attuned than a human's. "Six minutes is all we have to hold him here."

"Yield, Feltrino," Hansum said. "The Podesta's men are almost here."

"How does a lens apprentice play with me so?" he rasped, his eyes pleading.

"Yield," Hansum repeated.

Finally, the humans could hear the rumble of horses across the water. Each looked, a momentary truce called. There were ten horses in the distance, galloping along the shore of the bay towards them. The Podesta, Mastino della Scalla, was among them.

"All right, apprentice," Feltrino said, forcing his composure. "I cannot yield, but shall leave the girl and retreat." Hansum didn't say anything, but cocked his head, like he was asking for more. "And I shall leave the looker," Feltrino conceded, swinging the telescope case off his shoulder and dropping it.

"I don't think so," Hansum said. "I must keep you for the Podesta."

"I CANNOT YIELD TO A PEASANT!" Feltrino screamed, his body tensing and the tendons on his neck bulging. He reached down with his free hand and took a long dagger from its sheath, now aiming two weapons at his foe. "Kill me if you can, apprentice!"

The Podesta and his men were now galloping into the trees. At the pace they were moving they would be there in less than four minutes.

"Yield, Feltrino!" Hansum said. "Yield and live!"

"I'D RATHER DIE," and he ran, completely without form, toward Hansum. He slashed his sword and dagger, screaming at the top of his lungs. But Pedang intercepted the sword's blade, slid down to the hilt and flung the sword out of Feltrino's hand. It flew into the river. Feltrino, armed with only the dagger, and now at close quarters with Hansum, thrust the blade toward Hansum's throat. It was stopped dead as Pedang's steel instantly appeared in front of it. Feltrino twisted his body, trying to make a second stab, this one at Hansum's gut, but found his blade once again blocked.

"Yield, Feltrino, yield!" Hansum shouted, almost pleading.

Feltrino looked down, exhaled and relaxed, his arm with the dagger going limp.

"Romero," Guilietta called, relief in her voice.

Hansum looked over at Guilietta and smiled. Feltrino looked at him, over at the girl and then back to Hansum. His arm with the long dagger tensed. Hansum saw it, but did not flinch. He already felt Pedang moving to intercept. Pedang levitated to defend Hansum, and then, with a flick of Feltrino's wrist, the dagger flew in the opposite direction.

In horror, Hansum wrenched his head around and saw the dagger spinning through the air. As if in slow motion, he watched it turn tip-over-end several times, the point finally coming into contact, penetrating, and then embedding itself in its target. Like a hot knife through butter, it entered Guilietta's thigh and went straight through into the horse. Guilietta and the horse screamed as one and the animal reared. Hansum instantly dropped Pedang and sprang towards the horse, grabbing for its reins, but its hooves came down onto Hansum's chest. Hansum felt Sideways stiffen, to protect him from the flailing hooves, but was the A.I. strong enough to keep him from being crushed? Hansum fell to the ground, the full weight of the horse about to land on him. Sideways instantaneously transported Hansum two feet to the side as the hooves cracked the ground. Hansum had himself up and trying to stop the horse from bolting into the forest, getting in front of the terrified beast. He waved his hands frantically, but this only caused it to rear again.

"ROMERO!" Guilietta screamed, halfway on and off the horse. Hansum knew if he let the animal run off, Guilietta would end up being dragged and crushed as the animal ran through the trees.

"GUILIETTA!" Hansum cried back, waving his hands desperately at the horse, trying to block him.

Feltrino now dove to the ground for Pedang. As soon as he touched it, he could sense the presence of another will take control of the blade. Even with a firm grasp on the hilt, he felt it being pulled away from him.

Pedang began trying to help Hansum stop the horse from running off, moving left and then right, all the while dragging Feltrino behind.

The horse reared again and Hansum dove for the saddle, wanting to get hold on the ropes binding Guilietta and somehow loosen them. For some brief seconds he got a grasp of the rough cord and his hands touched Guilietta's. As Hansum was buffeted and twisted, he came face to face with Guilietta, each of them looking into the other's terrified eyes. One of the animal's twists pushed Hansum's cheek against Guilietta's face. In that instant he felt how her lips were swollen and rough from Feltrino's brutality. Guilietta screamed in pain as the horse kicked out violently. Hansum was thrown off, landing hard on the ground.

Covered in Guilietta's and the horse's blood, Hansum saw the horse was now perilously close to the twenty-foot cliff over the water. He winced as Guilietta slipped off its back, causing her to hang over the cliff. Tied to the saddle, her weight started dragging the tired animal with her. The horse's back hoof slipped off the cliff edge and its torso came crashing down. It pawed the ground furiously, trying to save itself. As the horse screamed and struggled to keep its footing, Hansum had no choice but to grab its mane and dig his heel into the ground. He started pulling landward, hoping every bit of force in that direction would help. Miraculously, the horse was able to inch itself back so all four legs were on solid ground and it began scrambling to its feet.

"THE HORSE, PEDANG!" Hansum screamed. "HELP WITH THE HORSE!"

Feltrino's teeth were clenched as he continued struggling with what must be an enchanted sword. He felt the sword pull away from him so hard that even his toughened hands couldn't hold on. He watched in horror as the thing flew through the air by itself.

"DEVILS FROM HELL!" he screamed. "ALL OF YOU ARE DEVILS FROM HELL!"

"CUT THE ROPE, PEDANG, CUT THE ROPE!" Hansum cried, feverishly grasping the horse's mane and trying to hold it down. Guilietta, now gone limp, was reduced to a gouged and bleeding rag doll, flopping off the side of the animal's back. Pedang flew to the horse, whose huge round eyes expanded even more as the strange, sharp object approached it. Ignoring Hansum's weight, it somehow found the strength to rear straight up on its back legs one more time, roaring in fear and pawing the air as if it wanted to fly. Pedang and Hansum quickly backed off, terrified and powerless to get to the now unconscious Guilietta.

"DEVILS!" Hansum turned just in time to see Feltrino coming at him with a huge rock over his head. "DIE DEVILS!" the Gonzaga screamed as his body smashed into Hansum's shoulder and the rock crashed into his skull. The buzzing and sparks off Sideways's energy shield glowed around Hansum's head, absorbing that blow, but Feltrino's momentum pushed Hansum into the horse just as it reared at full extension. The horse fell sideways and, for a split second, the heavy animal's only contact to the cliff was a single back hoof. Hansum, squashed between the horse and Feltrino, looked down to see the roiling water.

"Grab hold of me," he heard an infant's voice say, and there was Pedang, hovering next to his hand. Hansum grabbed the hilt but felt a strong hand smash into his, forcing it off the handle.

Hansum was now falling, tumbling with the bulk of the beast beside him. Looking up, the last thing he saw was Feltrino hanging in the air and holding onto the A.I. sword.

As the fast-running water swallowed Hansum, Guilietta and the horse, and as all three submerged into the cold and dark, Hansum twisted his body around, trying to get hold of some part of the animal, his only concern being to get to Guilietta before she drowned.

Chapter 8

Pedang, allowing his eyes to show on the flat of his blade, looked down as Hansum and the others disappeared into the black waters of the fast-moving river. While imbued with the knowledge and experiences of millions of other A.I.s, and full of the recorded knowledge of human kind, his infant mind felt shock at the loss of the people he was charged to protect. He watched as the horse, Hansum, Guilietta and Sideways reemerge from the water a good distance down the river. Both the horse and Hansum were thrashing wildly, but Guilietta was limp and being carried down the river as so much flotsam. Pedang's first impulse was to speed to them, like an arrow, to render assistance. But then he looked down and saw the bruised and bloodied hand of

Feltrino still holding onto his sword hilt. Feltrino's feet were dangling over the water and his shocked face was looking up into Pedang's eyes.

The mission had been to detain Feltrino so the Podesta could arrest and hold him until Hansum and the other teens somehow got back to the 24th-century. As well, the older Hansum would stay in place of the younger one for the next few hours, making sure there was no promise to help the Podesta develop cannons and black powder. This way, because the younger Hansum now had the temporal protection necklace, when the time continuum changed, the younger Hansum would go forward into history, while the older Hansum, without the necklace, would disappear into nothingness, a noble and excellent sacrifice. But it was not being seen as a suicide. The younger Hansum would take his place. That's why the Council had accepted the plan and why the sentient beings of Earth and beyond, both human and A.I., had become so intrigued with the continued story of Hansum and Guilietta. Guilietta would be saved, there would still be a Hansum, and history would resume as it had before all this happened.

Now the fine plan was in a shambles and Pedang had to make lightning choices: let Feltrino go and render assistance, or stay with Feltrino until the Podesta came.

His conundrum answered itself. Pedang saw Feltrino's eyes widen and felt his grip loosen. Feltrino was going to escape into the water, as he had done in the first version of this reality. Instantly, Pedang shot out a grasping force field, encircling Feltrino's hand and wrist. He then shot a small jolt of electricity into the man's limb, forcing it to re-grasp the hilt. Feltrino now hung, trapped and helpless, horror in his eyes.

Pedang's acute A.I. hearing told him to look over toward the bushes. He could hear the Podesta was almost there. Less than a minute, he calculated. He levitated back over the ground and released Feltrino from four feet up, letting him fall into a heap. Feltrino could now also hear the rumble of horses and shot to his feet. He looked at the levitating Pedang, meeting his eyes again, then over at his own horse. Feltrino leaned towards the animal but, in a flash, Pedang was between the Gonzaga and his mount.

"Sword of Satan!" Feltrino gasped, and he whirled around and headed for the water again. But Pedang zoomed around him and the Gonzaga ran right into the edge of the blade. The sharp steel cut through his shirt and stopped. A stain of blood rose through the fabric.

"Yield!" Pedang said, his child's voice sounding angry. "YIELD!"

"I yield, evil spirit!" Feltrino said, getting to one knee.

"Lie down," Pedang added.

"What?"

"I said lie down! On your back! NOW!"

Feltrino obeyed just as the Podesta, Captain Caesar and the other soldiers came thundering into the open. Pedang let himself fall onto Feltrino's chest, inert, so nobody else would see him hovering. As the horses surrounded Feltrino, Pedang's eyes scowled at Feltrino and then he let his image fade. Four soldiers leapt off their horses and yanked Feltrino to his feet, letting Pedang fall to the ground.

Captain Caesar, on his horse, was already looking down river with his own looker.

"The savant and one of the horses . . . and the girl," he began. Then he shouted at two of his men. "Down the river. Go!" and the two men took off back through the forest.

Mastino jumped off his horse, running to look downriver. He turned, facing Feltrino.

"You killed my savant," he said, stomping back to him and seething with rage.

Feltrino, still paralyzed with fear, cried, "No, he was alive. He jumped in after the girl, when this thing . . ." he said, looking down at the sword.

"This thing what?" Mastino demanded angrily, coming close to the Gonzaga.

"Don't touch it. The sword is enchanted!" Feltrino cried to Mastino. "It's a devil. It flies and talks and fights."

Captain Caesar picked up Pedang. "It's da Silva's sword," he said, handing it to Mastino.

"I swear," Feltrino pleaded. "It fights and cannot be beaten."

Mastino ran his finger along the blade. "Quite . . . ordinary," Mastino replied, eyes burning.

"Listen to me," Feltrino cried. "I tell you it's of the devil!"

"Excellency, here's what we came for," a soldier said, handing Mastino the looker Feltrino had stolen. It was now battered and broken from being trampled in the fight.

"Well, our mission is accomplished," Mastino said, looking sternly into Feltrino's eyes. "But my savant is lost." He gestured to the soldiers, who renewed their hold of Feltrino's arms.

"I . . . I guess it's back to my cell," Feltrino said scowling. He looked down, defeated.

"Not for you," Mastino answered coolly. Feltrino looked up, confused. And then his eyes went wide as Mastino plunged Pedang under his ribcage and into his heart. Sounds came from two quarters. A low grunt emerged from Feltrino's lips and a terrified shriek emanated from Pedang. He was horrified at being used for murder. As Mastino went to pull the sword out, Pedang propelled himself into the air, making it appear that Mastino was throwing him into the river. As a shocked Pedang descended toward the water he saw, not only a surprised Podesta, but also Feltrino, slumping to the ground dead.

Chapter 9

"Guilietta! Guilietta!" Hansum gasped, as he held on to the horse's mane with one hand and incessantly beat the fast-moving water with the other. He was desperately trying to pull himself to his unconscious wife who was floating on the other side of the madly-thrashing horse. The poor animal was still trying to swim, but the river was moving so fast that nothing, animal or human, could fight its current. They bobbed up and down, like leaves, as the deep water rose and fell over the riverbed. And when they came to a bend in the waterway, the oddly configured assembly of horse and people spun in circles.

Hansum finally got two hands on the horse's mane as they approached another curve. So far the river had been clear of deadly obstructions, but Hansum saw many ugly, jagged rocks, broken tree trunks and branches protruding from the water ahead. As they began to spin, the centrifugal force threw Hansum toward the horse and he was able to grab the saddle. He pulled himself onto it and finally grabbed Guilietta's arms. His extra weight, however, caused the weakening animal to sink. As the horrified animal's back and neck submerged, it stretched its head straight up to keep its mouth and nose in the air. Hansum pulled Guilietta over the horse and let himself slide off. The animal came up some, but it was obvious the poor thing was weakening. Hansum had to act quickly, before the horse died and dragged Guilietta down.

"Sideways," Hansum shouted. "Site transport. Quickly."

"I can't," the AI cloak said, it's face on Hansum's chest bobbing in and out of the water. "The horse is too big. We must get the girl's hands unbound first."

Hansum pulled himself onto the horse again, in an effort to steady himself and find some purchase against the ropes, but they were so wet and tightened from all the stretching, he had no luck.

"Pedang!" Hansum said, as if cursing. "Where's that Pedang? I need some help . . ."

He saw someone running along the riverbank towards them. It was him, his younger self, running toward the water. He must have escaped from Lincoln, who was nowhere in sight. And then Hansum heard a deep rumbling. He looked up. There was a heavy cloud of mist ahead. This could only mean one thing. Rapids. The river was going to run downhill through rocks and broken trees.

"HELP! QUICKLY! HANSUM!" he called to his other self. "HURRY!" He looked down briefly and saw Guilietta's eyes flutter. Perhaps it was the sound of his voice, but Guilietta was trying to regain consciousness. "Hold on, Guil," he said into her ear. "Hold on, sweetheart." She opened her eyes for a moment, recognition showing. She mouthed her name for him, 'Romero'. Hansum bowed his head and kissed her hands and she smiled faintly, and then he felt the horse sink. He threw his weight off the horse but kept hold of the saddle. "HURRY!" he screamed again. He watched his younger self dive from the shore and into the water. "Help's coming, Guilietta. Help's coming," Hansum said encouragingly. "We're going to get you out . . ."

That's when the partly submerged tree appeared, looming over them like a demon from the depths. The horse's head took the brunt of it with a disgusting and brutal crack. It was killed instantly. The animal turned on to its side, whirling Guilietta off her perch and tossing her straight into a tangle of sharp, broken branches that stuck out like spears. Then, as the horse's carcass spun away from the tree, it yanked her off the sharp, wooden spikes.

Hansum was thrown off too, but was able to catch hold of the horse's tail. As the dead horse spun around in an eddy, Hansum caught hold of the saddle again. With the horse now on its side, Hansum saw another opportunity. He could see the girth strap for the saddle exposed. If he could unbuckle the cinches before the animal sank and before they hit the main part of the rapids, he could free Guilietta and only have the saddle to contend with. It was still an impossible situation, but less impossible than the present one.

That's when the younger Hansum reached them.

"YOU BLOODY . . ."

"KEEP HER ABOVE WATER," the older Hansum screamed above the din of the approaching rapids. "I'VE GOT TO GET THE SADDLE LOOSE."

The younger Hansum grabbed the saddle where Guilietta was tied and flipped her onto her back. Her arms and hands were now stretched unnaturally over her head. Ducking below the water, he went under Guilietta, coming up with his chest under her back and his head next to her unconscious face. He was treading furiously to keep them both afloat, the rushing water spilling across his face and mouth. It was obvious he would go under before he let her do so.

The older Hansum took a deep breath and submerged, searching for the saddle's cinch buckles. He grabbed hold of the girth strap and ran his hands along its length, but didn't find any. He searched again and again, grasping under one side of the saddle and then the other, trying to find them. Finally, out of breath, he kicked and burst through the surface of the water to get more air. In that brief second he saw his younger counterpart, desperation and justifiable anger in his eyes. And he saw Guilietta, still out cold on her back, her mouth and eyes slightly open.

The roar of the rapids was now deafening and they were moving even faster. He plunged back into the water, running his hands along the saddle girth, still finding no clips, and then he froze as the truth of the matter seized him. He would find no brass cinches on this saddle girth because it wasn't made of leather. It was a cheap rope girth, tied with a knot. It too was wet and as impossible to untie as Guilietta's wrists. A rush of true panic buzzed up Hansum's spine and burst in his brain. He kicked hard again, pushing himself upwards. His lungs were bursting with pain as he broke the surface, and when he did he screamed. He screamed so loud and hard it echoed over the rocky shore, and even over the sounds of the rapids.

His look of desperation was mirrored in the identical face that was staring back at him. Young Hansum's teeth were gritted, determination and anger showing. Suddenly another set of eyes were looking at him. These other eyes were hovering right in front of his face, now blocking the younger Hansum and Guilietta.

"Pedang!"

"We must hurry, sir," the young sword said. "Rapids."

"The saddle cinch," Hansum shouted. "Cut it. Follow me," and he ducked underwater.

Even under water, the roar of the rapids was deafening. It was like they were in a large drum that was being constantly beaten. Hansum grabbed the flat, woven rope cinch and pulled at it with all his might. He pointed and Pedang slid under it. The A.I. sword twisted and the rope sliced apart. Independent now, the dead horse started to float away. Hansum kept hold of the rope cinch and wound it around his fist, to make sure it wouldn't get away from him. Then he held out his hand and looked at Pedang, willing him to understand what he wanted. Pedang spun his blade around and placed his grip in Hansum's hand. Hansum pointed upward with his chin and Pedang started pulling him. As they broke the surface, Hansum saw they were just entering the rapids. There were huge rocks and trunks of trees just a few paces from them.

"Pull us to the shore!" he shouted to Pedang. "Secure Guilietta," he cried to the younger Hansum. He tensed as Pedang began pulling one arm toward land, while the current forced his other arm to bear the weight of a waterlogged saddle and two people being pulled in the opposite direction. The younger Hansum grabbed Guilietta around the waist and hugged the saddle to himself, so when the saddle was pulled, it wouldn't strain her wrists. As they slowly made their way out of the rapids and toward the shore, the older Hansum looked back to see the poor dead horse tumble into the rocks, slamming and breaking against them. Its four limbs spun upward to the sky and then back into the water before being crushed against another huge bolder. As Hansum looked away, it was disappearing underwater.

As the shore came nearer, the current slowed somewhat, but it was still too fast to swim in.

"Transport us, Sideways," Hansum called, and the A.I. cloak's face appeared in the fabric.

"I can't yet, Master Hansum. You're too spread out. When you can stand in the water together . . ."

Hansum turned to see how Guilietta was doing. His younger self was lying on his back, the saddle in one arm, Guilietta in the other, her head on his shoulder. Her eyes were now closed, her lips blue. The younger Hansum caught his gaze and looked back at him with cold hatred, as if questioning, "How could you let this happen?"

Hansum felt the bottom, a few slippery rocks and submerged tree trunks at first, and then sand and stone. He nodded to his other self.

"Can you touch bottom yet?" The younger Hansum struggled with his feet and then stood. "Stop!" the older Hansum shouted to Pedang. When he felt he could stand against the remaining current, he let go of the sword and pulled himself toward his other self. He grabbed the saddle with both hands, allowing his younger self to get a better hold of Guilietta. "Pedang, the saddle. Cut Guil's rope." Pedang was there in an instant and the older Hansum moved his hand to Guilietta's. He hesitated before he touched them. They were raw and blue. Emotion caught in his chest, but he pushed it down and, as gently as possible, forced his way between her hands and the saddle. The opening created, Pedang slipped under and, without hesitation, cut the bonds. Just like that, Guilietta was free.

The older Hansum now pulled the saddle away and released it into the current. It instantly took off down river, sinking before it got far. Then the two Hansums moved together, each putting their arms under Guilietta, forming a sling and raising her up. They started stepping toward the shore.

"I can transport now," Sideways said and, instantly, they were on the shore, standing on a patch of soft grass. There was still a roar in the air, but they could already feel the radiant heat from the sun. They put Guilietta gently down on the ground and knelt beside her.

"She not breathing," the younger Hansum shouted.

"Give her artificial respiration," Sideways said.

"I don't know how," the younger one cried.

"I do!" the older Hansum said, that being one of the first classes during general training.

Hansum breathed into Guilietta's mouth and alternatively pumped her chest. As he did, he could hear his younger self cursing him.

"How could you, how could you let this happen? Come on, come on, breathe Guilietta, breathe. Please Cristo, let her breathe," and, as the older Hansum switched from breathing to pumping, he could see his younger self cross himself.

Finally Guilietta coughed, convulsing as she did, and water came up from her lungs. The older Hansum quickly turned her on her side, and she winced. As she continued to cough up water, both Hansums noticed her dress was torn and a circle of red was forming. She had been speared by one of the broken branches. The younger Hansum gently put his hand there and Guilietta winced again.

Suddenly, Sideways moved away from Hansum, morphing from a tunic into a heavy blanket.

"What the . . ." the younger Hansum cried.

"It's okay," shouted the older one, the bright scar cross now exposed on his bared chest.

"I'm going to warm her and scan her injuries," Sideways called, and he lay himself over Guilietta.

The older Hansum watched as the younger one went to Guil's head and tucked the edge of the blanket under her, like a pillow. Then he moved her wet hair from her eyes and spoke soothingly.

"It's all right. I'm here now, sweetheart. I'm here. You're going to be all right."

The older Hansum had to shake his own head and refocus. He looked down at the blanket and Sideways's face formed.

"She's got internal injuries," he whispered. "A punctured lung."

"A punctured lung!" the younger Hansum yelled. "She has to be operated on. Take her back. Take her back with you." Guilietta coughed again, cringing in pain. More liquid came out from her mouth, but this time it was a frothy pink. "Don't just stand there, do it now!" the young Hansum shouted.

The older Hansum looked at the younger one. "You've got the pendant. You'll go back with her."

"What?" the younger one said, exasperated.

"You're supposed to take her back. It will make things right."

Guilietta coughed again. The younger Hansum put his hand to her mouth and his fingers turned bright red.

"I don't care who takes her," he screamed. "Do it now!"

"Sideways, take them home," the older Hansum said, and he bent down and put his face close to Guilietta's. "Take them home."

"Good bye, Master Hansum," Sideways said. "It was an honor." Sideways looked over at the younger Hansum. "Sir, you must take hold of me. A vortex will form."

Both Hansums' faces were close to Guilietta's now.

"Good bye, Guilietta," the older Hansum said. "I love you," and he kissed her gently on the temple. Her eyelids fluttered.

"Please step back, Master Hansum," Sideways said. "The vortex. Come, Pedang."

"Goodbye, sir," Pedang said. "I'm sorry that . . ."

"Go," the older Hansum shouted, and he raised his hand in farewell. He stood there, wet and shirtless, his face showing serene sadness.

"And thus I call the vortex," Sideways said. A wind came up, lifting leaves and sand off the ground. A circle started, but then it died. "I call the vortex," Sideways called again, but this time absolutely nothing happened.

"What's going on?" the younger Hansum asked in frustration.

The older Hansum stepped forward.

"It's like the first time Arimus and I tried to save her," Sideways said. "Guilietta just can't seem to go through a time vortex."

"What first time?" the younger Hansum shouted. "I don't understand."

The older Hansum fell to his knees.

"My plan didn't work," he said. "I've failed again."

"What first time?" the younger Hansum screamed. "What plan?" and he was up and at his older self. He got down on his knees and grabbed the other Hansum, shaking him. "Tell me what's going on! We've got to save her."

"I can't," Hansum moaned pitifully.

"Don't tell me that!" the younger Hansum screamed. "I'll kill . . ."

"Romero," the weak voice of Guilietta whispered. "Is that you, Romero?"

Instantly, both Hansums were back to Guilietta, one on each side.

"Don't turn her on her back," Sideways said.

The younger Hansum lay on the ground, looking straight into Guilietta's eyes. The older one hovered above.

"I'm here, Guilietta, I'm here, my love."

"My . . . husband," Guilietta whispered painfully. "You came to rescue me."

"Of course, of course. I would travel across time for you, my darling."

"You are all right?" she asked.

"I'm fine. Don't worry about me, darling."

"You're safe. That's good." She coughed again. More blood.

"We've got to get you home. I'll make a litter. Go find the Podesta . . ." He started to stand, but Guilietta's hand came out and touched his.

"No, stay with me, my husband. Stay with me while I go to Jesus."

"No, Guilietta, no," the younger Hansum pleaded, his eyes instantly full of tears. "You can't die. I haven't had enough."

"Who's to say what's enough?" Guilietta said, trying to smile. "Not those who say it. I am content that yours is the last voice . . ."

"Can't you do something?" the older Hansum said to Sideways.

"I've been trying, sir," Sideways said.

Guilietta looked up and saw the second Hansum. Her eyes widened and her composure left her. She became terrified. "What?" she gasped. She looked back to the younger Hansum, then back at the older. Fear filled her eyes. "Am I already dead? Am I in Hell? Am I in purgatory? Sweet Jesus, save me," and she began coughing, spatters of blood spraying on both Hansums. "I'm afraid of Hell!" she wheezed, then began gasping for breath, unable to speak.

"Her lungs are hemorrhaging," Sideways said.

"Guilietta, Guilietta!" the younger Hansum cried, cradling her in his arms. She looked up at him, her eyes wide with fear, her mouth moving but unable to form words as blood and mucus began to bubble from it. She saw the second Hansum and her face contorted. She closed her eyes, burying her head in the younger Hansum's chest.

"Guilietta," the older Hansum screamed, but as he came to her he felt his counterpart's hand shoving him away. He fell back to the ground, out of her sight. He stayed there.

"Hush my darling, hush," the younger Hansum cried. "Hush my darling, hush my . . ." and in a fit of pain her body, trying to breathe, broke free of her husband. It arched up off the ground, even throwing Sideways off. Her face, a bloody mask of pain, hung there frozen. Her heart was pounding, her body screaming for oxygen that her blood-filled lungs couldn't deliver. Her eyes focused on her husband's pleading and helpless face . . . and then . . . and then her gaze went blank. She collapsed to the ground, still. The A.I. cloak slowly rose off the ground and gently wrapped itself around the now-still body and face.

"I'm sorry, Master Hansum," Sideways said to the younger man.

He was sitting there, his unbelieving eyes in shock. Finally he grimaced and screamed.

"GUILIETTA!"

The older Hansum lay on the ground in a fog of exhaustion, unable to move as the white terror he had worked so hard to master, reclaimed him. The terror swelled up from the depths of his soul, the fear and grief from his first two losses, hidden by his training, raced up like ghosts from the grave and devoured his entire being.

But his countless hours of training *was* still with him. He ground his teeth and forced himself not to succumb to the situation. "Not yet!" His face pale and drained of blood, the older Hansum looked at the young man bent over Guilietta. He saw the dangling pendant around the other's neck, the temporal time protection. He knew that new waves of time were rolling across the cosmos and that they would soon catch up to the 24th-century, changing everything. Any second now, without that device around his neck, he would disappear and the Hansum in front of him would take his place.

That had been the plan, but could he let it happen now? Guilietta had died sooner. No cannons would be made before their time. But without his wife or the experience with the Podesta, perhaps the Hansum he saw in front of him would be so different, when he finally did get back to his century, maybe he wouldn't make the same decisions and come back to save Guilietta. Could he take that chance?

In his grief, the thought crossed his mind that perhaps that would be better. Guilietta was out of pain now. Maybe it was best. But then the older Hansum forced himself to stand, his conditioning to complete his mission coming to the fore. He walked over to his younger self and kneeled, putting a hand on the other's shoulder. The younger Hansum tensed and looked up, tears streaming from his eyes, grief, confusion and anger on his face.

"I made things worse," the older Hansum said. "I'm sorry."

Anger took over what was on the younger one's face.

"Who the hell are you?" he growled. "Who the . . ." Pedang levitated beside them both, his eyes moving between the two.

"I'm you," the older Hansum said quietly. "About a year from now. I . . . I came back to fix things, to save Guil . . . I made them worse." The younger Hansum's eyes flared. He looked down at the blanket covering Guilietta. The older Hansum reached and took hold of the chain of the time pendant necklace. "I need this, so I can try agai . . ." but before he could finish his sentence, a fist from the younger Hansum smashed into his face, driving him onto his back. The younger Hansum leapt upon him, throwing more punches.

"I'll kill you, you bloody liar! I'll kill you, I'll kill you."

"Stop it, stop it!" Pedang shouted.

"Desist, Master Hansum," Sideways's face cried from the blanket.

"I'll kill you, I'll kill you," the younger Hansum screamed as he continued to punch.

"Stop! Stop it," another voice called. It was Lincoln, still a distance away, hobbling and obviously in pain. "Stop it. Hansum. Stop!" But the younger Hansum continued to pummel his older self, who just lay there taking it. As Lincoln got to them, he awkwardly dove at the younger Hansum, tackling him around the shoulders and taking him to ground. "Please, buddy, please. Please stop," he said firmly, grabbing the younger Hansum's shoulders. Amazingly, he stopped, his red eyes burning up at Lincoln. "Where's Guil?" Lincoln asked, and neither Hansum answered. "Where's . . ." and then he looked around, seeing the blanket with Sideways sad face looking back at him. A hand and a foot were sticking out from beneath. Lincoln went pale as he flopped down to the ground, stunned. The younger Hansum, now free, turned toward Guilietta's covered body and lay himself back on the ground, facing her in the fetal position. All was silence until Pedang levitated over to Lincoln.

"Master Lincoln. The pendant. It must be put on your Hansum. Quickly."

Lincoln looked back at the younger Hansum lying awkwardly on the ground by Guilietta. He crawled over the few feet to him.

"Hey man," he said softly. "I need that pendant. If we've any chance to try again . . ."

The young Hansum grabbed the pendant around his neck and tried pulling the chain so hard it would break. But it was unbreakable. In frustration, he finally pulled it over his head and threw it at Lincoln.

"Take it, you bloody liars," he shouted.

Lincoln quickly went over to the older Hansum. He tried to put the necklace over him, but Hansum put a hand up to stop him.

"You must put the necklace on him, sir," Sideways said with urgency. "The wave containing the changes we've made to the timeline is speeding toward the 24th-century. If you want another try at saving Guilietta, you must put it on . . . now."

"What do you want me to do, pal?" Lincoln asked. "It's up to you. Try again or let it be?"

Hansum looked up at Lincoln with eyes that were now swollen and black.

"What is he talking about?" the younger Hansum asked, his voice choking. "Tell me."

The older Hansum looked from Lincoln to his younger self, and then to Guilietta. He felt so defeated, like he wanted to just give in to the universe. It would be so peaceful to just fade away and . . ."

"Over there," they heard a man shout in the distance. It was the two soldiers sent by Captain Caesar. They were galloping toward them.

"Quickly!" Lincoln said. "Decide."

Hansum nodded, putting his hand down and letting Lincoln slip the necklace over his head.

"Sideways. Pedang," Lincoln called. "To me." Pedang flew close to Lincoln and the older Hansum. Sideways slowly withdrew from Guilietta, exposing her still body. The younger Hansum crawled closer to her, still lying in the grass, now face to face with her unseeing eyes. He took her hand. Lincoln helped the older Hansum sit up and Pedang pressed himself against them.

"I'm sorry," the older Hansum said.

The younger Hansum turned and looked at him, stone-faced.

"Now," Lincoln said and Sideways blinked, calling for the vortex.

Immediately, a wind tunnel formed around the group.

"It's working this time," Pedang announced.

The two Hansums stared at each other as the large yellow Sands of Time appeared. They stared with eyes which had flowed from the same source, watched the same world and imagined the same dreams. Now they contained the same grief and wordless questions. As the Sands of Time gained speed, the ground fell away.

BOOK THREE
Fears of the Brave

Chapter 1

Hansum was awakened in the middle of the night by the touch of a familiar force field on his shoulder. He rolled over on his levitation mattress and saw exactly who he thought he would see.

"Charlene, I'm trying to sleep," he complained hoarsely. "I've got to catch the transport early in the morning."

"And I've got to talk some sense into you," she replied.

"Oh, for Gia sakes!" Hansum flopped back over and pulled the blanket over his head.

Using her force field, Charlene sucked the cover off him, causing it to fly up in the air.

"You *will* listen to me!" Charlene pronounced, her animated brows coming together above two angry, drawn eyes. Hansum sprang to his feet, clad only in a pair of boxer shorts.

"That's all I've been doing since I got back over two months ago," he snapped. "I've been listening to you, to Mom and Dad, the village elders, everyone. And when I do get a few words in, you all just talk over me."

"But going back for more punishment . . . a third time . . . it's obsessive!"

"I'm not obsessed. Both our family doctor and the Council agree I'm just trying to complete a difficult task. I want to save Guilietta. I'm not crazy."

"One time you come back and you've been skewered through the heart and the next your face is beaten to a pulp . . . by yourself. And you're going back for more?"

"You listen to me and you listen to me good, Charlene. Whatever I've been through, I'm healed. I'm fine and I'm going to keep trying. So get off my case!"

"You're not healed on the inside. I know you better than all those doctors put together. Oh, you're so stubborn! Worse than when you were a child. Something terrible is eating at you and I don't know what it is. I wish I could mind-delve you," Charlene grumbled. "I really want to know what's going on inside that brain of yours."

"Charlene, I've told you what I'm thinking. Believe me — please. Now," he said snatching the blanket from the floor, "will you please get out of my room and let me sleep? Lincoln, Shamira and Kingsley will be here in three hours."

"At least stay for another month," Charlene pleaded as he crawled back onto his invisible bed.

"Charlene, it's time to get on with things."

"For our family's sake. For my sake," she begged.

"Time travel is still open and we don't know if and when it will close. We've got to submit another plan to the Council and it's meeting the day after tomorrow." And with that, Hansum pulled the covers around him and turned toward the wall.

"But," Charlene started.

Hansum whirled around. "Arimus has already made the arrangements," he said. "I won't change them. Now let me sleep and go away!" And with that, he turned toward the wall.

Hansum lay there, listening. He heard Charlene's mouse-like snuffling for a few seconds, followed by the sound of the bedroom door opening and closing. He was alone in the dark again, but sleep didn't come quickly because Charlene was right. Something deep down was bothering him. And the problem was he didn't know what it was either. But he couldn't risk admitting that to anyone.

At first he thought it was just the images of the last mission. They kept jumping into his mind's eye; every horrifying part of the fight with Feltrino, the horse and the river, Guilietta lying dead on the bank. But there was something else, some phantom was haunting him, and he had to hunt it down and kill it himself.

Hansum received little comfort knowing that correcting the situation had, once again, been relatively easy. Arimus simply sent Sideways back to tell the earlier version of the A.I. cloak not transport Hansum to intercept his younger self. It worked. The timeline reset and played out as before. Guilietta was alive again and so was Feltrino.

Correcting the mistakes easily continued to surprise everyone involved, given that time seemed to be blocking them in so many other ways. But it piqued the curiosity of the 24th-century scientists advising the Council. They all found it fascinating and theories abounded. They hypothesized that Guilietta could be an example of some not-yet-understood force that made it impossible for some people to travel through a vortex, except at specific times. Perhaps it was a phenomenon the universe employed to protect key parts of the timeline, and they even developed equations to prove it. Maybe Guilietta was one of these people and they would have to devise a way to find when she could come through what they were calling "nexus points." As a result, the scientists were enthusiastically asking that more attempts be made as soon as possible to test this theory. The public also wanted more of the Romero and Guilietta story.

The only objection to mounting another mission was coming from a faction of the History Camp Time Travel Council. Elder Parmatheon Olama had gained more support from other members, so had become a power to reckon with. Arimus told Hansum not to worry. Hansum presumed it was because the 31st-century Elder Cassian Olama could veto his multi-generational grandson's vote. But Hansum still worried. He worried because he lived every day and night with the feeling that a demon was devouring him from the inside.

Finally, sleep came an hour before he had to get up.

When Lincoln found out what the new type of transport could do, he enthusiastically asked it to transmute into the shape of a Buck Rogers-style space ship. The A.I. ship captain laughed.

"Stand back, young people," he said, and immediately transmuted himself from a regular sized A.I. orb, wearing an old-fashioned leather aviator's helmet and goggles, to the sleek early 20th-century science-fiction version of a rocket ship, complete with a pointy front and long tailfins.

"Oh, I get it," Lincoln laughed. "You're not just the pilot, you're the ship."

As Lincoln, Medeea, Hansum, Shamira and Kingsley boarded the vessel, they saw five passenger seats.

"There's a chair for Medeea too," Kingsley observed.

"Tell Captain Orville that was very thoughtful," Medeea said to Lincoln. *"Very sweet."*

"Medeea says you're sweet, Captain," Lincoln joked. "But I was hoping she'd sit on my lap."

"Thoughtfulness is all part of Haudenosaunee hospitality," the now disembodied voice of the captain said. "Have a seat and here we go," and the ship took off.

"Man, this is fast," Lincoln said as he looked out the window. "We're already above the clouds and, Hell's bells, we're over the ocean already."

"I was going to sketch the Cliffs of Dover but . . ." Shamira began, pressing her nose to the porthole.

"Already passed 'em," Lincoln finished.

"There's no sense of acceleration," Kingsley added. "Those Haudenosaunee engineers certainly come up with great things."

"My makers are the best," Captain Orville's voice boasted.

Hansum gave a loud yawn and stretched. "Let me know when they've perfected site to site transport," he said lazily. "Then you can say they're fast."

"Sorry I don't meet your expectations, sir," the ship said without a hint of disdain. "Please enjoy the ride. I must attend to my duties."

Hansum stretched again and scratched at his chest.

"Wow, I think Hansum is actually getting ruder," Lincoln thought to Medeea.

"I agree," Medeea answered. Shamira and Kingsley looked like they were worried about their friend too.

"Man oh man, I wish I had a better sleep last night," Hansum yawned.

"What's the problem, bro?" Lincoln asked.

"Charlene woke me up and went on a tirade about what we're doing."

"I'm sure she's just concerned," Kingsley said.

"Concern doesn't begin to describe it. She even wished she could mind-delve me, to really see what I was thinking," Hansum looked out the window as they flew over Greenland. They were on their way to North America and what was still known as the Finger Lakes. "Man, taking this long to get from one place to the other is getting on my nerves."

Medeea raised an eyebrow to Lincoln.

"Maybe mind-delving Hansum would be a good idea," she thought.

"Charlene just loves you," Shamira suggested. "My Perminia was at me every day. 'Settle down,' she said. 'Do your art. Have a baby.' "

"You didn't tell me that part," Kingsley said.

"Oops." Shamira blushed and everyone laughed.

"You guys are lucky," Kingsley continued unabashed. "When I couldn't travel home during the blackout, I would have given anything to have my family badgering me."

When the blackout ended, people from the 24th to the 28th-century could time travel again. However, the 31st-century Arimus still couldn't, and that meant history was still unfolding differently. Arimus seemed to be taking it well now, confident things would work out.

"The next time you miss being badgered, you can have Charlene," Hansum said. "Hey, you can have my whole family."

Lincoln and Medeea looked at each other again.

"Hansum really is getting coarse," she thought.

"Yeah. He'd never say anything as thoughtless as that before. I mean, I would, but I was just a kid."

"Transport," Hansum called out impatiently. "How much longer before we get to Haudenosaunee? Have you slowed down?"

"Four minutes, sir," the ship's voice answered. "We're right on time . . . sir, and my name is Captain Orville."

"What I wouldn't give for my own A.I. cloak so I could site transport," Hansum said, snapping his fingers to indicate how long that would take him to get anywhere on the planet. "So, you guys ready to do this all over again?"

"Do what?" Lincoln asked. "The application to the Council or the trip back?"

"Both, for Gia sakes."

"We're here for ya to the end, pal," Lincoln said. *"Although you are getting to be a royal pain in the rear,"* he thought to Med.

"At least we don't have to do the application in that big amphitheater," Shamira said. "I hated being in front of all those people."

"Just because we'll be in an elder's longhouse with a few dozen people and A.I.s," Hansum countered, "doesn't mean there won't be millions of people watching from their homes."

"I . . . hadn't thought of that," Shamira said, going pale.

Lincoln and Medeea were once again surprised at Hansum's tactlessness. Medeea sat next to Shamira and linked arms, while Lincoln said something encouraging.

"Won't it be great, Sham," he said cheerfully, "if we can do what Hansum's going to propose for the next rescue? Bring Guilietta and her parents back with us? Can you imagine the Master and Signora in the 24th-century? What a hoot."

"That would be great," Shamira agreed. "The Signora could become healthy in her mind."

"First things first," Hansum said firmly. "Arimus was telling me yesterday the Council is equally divided on whether we should have another go at things, even though the scientists and public want it: the scientists, so they can study what they're calling these "nexus points" and the public, because they want more of our Romero and Guilietta story. We'll have to play all that up. But it's that Parmatheon Olama who's the real problem. He's such a friggin' bureaucrat."

"Landing at Haudenosaunee in one minute," the voice of the ship chimed.

"Finally," Hansum sighed, looking out the window, but he needn't have.

"Realigning atomic particles for a bottom view," Captain Orville announced. The floor of the ship suddenly became transparent.

"Oh, we're up high," Shamira said.

Haudenosaunee was the main settlement of what was originally called the Iroquois Confederacy or the League of Six Nations. While the original settlement had disappeared under a city called Syracuse, that was gone now too. As the Earth's human population shrank to one-thirtieth of what it was at its peak, nature began to reclaim everything. But it wasn't a wilderness. It was now much the same as it had been a thousand years earlier, when Europeans first came to North America *en mass.*

Still high in the sky, everyone could see Haudenosaunee, a fifty hectare settlement of twenty-five hundred people nestled on the shore of Lake Onondaga. At that height, they could just see Lake Ontario to the north and, to the south-west, a few of what were known as the Finger Lakes. As the transport descended, it became clear the settlement was ringed by hundreds of hectares of planted fields. Beyond that, and running west, there was a neat line showing the border of a heavy forest stretching to the horizon.

"As I'm sure you already know," the voice of the A.I. captain narrated, "the Haudenosaunee practiced one of the first and longest-lasting democracies on Earth. They were, and are again, known as The People of the Longhouse."

"I have Haudenosaunee blood," Kingsley said.

"The Haudenosaunee nation is about a third the size of what it was when Europeans came," Captain Orville continued. "It is comprised of what were known as upper New York State and Ohio, when they were part of the short-lived United States Empire. It has recently gained population and land from north of Lake Ontario and along the St. Lawrence River, from the now defunct country of Canada.

"When you are among the people here," the voice of the ship continued, "remember, you are not at a History Camp. The people here have agreed to live the way people lived before European contact, especially in food, clothing and housing, although technologically they are among the most advanced on the planet. This transport in fact . . . I," Captain Orville's voice went on, "am an innovation designed and birthed in one of the longhouses right below us."

Now, less than a thousand feet below them, the layout of Haudenosaunee became clear. There were about forty-five longhouses in a clearing, surrounded by a low palisade to keep out farm and wild animals. As the transport reached about two hundred feet, it slowed to a halt for a few seconds. The whole transport became transparent now, making it look like the passengers were sitting in mid-air. This gave everyone a chance to get a good look at where they were. With people now discernible below, it gave a human scale to the place and Lincoln was amazed how large the longhouses were. They ranged from eighty to two-hundred feet in length and were some twenty feet wide and high, impressive as they were made of elm and ash poles, covered with large, flattened pieces of tree bark. Ever since he had been in charge of making the cannon fuses from the hollow flight feathers of a goose, Lincoln had been fascinated with anything people made totally from natural products.

"Yes, they will be very interesting to study," Medeea thought to him.

He squeezed her hand and smiled. With absolutely nothing to hide from his A.I. girlfriend, Lincoln was free of guilt and self-doubt. Even his family, including his Nan, had commented on his personal growth to manhood.

The transport proceeded to land in an open field just outside the front gate of the village. They were next to several other transports, except these were older, solid vehicles, not like Captain Orville. Their rear ramps were down and perhaps another one hundred people and ten A.I.s were around them.

"Oh look, Shamira," Medeea said. "There's a wedding party getting off the transports. See the groom dressed a suit of pure white rabbit pelts? He must be Mohawk."

"Oh, how exciting," Shamira said. "And that must be the bride. She has old-fashioned European clothes on . . . and a veil too." She leaned against Kingsley, smiling.

"It's great when cultures mix," he said. "Like us."

A few feet above ground, the transparent walls and ceiling completely dematerialized and the fresh breeze of Lake Onondaga washed over everyone. As the floor touched down, it too evaporated and everyone was left sitting on their chair in the grass. The seats disappeared as each person stood and Captain Orville rematerialized, aviator helmet and all.

"Thank you for the interesting flight, Captain," Lincoln said. "You're one heck of a ship."

"I can transform my mass into a transport that carries up to one hundred passengers. I'm the first of my kind, born right here in Haudenosaunee. And it's an honor to have such renowned celebrities traveling in me. I bid you all a good rest of your journey. It was nice having you."

"It was nice being had," Lincoln answered, to which the captain roared with laughter as he levitated into the village.

"I hope I'm not bothering you," a woman's voice said. Shamira turned to find the bride and her groom smiling at her.

"Hello," Shamira said.

"Hello, Shamira. My name is Miriama and this is my fiancé, Charlie. We're getting married today."

"Congratulations," Shamira said. "This is . . ."

"Yes, Lincoln, Kingsley and Hansum," Charlie said putting out his hand. Hansum hesitated before shaking hands.

"And Medeea is here too," Lincoln added, motioning beside him, "She adds her congratulations to ours."

"Listen guys, we should find Arimus," Hansum interrupted.

Just then several more people rushed up to the group. A large man, looking like an older version of the groom, was among them.

"Son, you made it," he said throwing his arms around Charlie. "Look at him in my old wedding suit, Mother" he said to the woman greeting her future daughter-in-law.

"Yep, we made it, Pops."

"We're all so glad you and Miriama are here to stay," the father said. "It's a dream come true to work on deep space environmental equipment with my own son. Just like I did with my father and he before him."

"Guys. Let's go find Arimus," Hansum repeated.

That's when the father and mother noticed who they were standing by.

"Oh, excuse me," the father said deferentially. "I hope I didn't interrupt . . ."

"We've got to get to a meeting," Hansum said.

"Before you go," Miriama added, "If you have time, Charlie and I would be honored if you would all attend our wedding." As she said this, Miriama put her hand on Hansum's arm. Her eyes exuded happiness. "I've watched your wedding with Guilietta, I don't know how many times."

Hansum stared back at the bride, showing little of how her comment stung him to his core. After many long seconds you could see Miriama and Charlie become nervous. Then Hansum forced a smile.

"Thank you both very much," he said. "However, I have to prepare for something. I wish you both joy," and he turned and walked away.

"Hansum . . ." Lincoln called after him.

"I'll be over there," he said pointing to the village's open palisade gate.

"You'll have to excuse him," Hansum heard Shamira say. "He has a lot on his mind."

Chapter 2

Hansum was standing by the city gate, tapping his communications node off and on for a good five minutes.

"Why isn't Arimus answering?" he grumbled. He felt even testier when he saw Lincoln, Shamira and Kingsley among the hundreds of noisy people now gathered to celebrate the wedding. Children were running around, adults were laughing and greeting, and it even looked like a few romances were starting. "C'mon, Arimus. Answer me already," Hansum complained, tapping again. "Oh, finally. Arimus, why didn't you answer? We're here at the . . . what? What? Why? How long? This afternoon or tomorrow? Why the . . . Oh, all right, all right," Hansum said impatiently, clicking his communications implant off.

Just then a tall, handsome man of around seventy strolled out of the village, passing Hansum and standing before the assembly. He was dressed in the highly decorative regalia of an Onandoga chief. His outstretched arms revealed a jacket and trousers made of deerskin and covered with intricate beading and lapidary work. His hat was a collection of hundreds of hawk and eagle feathers, all radiating out from a center point. But the man himself was surprisingly light skinned, almost like Shamira.

"Welcome," he called out. "I'm here to welcome you to Haudenosaunee. My name is Sam Goldman, the Tadodaho of Haudenosaunee."

There was a gasp of surprise from behind Hansum. He turned and saw two men coming out of the village, apparently to see what the excitement was all about.

"The Tadodaho himself is greeting them? It's probably because . . . they're here," one of the men said, pointing to Shamira, Lincoln and Kingsley. The man caught Hansum's eye and gave a start, realizing he had been overheard. He looked embarrassed and turned away.

"Not everyone will love ya," Hansum said under his breath. "So don't even try."

"We're all here to celebrate Miriama and Charlie's wedding and to welcome them to their new home," Sam Goldman continued. "So, if you will all follow me, we shall proceed to the celebration longhouse. It's much cooler in there and we have refreshments for everyone." Elder Goldman, the Tadodaho of the entire Haudenosaunee nation turned, his arms still outstretched, and led everyone into the village. As the crowd passed the gate, Lincoln, Shamira and Kingsley stopped in front of Hansum.

"You might as well keep on enjoying what you're doing," Hansum said. "Arimus says it will be later today or even tomorrow before they need us."

"That's fantastic," Shamira gushed, smiling at Kingsley. "I've never been to a wedding like this."

"I have," Kingsley said. "C'mon. Let's get some pointers, babe."

"You coming, Hansum?" Shamira asked.

"No, no. I'm fine. I'm going to find my room and prepare," he said leaning against the open palisade.

"Prepare for what?" Lincoln asked.

"Yes, please, Hansum . . ." Kingsley began.

"I just want to rest. You guys have fun."

"Go ahead you two," Lincoln said to Kingsley and Shamira. "I'll catch up in a minute."

"All right," Kingsley replied, "But there will be venison at the feast," and he and Shamira rejoined the crowd.

"Venison is deer meat, isn't it," Hansum heard Shamira ask enthusiastically as they left.

"Yes. That's the main meat source around here in my time," Kingsley said, their voices trailing off. "I'm sure it's the same now."

"Hey man, what's up?" Lincoln asked. "What you did to Miriama and Charlie was pretty rude."

"What's rude is Arimus not being here," Hansum replied, looking through the gates and into the village proper. "He says he's having difficulty with the pre-negotiation, whatever that is."

"Well, tomorrow or whenever will come soon enough," Lincoln said. "C'mon and have some fun."

"Lincoln, please. Just go ahead."

"Okay, buddy," Lincoln replied. "We're just worried for ya, man. We love ya."

"I know," Hansum answered. "Go."

Hansum watched Lincoln run through the gates and catch up to the crowd, which was funneling into a very large longhouse off the main square. When the last of the throng disappeared inside the cedar bark building, a single man was left standing by its entrance. He was looking right at Hansum. His skin was deep brown and he wore long straight hair to his shoulders. His black eyes were like coal and, even from a distance, gave the impression they could ignite and glow red hot at any second. His mouth was a long, wide slit turned down in what seemed a permanent frown. For the first time in a long time, and despite all his recent training, Hansum felt surprised. He took a deep breath and was about to call out, but the man turned and walked in among the other longhouses, disappearing.

'That was weird,' Hansum thought, and then walked through the gate and into the village. He touched his communications device. "Can someone tell me where my lodgings are?"

A few longhouses down, a boy and a girl, both about twelve, were playing keep-away with a soccer ball. They stopped and touched their communications nodes. Hansum knew the local communications A.I. had found some errand runners to show hospitality to a visitor. They seemed to listen to some silent instruction before looking around. When they saw Hansum, both came running with big smiles on their faces.

"Hey, you're him," the boy said, sliding to a halt, his bare feet kicking up dust.

"Yes, I am," Hansum replied. The girl was staring gap-mouthed at him, up at his face and then down at his scarred hand. Hansum held it out and she looked away.

"Sorry for staring," she said. "It's rude."

"No problem. Can you show me where I'm staying?"

"Follow us," the boy said. "It's on the other side of the village. Want to run? I watched you run through the forests the other month. I'm a good runner too," and the kids turned and started jogging. Hansum felt good to be getting exercise. They ran left and right, twisting around the longhouses that were definitely not laid out in any specific fashion, neither in a grid nor a wheel. It was all willy-nilly. "Too bad we can't run through the longhouses," the boy called out. "What's it like running through trees?"

"Zippy!" Hansum answered, and he and the children laughed. It took several minutes to get across the village and many people stopped to watch, but Hansum paid them no attention.

As his escorts slowed down, Hansum noticed one set of eyes he couldn't ignore. The man with the eyes of coal was again staring at him. He was standing at the base of a very large black walnut tree. The tree's trunk was at least five feet across and its canopy spread out a good fifty feet in diameter.

"We're here," the boy said, puffing as they came to a halt in front of the guest longhouse. The two children watched Hansum and the man staring at each other. Then the man turned and walked away, again disappearing between the narrow paths between the buildings.

"Who's that?" Hansum asked. The kids twisted their tanned faces, as if to ask, 'You don't know?'

"That's the Deganawida," the girl said with awe in her voice. "The spiritual leader of our *whole* territory."

"When he's around, us kids don't mess around." the boy added. "He gives me the heebie jeebies."

"Bandy, don't talk like that," the girl scolded.

Hansum laughed. "Thanks for bringing me here. Where's my room?"

Bandy touched his node again, muttering. "In here . . . sir. Yes, I called him sir," he added testily to whomever he was talking to. Hansum smiled. Bandy reminded him of a younger Lincoln.

The interior of the guest lodge had a walkway down its length, with woven willow-strip walls separating the hall from the guest rooms. Colorful woven blankets acted as doors to each room, reminding Hansum somewhat of the curtained doors back at the della Cappa home. He found his quarters roomy and high, the walls and roof supported by a series of cedar and hickory poles. Other poles were lashed horizontally to create platforms for sleeping and storage. A thickly-padded sleeping mat and beautifully hand-woven blankets were neatly folded, waiting for Hansum's comfort.

There was also a bowl of water and soft towel on a small ash sideboard. Hansum washed his hands and face, dried them, and then sat on the edge of the sleeping platform. He drummed his fingers, thinking what to do. He reached over to his luggage. It was a long and narrow case, custom built to suit his needs. Loosening the woven ties, he opened the lid and took out a top layer of shirts and trousers. Below was the reason he needed the case to be so long, his sword with its scabbard and belt. He placed them on the bed, hung his clothing on pegs, and then lay down to nap.

His head instantly burst with images and sounds from the river . . . again. Hansum cursed, gritting his teeth and pulling the pillow over his head. He kept his eyes shut, determined to sleep, but it was no good. He couldn't stop the stream of images that came at him every time he tried to relax. And the sounds from those memories, they seemed to ring louder in his ears than when he lived them. The thundering of the horse's hooves, the clash of the swords, the screams of the dying animals and the roar of the river, they just wouldn't let him be.

Hansum kept telling himself he must be overcoming these ghosts in some ways though. He was succeeding brilliantly in his training and had even been given the accreditation of "journeyman" the other day. But was suppressing all he had gone through really working? If so, why was he acting harshly to everyone? Why did he constantly walk around feeling like he was going to explode? He knew his friends realized something was wrong. They were taking the brunt of it. And there was a practical danger. As the group leader, he knew his bad attitude could cause a diminishment of trust. This could compromise the mission. And most critical, he knew Arimus realized there was a problem. Maybe that was why he didn't want him to be at the meeting earlier. Why wouldn't his head stop spinning?

Less than a minute after lying down, Hansum opened his eyes and stared at the curved posts and bark covering of the longhouse roof. More awake than ever, he continued drumming his fingers and then sat up. He sighed. Perhaps a walk would help. More exercise might clear his head and allow him to sleep. Almost out the door, he turned and went back to his bed, picked up his sword and clipped the belt around his waist. In the corridor, he passed by several staring guests.

Walking into the bright sunlight, Hansum looked around to get his bearings. He remembered how the village was laid out from the air, Lake Onondaga to the east, fields and forests to the north and west. He turned away from the busy part of the village and worked his way through the tight spaces between several longhouses till he reached the palisade. Hansum pulled himself up to see the broad expanse of crops and, beyond that, a line of trees. Grasping the pointed tops of the fence stakes, he pulled himself over and dropped to the other side.

"Is everything all right?" a voice in his head asked, obviously a local security A.I.

"I'm fine, thanks," Hansum answered. "I just want some privacy and exercise."

"Very good, honored guest," the voice replied. *"You shall have it. Call if you need assistance."*

"Thank you."

As soon as Hansum walked in among the tall maize plants, he was again in shadow. It felt quite fine to be on his own for a while, outside and hidden from staring eyes. It was also interesting to see these fields close up. Hansum's father was the head fruit and vegetable elder of his village, and had told him about the ancient Haudenosaunee society's feat of terraforming hundreds of thousands of hectares into a productive commons of farms, hunting grounds, orchards and woodlands. When Europeans arrived, they found a whole territory of well-tended lands. The Europeans marveled how, outside the fields of crops, there were forests with huge trees, selected for their bark for housing, and nuts and fruits for eating. And there was little undergrowth because of a yearly, skillful burning. Europeans wrote about forests they could drive a wagon through for miles. The burning also encouraged certain game animals to come for the tender greenery that sprouted after the undergrowth was cleared. There were also stands of trees grown as poles for housing and fencing, to be harvested every few years.

The agriculture of the field crops was also very sophisticated. The field that Hansum was walking through contained what were known as the "three sisters." Hansum's father explained how maize, climbing beans and squash were grown together in what was called "companion farming." The beans climbed up the stalks of the maize and the squash leaves acted as a mulch to keep the soil from drying out. As well, and one wonders how many hundreds of years it took for the ancients to figure this out, the elements which one plant took from the ground, the other replaced, allowing the field's nutrients to diminish more slowly.

After about ten minutes of walking, the field of three sisters ended and another one, also with heritage crops, began. A field of little-barley was followed by a mixed field of maygrass, chenopod and knotweed. The heritage crops were kept close to the village for visitors to see.

Hansum then came to large plots of mixed crops, vegetables from all over the world. The citizens of this area were certainly proud of the Haudenosaunee heritage, and showed it, but it couldn't be said they didn't welcome food gifts from around the globe. There were carrots, beets, sweet and hot peppers of all colors, blueberries, huckleberries, potatoes, asparagus, broccoli, cabbage, cauliflower, celery, chard, cucumbers, okra, onions, peas, radicchio, radish, rhubarb, shallots, spinach, sweet potato, tomatoes, turnips, and even watermelon and yams. Hansum, like most children growing up in a village, knew them all, for part of all of Earth's cultures now was to have youth work in the fields that fed their region.

"Finally," Hansum said, feeling relaxed. "I'm thinking about something else." Hansum stopped and took in a deep breath, attempting to sense everything around him: the song birds, the insects, the rustling of the plants in the wind. He felt a calm coming over him. But as soon as he stopped thinking about the Haudenosaunee horticultural practices, his mission forced itself back into his mind. He put a hand on his chest to stay his anxiety. Why was he getting anxiety attacks and what was taking Arimus so frigging long to contact him?

Hansum broke out into a trot, running for a good ten minutes, trying to tire himself out. Finally he came to the end of the fields and walked into the forest. Most of the trees had massive trunks, four to eight feet thick and reached well over a hundred feet high. Their widespread canopies intersected with each other, making an immense open space below, like the interior of a great building. The massive trunks and high ceilings made Hansum think about the unforgettable churches of medieval Europe. Alone and hidden in this glorious cathedral of nature, Hansum slid his sword from its scabbard and began running through one of his warm-up routines, lunging, slashing, moving his feet agilely over and around the massive roots, skills that he would no doubt find himself using one day.

Then Hansum heard noises, a bleating and hooves running. He froze and listened carefully. The source of the noises was close by. He stepped behind a tree as a man's voice called out.

"Hurry, hurry. We must run him down. Don't let him rest," and then there were more footfalls through the leaves.

Hansum picked his way carefully around one tree and then the next, practicing his stealth. As he came around the great trunk of a shagbark hickory, he stopped and looked on in silence.

About fifty feet away were two men bent over a roan-colored lump on the ground. He could tell the man with his back to him was older. He pulled an arrow from a good sized white-tailed buck and patted the dead creature kindly on its shoulder. Without pause, he then pulled the animal's front legs forward and pointed to the back legs, indicating to a young man of about fourteen to pull on them, to expose the animal's belly. The young man stood up, but did not move.

"Come now, slave," Hansum heard the gentle voice of the older man say. "We must do this before the blood settles. Do not worry. This is something you will get used to and one day enjoy. I promise you."

The young man blew out a breath to steel his courage. He grabbed hold of the animal's large muscular legs and pulled. As he did so, he slipped and fell back on his backside. Hansum chuckled to himself.

The older man raised his head and looked at the youth. Hansum was surprised when he saw who it was. It was the stone-faced man, the region's spiritual leader, known as the Deganawida. Now that Hansum heard how gently he instructed the young man, the hard face seemed less ominous.

"Come. Get up and watch, slave."

Hansum knew that being a slave in some of the native cultures of North America was not as evil a thing as it had been in others. This had been a culture that didn't use money as its social glue. Therefore, when people needed help, were captured in war, or were just failures in making a living for themselves, they could become slaves of another family or elder. It was similar to being an indentured servant or apprentice, as Hansum had been. A slave could end up marrying into a former owner's family or buying his freedom through work or goods. Often, slaves didn't live with their owners and only owed them work part-time.

In the situation in front of him, Hansum presumed this was a hard case boy from another community who had been given to the Deganawida to learn life skills. Hunting and providing for one's self was a sure lesson to that end — not as severe as a Hard Time History Camp, but maybe this boy wasn't as bad as Hansum had been.

The young man was up on his feet, but still several paces from the carcass. The Deganawida took out a sharp hunting knife from a beautifully beaded sheath on his leg. Hansum could see, even at a distance, the gray-silver glint of the hand-forged, multi-folded steel. "Come, come closer slave. That's better. Now watch carefully, for you will do it next time."

The Deganawida turned the buck on its back and placed the tip of his sharp knife between the animal's scrotum and anus, and then pushed the tip into the hide. "You must make sure you don't cut into the urethra or bowel." Hansum could hear the teen suck in his breath.

"Don't be squeamish. Watch. Watch." Now the Deganawida cut under and around the animal's anus, pulling and separating it from the connective tissue. Hansum, who was relaxed, looked at the boy squinting like he was trying to see only half of what was happening before him. "Now I must cut up to the sternum, but being careful not to break through the abdominal wall. You don't want to contaminate the meat with fecal matter or bile. See? I turn my blade upside down, so the sharp edge cuts the upper hide only." As the blade moved up the chest, the Deganawida folded open the flap of skin he was creating. Finally, with the knife at the sternum, Hansum could see the fully-exposed abdominal wall, the sac holding in the guts.

The Deganawida then took half an arm's length of fine hemp string from a pouch on his belt and tied up the urethra and bowel. "You know why I do this?" he asked the teen.

"To keep the poop and pee in?" the boy ventured, crinkling his nose.

The older man then put both hands on the knife handle and started slicing through both the hide and sternum bone, right up to the throat. He quickly opened the neck completely and fished out the esophagus, a corrugated white tube of cartilage. He cut it away, so it hung out the neck. Then he turned back to the abdomen, reaching in and worming his hand, and then his whole arm, into the chest cavity.

"We reach up, like so . . . separate the diaphragm from the upper cavity . . . past the lungs, yes, the heart . . . got it . . . and . . ." he gave a little grunt as his hand worked around. "And then firmly, but gently . . . pull . . ." The esophagus disappeared from the throat region, suddenly popping out above the intestinal sack. Then the Daginawida tipped the carcass back on its side and, with one last gentle pull, all the internal organs fell out onto the ground in a neat bundle, with surprisingly little blood.

But this didn't matter. The young man scrambled to a tree and began throwing up. Hansum laughed, remembering how, back in Verona, it had taken him time to get used to all the butchering in the market place and down the street in front of Master Spagnoli's.

The Deganawida turned at the sound of Hansum's laugh and looked at him. For a moment his black eyes burned into Hansum's. Then a slow smile came to his lips and his face transformed, with large square teeth shining out from dark skin. He motioned for Hansum to join them. The

Deganawida's eyes followed Hansum as he approached, and Hansum could tell the older man was watching to see how he would react to the dead animal and fresh pile of guts. Hansum looked to the mound but did not flinch.

"So, you found *me* this time," the Deganawida said quietly.

"Greetings elder," Hansum said.

"Slave, what are you being sick for?" the Deganawida called, turning back to the younger man. His voice was still soft, but firm. "You weren't squeamish tucking into that deer steak the other night. Come now, we've got to butcher the meat and we've got company. Stand up and show respect to my visitor."

The young man, wiping his mouth with the back of his hand, turned. His eyes went wide when he saw Hansum. He jumped to his feet.

"You're . . . you're . . ."

"I didn't say to speak, slave. Now you must stand and be quiet." The older man turned back to Hansum, smiling again. Hansum held out his hand.

"Hello. I'm . . ."

"Yes, I know who you are," he said clasping Hansum's hand. He grasped it with both of his and took time to inspect the famous scar. "I've got one of those here," he said pulling up his shirt. "Got it when I was fourteen, from a buck not far from here. That was a lesson worth keeping too."

"Impressive," Hansum said.

"You, slave. Come here. Mind if I show him this?" he asked Hansum about the thumb.

"That's fine."

The boy walked over tentatively, looking down at the thumb, and then at something else. Hansum realized he was looking at his sword. The Deganawida realized it too and laughed.

"I caught this one watching your first sword fight by the river the other night. He had a stick in his hand and was slashing away at the air. 'What are you doing, slave,' I asked? 'I'm going to be a time traveler,' he said like the grown child he is. 'Maybe you need a stint at a Hard Time History Camp?' I asked him, and he pouted. Pouted." Hansum knew what the Deganawida was saying was not meant cruelly. It was the job of a mentor to point out hard realities, something a parent couldn't always do. "Look again at Journeyman Hansum's thumb and think of what he went through to get his scars." You could see the boy's imagination working and he went discernibly paler. "You can't even stand seeing a deer cleaned and you think you're fit for exploits? Now, look into Journeyman Hansum's eyes."

What Deganawida was doing to his slave had been done many times to Hansum when he was a hard case, trying to make the boy think outside his own ego-driven fantasies. Hansum stared back at the boy, his hard eyes, eyes that had seen so much in the past year, looking into the soft self-deluded eyes of a teen maybe three years his junior. The boy blinked, and then looked down.

"Good, good," the Deganawida said softly. "This one, my slave, back in his territory had won an archery contest and crowed about it when we got here. But could he shoot this deer when he had it in his sights? No, I had to. Do you think you will be able to do it next time? Eh? Answer me."

"I'll try, Master."

Hansum looked over at the boy, who had a tear running down his face.

"You know, Elder, I've just realized something," Hansum said.

"What's that, my son?"

"In all my experiences on missions, in all I've been through, I've never killed anyone . . . or anything. Not even a deer." The young man, the slave, looked up surprised. "Can I help finish dressing the animal?" Hansum asked. "We could learn together," he said to the youth.

Chapter 3

"I've never been to a wedding like this before," Shamira whispered to Kingsley. Her eyes were wide. "Is this where they cut into their arms?"

"Yes, that's coming up, sweetie," Kingsley whispered, and gave her a loving squeeze.

The ceremony had been so romantic. Charlie was in his tribe's wedding regalia of white rabbit fur and Miriama wore a modest, but beautifully tailored suit of an East European Jewish bride. The wedding had been conducted by both the Tadodahoe, to administer the Haudenosaunee rites, and a rabbi for the Jewish ones. And it all took place under a wedding canopy, or chuppah. The bride and groom were paraded in to the hauntingly beautiful sounds of a Haudenosaunee courting flute.

It had taken the better part of an hour to get through the two ceremonies and, while the traditions had been continents apart in origin, they were surprising close in emphasizing the building of familial ties and mutual respect between men and women.

Even though Shamira and Kingsley were standing among some two hundred guests, Shamira felt an incredible intimacy. Kingsley's warm arms were wrapped around her and every few minutes he would kiss her hair.

But now, after the ancient wedding rites, came the modern part of the ceremony. Back in the part of the world where Shamira and Lincoln grew up, what came next was usually done later and by a doctor. But here it was done as part of the marriage ritual and in full view of the community.

Their work completed, the Tadodaho and rabbi stepped aside and the angel, Laylah, flew into the longhouse. Laylah was an A.I. in the shape of a renaissance cherub, a plump little baby with golden hair, rosy cheeks, black eyes and a pink toga. After joyfully dive-bombing the crowd, he took his place, hovering in front of the couple.

"So, you want to have a child, do you?" he challenged the new couple. His voice was that of a boy of perhaps six, but harsh.

"Yes, we do," Charlie and Miriama cried loudly.

"I am here to grant your wish," Laylah replied. "But first I must remind you of the seriousness of this undertaking." He turned and started to fly slowly about the crowd, his little wings beating away. "In prehistoric times, before the human animal gained sentience, its reproduction, like that of all living things, had to be in great enough numbers to overcome a high mortality rate. But after the invention of agriculture," Laylah snapped his fingers, "within the blink of a galactic eye, the short space of ten thousand years, your kind's ingenuity outstripped its biology and the human population grew from a few million to over twelve *billion*." He paused for effect. "That's when your ancestors finally came to their collective senses and adopted binding population targets. They also called upon us, the A.I.s, to enforce this law. Since then, when a child is born an implant is placed within its body, not allowing that individual to reproduce . . . until a day like this."

In a blur, the angel sped back to the couple, stopping in a flash and hovering with a serious expression on his baby face.

"Put forward the limb from which you want me to cut the constraining device," he said solemnly. Both Miriama and Charlie pulled back their sleeves and exposed their upturned forearms. "Do you both vow that, come what may, you will love and support any child that comes from this action?"

"Yes, we vow," the couple replied together.

Without taking his serious little eyes from the couple, Laylah cried in a sonorous voice, "And does the community likewise vow to be loving and supportive in helping raise Miriama and Charlie's child?"

A great shout came up from all the people in congregation. Old and young alike knew what they were to respond and why.

"Miriama, Charlie and the child have our support!" several hundred people cried in unison.

The room went silent again. All that was heard was the rhythmic beating of Laylah's wings. Even the birds outside seemed to have stopped chirping. Laylah continued looking between Mariama and Charlie, his face a child's, but his eyes those of a terribly serious adult.

"Layla actually symbolizes the unborn child," Kingsley whispered, "looking at his future parents and questioning what type of world he will be brought into."

Hovering in the air, Layla now reached over his shoulder and took a short, sharp golden knife from his robes. It had a ruby encrusted hilt. Of course, everybody knew it was really a bloodless skin scalpel. The cherub placed the blade on Charlie's arm. The rubies glowed as he stuck the tip into his flesh. Charlie winced, for this was not to be a completely painless procedure. The skin opened up in a perfect oval. There, among the exposed muscles and tendons were two small spheres, each the size of a pea, one gold and one black. With the tip of the knife, Laylah flicked out the black one, catching it in the air and placing it within his robes. The cherub then turned to Miriama and placed the tip of the blade on her forearm, staring hard into her eyes. The bride smiled and the blade was pushed in. Miriama winced, but her smile never left her. Laylah removed her black sphere and held up both of their arms, so the congregation could see the open flesh.

"And now they can have a baby," Shamira whispered, squeezing Kingsley's massive arm and melting back into his warmth.

Laylah took Charlie's arm and moved it so his opened wound was covering Miriama's. He pressed the two together and a glow appeared. As he separated them, the skin was whole and fresh.

"No matter how many times I see that, I'm always amazed," Kingsley whispered.

"Elder Sam, my brother," the cherub called to the Tadodaho, "I believe there is one more piece of business."

Sam Goldman took a small empty wine glass and wrapped it in a linen. He placed it on the floor.

"Charlie," he said, motioning downward.

"With pleasure," Charlie answered, smiling at his bride. He lifted up his foot and came down on the tiny bundle with all his might. It made a loud crunch.

"MAZEL TOV!" the crowd screamed, as Miriama and Charlie kissed for the first time as man and wife.

Now Laylah lost all his seriousness. "All right then," he laughed loudly. "The rest you must do the old fashioned way. I've got to get to another wedding," and he flew out of the longhouse as a klezmer band struck up a lively tune and everybody started dancing.

Shamira watched as Lincoln and Medeea, who were standing next to them, turned to each other and started gallivanting with the crowd. She turned to Kingsley to start dancing with him, but he was looking at her seriously.

"What?" she asked.

He bent down and whispered in her ear.

"I know it's dangerous to do this at a wedding, because a person's emotions are so high, but I've never been more sure of anything in my life." Shamira's eyes went wide. And when Kingsley went down on one knee, her whole body started to quiver. "Shamira. I love you. I love you so much. Will you be my wife?" She tried but couldn't get the word out. That single word. Kingsley looked at her oddly. Then she noticed Medeea and Lincoln staring at them, amazement and expectation on both their faces. Many of the revelers noticed as well and turned their smiling faces to them, every eye beaming.

"Yes. Yes, I'll marry you, Kingsley."

Shamira heard Medeea screech with excitement, and the crowd roared its approval. Shamira felt herself being raised off the ground and the room began to spin as Kingsley whirled her around. As all the laughing and dancing people sped past her vision in a blur, as her ears were filled with laughter and music, Shamira threw back her head and squealed with an immense joy that permeated her entire being. Around and around she twirled, and then Kingsley brought her into his arms and their mouths met, to seal the happy promise.

Then another voice spoke to her.

"Sorry to disturb, my dears,"
Arimus's voice said in all the teen's minds.
"Sideways will now transport you unimpeded,
as your presence at the meeting is now needed."

Chapter 4

The deer was now skinned and cut into large pieces, ready to be wrapped in foil-like envelopes and put into backpacks for carrying to the village.

"There, slave, was it as bad as you imagined?" the Deganawida asked.

"No, Master. It wasn't. Thank you, Master."

The interaction between this master and slave reminded Hansum of his late father-in-law, Agistino della Cappa, and how he and Lincoln had to behave as apprentices.

"Good, slave," the Deganawida said slowly. "Another five or six hunts and I shall be able to trust you to do this by yourself." The boy beamed. "Now, put everything into our two packs so we can carry them back."

"They'll be heavy, Master. Can't we call a transport to come and get them?" the Deganawida looked at him, saying nothing. "Sorry, Master," and he lowered his eyes.

"Come, Journeyman Hansum. Let us walk and chat for a few minutes, while my slave does his work."

"It was nice meeting you, sir," the young man said to Hansum. "You've been a hero of mine." Hansum and The Deganawida looked back at the boy.

"Heroes?" the Deganawida questioned, almost with disgust. "Get back to work."

The two men began walking through the woods in silence, Hansum thinking how the Deganawida had referred to him as a journeyman several times. It had only been days since he earned that accreditation and was one of the few facts the world didn't know about him yet. Obviously, something was up.

"So, since you've been following my progress and have access to my training records. . ." Hansum began.

"I hope you are not offended," the Deganawida replied gently.

"No Elder. I'm just curious as to why."

The elder laughed. "I can usually do my job more stealthily. It's better if those whom I counsel come to their own conclusions. But you have seen through it all. What was it? Oh, of course. I called you a journeyman."

Hansum stopped and turned.

"Sir, I doubt you did it by mistake. It was a test, as is your last statement about it being a mistake."

The Deganawida laughed again. "You've had good teaching about reading between the lines and understanding motives. I did not see that on your curriculum."

"My mentor for that skill was Mastino della Scalla."

"Perhaps I'm not equal to the task I've been given with you."

"What task is that, Elder?"

"My old friend, Arimus, asked me to see what I can do about your recent hardening of temperament."

Suddenly, without apparent reason, a wave of emotion swept over Hansum. It was stronger than any he had experienced so far. He stopped walking and shut his eyes tightly. He felt completely blindsided by this seemingly innocent comment. 'Why?' an inner voice screamed. Part of him knew. He was standing with one of the most experienced mentors on the planet, most probably a doctor of psychology, the spiritual head of a whole people, and also someone trusted by Arimus. This had to be why Arimus arranged the meeting with the Council to be here. Hansum suddenly felt vulnerable. He put a hand to his chest.

"Are you ill?" the Deganawida asked.

"No sir. Just dizzy," Hansum replied, reaching out for the nearest tree. The Deganawida took Hansum's arm and walked him to the towering oak. Hansum grabbed the rough bark to steady himself.

"Whatever it is, *it* wants to come out, my son."

This simple statement caused Hansum to fall against the tree. His hands flew up and he grabbed great clumps of his hair.

"I know, I know," Hansum answered in a constricted voice. "But I don't know what *it* is."

"Arimus fears that whatever is troubling you will affect your judgment in the field and also the trust your comrades have in you!"

Upon hearing that Arimus's worries mirrored his own, Hansum ground his teeth and squeezed his eyes shut harder. Why, why was this conversation causing him to fall apart?

"I . . . I fear that too!" he said breathlessly.

The Deganawida brought his face close.

"And the way you are acting to others, is this what's causing your mind to be troubled?"

Hansum held his breath, staring into space. "No," he said, then, "Yes. Maybe. I mean," Hansum's confusion was palpable. "I mean I don't know. No, no, no, I don't know."

The Deganawida didn't rush. He contemplated before asking his next question. "Do you think the way you are acting could be a symptom and not a cause?"

"A what?" There was a catch in Hansum's voice.

"A symptom of the cause. The . . . true cause."

"I . . . I don't understand."

"Perhaps these actions toward others are an indication of something that is troubling you. Something you don't want to face. So your subconscious makes you act out in . . . odd ways."

Hansum shivered. He leaned back against the oak, trying to breathe slowly. He had practiced this in battle classes, calming himself before an assault on some objective. Was he attacking an objective here?

"I . . . I don't know what you're talking about," Hansum answered. He could feel the demon lurking in his mind, looking for the bottomless pit of his subconscious, a place where the light of truth could never shine. Hansum stared at the Deganawida. This man's countenance seemed to exude a power to draw the best out of people . . . no matter how much it hurt.

"Most know the answers to the things they are struggling with. They only balk at admitting these answers to themselves . . . because of an inner fear."

A flash of anger flared up in Hansum. "I'm not afraid!" he bellowed defensively. He glared fiercely and thrust out the hand with the scar. "I would do this a thousand times without hesitation if . . ." Hansum froze.

"If what, my son?"

"If I thought . . ."

"If you thought what?" the mentor prompted. Hansum remained silent for some seconds.

"If I thought I had a . . ."

"Had a?"

"Chance. A chance," Hansum finally admitted quietly. "If I thought I had a chance."

"A chance for what, Hansum?"

Hansum looked away, staring into space, bereft of words. His breaths were long and slow. After a while the Deganawida leaned around, so he could look him squarely in the face. The spiritual man's movement was enough to repeat his question without words. Finally Hansum spoke, still very quietly. And as he did, his hands, and then his whole body, began to shake.

"If I thought I had a chance . . . of success." And then Hansum began to weep. Large tears welled up in his eyes and spilled down his cheeks. His face contorted and a sob wrenched itself up from his chest. He expelled two, then three more sobs, tears flowing until he no longer had the breath to make a sound, and when finally he could inhale, a pitiful rasping sound hurt his throat. Still shaking, and through clouded eyes, Hansum peered at the Deganawida. The spiritual leader was looking back at him with such quiet and compassionate eyes that he seemed to give Hansum permission to continue crying. He slid down the tree trunk, onto the ground and began to wail. The Deganawida sat down next to him, cross-legged and looking away, patiently waiting for Hansum to release whatever was pent-up inside him. This went on for several minutes, Hansum gasping for breath and clasping and re-clasping his hands. Finally the Deganawida turned and faced Hansum.

"Say it out loud, my son. It is important to say with your own mouth what is troubling you."

"I'm . . . I'm afraid, Elder."

"Afraid of what?"

"Of . . ." Hansum's lips quivered. ". . . failure," he finally whispered. ". . . again. I've failed Guilietta . . . I've failed her three times. Because of me, she's died in pain. Awful . . ." and he exploded with sobs again, ". . . pain! I failed her and she died in agony. I failed her and she died in agony," he repeated. "I failed her and . . . she died. I'm afraid . . . I'll fail . . . and she'll have . . . more pain." And he began to cry again, this time without constraint, his long wail echoing through the canopy of nature's temple.

"Good," the Deganawida said. "Good," and he put his hand on Hansum's knee and sat as the sobbing continued.

After several minutes they heard footsteps. They looked up and there was the boy, the slave. He had one of the packs on his back and was lugging the second.

"Here you are, Master. I've brought your . . ." He saw the state Hansum was in and stood transfixed.

"Leave the one pack and go back to the village, Daniel," the Deganawida said. "I will follow soon."

"Yes, Master," the slave named Daniel answered. He dropped the second pack and, still staring, continued on. Hansum locked eyes with him, unashamed of his circumstances. Then Daniel turned and continued through the wide, open walkway under the trees.

"Slave," the mentor called out, and the boy stopped and turned. "You referred to our friend as a hero. Do you use that word because you wish to honor his strengths?"

Daniel seemed to think about it and then spoke. "Not just because of his strengths, Master. I admire him and call him a hero because he persists through his struggles."

"Ah. Very good. Then this man is a hero," the Deganawida said, and he patted Hansum's knee again. Daniel smiled, turned and left.

Hansum was sitting motionless. The Deganawida got up and went to the backpack. He removed a bronze canteen from an outside pocket, unscrewed the horn cap and brought it to Hansum.

"Wash your face, my son. You'll feel better." Hansum cupped his hands. He splashed cold water on his face three times. It did feel good. "Now drink." Hansum drank deep, feeling cleansed. He sighed and passed the canteen to the Deganawida, who also took a long drink.

"Thank you, Elder," Hansum said. "I feel much better."

"Good," the Deganawida replied. "Remember that a person's critical mind and their emotions are two distinct things, but living in one body. The mind knows what must be done, while the heart cries out for what it craves. In time you will gain the wisdom to know when . . ."

But there was to be no time for Hansum. Arimus, with Sideways looking out from his cloak, site transported in front of them.

"Ah, Hansum, here you are.
We've been looking for you, near and far."

"Arimus, you old rattlesnake," the Deganawida said. "It's nice to see you again."

"And you too, Andy . . . oh, forgive me, I mean,
Deganawida, Great Peacemaker.
I see you found our boy."

"He found me, actually, and we've had a good talk. He'll be fine."

"He found you?
A coincidence or of nature a quirk?
Isn't it fascinating how these things seem to work?
How are you, son?"

Hansum began to say something, but Sideways interrupted. "There's no time to catch up."

"Quite right, my friend.
Come, Hansum, it's that time again,
to beard the lion in his den."

"The Council? Now?" Hansum asked, jumping to his feet. "Are we going to pick up the others first?"

"They're awaiting us there already.
Come, of Sideways take hold his sleeve.
Andy, have you reconsidered my proposal?
With your skills, a great time traveling elder you'd be."

While Hansum moved to Arimus, the Deganawida stayed cross-legged on the ground.

"No, I must refuse again," he answered. "There's enough guidance to be done in this one era. I'll leave the rest of time to you."

"Come on, we have to go," Sideways complained. "You saw the mood those fool Council members are in. We don't want to give them more time to confuse themselves."

"Thank you again, Elder," Hansum said, taking a handful of Sideways's cloak.

"You are welcome, young friend. When one faces and understands one's fears, one goes a long way to alleviating them. He's all yours, Arimus." Arimus looked straight into Hansum's face.

"There's the old Hansum I've missed.
Sideways, away."

Chapter 5

The first things Hansum noticed when he appeared in the long-house with Arimus and Sideways were a long, hand-hewn table with twelve chairs, six a side. Half were occupied by men and half by women, and all their A.I.s were backed up against the longhouse wall, giving their humans a wide berth. This separation of humans and A.I.s was strange enough, but nobody was smiling.

Actually, one person did look happy. It was Elder Cassian Olama, the aged representative from the future. He sat contentedly in a thirteenth chair at the head of the table, his chin resting on an upraised palm, his eyes closed. He once again appeared fast asleep. Talos was hovering at the other end of the table with Shamira, Kingsley and Lincoln. He presumed Medeea was there too.

As the History Camp Time Travel Council members noticed the new arrivals, Elder Cynthia Barnes turned around. She was gracious enough to smile.

"Ah, here you are," she said pleasantly to Hansum. "We thought you had become lost."

"I was out in the woods with the Deganawida, helping butcher a deer," Hansum explained.

"Yuck!" Elder Parmatheon Olama said, making a face. "I'm a vegan. It's been horrible getting meals here."

"Nonsense," Elder Barnes laughed. "I'm vegetarian and find this community has the largest selection of fresh produce I've ever seen."

"We disagree again," Parmatheon Olama said. "Now, let's get on with the meeting so we can vote against the proposal and I can go home. So we can all go home. I've already got the votes."

This took Hansum aback. He wasn't so much surprised Parmatheon was against him as he was that he would say it so blatantly, even before Hansum was allowed to make his presentation.

"The results of Journeyman Hansum's proposal,
let us not presume," Arimus suggested, smiling sincerely.
"After all, the feed to the public started
as soon as he entered the room."

This startled Elder Parmatheon and he sat up straight.
"They heard what I said?" he asked.

"Of course," Arimus answered with a smile.
"Uh, shall we take a seat?"
he said looking around. There were no extra chairs.

"You can speak standing," Parmatheon said bluntly. He had obviously arranged this.

"Elder Parmatheon," Cynthia Barnes interrupted. "I am the chairperson of this Council. I'll direct things, if you please." Parmatheon gave a wave of his hand and sat back belligerently. Elder Barnes turned to Hansum and Arimus. "Please forgive us. I'll call for more seats."

"No need," Hansum said, striding to the foot of the table. There he took a deep breath, found his center and allowed a relaxed smile to spread across his face. He was feeling a lightness he hadn't enjoyed in a long time and, as he made eye contact with each person, not reacting to any of the hostility he saw in many of their glances, he channeled Mastino della Scalla. He would try to act as he thought the long-dead noble would have done when facing a hostile group such as this.

"Thank you very much Madame Chair and honored Council members, for the chance to present a proposal for another trip back to the 14th-century. Its objective will be to appraise when the best place would be to intervene and rescue my wife, Guilietta. I would also like to thank the public, whose interest in this matter means a great deal to me. It gives me added courage to go on and . . ."

"The delegate will refrain from playing to the public," Parmatheon interjected.

"Elder Parmatheon Olama," Cynthia Barnes chastised. "I warn you again to not speak out of turn. However, Journeyman Hansum, the elder is correct. Please confine your presentation to the Council."

"Of course, Madame Chair. My apologies." But Hansum wasn't sorry. He had mentioned the public on purpose, to make his point that the public was with him. He wanted the Council to remember that. He smiled and continued. "I would emphasize that this mission will not be a mission of action, but one of reconnaissance only. No unforeseen events can happen, as we will not be coming out of phase."

"We've heard that before," Parmatheon said blithely. Cynthia glared at him.

"Journeyman Hansum, continue, please," she said.

He nodded and did so. "I was fascinated to hear how scientists studying time travel are anxious to continue this . . . project. While for me, it's a mission to save my family, it has also become an experiment to find out more about time travel, in this case the nexus points."

"Those are the theorized points in time when, people who otherwise can't travel through time, may be able to do so?" Elder Barnes asked.

"As I understand it, yes, Madam Chair," Hansum said.

"Theory," Parmatheon said. "Only theory."

"As I said," Hansum continued, "this is to be an exploratory mission. To begin with, we won't even send people back. Your scientists have proposed, and received, preliminary agreement from their A.I. counterparts, to send back any number of out-of-phase cameras. They will follow multiple situations and hundreds of people for extended periods of time. The purpose of this would be to make sure that some unsuspected individual, who only looked peripherally involved with a situation, wasn't really the cause of some major action. Only after identifying every possible juncture, and these hitherto unsuspected free agents, would we personally go back for a closer examination to see if we could find a nexus point there. That's when, and only when, we would begin to formulate a final plan of intervention."

"Any number of out-of-phase cameras?" Elder Parmatheon guffawed. "And all the Mists of Time viewers and people to watch them? Watching hundreds of situations and people for extended periods of time? You want us to commit all these resources?"

"As your scientists suggest," Hansum smiled.

"It sounds like a careful, step-by-step plan to me," Elder Barnes observed.

The scarecrow-shaped Demos floated over and whispered in Elder Barnes' ear. Her eyebrows rose in surprise and she put two fingers to her temple, to take in more information.

"I am informed that one hundred and fifty million people, half the population of the planet, are watching these proceedings," she announced. With her hand still to her temple, she continued. "And well over ninety percent are communicating they want us to approve Journeyman Hansum's proposal."

"Irrelevant poppycock," Parmatheon objected. "The public is not knowledgeable about all the nuances of time travel or aware of the great responsibilities . . ."

"You're the one talking poppycock, Elder Parmatheon," Cynthia Barnes rebutted. "Time travel is new for us too. This Council is new. We don't have any experience in a situation like this."

"By law, the Council has the legal right to make the rules . . ." Parmatheon argued.

"How can you make rules for situations you've never experienced," Hansum queried.

"What's more important than sticking to protocol?" Parmatheon shot back. "Besides, you're just a hard case troublemaker who caught the imagination of the pub. . ."

"Order! This meeting will come to order," Elder Barnes demanded. "Journeyman Hansum, do you have any more to add to your proposal?"

"Well, Madam Chair, there is one other thing that wasn't in our proposal."

"I knew it," Parmatheon grumbled, and Hansum continued.

"I think the Council might like to know," he was again aiming this at the public, "that besides trying to rescue Guilietta, we would now like to ask permission to bring back Guilietta's parents at the same time." The Signora had become a well-loved figure to the public. She reminded people how mental illnesses used to destroy so many wonderful people. Hansum was counting on the public to be further enthralled with the idea of rescuing and curing her. But not so Elder Parmatheon Olama.

"And now he wants to bring back a crazy old lady who's been dead a thousand years?"

"Excuse me, elder. That is my mother-law," Hansum retorted, surprising himself at his anger, but also playing it up.

"Elder Olama, apologize," Cynthia demanded.

"Yeah, yeah. No hard feelings. Now, are you finished?" he asked Hansum.

"Yes, sir. I suppose I . . ."

"He's finished, let's have a vote."

"Elder, I warn you . . ."

"I demand a vote this instant," Parmatheon insisted.

"I think you have to take the public into . . ." Hansum started, but the Council's chairperson and co-chair were starting to argue in earnest. He tried to butt in, but stopped when he felt Arimus's hand on his shoulder.

"I will run this meeting," Cynthia shouted.

"I demand a vote!" Parmatheon insisted. "I demand it!"

"Parma, you're such a . . ."

"I demand it." he repeated. "It's within my rights." There was a silence "It's . . . within . . . my rights." Parmatheon looked to Demos and the A.I. nodded reluctantly.

"Very well," Elder Barnes conceded.

Hansum went to object again, but Arimus shook his head, motioning with his chin toward the sleeping Cassian Olama. 'Of course,' Hansum thought. 'The old guy from the 31st-century will veto any negative vote.'

"Okay, let's have the vote," Parmatheon began. "All who agree that . . ."

"I'll call the vote, if you please," Cynthia corrected. "All who are in agreement with Journeyman Hansum's plan, please raise your hand." Hansum looked down the table. Two hands went right up, including the chairwoman's, followed by a third, fourth and fifth. Then, Elder Barnes asked, "Those against?" Parmatheon's arm shot up. Then six more went up, albeit more slowly.

"Finally!" Parmatheon said smugly, standing. "Now we can go home before that Tadodaho makes good on his promise to get me into a sweat lodge . . ."

"Not quite, my fellow, it's not the last word," Arimus said.
"There's one more at this table, whose voice must be heard."

He gestured to Elder Cassian Olama.

"Oh come now, he hasn't even been listening," Parmatheon spat. "The legal and rightful Council has ruled."

"Twelve people voting on something they're ignorant about doesn't make their decision right," Hansum argued, "just because you're the . . . **authorized** Council."

"Watch your tone, young man," Parmatheon warned.

"Quiet, both of you," Cynthia Barnes broke in. "Elder Arimus is right. Wake Elder Olama and explain . . ."

"He doesn't want to know what's going on," Parmatheon continued arguing. "He just does what Arimus tells him."

"I said wake him up."

Arimus tapped his sub-dermal, to send the sleeping Olama a message. The old man didn't stir. He tapped again. Still no answer. He went over and put a hand gently on his shoulder, looking directly at the old fellow's smiling face.

"Excuse the disturbance of your most happy dream.
It's time to wake up and . . ."

Elder Cassian Olama's head slipped off his upturned palm and crashed to the table.

"Call a medical A.I. Quickly!" Elder Barnes shouted. "Lay him out on the . . ." Arimus put up a hand.

"Please don't bother," he said,
putting two fingers to the neck of the still-smiling corpse.
"The grand old man told me just the other day
his implants advised death was about a week away.
He told me to tell that more time in this mortal coil he's forsaken,
and that no extraordinary measures are to be taken."

"Well, that's it then," Parmatheon said, slapping his hands on the table and standing. "No veto and the vote stands."

Hansum exploded with anger. "You can't do this! It's not right! And . . . and you still have an elder from the future here. Elder Arimus can take Elder Cassian's place!"

"I don't think so . . ." Parmatheon said, smiling and wagging a finger knowingly. "He might be qualified, but he's not certified." The room was silent and looked to Arimus.

> "Unfortunately, he is correct.
> Although an elder from forward in time is my lot,
> A member of my own era's Time Travel Council, I am not."

"And you can't bring one back because of the blackout," Parmatheon added. "Well, at least he sticks to the rules."

"NO!" Hansum screamed.

"Quiet, insolent boy," Parmatheon scolded.

"Elder Parmatheon," Chairwoman Barnes said harshly. "The Council may have voted one way on a particular item, but I am still the head of it."

"As to that, I have another vote to put forward." And then Parmatheon spoke very slowly. "I call for a vote on the installation of a new chairperson for the Council." The room went dead silent and Cynthia's eyes went wide.

"I nominate Elder Parmatheon," a woman from Central America said, obviously as planned.

"I second," a man from Northern Europe added.

Parmatheon looked hard at Cynthia. "Well, you've been insisting you run the meetings. Call the vote, Madam . . . chair."

"All . . . all in favor?" Cynthia asked, and seven hands went up.

"Carried!" Parmatheon cried, and he quickly went to work. "Arimus, you and your radicals will be put under house surveillance until the Council can decide, once and for all, what we should do with you."

"Demos," Cynthia Barnes shouted to her A.I., "Aren't the A.I.s going to take action?"

"Tell her, Demos," Parmatheon said confidently. He had obviously done his homework.

Demos looked at her human straight in the eye.

"Cynthia. All three hundred million A.I.s have communed and debated this. We have decided," she turned and looked at Arimus. "As people from your future can neither travel forward nor backward in time, and admit time is unfolding differently from what you know of as history, we believe it would be better for humankind to err on the side of caution and . . . do nothing at the moment." And with that all the A.I.s backed themselves up against the longhouse wall and fell silent.

"That's right," Parmatheon said. "Sometimes it's best to do nothing!"

"It's not . . ." Hansum began, but Arimus pulled him aside.

"Sideways, attend.
Transfer yourself to our friend."

Instantaneously, Sideways site transported onto Hansum.

"What are you doing?" Parmatheon asked. "No funny business." Arimus ignored him.

"Shamira and Kingsley, Lincoln and Medeea,
My children, go to Hansum and of Sideways take hold.
It is time to just do something bold."

"Stop! In the name of the Council I demand . . ." Parmatheon shouted, but it was already too late.

The Sands of Time were spinning around Hansum and the other teens. The members of the Council backed away, Parmatheon's supporters screaming at their A.I.s to do something. The twelve A.I.s all looked at Talos and Sideways, straining their faces. They were trying to exert some control, but the two A.I.s from the future just laughed.

"I am the leader of this Council and you must obey me," Parmatheon Olama shouted frantically, but nobody was listening. Arimus touched his communications node and silently communicated with the teens.

"I cannot travel back in time, my children,
but in your collective abilities, I have full trust.
Go back to Verona and, without hesitation,
do what you must."

"How about you and Talos," Hansum asked. "Will you be okay?"

"Do not fear, be off on your way.
We'll find fine amusements
in Parmatheon's angry display."

"We're off on another adventure, Med," Lincoln said, smiling.
"Life with you is one big adventure," she thought back.

"Kingsley, why are you joining them?" Parmatheon called over the din of the vortex. "You're not of the 24th-century."

"The same reason as Hansum," the big man shouted back, pulling Shamira close to him. "For love."

The ground fell away and they were gone.

Chapter 6

How long ago was it that Shamira had felt so impossibly happy? An hour? She had been at the wedding, wrapped in the arms of her lover, secure in a community where people lived their lives fulfilling themselves by meeting challenges to make the world a better place. And she was engaged to be married. Married! There was so much to live for.

But now, here she was a short time later, traveling back in a vortex to the unknown dangers of the 14th-century.

"Snap out of it!" she said out loud.

"What did you say, love?" Kingsley shouted over the noise of the vortex. They were again half floating, half falling. She squeezed his hand and forced a smile.

"Nothing."

"Everybody," Hansum shouted, getting their attention. He pointed to his sub-dermal and tapped it.

'At least Hansum's in the proper mindset to get right to work,' she thought. But he'd been such a pain lately. Shamira loved him and certainly understood where his melancholy and morose attitude came from, but what was he going to be like leading this foray, especially now that they would be winging it? She knew everyone was thinking the same thing.

"Here we are again, kids," Hansum said through his communications implant, and there was a different tone in his inflection. *"The idea of this mission was just to do reconnaissance and determine where we can intervene, and do it using out-of-phase cameras. We don't have that option now. However, the concept is still good, except now we have to do it ourselves. So, I'm thinking we check things out carefully and come to a concensus before we act."*

"Agreed," Shamira said through her communications node, and she thought, 'Hansum seems different.'

"But now we have an added problem," Hansum continued. *"We have to be on guard in case people from the History Camp Time Council follow us."*

"But they can't follow easily," Lincoln put in. *"They have to use their less accurate technology. They can't pinpoint where or when they'll land, like we can with Sideways."*

"Absolutely," Hansum acknowleded. *"But still we'll have to be aware they can show up at any time."*

"Where do you think we should start?" Kingsley asked.

"I'm thinking we go to the cannon testing grounds, to when Feltrino attacked, and work forward from there."

"What are we looking for?" Shamira asked.

"I really don't know," Hansum said, and as she looked across the vortex at him, there was a little smile on his face.

"Ninety seconds," Sideways said. *"I'll put us in the woods where we can see the battle, but still be hidden."*

"All agreed?" Hansum asked.

"You're in charge," Kingsley said.

"One more thing," Hansum added. *"I'd like to apologize for my attitude the last while. The truth is I've been afraid of failure and it was affecting me. Now that I know worrying about it will make things worse, for some reason my mind has cleared."*

"Hey, bro, I already told you," Lincoln laughed. *"We're with ya till the end."*

"Hey, Shamira and I haven't had time to tell you our big news," Kingsley crowed. *"Do you mind?"* Shamira smiled. *"We're going to get married."*

The whoop of joy from everybody was so loud, they didn't need their communicators to hear it.

"Fantastic!" Hansum laughed. *"Finally, some good news. When's the big day?"*

"We haven't made a date," Shamira said. *"This only happened at the wedding."*

"How about . . . as soon as we succeed in this mission?" Kingsley suggested. *"That way, Guilietta can be there."*

"And her parents," Lincoln added, a huge grin on his face.

"Okay, kids," Hansum said. *"Now we have more incentive to make this thing work."*

"Five seconds," Sideways announced. *"And we're here."*

The vortex dissipated and their feet touched the soft humus of a forest floor. They were hidden among the trees and dense undergrowth. The whirlwind's roar was replaced by the rustling of leaves and song birds. Then "BOOM!"

"Gina!" Lincoln said, an instant smile flashing on his face. He turned toward the sound and peeked through some branches. "There we are."

Everybody knelt down and carefully peered through the foliage. Below them in the valley was the cannon named Gina. A huge billow of smoke was wafting away from it, exposing the familiar soldiers and officers who tended her, the younger Lincoln included. Not far from them were the captain and the lieutenant keeping track of statistics, and more soldiers and mounted knights led by Lieutenant Raguso. And finally, in his brown hat and the clothes of a noble, there stood the younger Hansum.

"I was cute in my uniform," Lincoln observed wryly. "And that kettle helmet saved my life. Oh, and there's Georgio and Daveed and Caliveeta," he added enthusiastically, and then it struck him hard. "They're going to be dead in a few minutes."

Hansum put his hand on Lincoln's shoulder. "Are you going to be okay with this, pal?" he asked.

"No, no. I'll be fine," and Lincoln put on a serious face.

"Good man."

"What are we looking for?" Kingsley asked.

"Like I said, I don't really know," Hansum answered, and then he looked thoughtful. "We should split up, maybe leave one person here and place the others elsewhere."

"Like where?" Lincoln asked.

"The Master's house," Hansum said.

"Yes," Sideways agreed. "Mistress Guilietta and her mother will be ill at this juncture. Perhaps if we watched here and there at the same time we could see if the incidents are linked."

"Right," Hansum said. "Sideways, switch over to Lincoln and take everybody to Verona. Sham, you and Kingsley watch Guil. Lincoln, you and Medeea the Master, the Signora and the others at the house. And look around the neighborhood too. Sideways, after everyone's settled, come and get me and we'll take it from there. And remember to watch out for Parmatheon's men. They can screw up everything."

In a flash, Sideways's protective cloak was off Hansum and on Lincoln.

"Good fit," Lincoln said. "All right. Everyone take hold."

"Should we go out of phase?" Kingsley asked.

"Excellent idea," Lincoln agreed, and they all put a finger to the base of their necks. Lincoln took one last look down at the valley, where he and his old team were reloading the cannon. "G'bye guys."

"Be careful, Hansum," Shamira said, and they winked out of sight.

Hansum took a lungful of forest air. It smelled and tasted so good, similar to the forest at Haudenosaunee.

"So, let's see what we can see," he said to himself softly, and went back to spying.

This was when they were testing the cannon as an antipersonnel weapon, filling it with thirty egg-sized river stones. They had set up a target of one hundred sapling poles in a square, and shot the cannon at it from two-hundred and fifty paces. The first shot was done with the loose stones and the results were poor, just as Pan had predicted. The second shot was the "Boom" they had just heard. Stones had been shot out of the cannon in a canvas sack, but the material disintegrated and the results were little better. Hansum watched his younger self checking the soldering of a tin cylinder containing the same number of stones. He found it curious to see himself dressed as a noble, walking around quiet and confident, while others stood back and showed him deference. He saw himself nod to the lieutenant in charge of the cannon, smile at the younger Lincoln, and then walk back to Lieutenant Raguso. He was leaning over and saying something to Raguso. What was it? Oh yes. "Never be afraid to fail when testing something."

"Never be afraid," Hansum repeated to himself.

He heard the soldier-Lincoln shouting. "Thirty stones in tin canister," and then go through the regular routine. The cannon shot and a second later the target exploded as the canister burst out its ammunition in all directions, snapping many of the branches and . . .

"Aha. I've caught you," came a voice behind Hansum. Hansum spun around, one hand instantly grabbing for and withdrawing his sword from its scabbard, the other going to the node to take him out of phase. But there, standing before him, was Elder Parmatheon Olama, disheveled and mud-splattered, his clothing badly torn. Beside him was an equally untidy man in the uniform of a commissionaire from a government office. The man's eyes and mouth went round with wonder when he caught sight of the armed soldiers and cannon below.

"Elder Parmatheon," Hansum said in a loud whisper. "What are you . . ."

"I've found you," Parmatheon said loudly. "Now you must come back with us."

"Elder, get down! Be quiet!" Hansum whispered, reaching forward and trying to pull the bureaucrat by the sleeve. "They'll hear you."

Parmatheon pulled his arm back. "Don't tell me what to do, you rapscallion. We've spent three days traipsing all over Italy trying to find you. I started out with ten men and now look. Only one left. The others were either hurt or scared and pressed their escape buttons."

"If you're not quiet, you'll get us . . ."

"Guard, seize him," Parmatheon said to the man with him. This fellow was most likely used to standing in the hallways of public buildings, giving out directions and trying not to be caught napping. He was hardly the muscle needed to arrest anybody, let alone a well-trained fighter like Hansum was now.

The man came over and hesitantly put his hand on Hansum's muscular shoulder.

"You're kidding, right?" Hansum asked, lifting the man's hand with the flat of his sword.

"You must submit to me," Parmatheon said sternly.

"I said get down, both of you!" Hansum ordered, pulling the commissionaire down by the sleeve.

Suddenly there was a cry from the valley. "Captain, someone in the bushes," a soldier shouted. Hansum spun around and looked.

"Now you've done it," Hansum said, "Here comes Lieutenant Raguso and his men."

"Submit! You must submit." Parmatheon repeated.

"Are you insane? Raguso can't come after us. He's got to leave with his men so Feltrino will attack and . . ." It was almost too late. "We better go out of phase. Quickly. They're almost . . ."

"I'm not going out of phase. You push that return button back to our time or there will be trouble. I have the authority . . ."

"Your authority won't do you any good against a sword or a pike," Hansum warned. Just then, a soldier on horseback, one who had circled around them unseen, came crashing out from the trees. "Press your . . ." Hansum and the commissionaire pressed their out of phase nodes and disappeared. But Parmatheon wasn't fast enough and the horse ran right into him, knocking him off his feet and throwing him against a tree. He dropped like a rag doll. Hansum and the commissionaire watched as Lieutenant Raguso and his men fell upon the unconscious Council head.

"More footprints, brother," one of the soldiers called to Lieutenant Raguso.

"Search the woods," Raguso shouted. "They can't be far. Is this one alive? No, fools, don't kill him. Stand him up. Tie his hands."

If Parmatheon appeared disheveled before, now he looked absolutely gruesome. His face was bruised and swollen. Blood was coming from his nose and mouth. And his eyes? As officious and mean as they were before, now they were the exact opposite, filled with stark terror. His hands were being tied in front of him with a length of rope and the soldier holding it got back on his horse. "To the captain!" Raguso shouted, and three of the horses began their way back down the hill, Parmatheon being pulled along on foot.

"Help me," Hansum heard him mumble in Earth Common through bloodied and enlarged lips. "Help me."

As Parmatheon stumbled down the hill, Hansum pointed the tip of his sword at the base of the gape-mouthed commissionaire's neck.

"You'd better push that escape node. I'll try to rescue Elder Parmatheon, although I can't think why."

"But our nodes aren't that accurate," the commissionaire whined. "It took us ten jumps to find you, and a few of us ended us up in the water or high in trees."

"Practice makes perfect," Hansum said, putting his hand up to the man's neck to do it for him. The man took the hint and pressed the button himself. With one last desperate look, he disappeared.

Parmatheon was now at the bottom of the hill and being slapped hard by the captain. The 24th-century functionary fell to his knees and Hansum heard him cry out in Earth Common. He watched the younger Hansum and Lincoln look startled when they heard him talking in their native tongue and then quickly come to intervene.

'Now what should I do?' the older Hansum thought. 'This was supposed to be a recon mission and things have changed already.' Bile rose into his mouth, but his training kicked in and he swallowed it down. "Get to it," he said out loud, and began jogging, out of phase, down the hill. As he did he turned toward where he knew Feltrino and his men had been hiding. Would they still attack? Were they fleeing? 'What can go wrong next?'

By the time Hansum got to the bottom of the hill, Parmatheon was surrounded by the entire cannon crew. Lieutenant Raguso was looking down at the scene from his horse and the captain was leaning menacingly over the terrified man, screaming in Italian.

"Where are you from? The Este? Florence? Tell me or I'll flay you!" he demanded while holding a knife to the terrified man's neck. Parmatheon screamed shrilly, and the surrounding men wrinkled their noses. Their prisoner had soiled himself.

The younger Hansum, with Lincoln by his side, stepped forward and put a hand on the captain's arm.

"Allow me, Captain," Hansum said in Italian, and he knelt down, putting his hand to his language node and touching it discreetly. "Where are you from?" he asked in Earth Common.

"Why, you're . . . I just saw you up there . . ."

The younger Lincoln, in his kettle helmet and chainmail, knelt down too. "Look how he's dressed. He's from our time," he said in Earth Common. "Maybe they've come to rescue us."

"Well, have you?" Hansum asked.

"I'm not supposed to tell. . . I might change the . . . oh this is more complicated than I . . . I didn't truly understand . . ."

"What's he saying?" the captain demanded in Italian. "Who's he working for?"

"He's from our home country," Hansum lied. "I think he was alone, just lost in the woods, trying to make it from one city to the other."

"There are signs of others in the wood," Lieutenant Raguso said from his saddle. "My men are searching for them."

"Alone, eh," the captain scoffed. "Call all the men and scour the woods!" he shouted. "There are spies about. Take this one to the Podesta. We'll find out what he knows."

Parmatheon was grabbed by several more soldiers and yelped as they started dragging him toward the manor house. The younger Lincoln took hold of the older man's arm, looking like he was helping guard him.

"Where and when are you from, pally?" Lincoln whispered in Earth Common.

Parmatheon looked at him with wide eyes.

"I . . . I can't tell," he said pathetically. "I'm, I'm not supposed to . . . Oh dear. What are they going to do to me?"

"They're probably going to stick a pike up your . . ."

Chapter 7

"I think this is Master Calabreezi's carriage," Shamira said. She, Kingsley, Lincoln and Medeea had just site transported to the front of the della Cappa home. "This is when he came and we found out the Podesta had hired Devlena to poison Guil."

"Good Gia," Kingsley said. "I just can't get my head around poisoning someone."

"It wasn't that uncommon among nobles," Sideways put in, "and with their primitive knowledge of chemistry, it was hard to guard against."

The door to the house opened and Master Calabreezi walked out, closely followed by Agistino and a younger Shamira. She was in her kitchen-girl clothes, including a veil covering her hair. A very solemn Calabreezi turned and took Master della Cappa's hand.

"Remember, my friend," Calabreezi advised, "We must not mention the fact we have discovered Devlena is working on behalf of the Podesta, or that I was even here. The safety of both our families depends on it."

"You have my word, Master Calabreezi," a somber Agistino answered, crossing himself to seal his oath.

"And you, Carmella," Calabreezi said to the younger Shamira. "If you still think it absolutely necessary, write your note to Romero and take it to the courier I suggested. And when all this settles down, I shall introduce you to some fresco masters. Your talents must be put to better use."

"I look forward to meeting you again, Master," the younger Shamira answered.

"Farewell then," Calabreezi said.

The older Shamira and the others watched as Master della Cappa and the younger Shamira went back into the house.

"Amazing, Sham," Kingsley said, "Master Calabreezi thought you were good enough to put you in the circles of church painters."

"It was the first and last time I ever met him. He's going to die in a few hours of a heart attack."

"Okay, back at it," Lincoln said. "Medeea and I will check on Guil. You two, young Shamira, the Signora and Master."

They walked through the door into the house. The younger Shamira was already sitting at the table, writing her note. Master della Cappa was almost up the steps, going to his girls.

"I'll watch here for a minute," Shamira said while Lincoln and Medeea followed the Master.

Kingsley went over and leaned close to the younger Shamira. The older one went to the other side of herself and looked at Kingsley, who had a big grin on his face.

"When I was a kid and saw you dressed like this, I had such a crush on you."

"You like the younger girls, do you?" Shamira teased.

"I was ten, so you were an older woman," he replied, and then put his hand where the younger Shamira's cheek was. It went right through. She scratched an itch.

"I'm going to marry you, little girl," Kingsley said.

Lincoln and Medeea were in the doorway to Guilietta's sickroom, watching Master della Cappa standing over his sleeping daughter. The family had just found out the truth about Guilietta being poisoned and then saved by her mother's delusion of the Archangel Michael. Agistino was standing, head bowed and face buried in his hands, reciting his Hail Marys. His hands lowered and he stared at his daughter, tears accentuating a look of wonder in his eyes. It was the look of a man appreciating something he had taken for granted — the life of his child.

"I must attend to your saintly mother," Agistino said to his sleeping daughter. "She sleeps in the other room. I fear I have much to make up to her." As the contrite husband turned to the door, Lincoln felt as if Agistino's eyes looked right into his.

"We're here to save them, Master," Lincoln said, and the old man walked right through his former apprentice.

As Lincoln and Medeea turned to watch the Master go to the other bedroom, Kingsley and Shamira were coming up the stairs.

"Nothing seems to be changed here," Lincoln said. "No anomalies, as far as I can tell."

"My younger self just took the letter to the courier with Bembo," Shamira reported. "That's the same as it was before too. We'll sit with the Master and Signora for a bit, to check on them."

"If you get a chance with the Signora alone, try to take her out of phase," Lincoln said. "If you can, that should mean we've found a nexus point. We'll do the same with Guil."

"Right," Shamira answered.

"Lincoln and I shall walk around the neighborhood, checking for anything untoward," Sideways added. "Then I shall return to Master Hansum. Darn it all, this is much less efficient than having hundreds of cameras."

"It's the best we can do," Lincoln said pragmatically. "C'mon. Let's go."

After walking around the neighborhood, Lincoln and Medeea returned to Guilietta's room. Sideways transported back to Hansum. The sleeping Guilietta had a small smile on her lips.

"Maybe it's because Master Calabreezi told her she'd recover," Lincoln mused.

"I bet it's because a note's been sent to Hansum, telling him to come home right away," Medeea countered.

"Could be. I'll try to bring her out of phase," Lincoln thought, and he opened up a small portal and reached through. "No luck," he grimaced.

Guilietta became restless, running her tongue over her parched lips.

"She looks thirsty," Lincoln said to Medeea. "Should I pour her some water, for when she wakes?"

Medeea looked over at Lincoln, her impish, sixteen-year-old face grinning at him.

"Okay. But let's put a drop of me in her too. I'd like to get to know her. And then you can be in her head too."

"Naw. You go ahead, but don't connect me," Lincoln replied. "Guil's like a sister to me. It would be too weird." Lincoln tapped his node and created a small portal. Then he reached through and poured some water from the jug on the table into a wooden cup. "How can we get her to wake up and drink without seeing us?" he asked.

"Don't put me into the water." Medeea thought back. *"Just let a drop fall on her lips and I'll enter through the skin. I'll use my powers of suggestion to have her wake up and take a drink."* Lincoln took out Medeea's tear vessel and held it carefully over Guilietta's mouth. As the single drop fell between her slightly parted lips, he gingerly pulled his hand back and snapped his fingers, making the portal disappear. Guilietta moved her head as the liquid touched her tongue. *"Ah,"* Medeea said, smiling as she read the sleeping girl's mind. *"She really is a sweet person. Oh, but she's tougher than she lets on. I'd love to get to know..."* but before she could finish the sentence, Medeea's eyes went wide.

"What is it?" Lincoln started to ask, but then he saw what Medeea did.

"Guilietta. She's ... pregnant."

Chapter 8

The out-of-phase Hansum followed as the soldiers manhandled Parmatheon into the planning room and started working on him in earnest. The once-haughty bureaucrat was tied to the same chair Hansum had seen Master Bernarius trussed up in before Podesta della Scalla ordered him killed. Parmatheon's shirt was stripped off and they were about to slash his chest to make him speak. Podesta della Scalla was standing next to the captain and several other soldiers. General Chavelerio had taken over screaming in Parmatheon's face.

"Stop pretending you don't understand what we are saying," he shouted, spittle flying on to the bound prisoner. The tip of his dagger was already pressed onto Parmatheon's chest and a trickle of blood was running down his front. The general looked to the Podesta, asking permission to proceed with the torture. Mastino nodded.

"Excellency," the younger Hansum interrupted. "Before you do this, allow me to talk with him. We speak the same dialect."

"Very well. General," Mastino said.

Everyone stepped back as the young savant took another chair and sat before Parmatheon. Making like he was straightening his brown hat, he pressed the language node again. Parmatheon's jaw was trembling in terror.

"So, what are you doing here?" Hansum asked. "You'd better tell me so I can figure out a way for all of us to get back home, you with your skin."

Parmatheon could barely get words out. When he did, he stammered. "It, it, it . . . it looked so simple . . . to make de . . . decisions . . . f, f, from, from a seat on . . . on the Council." The captain kicked the chair and the prisoner yelped.

Hansum held up a hand to ask the captain to refrain. "What Council?" Hansum asked.

"The, the . . . the History Camp Time Travel Council."

The younger Hansum looked confused, as did Lincoln.

The out-of-phase older Hansum realized his younger self had been sent back before the announcement that the 24th-century scientists had already discovered rudimentary time travel and were secretly working with the people from the future. The younger Hansum looked back at Parmatheon.

"You mean a Council from Elder Arimus's time?"

Even his present predicament couldn't cause Parmatheon to hide his disdain for Arimus.

"That troublemaker? No. Not from his time. Our time. Yours and mine."

'Oh no,' the older Hansum thought. 'If I find out about all this earlier, who knows how it can screw things up more.'

The younger Hansum looked to Lincoln, to see if this was making any sense to him. Lincoln shrugged.

"You better make something up for the Podesta, though," Lincoln said.

"Excellency," Hansum said. "Apparently this fellow was just coincidentally walking through the woods when he ran into some, I guess, real spies. He says he was an indentured servant in Mantua, sold by some slavers from around . . . Greece. This fellow escaped and was trying to make his way back to Venice, to hopefully find a ship to get home on."

"He's not speaking Greek," Mastino della Cappa said. "And how the devil would he get from Greece to here?"

The Hansum in the brown hat looked worried. He turned to Parmatheon.

"Just say something. Babble for a minute, like you're telling me something," he said.

"I'm the head of the Time Travel Council," Parmatheon said. "I come from about a year after you came back. Your other, older self is trying to get back and save your wife." The younger Hansum and Lincoln looked at each other, shocked.

"Save Guilietta? Why? What's wrong?" the younger Hansum asked.

The older, out-of-phase Hansum was shaking his head in despair. Mentioning Guilietta was probably the worst thing to do. That could really spook the younger Hansum. He looked intently at his younger self, who was staring at Parmatheon, obviously trying to weigh what he should say and how he should act.

"Well? Tell me what's going on!" the Podesta demanded.

The younger Hansum looked purposefully at the Podesta. "I believe him," he said with resolve. "He says he doesn't speak Greek. He speaks . . . Atlantean." Hopefully Mastino didn't know his Greek myths that well. "It's an island in the Aegean Sea. We only saw this fellow because, as he was trying to stay unseen walking through the forest, he ran into whoever was really spying on us. They made chase after him and that's when we saw him." He pressed his node again and asked Parmatheon, "Who was up there with you?"

"You were," Parmatheon answered, which caused young Hansum to startle. "And apparently somebody named Feltrino was about to attack you." Hansum really looked shocked now, but didn't have time to react because the door to the room pounded open and Lieutenant Raguso came in.

"We've found many tracks, Excellency. Many horses and men, but they are gone. We didn't pursue because I was following with far fewer men. I thought it best to return and post patrols around the property instead."

"You didn't pursue?"

"Whoever they were, they had heavy horses and many men. Perhaps three times as many as I had in my unit. They must be far away by now."

"Well, they left one," the captain said, obviously not convinced by Hansum's story.

"Look, look at his hands, Excellency," Hansum said to Mastino. "They are soft. Uncalloused. He can't be a soldier. And his footware." Although Parmatheon's ordeal had left him with only one shoe, it was made of woven hemp, the sole, the upper and the laces. It was a fashion back home.

"Why would an indentured servant have smooth hands?" Mastino asked. "What did he do for the Gonzaga?"

Hansum looked back to Parmatheon, touching his node. "What can I say you did?"

"I . . . don't even know . . . what you're talking about."

"He's, he's a mathematician, Excellency. Educated by the Saracens, so quite sought after. He was helping the Gonzagas design their buildings. That's why they bought him."

"A mathematician for buildings?"

"Excellency, this story is *merda*," the General argued. "Let's just cut this one's throat and get all our men stationed around the property."

"I could use a good mathematician," Hansum interjected. "Let me talk to him further." Mastino hesitated. "I have larger cannon planned," Hansum added, "but can't do it without someone to help me calculate greater stress loads and longer trajectories." The older Hansum was impressed by his younger self. He always could cook up convincing lies quickly.

"Very well," Mastino conceded. "Talk to him. But leave him tied. Captain, let's get outside and reorganize the men. And General, you order more." And with that he turned and left, followed by the soldiers.

Lincoln closed the door. The older Hansum watched his younger self staring at Parmatheon.

"Untie my hands," the older man begged, "so I can touch my emergency escape sub-dermal."

"In a minute," Hansum said. "First, tell me what's going on."

"I . . . I'm not supposed to tell," Parmatheon said, wide-eyed.

"Well, okay then," Hansum said, motioning for Lincoln to go to the door. As Lincoln turned, Parmatheon recanted.

"Wait. I'm really not supposed to tell, but . . ."

"Go on," the younger Hansum urged.

"We are trying to . . . well, at least some people, including both of you, are trying to . . ."

The older Hansum couldn't risk letting his younger counterparts know more than they already did. He quickly tapped on one of his emergency nodes and a small circle of blue static appeared in the air. It was about the size of a fist, and he thrust an arm through. He held his hand right in front of Parmatheon's face in the universal sign for ***"Stop!"***

"What the . . ." Lincoln said.

Hansum knew that, to his counterparts, his arm seemed to be floating in the air.

"You see, I'm not supposed to say anything," Parmatheon said excitedly.

"So, we're being watched," the younger Hansum said. "Why aren't we being rescued? Why are they leaving us . . ." The older Hansum quickly rotated his hand and held it in the same position in front of his younger self, silencing him. Then he pointed to Parmatheon's hands, as if to say to untie them. "Not until someone tells me what's going on," the younger Hansum insisted. The hand began to move towards Parmatheon's neck.

"Wait a minute," Lincoln said, grabbing it. The hand grabbed him back. "I recognize this hand. Hansum, hold yours up." The younger Hansum did. "It's you, man, but with a honking big scar."

"Tell me what's going on!" Hansum shouted.

The hand pulled away from Lincoln's grasp and disappeared back into the hole.

"Come back here, whoever you are," Lincoln shouted into the opening, which immediately shrunk to the size of a peephole. He put his eye to it and looked around. "I think he's still in there. I think it really is you."

"But the scar on the hand . . ." Hansum looked at Parmatheon. "If you want my help, tell me what's going on," he ordered. "Now, before the others come back. They won't be as nice as me."

"Hey!" a voice from the air said. The boys looked around. There was a familiar hazel eye looking at them from the small hole in the air.

"Hansum, it *is* you!" Lincoln said definitively.

"Let him go," the voice from the hole said. "I'm trying to help, but things are going to get too complicated if that idiot stays here."

"Tell me what's happening first," the younger Hansum demanded.

"I can't," the older one insisted.

"This is ridiculous. Make this opening bigger!" and young Hansum poked his finger into the orifice. Static sparked brightly on the younger Hansum's flesh and he pulled it back as if he were burned. "Ouch!" Then, with another pop, the blue ring of static shrank to nothing and was gone. Shaking his finger with pain, the young Hansum turned an angry gaze to the still-bound Parmatheon. "Where is he, me? Back in the future?"

"I told you, I'm not supposed to say," Elder Parmatheon Olama replied fearfully. "It's against . . ."

"Call the others back in," Hansum ordered Lincoln.

"He's not in the future," Parmatheon said quickly. "He's hiding out of phase. Please don't call in those murderers. I beg you."

"What do you mean out of phase?" the young Hansum asked, not familiar with the term yet.

"He's here, watching us," Parmatheon admitted, looking around fearfully. "In this room, but invisible. He's trying to save you, but there are technical problems. I can get back though. I'm here by mistake. Let me go. Please. And he's right. I am an idiot. I messed everything up."

"What do you mean, technical problems?"

"Something's screwed up with time. And they're trying to avoid other disasters."

"What disaster?"

"Disasters," Parmatheon corrected. "Believe me, so much has gone wrong for you already and he's really here to help."

"How can you get back?" Lincoln asked.

"There's a sub-dermal on my neck. It's an emergency return node. Please, untie me so I can press it." Hansum and Lincoln looked at each other cautiously. "Or one of you press it. Here, right at the base," Parmatheon said, stretching his neck and twisting it, to make the faint outline of the sub-dermal visible. Lincoln leaned forward and checked it out.

"Sure looks like one," Lincoln said.

"And if you help me, I promise I'll do my best to help you when I get back." And then he said more loudly, looking around like he was talking to someone hiding in the room. "Journeyman Hansum. See, I haven't told them anything really important. And if I get out of here, I won't stand in your way anymore. I'll . . . I'll be good. I'll help with the Council."

The younger Hansum looked like he was thinking. He turned to Lincoln.

"If I'm really here watching," he asked thoughtfully, "how did I get back originally and how can I be stuck here now?"

"It's time travel," Parmatheon said pathetically. "It doesn't make any sense . . . at least to me."

"And whoever this other me is, he really is trying to save us?"

"Yes, yes, he is. And I was wrong to block him. I see that now. I'll be good, I'll be good," he pleaded.

"How can we explain his disappearance?" Lincoln asked.

"We'll say he got loose and escaped. We'll break a window."

"They won't believe he got away without a fight."

The two boys, having worked together as a team, looked like they were reading each other's minds, even without communications implants. Hansum blew out a breath. "I guess I'll do you and you do me."

"You better come through for us, pally," Lincoln said, pointing a finger in Parmatheon's face. Then the two boys looked at each other.

"This is going to hurt . . ." Hansum said, pulling back his arm and making a fist. "Make it show, but not the nose."

"Same here," Lincoln agreed.

They pulled back and swung. "THWACK!" They hit each her so hard, both fell to the ground.

"You two have gone native!" Parmatheon gasped, his face going whiter than it already was. Lincoln got up, rubbing a big welt under his eye. He stared menacingly at the bureaucrat, who quivered as Lincoln's hand came toward him. "Are you going to untie me?" Parmatheon asked. "Can I clean myself up first?" and, without another word, the younger Lincoln pressed the emergency nodule. "I hope I land softly this time. Oh dear, oh . . ." and the less-developed technology caused his image to disintegrate into wavy bits before it faded out of the 14th-century.

Hansum, still on the floor, ordered, "Throw that chair through the window."

Lincoln picked up a heavy chair, took a few steps back and ran at the lead and glass frame. It took three tries before he broke open a hole large enough for a man to get through. The noise caused the general and three of his officers to burst through the door just as the chair fell out. Lincoln was leaning on the remaining broken glass in the window and Hansum was still on the ground, a hand to his new black eye.

"He got loose and escaped," Hansum said from the ground.

"That pants-pissing craven?" the captain challenged.

"You were right, sir. He was faking," Lincoln said, blood dripping from his hand as he took it away from the glass. "But he fought like a demon. I think he was . . . a wizard." Then he looked out the window and cried. "Yikers, he made it to the woods!"

"After him," the general shouted, and all the men took off.

"We better go too," the younger Hansum said getting up. As he and Lincoln started for the door, they turned. "You better get us out of here," Hansum said to the air, and they left the room.

The older Hansum thought what he had just witnessed could be funny, except events were getting more out of hand every minute. But, until Sideways returned, Hansum could do nothing.

He walked over to the table and looked at his old plans on the desk, suddenly feeling a nostalgic urge to see them. However, they had been turned face down for secrecy. Hansum reached out, his hand going right through the plans and desk. Looking out the window, he saw all the soldiers running into the woods, followed by his younger self and Lincoln. He went to the door and looked up and down the hall, seeing nobody. Then he came back to the table and put his hand to one of his sub-dermals. He pushed it hard. A blue flash filled his vision and he was back fully in the 14th-century. The familiar moldy smell of an older building filled his nostrils. Then, he reached down and turned over the plans, spreading the large parchments in front of him.

Here were the advanced instructions for making saltpeter and black powder next year; large copper vats for boiling ley, and a stone building with many racks for drying finished black powder, as well as a drawing for the incorporation mill. This was the large machine for crushing saltpeter, charcoal and sulfur together. These projects were never completed. Hansum let out a tired sigh.

"Master Monticelli?" a feminine voice spoke behind him.

Hansum turned and gulped, his eyes going wide. "Lady Beatrice," he said, trying to collect himself.

"I thought I saw you chasing after someone. A spy, I understand."

"Yes, there was much excitement. He got away, but I think he's harmless . . . and I'm right here, as you can see."

She walked toward him regally, her eyes with the look of a woman asking what was taking him so long to show interest in her. Then she looked down at the plans, upon which one of his hands still lay.

"Did the spy see these or get any intelligence?" she asked.

"I don't believe so, my lady."

Then Beatrice looked at something else. She reached forward and touched his hand and the scar surrounding his thumb. Too late, Hansum pulled his hand away and put it in his pocket.

"I never observed that," she said, looking up at him.

"I try to hide it, my lady. Most don't notice."

Then Beatrice's gaze studied Hansum's face.

"Most odd," she said. "You look somehow different."

"I can't imagine how," he answered. She considered.

"A bit older. More seasoned."

"Perhaps it's merely the dirt from working with the black powder."

"Perhaps," she replied, not sounding convinced. "Let me see that hand again."

Hansum had no choice but to bring out his repaired hand. It was dirty from rambling around in the woods. Beatrice took the hand in hers, holding it and turning it over, inspecting it thoroughly. She moved one of her soft thumbs around the scar that circumscribed his thumb. She looked up at him, her delicate eyebrows knit together in a question. Then she looked down again and opened his hand flat, running the tips of her fingers along the palm and turning it this way and that.

"Your callouses are different too. Not those of a laborer, but a soldier's."

Hansum forced a snicker. "Is that so? I hadn't noticed you were so observant or interested."

"Oh, I am. But you are obviously . . ." her sentence trailed off. Then she turned the palm up again. "You have an exceeding long life line, Signor," she observed. "I see much travel for you and . . . much sorrow."

"Ah, you practice the science of palmistry," Hansum said.

"It's more of an art," Beatrice replied. She turned his hand and gently scraped her thumbnail along the hand's edge, sending an erotic tickle up Hansum's spine. "And I see children in your future, Signor." She looked up at him, somewhat surprised. "Two?" Coming from a time when the vast majority of people only had one child, this registered with Hansum in a different way than in the medieval woman in front of him. "So few progeny during such a long life?"

"We shall see," Hansum said, finally smiling. He took one of Beatrice's hands. She allowed it and he spread her palm. "Let's see what I can see in your hand, my lady."

"Your savant knowledge knows no bounds," she replied.

Having studied Beatrice's life after returning home, Hansum observed, "You too will have a long and interesting life, Lady Beatrice. Here, observe, eight children."

"Oh really, Signor. That many?"

"Very prolific," he replied. "Ah. And your life will not be one of just a dutiful wife, although you will be that. I see you shall be a great woman of business, finance, and a commander of armies." He ran his fingers over her palm again, splaying her fingers. "And the line that follows you, you shall be the grandmother of many famous and great kings, queens and statesmen, all of whom will change and impress the world."

Hansum looked up and found Beatrice with a most curious look on her face. For the first time since he met her, she seemed vulnerable.

"Signor, I have a question," she started. "No, a bold proposal, I am ashamed to say. But please vow to take it seriously and not scorn me."

"What is it, my lady?"

"Vow first," she said, squeezing his hand.

"I vow."

Beatrice looked down and blushed. Then she looked up again. "All these generations of kings, queens and the other great doers I shall be grandmother to. Could you not be . . . their grandfather?"

Hansum, true to his word, smiled kindly at her. Then he held up his palm to her. "That is not in my future, dear lady."

Just then there was a commotion in the hallway. People were returning.

Beatrice turned away from Hansum, letting go of his hand and running to the door. Just as she got there, she was blocked by people entering. She looked up in astonishment as she walked right into one. It was Hansum, the younger one, complete with his brown hat.

"But you . . ." she turned and looked behind her. All she saw was the large desk and plans. "You were just . . ." She looked back and forth several times. The younger Hansum, Lincoln, the general and her father looked back at her quizzically. "I was just talking to . . ."

"My lady?" the younger Hansum asked.

Beatrice stared at the slightly younger face. Then she grabbed one of his hands, looking for the scar, and then the other. Letting them go, she clasped her hands to her mouth, muffling a scream. Then she crossed herself and ran from the room. All the men followed.

Having gone out of phase as soon as Lady Beatrice turned away, Hansum had been standing right next to her when she couldn't see him.

"Ahem!"

Now Hansum turned to find another out-of-phase presence. It was Sideways, his astonished face looking out from the hovering cloak.

"What in the world is going on?" the A.I. asked.

"Everything has gone wrong," and Hansum spewed it all out. "Elder Parmatheon showed up in the woods and della Scalla's men caught him. I helped him escape back to the future. But when Lieutenant

Raguso didn't leave the firing range, Feltrino didn't attack. I think he's run away."

Sideways's eyes went wide. "You mean the battle didn't take place? The cannon is still intact and all those men alive? This, this could change the future irrevocably. It couldn't be worse."

"Yes it can. Hansum and Lincoln, the younger ones . . . they saw me. Beatrice too."

"Worse and worse!"

"What's happening in Verona?"

"From what I've seen, all is as before. I left the others there." Sideways gritted his A.I. teeth. "Now changes will happen fast and furious."

"I tried touching the Lincoln and other me, but couldn't put them out of phase. So I guess the nexus point isn't here, at least now. Should we get back to Verona and keep searching there? The changes here are bound to multiply by the time the people here get back to the city."

"I don't disagree, Master, but shouldn't we check on the most likely variables that could screw things up?"

"Like what?"

"You said Feltrino didn't attack."

Hansum felt a rush of panic. "You're right! We've got to find out what he's up to. We've got to hurry!" Hansum grabbed Sideways and quickly put him on. "Let's fly over all the roads and fields within a radius of where Feltrino could have gotten to in this time. Then we'll go to Verona."

Chapter 9

Feltrino Gonzaga sat on his horse in a thickly wooded area by a road, an hour away from Bella Flora. Night was falling. He and his men had stayed in the area hoping the cannon would remain in the valley and be lightly protected, but his stealthy spy had just returned and said it was taken back to the estate and now was under heavy guard.

'Porka vacca!' Feltrino swore to himself. His men had been primed and ready for battle. Who had della Scalla's men seen and chased? A spy from another rival family?

"What do you want to do, Excellency?" his captain asked. "We can't stay too long on della Scalla's land with such a host of men as this."

"If we don't do something about that cannon or savant now, the next time we fight this family, we'll be up against their new weapon."

"True enough," the captain answered, "but we've lost the advantage."

Feltrino scowled, the foul taste of bile building in his mouth. He spat it out. "Send the men home with the lieutenant," Feltrino ordered. "You and Testa stay here with me. We'll poke about and make a new plan."

As the captain gave the orders for his men to return to Mantua, Feltrino got off his horse, tied it to a tree and stretched. He had hardly slept in three days and his phantom thumb was throbbing. It always did when he thought about the lowly apprentice who had inexplicably bested him in a sword fight.

'Why didn't I just kill him quickly? That weapon could smash my family's hold on Mantua. Why is God thwarting me so?' As he thought all this, his missing thumb ached even more. 'And how can something that doesn't exist hurt?'

"Keep to the woods till you reach the River Po," the captain called as his twenty knights thundered off. He and the spy, Testa, returned to Feltrino and got off their horses, waiting for the Gonzaga prince to speak.

The captain was in full armor. Testa wore the plain-spun clothes of a commoner, and a buckskin jacket. He was a local known as a woodsman, but actually worked as a Gonzaga spy, roaming the area and gathering any information he could. He was the one who had picked up on the fact that something special was happening at Bella Flora, when all the wagons of rot and waste were transported there. Then, hanging around the local church and tavern, he heard the peasants talking about how they were making something called saltpeter beds, about a young savant who wore a brown cap and then about grinding great quantities of black powder. Testa had slipped onto the property only two days ago and had seen the first enormous test explosion blowing up a donkey. He rushed to Mantua to warn his masters.

"It was ill luck that another's poorly trained spy was seen, Excellency," the captain said.

"Very ill luck," Testa agreed. "I shall watch for another chance."

Feltrino spit again, looking at the two as if they were imbeciles. "We don't have time to wait!" he shouted. "There won't be another chance. They're on their guard now."

"What would you have us do then?" the captain asked.

"My father says that I must not be distracted by revenge, even though I have a rightful claim to it," he said, holding up his thumbless hand, "and I shall honor this wisdom. But both the weapon and the savant are now well-protected. We cannot do much about the weapon, but the man, he can be . . ."

There was the rumbling of many heavy hooves on the road, coming from the direction of Bella Flora. The Gonzagas took cover, but could see who was passing. To Feltrino's amazement he saw six della Scalla knights and soldiers riding before and after a seventh animal carrying . . . the savant and his small friend on the same horse. After they passed, Feltrino became livid.

"Curse my fortune!" he screamed to the heavens. "If I still had my twenty men we could overtake them and have the savant! Why is God being so cruel to me?" Feltrino looked hard at the captain. "Verona," he said firmly. "He'll be in Verona and most likely at the lens maker's."

"He could be going to della Scalla's palace," the spy suggested.

"Sooner or later he'll be at the lens maker's," Feltrino retorted angrily. "And when he is, we'll be there."

"After last time, it will be hard enough to get you two into Verona, let alone getting you out with an unwilling prisoner," Testa warned.

"We won't have a prisoner," Feltrino said, and he drove the point of his sword deep into the bark.

"But your father said it's a sin to kill a savant," the captain reminded him.

"Mastino cannot be allowed to have this advantage!" Feltrino yelled. "Do we still have men on their wall?" he asked Testa.

"Si, Feltrino."

"Good. We will approach Verona and, while the captain and I hide our armor in the woods, you will go and make arrangements to get us and our swords in. We will strike and be gone before Mastino knows what has become of his prized pet."

There was a silence. Finally the captain spoke.

"My job is to follow orders," he began, "but I have been with your father since I was a boy. He is a hard man of action, often bold, but I know what he would counsel before he committed to something."

Feltrino didn't like being challenged. He took hold of the hilt of his sword, pulled it out of the tree and pointed it at the captain. The soldier didn't flinch. He looked back at Feltrino with the same gaze he was getting. Feltrino laughed and put his weapon back in its scabbard. Then he chucked the captain on shoulder.

"Yes, you are right. He is right. I must consider what my father would say." Feltrino put his hands behind his back and began pacing back and forth, making a show of weighing the different options. "Let's see, what would he say?" he mused, an ironic smile on his face. "Ah, firstly he'd advise, view the situation, making sure you are seeing it truly and then consider your options. As to the situation, the fact is we've lost our opportunity to obtain the cannon and savant by stealth. Also, we have just witnessed seeing the savant pass on the road and know he is less guarded. The options? We can risk fighting him on the road, but there are six guards and we are only three, two fighting men. Another course of action would be to sneak into Verona and . . . ."

"Where is Feltrino?" Hansum spat as he and Sideways skimmed, out of phase, just over the treetops. They had already been flying for over an hour, checking the forest between Mastino's Bella Flora estate and Mantua. About ten minutes earlier, they found the bulk of the men they sought, at first happy the Gonzagas were headed away from Verona. But coming closer, they saw Feltrino was not with them. They hurriedly levitated back above the trees and made a beeline for the road to Verona, Sideways still complaining about how inconvenient it was not to have a full array of technology at his disposal. They quickly came upon the younger Hansum and Lincoln, riding with the della Scalla soldiers.

"They're heading back to Verona several hours earlier than before," Hansum said. "Mastino didn't make them wait, probably because there was no attack. They'll be in Verona sooner than expected."

"Thirty or forty minutes," Sideways advised. "Feltrino might be following them. We'd better backtrack." They reversed direction, crisscrossing the road, the A.I. using his enhanced sensory capabilities to find their temporal wild card. As they flew, Hansum's communications implant buzzed.

"It's Lincoln," Hansum told Sideways. "Hey man, what's up?"

"Boy, using this old communications implant instead of Medeea's telepathy is so archaic," Lincoln said in Hansum's head. *"What's taking you guys so long?"*

"Things have gotten complicated. Events have changed big time and we're held up trying to find Feltrino."

"What do you mean things got complicated. How?"

"There's Feltrino," Sideways said. "We found him."

"Lincoln, I have to go," Hansum said. "We'll be there as soon as we can."

"Will you be here before our other selves arrive?" Lincoln added hurriedly. *"That's three hours from now."*

"Sweet Gia, no," Hansum said. "No, that's one of the things that changed. We've left early, our other selves, that is. They'll probably be there in less than half an hour."

"What in the world happened?" Lincoln gasped.

Sideways was swooping down into the woods beside the road. Not having to go around the trees, the out-of-phase travelers went right through a thick canopy of forest. When they emerged into the small clearing below, there was Feltrino, an officer and a man in peasant clothes. Feltrino was talking to them, a perplexing smile on his face.

"Gotta go. Fill you in later," Hansum said, disconnecting from Lincoln as they hovered a dozen feet above the ground.

"Yes, you are right," Feltrino was saying, smiling hard at the officer and chucking him on the shoulder. "He is right," he added to the peasant. "I must consider what my father would say. Let's see, what would he say?" Feltrino looked thoughtful and began pacing. "Ah, firstly he'd advise, view the situation, making sure you are seeing it truly and then consider your options. As to the situation, the fact is we've lost our opportunity to obtain the cannon and savant by stealth. Also, we have just witnessed seeing the savant pass on the road and know he is less guarded. The options? We can risk fighting him on the road, but there are six guards and we are only three, two fighting men. Another course of action would be to sneak into Verona and wait for our chance to obtain the savant there. But, even if we could kidnap him, it would be impossible to get an unwilling prisoner out without being caught ourselves. So, we also have the additional option of simply getting into the city and slitting the savant's throat." Hansum looked down at Sideways and the A.I. back at him. Feltrino started to consider again. "Ah, but then I hear my papa saying something. What would he say, Captain?"

"He would say it is a sin to kill a savant."

"Si, that's exactly what he would say," Feltrino said with mirth. "The only thing left, I suppose, is to go back to Mantua and regroup. Build up a force, go to our allies and let them know of this new and dangerous weapon. Then, together we will crush Mastino before he builds up a number of them." Feltrino stopped speaking and raised his eyebrows at the officer, waiting on his comment.

"Yes, Feltrino," the captain said. "I believe that is exactly what your father would counsel."

"And, as a good soldier, if I said this is the best course of action, would you do as I say?"

"I would follow those orders, or any others you or your father gave me, Excellency."

"Good, then let's go," Feltrino said. "Let us mount our horses and ride."

The three men went to their mounts and untied them.

"I confess," the captain said, getting on his huge horse and starting to walk to the road, "I like the idea of sleeping in my own bed more than in the forest again, Excellency."

"Who wouldn't?" Feltrino agreed, riding with the others toward the road. "And there's a new kitchen girl at the palace. A comely thing. Maybe even a virgin. When I am next in my bed, I think she will warm it too."

"Then let's away," the captain laughed, pulling on his animal's reins."

"I think we've seen enough," Hansum said. "Our other selves should almost be at the Verona gates. Let's get there ahead of them."

"We can site transport there in a split second," Sideways said.

"Let's do it." Hansum took one last look at Feltrino and his men riding their horses across the road toward the forest and Mantua. "Finally we've caught some luck," Hansum said, and they winked away.

The captain was now on the road and just about to ride his horse into the trees.

"Where are you going?" Feltrino called.

"Back to Mantua," the captain answered, turning to face his young master.

"I didn't give that command," Feltrino replied, a certain tone in his voice.

The captain looked confused. "But you said . . . Mantua."

"True, I said it, but that was not my command," Feltrino smiled sardonically.

"Your bed? The girl?" the spy reminded.

"They will have to wait," Feltrino replied.

"Where are we to go then?" the captain asked.

"To Verona," Feltrino answered, pulling his horse around and spurring it. It took off in the direction that Hansum and Lincoln had ridden.

"To what end?" the captain shouted, whipping his horse to follow. The spy shook his head ruefully and got his animal galloping too.

"To what end?" Feltrino shouted back. "To kill the savant, of course."

Chapter 10

When Hansum and Sideways site transported into Guilietta's sick room, Lincoln and Medeea were not the only ones watching the sleeping girl. Shamira and Kingsley were there as well. But even though they were all out of phase, and thus invisible, the room was small and Kingsley had to stand half in and out of the room, his out-of-phase body visually sliced in half by the wall common to the hallway. As well, the younger Shamira was just entering with a steaming wash basin and clean linens. The place was packed.

"Finally," Lincoln said as Hansum appeared. "What the heck went so wrong?"

But Hansum didn't answer. He was shocked to see Guilietta looking so poorly.

"When I got here last time, she didn't look this sick," Hansum said.

"That's because I cleaned her up before you arrived," the older Shamira replied, gesturing to her other self. Hansum stood, wide-eyed and silent, as the young Shamira bent down and put her hand on the sleeping Guilietta's arm.

"Wake up, Guil. Wake up," the Shamira in the 14th-century said gently. Guilietta stirred, but did not open her eyes. "It's time to get ready for Romero. Romero's coming." At that Guilietta's eyes opened, expectation on her face.

"Is he . . ." Guilietta asked, her voice weak.

"Not yet. The courier said if he comes right away, he could be here within four hours. That could be soon now."

"Oh dear," Guilietta said, trying to raise herself up. "He mustn't see me like this. Help me get out of bed so I can wash and fix my hair."

Shamira helped her sit but, when Guilietta swung her feet over the side of the bed and tried to stand, she got dizzy and fell back. Shamira helped her on to the bed, going to her knees and waiting while Guilietta caught her breath. The out-of-phase Hansum gritted his teeth.

"Let's prop you up against the headboard," young Shamira suggested, helping her move. "Master Calabreezi said the best medicine for you now is good food," Shamira said, tucking in the blanket and smoothing it down. "Nuca's at her house preparing some. In the meantime, I'll give you a sponge bath."

"You really are like sisters," Kingsley said, putting a hand on his sad-faced, older Shamira.

"So, what happened, man?" Lincoln asked Hansum again. "Medeea says the changes at Bella Flora can quickly impact things here."

Hansum explained as he kept a close eye on Guilietta. "Parmatheon found me and wouldn't keep his mouth shut. The Podesta's men caught him. I helped him escape, but Lieutenant Raguso started checking the woods for spies and Feltrino didn't attack."

Lincoln smiled. "So my crew didn't get killed?"

"*I know it's pleasant to think how your friends didn't die, dear,*" Medeea said, "*But remember, each man still alive is an agent of change in the universe. Each thing they do, each person they interact with, causes*

the universe to be different. Within days, hundreds of deviations will rip-
ple down, then millions and billions."

"Man, these time travel conundrums are really screwing with my head," Lincoln said, slapping his forehead.

"Do we know what Feltrino's up to?" Kingsley asked. "He's not one to give up so easily."

"That's what took so long, finding him," Hansum explained. "He's on his way back to Mantua, so at least we don't have him to worry about. But our other selves have already left the estate. They're on their way back here."

"That's changed too?" Shamira asked. "When should you, I mean they, be here?"

"Any minute."

"Do we have to worry about Elder Parmatheon anymore?" Kingsley asked.

"No, I don't think so. I believe he's learned his lesson," Sideways added. "However . . . while maneuvering to rescue him, the younger Hansum and Lincoln saw our Hansum here and . . . so did Lady Beatrice."

"They saw you too?" Lincoln slapped the side of his head again. "Man oh man."

"So, we came to just observe and instead, made everything change," Kingsley recapped.

"Parmatheon caused it," Hansum said defensively.

"It doesn't matter who started the changes," Sideways said. "The question still remains, if we see a nexus point, should we transport the della Cappas back to our time, or should we wait?"

"All I want to do is keep Guil safe," Hansum confessed, his eyes still locked on her. "I've gotten her killed three times so far. I don't want to put her through more pain. Did you try taking them out of phase?"

"Ya, but no luck," Lincoln said.

Just then the curtain door to the room was pulled back and Master della Cappa came in. His eyes welled up at seeing his daughter sitting up.

"You're awake," he said as if seeing a miracle. He walked through the out-of-phase onlookers and knelt beside her.

"It's getting crowded in here," Kingsley said, stepping back a few more inches.

Agistino gently sat down on the edge of the bed and cupped Guiliet-ta's pale face in his hands. "How do you feel, my daughter?"

"Weak, Papa, but happy now that Master Calabreezi says I will recover."

"That bastardo, della Scalla," Agistino cursed. "He sat in my house and drank my wine, made his pledges — and he does this?"

"Master, you must control your anger," the younger Shamira advised. "Remember, Master Calabreezi says we must act like nothing has happened. If the Podesta feels slighted, he could cause us, and even Master Calabreezi's family, great harm. Let us just be happy that everyone is going to get better."

Agistino didn't respond, but trying to contain his rage caused his scowl to deepen. This, along with his wet eyes, made the big man look very fragile.

"How is Mama?" Guilietta asked, putting her hand on his arm.

The question about his wife's heroics caused Agistino's brittle emotions to crack even further. He could do nothing but choke out his reply.

"Your saintly mother is sleeping now. And who knows? Maybe we owe a debt to her Archangel Michael. Let, let us pray to him."

Guilietta and Agistino clasped one another's hands and bowed their foreheads together. As they muttered their thanks, the younger Shamira continued to slowly comb her sister's hair.

The sound of the front door to the house opening was heard and a familiar voice spoke.

"Romero!" Guilietta said, excitedly. She propped herself up straight and folded her hands demurely. The Master stood and wiped his eyes with his sleeve.

"Where is everybody?" the voice of the younger Hansum was heard asking in the lower room.

"They're upstairs, Romero," Bembo's voice answered.

"Did you bring presents this time?" came Ugilino's voice.

"Shut up, meathead," the younger Lincoln said, and there were quick footsteps up the stairs.

As before, Hansum rushed into the room, fell to his knees and began crying as his head dropped onto Guilietta's lap. The older Hansum noticed one distinct difference from before. His younger self had on a belt with a sword hanging from it. The younger Lincoln, still wearing his chainmail balaclava, stood next to the younger Shamira, his eyes full of worry.

"My darling, I'm fine. I'm fine, my love," Guilietta cooed, soothing the top of her husband's head.

"Your note," the younger Hansum said, looking up at Shamira. "It didn't say what the matter was. The Podesta let me come back right away, thank Cristo, but what's wrong?"

"The Podesta," the Master growled. "Bastardo!"

"What?" Hansum asked incredulously.

"We thought Guilietta was sick," the young Shamira explained, "But when Master Calabreezi came and saw what was going on, he figured out that Guil had been poisoned, with hemlock."

"Poisoned!" Hansum gasped. "Who . . . who would do that?"

"The bastardo! The Podesta, may he rot in Hades," Agistino said crossing himself.

"I don't understand," the 14th-century Hansum said.

"He sent a poisoner, acting as a herbalist," Shamira continued. "She befriended Nuca and then Guilietta. She tricked us."

"But why would he . . ." the younger Hansum stopped. He knew. "But you're going to be all right? You found out in time?"

"She will be all right, but no, it was not us that found her out," Agistino said, putting his hand on Guilietta head. "My daughter was saved by two angels . . ." and then he explained how his wife, with the help of her vision of the Archangel Michael, had prevented Guilietta's death.

With the extra people in the room, both in and out of phase, Kingsley's body was now mostly in the hallway, with only the front of his face peeking through the wall. He bent down to whisper into his Shamira's ear.

"It's crowded here," he whispered. "I'm going downstairs and maybe walk outside." She nodded, continuing to watch the highly-charged scene in front of her, very emotional herself. "I love you," Kingsley added, kissing her softly on the cheek. She looked up at him with limpid eyes and smiled, squeezing his hand as a tear rolled down her cheek. He wiped it away and Shamira looked back at the reunion. Kingsley backed up into the dark hallway, standing alone now.

'This is really heavy stuff,' he thought. 'Real life like we couldn't imagine in the 26th-century. And it's so different seeing it firsthand, instead of watching from afar. I wonder how it will affect my art?'

"Hey, let me out!" said a croaking voice from downstairs.

"You can't go out," another man's voice said sternly.

"But I gotta piss!" the first voice croaked again.

Kingsley quickly padded down the steps to see what was going on. There was the grotesque boy, Ugilino, at the door, facing two uniformed soldiers. The one who looked like an officer had his visor up and carried a short sword. The shorter soldier wore a kettle helmet and had several days of heavy beard growth. Both looked grimy from being on the road.

"You can't go out," the officer repeated.

"But I gotta piss and then I wanna go to my bed in the barn," Ugilino argued.

"Excuse me, Signor," Bembo, Master della Cappa's journeyman interjected. He was a well-spoken fellow with an easy and likeable manner, and very reliable in an emergency. "May I ask who you are and what is going on? Why can't we go out?"

"I'm Lieutenant Raguso. We're here to protect Master Monticelli, under orders from the Podesta," the officer said.

"Why does Romero need protection?" Bembo asked.

"He's the Podesta's savant," Lieutenant Raguso said.

"The Podesta's pet," the soldier next to him interrupted, and then he gave a great gaping yawn, exposing a mouth full of rotting teeth.

The officer cuffed him with the back of his heavy leather glove.

"Shut up! Imbecile! Excuse me, Signor. Master Monticelli is an important man and must be protected. There are spies and enemies about."

"**Master** Monticelli is it now?" Bembo said.

"Romero? Important?" Ugilino said, squinting.

"The Podesta's pet invented a grand new weapon," the tired soldier interrupted again. "Ta blow our bloody enemies ta bits. I seen it with me own eyes," and then he yawned again. "Loud too."

"Chinza! I said shut your mouth."

"But it's true, brother. As true as the fact that it was me who saw someone movin' in the trees, spyin' on us. And I helped catch that funny lookin' guy. And when we was chasin' all through the woods for his bloody friends, didn't you and I both see their horse markings and lots of droppings? Oh, there must have been fifty of them, brother."

"Twenty's more like it," the officer corrected. "But I said shut up!"

"All the same, it's true."

"As true as being ordered not to speak of this to anyone?"

"Oh, yeah," and the soldier yawned again, unperturbed.

"But I gotta piss," Ugilino protested.

"Well, do it in a pot in the house," Raguso told him.

"I gotta do more than that, and the Master don't allow the men to do it inside. Only the women."

"I gotta do it too," the soldier named Chinza said, yawning again. And then he winced, like his guts hurt.

"All right, all right" the lieutenant said. "You. Gargoyle face. Show us where to go and then get back in the house."

Ugilino exited into the night, shutting the door behind him, leaving Bembo and the unseen Kingsley inside. Kingsley had found this rustic interaction fascinating and wanted to see more, so he walked through the closed door, onto the stoop. Besides Ugi and the two soldiers, four more were standing on the road with the horses. The men all looked tired and mean.

"So, ugly one," Lieutenant Raguso began, "where does your master let you do it?"

"Behind the shop," Ugilino said, pointing down the lane.

"That's the shop?" the officer asked. "It looks like an old barn."

"Upstairs it still is," Ugilino croaked. "Downstairs is the shop, with the best lens making equipment in all of Europe, my master says. We make the lookers for the Podesta."

"They's made here?" the tired soldier asked Ugilino, sounding impressed. "The lieutenant, my brother here, let me try his. It's like witchcraft. And you help make 'em?"

"Uh . . . si," Ugilino lied.

"C'mon, let's go!" the lieutenant ordered. "You two, stay by the house. Our orders are to guard both the shop and house. You lot, bring the horses," and they began down the alley.

Kingsley clicked on his communications implant.

"Hansum, something's happening out here," he said. The image of the older Hansum in the small bedroom came into Kingsley's mind.

"What going on?"

"There are six soldiers down here. Armed to the teeth. Apparently they're guarding your younger self because you, he, may have been followed. Feltrino, I guess."

"Feltrino and his men are on their way back to Mantua."

"I understand," Kingsley replied. "But I thought you should know there are lots of soldiers around."

"Absolutely. Thanks. But I'm sure we're fine." Hansum's image disappeared.

"That sword looks sharp," Ugilino said to Chinza as they walked to the shop.

"It is," the perpetually yawning soldier answered. "I've gutted my share with it."

"I could be a soldier," Ugi said. "It would be fun riding around and killing people."

"Oh, yeah. And sleepin' in the mud or in your saddle for days, your ass bleedin' from the blisters. And wearin' hot, heavy armor, chasin' here and chasin' there, after someone who wants to stick a big sharp pike up your arse." He gave his biggest yawn yet, adding, "It's a treat."

"My master yells at me all the time."

"A skilled lens maker like you gets yelled at?"

Ugilino didn't answer. "Here's the barn. We're not supposed to do it out front, because of the customers. Come 'round back."

"You sleep in the shop?" Lieutenant Raguso asked.

"No, I have my own stall, with all the fresh straw I want and a wool blanket. It's 'round the back too."

"You go with him, Chinza. But don't be long."

"A wool blanket? Lucky," Chinza said as he followed Ugilino. "You got it lucky."

Kingsley was amazed at the interaction between the two not-so-brights. This truly would be fodder for some future piece of art. It made him think how, back home in his time, he spent hours in the tea houses with his friends, watching historical events and debating. He had always liked watching the big events, concentrating on glorified historical figures. But he was starting to appreciate how anonymous little people also made things change. What would have happened if this odd little fellow hadn't spotted Elder Parmatheon in the woods? Would the battle with Feltrino have gone on as before? And like Medeea said, now that all those soldiers hadn't been killed, would they have children who otherwise wouldn't have been born? Would they become free agents of time, siring even more free agents who'd cause more ripples of change? It was inevitable. And the soldiers who weren't killed would most likely kill people who weren't killed before. Such thoughts could go on and on.

These certainly were heavy and important ideas, ideas that History Camps and time travel were supposed to illuminate. They were ideas to be taken seriously. Kingsley frowned as he indeed did think about this seriously, but then . . . two huge farts echoed in unison from around the back of the barn. It was Ugilino and Chinza, relieving themselves. All the soldiers broke into gales of laughter. Kingsley's deep thoughts disappeared as he laughed along with the della Scalla knights, only a few feet away and out of phase.

Chapter 11

"Oh, this soup is good," Guilietta said, still perched up in bed. "More, husband," and the younger Hansum lifted the wooden spoon from the bowl, blowing on it gently before he put it to his wife's lips. As she sipped, her adoring eyes were locked on the similar warm looks of her Hansum. The older Hansum, Lincoln and Shamira had been watching them since Bembo brought up the soup Nuca prepared. Then Bembo left to sleep over at Nuca and her husband, Bruno's house, since the soldiers were forbidding anyone to sleep in the barn.

Meanwhile the younger Lincoln, Shamira and the Master were in with the Signora, giving her another dose of the vinegar Master Calabreezi had ordered to purge her bowels. It would take all of them to get it down her and then clean up, after it had sped through her system.

The older Hansum watched his younger self feed Guilietta another spoonful of soup and a morsel of fine, white bread, popping it in her mouth. Then he dabbed her lips with a linen.

"Maybe wait awhile before you have more, *mia amore*," the young husband suggested. "You haven't eaten much and your stomach will be sensitive."

"You take such good care of me," Guilietta sighed, leaning forward and kissing Hansum on the mouth.

"Oh, I've missed that," the younger Hansum said.

The older Hansum thought how he was speaking for both of them. He looked up to see his Lincoln and Shamira watching him. He smiled to show he was all right.

"Guilietta, you must sleep now," the younger Hansum said. "It's late. Close your eyes and . . ."

"I want you to stay here with me," she protested, taking his arm.

"I'll sit with you till you fall asleep, and then I have to talk with your father and the others. But I shall crawl into bed with you afterwards."

A smile came upon Guilietta that lit up the whole room and everybody's hearts, in and out of phase. She lay down, nestling her head into her pillow and Hansum tucked the covers over her shoulders. He kissed her forehead, her eyes, and then started humming a lullaby that wouldn't be composed for many centuries.

The older Hansum shook his head, to force himself to get serious.

"With things happening differently, I guess it doesn't matter if we change things further. We've got to get Guil medicine to stop the infection from flaring up."

"But the rule about modern . . ." the older Lincoln started.

"I don't give a fig about that now," Hansum said. "The only thing is to keep her healthy. I won't let her die again. But what to get and where to get it?"

"How about Signora Baroni?" out-of-phase Shamira suggested. "Remember, she's actually a colleague of Arimus from the 31st-century."

"Right," Hansum said, snapping his fingers.

The younger Hansum, seeing that Guilietta was asleep, stood, walked right through the out-of-phase Lincoln and Shamira and softly called for the younger Lincoln to join him. He took off his brown cap and stared at its secret compartment, the place where he kept Pan's home, the small brass lamp.

"Psst, Pan," he whispered, cocking an eye towards the sleeping Guil. "You can come out now."

A second later the familiar whirlwind spun out of the hat and all one meter of Pan spilled onto the floor. The older Hansum felt a pang of melancholy to see his old friend.

"What do you think, Pan? Is she okay?" the younger Hansum asked.

"Looking out from your hat, I was able to scan her eye," the gruff but musical voice said. "She still has a low grade infection that needs attending. However, Master, there's something else I should tell you. You see, she's . . ."

Lincoln entered, pulling the curtain tight behind him when he saw Pan.

"She's what, Pan?" Hansum asked.

"I'll tell you when we're alone, Master Hansum. Nothing to worry about."

The out-of-phase older Lincoln looked at Medeea.

"I think he knows she's preggers," he thought to his girlfriend.

"We'll find out soon enough," she thought back.

"Do you think I should tell Hansum? Our Hansum?" But before Medeea could answer, Pan said something that made everybody out of phase nervous.

"Young Masters," Pan said, "About those we saw at Bella Flora when we were alone with that bureaucratic fool. He and others may be . . ." and he waved his pudgy hand around the room.

Hansum and Lincoln, both sets of them, realized what he meant. The younger Lincoln took a few skulking steps around the room. "Come out, come out wherever you . . ."

"Lincoln," the younger Hansum chastised. "Not like that." Then he looked around in the air, searching, and said in a stage whisper. "Hansum, Shamira, Lincoln, Pan from our future. If you're here, there must be a reason. Please. Share it with us. Let's work together."

The older Hansum looked down at Sideways. "If we show ourselves, it would be easier to help Guil."

"No," Sideways answered. "If we bring them into our plans, things could change even more. And the more things change, the more out of hand they can get."

"I guess they're not here," the younger Lincoln said to Pan.

"I think they most probably are," Pan replied. "If I'm with them, I'd say not to expose yourselves . . . themselves. It could complicate matters."

"But they showed themselves before, or at least I did," the younger Hansum said.

"I think we can deduce that was not part of their plan, but only a necessity to rescue that fellow. No, I think the percentages are good that they're . . . very close."

"There, Excellency," Testa the spy said. "You are both in, as I promised."

"But we don't have our horses," Feltrino complained. He and his captain were wearing heavy tunics and breeches, like tradesmen. But they still had the tools of their trade, their swords and knives, wrapped up in burlap over the captain's shoulder.

"After your last entrance and exit from Verona," the spy commented, "they're on the lookout for you, so they'd notice good horses. And we were lucky to find one of our men on the north gate."

Feltrino's way of admitting one of his men was right was to scowl harshly, but say nothing.

"Well, let's go scout the lens maker's house. How far . . . on foot?"

Kingsley watched the interactions of the Podesta's soldiers with professional interest. As a sculptor, he was a people-watcher. He found the short, stocky fighting men of the 14th-century fascinating, especially their hard, weathered faces and even harder hands, the two things sculptors say express the most about a person. With two at the house, that left three unsaddling, grooming and tying up the horses, and one around the corner with Ugilino.

"How long can it take to empty their bowels?" Lieutenant Raguso complained.

"By the sound of them awhile ago," another soldier suggested, "the Podesta could have used them for cannon." This made all the soldiers and Kingsley laughed again.

"I 'eard that," Chinza protested, coming around the corner with Ugilino.

"Help with the horses," Raguso ordered.

"Oh, merda," Chinza went on. "The lens maker here just showed me the neat little nest he sleeps in. Nice warm straw and a clean blanket. He says his master gives all his men a clean blanket."

"My master makes me air it every day and wash it once a month," Ugilino said proudly.

"Cause the lens maker here's gotta sleep in the house tonight, he says I can use his stall to sleep in," Chinza announced, and he yawned once again, as if to make sure everyone knew he really was tired.

"Remember our deal," Ugilino said, "You can sleep there, but I get to ride your horse tomorrow and wear your helmet . . . and carry a pike."

"He'll not be sleeping in that stall," the lieutenant said. "It's too far around the building if there's trouble. You'll sleep on the floor of this shop with the rest of us. Can you get the key to the door, Gargoyle?"

"My name's Ugilino."

"Ugly it is then," Raguso said. "Get the key and maybe you'll still ride a horse tomorrow. And food. Can your master feed us?"

"Usually there's lots of food and we eat like princes," Ugilino said. "But with the Signora and her daughter sick, we been eatin' slim. I even ate at the *taverna* tonight."

"The taverna's the thing," Chinza said, brightening. "I'll go get food for all of us."

"I thought you were tired?" the lieutenant shot back.

"Now how long would I sleep with an empty stomach?" Chinza retorted. "I'll take this one with me to help carry."

"I'll get a basket from the house," Ugilino said excitedly. "Can we ride the horses there?"

"The horses have travelled enough today," Raguso answered, taking out a coin from a pouch. "And be quick about everything."

Still excited, Ugilino jumped to attention like a soldier.

"Si, General," he shouted, and then took off up the alley. "I'll be right back with the basket and key."

Kingsley decided to follow Ugilino, so began trotting after him. He should check in at the house anyway.

"That gargoyle is no more a lens maker than I am the Podesta," he heard the officer laugh.

"You're not the Podesta," a soldier laughed. "You're a general."

Easily catching up to Ugilino, Kingsley watched him snap to attention when he came to the two soldiers at the front door. They looked at him, boredom and exhaustion showing in their faces.

"Permission to enter the house?" Ugi asked loudly.

"*Idiota!* You live here. Get in and don't bother us again."

"No, I must leave again, on a mission for the general. I'm getting a basket to go to the taverna, to get food for all you soldiers."

That, at least, caused the soldiers to be less cranky.

"And drink too?" one asked.

Ugilino looked at the coin he was given, and made a gargoyle grimace. "Maybe not," he said. "I'll ask the Master. He's rich now and I know where he keeps . . ." he stopped. "Let me in."

"Open the door yourself."

Ugilino opened the door and burst in, Ugilino style. Kingsley followed. There, by the table, were the younger Hansum, Shamira and Lincoln, all leaning in, like they had been conferring in hushed tones. The second set of them, the out-of-phase older teens, were on the stairs, watching.

"Where's the Master?" Ugilino demanded. "I'm on a mission to get food from the tavern for the soldiers, but the general only gave me a *soldi*. I need more."

"Quiet!" the younger Hansum scolded. "The Master's upstairs. He's finally sleeping."

"He mustn't be disturbed," Shamira added. This put an instant frown on Ugilino's face.

"Ugi, it's late and we have to talk," Lincoln said. "Go to bed in the barn."

"The general said I couldn't," answered a clearly frustrated Ugilino. "I've got to get them food, and drink too, or they won't let me ride a horse. And they said I have to sleep in the house."

Hansum dug into his coin pouch and took out three very shiny silver coins.

"Here. Get lots of good food and drink and spend all of it. Don't keep any of it or give it to that taverna girl you visit. You understand?"

"Those are shiny soldi, Romero," an amazed and instantly happy Ugi pronounced. "You really must be the Podesta's pet. Oh, I need your basket, Carmella, and the shop key." Shamira pointed in the corner and he grabbed the wicker basket. Lincoln took the key from his pouch and tossed it to him. The energized Ugilino then ran back to the door, swinging it open wide and running right through Kingsley. "They gotta let me ride a horse in the morning now," and he was gone.

"I guess you haven't found a place to intercede?" Kingsley asked. The older Hansum shook his head. Then, all the teens looked over as Pan popped back into view.

"Pan, if you really think we're being watched by ourselves from the future, why do you think they won't reveal themselves or give us real medicine?" the younger Hansum asked.

"Maybe the fact that they're just watching their past means everything worked out," the younger Shamira suggested.

"Yeah," the young Lincoln agreed. "That's gotta be it. We got back, Guil's just fine and we're all living happily ever after. And we've, they've just come back to watch themselves — for fun like."

"No, I don't think so," Hansum the younger said, despondently. "The other me said they're here to rescue us."

"Well, if they're here to rescue us and they're from the future," Shamira offered, "then they must succeed and we'll be doing the same thing for another set of us in our future."

"We can't depend on that," Pan stated quite definitively. "Nobody knows whether time and events are fixed or pliable, and whether we can change things."

"We know," the older Hansum said forlornly. "And now we've got them second-guessing themselves. That could screw things up more."

"This is what I think." Pan was speaking a little louder and looking around, obviously aiming his comment at anyone who might be listening in covertly. "I think that, unless the people from the future contact us in the next few seconds, we must continue to carve out our own present and future, with no thought of them." They all stood silently looking around the room.

"Come out, come out . . ." Lincoln repeated cautiously.

"Nope," Pan finally said. "No sign of them. We act like we're on our own."

"Pan, for all his silliness, really was wise," the older Shamira observed. Then the younger Shamira spoke.

"Should we go wake up Signora Baroni now or wait till the morning?"

"Now is best," Pan said, just like before. "One never knows with infections, but I am quite positive if we start Guilietta on a course of what I have suggested tonight, we'll stop it from becoming full blown."

"Please, please . . ." the older Hansum prayed, knowing this measure was doomed to fail.

"Okay, Sham, let's go," said the kettle-helmeted Lincoln with authority.

"My, aren't you becoming the serious fellow," she said playfully.

"You should see me bossing guys around when we're firing the cannon."

"I'm going to be with Guilietta," a melancholy younger Hansum said, turning to the stairs.

"Good," Pan responded. "But switch me over to Mistress Shamira first."

After doing so, Shamira and Lincoln left, walking right through Kingsley at the door. As the younger Hansum ascended the stairs, he walked through his older counterpart.

"So, what do we do now?" the older Lincoln asked.

"I want to watch over Guil too," his Hansum said, turning to go up the stairs, "just in case her illness happens differently for some reason. After they're asleep, I'll try taking her out of phase every half hour."

"Medeea and I will do the same with the Signora and Master," Lincoln said.

"I want to go to the barn," Kingsley said with a smirk. "Those soldiers are a hoot. It should get even more interesting when Ugi comes back with the food and drink. Want to come with me, Sham? They'll give you a laugh and then we can bed down for a few hours . . . in the loft," he said winking.

Hansum stopped and turned back to the others. "Something just occurred to me. Elder Parmatheon was the worst of the Council, but now that he's had a taste of what happens in the field, maybe he'll get the others to support us. He said he would."

"He could have just said that to save his own skin," Kingsley suggested.

"We should find out," Hansum decided. "Sideways, can you pop back to our time and see what the situation is?"

"This is not a problem, Master Hansum."

"But if he hasn't changed his mind, or is even angrier, won't they stop you from coming back?" Shamira asked.

Sideways laughed. "You forget I'm from the 31st-century. Just because I haven't flexed my superior technological muscles, doesn't mean I don't have them. I'll be safe enough."

Lincoln looked at Medeea. "C'mon, Med. Let's go curl up in a corner of the Signora's room.

"*Sounds romantic,*" she thought to him. "*Too bad we can't go to the loft.*"

"*We can be in the loft. Or anywhere. In our minds,*" he thought back, winking. He reached out and they walked up the steps hand in hand.

"C'mon Sham. Wait'll you see this motley crew," Kingsley laughed. "They're hilarious."

Hansum watched as Lincoln climbed the stairs, his hand held out, obviously holding Medeea's hand. He turned and saw Shamira and Kingsley, also hand in hand, going toward the exit. Shamira turned back, smiled, and disappeared through the door.

"I should be off then," Sideways said. "Aren't you going to Guilietta's room?"

"I'll give them a bit more time alone," Hansum replied. "I won't intrude till they're asleep."

"I'll be back as soon as I determine the situation and we'll take it from there," Sideways said and, with that, Hansum was left wearing the tunic he had on at Haudenosaunee.

Hansum could hear Guilietta and his other self chatting and giggling in the bedroom, followed by long silences. While he couldn't hear exactly what they were saying, he remembered his similar sweet reunion when he lived this reality. He left the steps and sat at the table, so he'd hear even less. Leaning forward on his elbows, he thought of Shamira and Kingsley, what they had, and how even Lincoln's situation was making him happy. And then he thought how, if his plan worked, while the person he was now would cease to exist, perhaps the Hansum that emerged could experience a renewed and sustained love. He could only hope.

Chapter 12

The shadows were deep and dark in the back alley. From the distance they were at, they could see the lieutenant walking out of the shop, checking on the man who was sitting, his back against the wall. His head was down and he didn't notice his superior approach.

"Hey, get off your ass and walk around when you're on watch," Lieutenant Raguso barked. "I'll be sleeping in here with the others. When we spell the two at the door in a few hours, you can come inside then."

"Lieutenant, aren't we going to wait for the food?" the soldier asked as he rose.

Raguso snorted. "We sent my brother to a tavern. If Chinza comes back at all it will be a miracle. And the gargoyle he went with . . . they're one and the same."

"If you don't mind me saying, Lieutenant, two brothers and you're so different. You an officer and him an . . . an . . ."

"An ass? He's my father's bastard. But my father was an honorable man and looked out for him, much to my mother's anger," he said crossing himself, "May she rest in Cristo. And now that my papa is *morto* too, that blood of my father's blood has become my cross to bear."

"He did save your skin at Bresca."

"Oh, he's no coward and not afraid to use his sword, for sure. But all the other times, I'd like to," and he made the Italian salute. "Now don't fall asleep," and he went inside the darkened shop and closed the door.

"They're very foolish," one of the watchers said, invisible in their shadows.

"And they're going to be dead in a few minutes," the other added.

There was a scuttling sound behind them as a third companion crept up.

"There's just the two guards at the door, Excellency," Testa said. "One sat down and is sleeping. The other's almost asleep on his feet."

"And three here with a sixth at a tavern and likely not to come back soon. Okay, let's do our business here and then go to the house. When the guards are dead," Feltrino finished, "we'll kill the savant."

As Shamira walked through the door, she turned to say goodbye to Hansum. He was sitting on the stairs, staring at them forlornly. Poor Hansum, she thought, giving him a sympathetic smile. He smiled back, and then she and Kingsley were gone.

The first thing she heard on the porch was rough snoring. One soldier was sitting against the wall, his mouth wide and a guttural sound coming from the blackened cavern. His colleague was standing, eyes shut tight.

"It would appear the only reason the one standing is awake is his friend's snoring," Kingsley joked. The second soldier slid to the stoop and his head fell forward, as did his long pike.

"You're right," Shamira laughed. "They are funny."

"I told ya," Kingsley said, and he gathered Shamira in his arms and kissed her hard. As they parted, Shamira looked closely at Kingsley. This was the man she would marry.

"Oh, I love the way you kiss," she said.

"There's a poet in my time. He'll write, 'Kiss like every meeting of our lips will be their last.' "

"I thought you weren't supposed to tell me things about the future till we're . . . married."

"I feel we already are," and he took her in his arms and kissed her again.

"No, no. Not in there. The general is waiting for us," they heard Ugilino's voice from down the road.

"Nah, it's fine. Come!" Chinza's equally gruff voice replied. Shamira and Kingsley saw two very unsteady silhouettes.

"What are they up to now?" Kingsley said mirthfully. "Come on. This should be priceless." He took Shamira's hand and they ran laughing down the street.

"No, we'll sit in this alley," Chinza was saying, "and have our fill first." Ugilino was carrying a basket laden with loaves of bread, sausages and bottles of wine. The soldier had an open bottle in one hand, and was taking a long pull from it.

"No, this is Master Spagnolli's house," Ugilino whispered loudly. "It's late and he has a big cleaver."

"I have a big cleaver too," the drunken Chinza replied.

"Your sword?" Ugilino asked.

"Nah," and he looked down and winked. He and Ugi broke up laughing.

Shamira and Kingsley laughed so hard, they had to help each other stand.

"Shhh!" Ugi said, still snorting and spitting. "The butcher will tell my master."

"A valuable lens maker like you, afraid of his master? Eh? Maybe I should tell 'im how you gave that three *denarii* to the bar girl, eh?" and he spit on his grubby middle finger and poked into Ugilino's ear, which threw Ugi into more gales of snorts and honks. Chinza took the ceramic bottle and swigged more wine.

"Eh, shouldn't we get all this back to the general?" Ugi asked. "Won't he get mad and beat you?"

"All right, all right," Chinza said, starting to meander back to the workshop. "But that ain't no general. He's only a lieutenant . . . my big brother. Aldo Raguso. He don't never beat me."

"Wow. You knew your papa? I never knew my papa. I'm a bastard," Ugi said, taking the bottle from his new companion and upending it.

"I'm a bastard too," Gino said brightly. "Aldo and I got different mamas. Here, I'm going to have some *pane*," and he broke off a big piece of the bread as they walked and shoved it in his mouth.

"But you said . . ."

"Papa made sure my mama always had money, but she couldn't work in his wife's house no more. But when I growed up and my mama died, he got me in the army. He gave me this sword on his deathbed," he said patting his scabbard.

"Wow, you really is lucky," Ugilino said with awe. By this time they had staggered their way to the della Cappa home. "Hey, your friends are sleepin'," Ugilino said about the guards on the stoop.

"No friends of mine." Chinza spat. Then he looked happy. "More for us. They don't deserve it, sleepin' on duty." They tried tiptoeing by the house, but kept stumbling and laughing, which was very entertaining for Shamira and Kingsley. The two drunks looked up the alley. The moon was shining down on the shop. They could see another man lying against the wall and no lamps were lit in the workshop. "They's asleep too. I tell ya, let's go to your stall and we'll have all this to ourselves," Chinza said.

Ugilino gritted his teeth. "But then the general won't let me ride the horse tomorrow."

"Oh, all right," Chinza conceded. "Le's go wake my dear brother," and they continued stumbling down the alley.

"Poor Ugi," Shamira said. "You really do see another side of people when you watch them unawares. He's pathetic, but sweet somehow."

"Shamira. It's Lincoln," came a voice in her head.

"Yes, what's up?"

"It's the Signora. She's awake and acting really weird. You better come here. Medeea says we need a flesh and blood woman."

"I'll be right there. The Signora's acting out," she said to Kingsley. "Lincoln wants me to . . ." Kingsley was already a dozen steps down the alley, following the two entertaining drunks. He turned.

"I'll come with you," he said.

Shamira could see how happy he was observing these fools. He really was an ardent people-watcher. That's why he was such a good artist. "No, you go along," she said. "I'll come back as soon as I can. But, how about a goodbye kiss . . ."

"Owwwfff!" came a grunt up the alley, followed by an inebriated laugh.

"Shhhh!" Chinza hissed.

Ugilino had tripped and spilled the contents of the basket. Kingsley turned to see a giggling Ugi on his knees, collecting the now dusty bread and sausage. Kingsley quickly tiptoed toward them, shaking his head and laughing at the two clowns.

". . . a goodbye kiss?" Shamira finished saying, but to herself now. "Oh well."

"Shamira, are you coming?" Lincoln's voice asked with urgency.

"Right there," she said turning and starting to run.

'He really isn't a bad person,' Kingsley thought to himself. Ugi was gathering up the bread, banging the dust off with his hands and shoving the bread back in the basket. He stood and even spit on the sausages to clean them.

"You stay here," Chinza whispered as Ugilino got on his feet. "I want to surprise him." The soldier was sitting against the wall, slumped sideways, one arm flung out to the side and his sword still in its scabbard.

Ugi stood still, a moronic grin of anticipation on his face. Kingsley was right by him, looking closely at his face, his artist's eye taking in the unsymmetrical cheekbones and broken nose, wondering what harsh experiences made them that way. He looked over and watched Chinza slowly draw out his sword and tiptoe the last few feet to his comrade. Kingsley noted how everything looked black and white in the near dark, like ancient, pre-color photographs. Chinza reached out with his blade, grinning back at Ugi one last time before playing his prank. Ugilino tittered, spittle ejecting from his mouth. Then Chinza put the sword point under the other soldier's lowered chin and pushed gently.

"Eh! You ready to die hungry, ya sleepin . . ."

The soldier keeled over, his head unceremoniously hitting the dirt. There was a wet sound and something black splashed onto Chinza's boot. "Wha . . ." More black on the sword point. He pulled it back, his eyes going wide. "Blood!" he said and moved quickly to the door. It was ajar and he pushed it open. "Brother . . ." he began to shout.

Two men spun their heads toward them, looking up from the dead face of Lieutenant Raguso, whose throat was horribly carved from ear to ear.

Kingsley felt an instant chill flash up his spine as he caught his breath, horrified.

Chinza, without hesitation, turned on his heels and ran. "Attacked! We're being attacked!" he screamed into the night. He ran right through Kingsley and knocked into Ugilino, who dropped his basket and ran too. "Wake up, we're being attacked," Chinza shouted as he ran back up the alley, putting distance between himself and Ugi.

Kingsley started running towards the house. The assassins were following. Kingsley touched his communications node.

"Hansum. The shop's being robbed. They've killed the soldiers there. Wake up the guards. They're asleep on the porch. Then bar the door!" Kingsley had caught up to Ugilino and heard Hansum giving orders over his transplant. Chinza was now to the end of the alley. He started to turn the corner.

"Wake up you bastards," he screamed to the guards on the porch. "There's . . ." he stopped dead, a sword now sticking clear through him. Ugilino and Kingsley screeched to a halt as Chinza's arms jerked out and the sword his father gave him flew high in the air. It rose in an arc and landed point down in the dirt, right between Ugilino and Kingsley. As Chinza slumped, the sword was pulled out from him and the blade's wielder stepped forward.

Kingsley's hand flew to his temple, touching his communications node.

"Hansum. It's Feltrino! Feltrino's here. Don't open the door. I think the guards at the door are dead!"

"Hello, ugly one," Feltrino said to Ugilino, who looked quickly behind him. Two men were blocking the alley. Ugilino fell to his knees.

"Feltrino, please don't kill me," he begged, crossing himself.

Feltrino signaled to one of his men, drawing a hand across his throat. The smaller one, wearing a deerskin jacket, walked toward Ugilino, his bloody dagger raised.

Kingsley bit his lower lip and felt one of his hands rise up to his emergency node. The other lowered to the sword in the ground.

Chapter 13

Already running up the steps, Hansum clicked his communicator.

"Lincoln, make sure the Mistress stays in that room. You and Sham get her and the Master off the bed. Have the Master help you take the bed apart to barricade the stairs. I'll get Guil in there too."

"But that means we have to come out of phase."

"Just do it!"

Hansum was already up the stairs and in the room with Guilietta and the younger Hansum. He pressed his emergency node, causing a blue spark and snap. The younger Hansum, lying with his arm curled over his sleeping wife, spun around to find a hand clamping onto his mouth and a face he had often seen in the mirror staring down at him.

"I'm here to save Guilietta. Feltrino's outside."

With that, the younger Hansum spun further around in bed, reaching for his sword on the floor. The older Hansum reached down and put his hand on the hilt first. "You let me handle that. I'm better than you now."

The younger Hansum got up quickly. "Tell me what's going on."

"No time for details. You get Guil into the other bedroom. My Lincoln and I will hold them off till help arrives." Before Hansum could go out of phase again, the younger man spoke.

"Where's Pan? Your Pan? Use his friggin' laser, like he did at the river."

"We're alone here for a while. No A.I.s. Bad timing." He touched his node and was disappearing as he said, "I won't let it happen to her again . . ." and he was running through the walls. As he entered the other bedroom he watched Shamira and Lincoln coming out of phase. The Signora had a sheet wrapped around her face, her blubbery cheeks and tightly closed eyes the only parts showing.

"Something bad is going to happen," the old woman was crying. "Something bad is going to happen."

The Master was sitting, his back to Shamira and Lincoln, trying to comfort his wife.

"No, my dear. All is well, all is . . . Carmella, Marucio. I didn't hear you come in."

"There's trouble, Master," Shamira said. "Feltrino's outside," at which the Signora flung off the sheet and screamed shrilly.

"Master, let's get the Signora on the floor," Lincoln said. "We must use the beds to block the stairs."

"Come Mistress. Off the bed," Shamira urged. "Sit on the floor."

As the older Hansum watch from out of phase, he racked his brain on how to proceed. He looked at the sword in his hand, realizing it was from the Podesta's own collection. What would Mastino do if he were in this predicament? He bit his lip with resolve and clicked his communications node.

"Lincoln, I'm going downstairs. When the other Hansum comes in, have him help with the barricades, but don't, I say, don't let anyone come help me. Do you hear? Nobody!" He turned and was gone through the wall.

As the Master was helping Lincoln move his wife, he looked at Lincoln oddly.

"You look . . ." he started, but his wife saw something too.

"Such strange clothes, Carmella. Such strange eyes," the Signora said, and she winced as they sat her on the floor.

The younger Hansum entered, helping Guilietta walk. As soon as they had her on the floor, a pounding started at the front door.

"Master. Romero. Quickly. The bedframes and mattresses from both rooms," Lincoln ordered. "Barricade the top of the stairs."

Shamira grabbed the straw-filled mattress off the bed and the men heaved the heavy bedframe on its side. They muscled it across the floor and through the doorway, ripping down the curtain, Shamira right behind. Manhandling the frame, they wedged it tightly into the narrow passage.

"I will go down and confront him," the Master said. "I'll give him my gold and as many lookers as he . . ."

"That's not what he wants now, Master," Shamira said sternly. "He's here to kill Hansum, I mean Romero."

"No!" Guilietta screamed from the bedroom. The Signora started praying.

The pounding on the door became more fierce.

"Still, I shall confront him," Agistino insisted.

"Husband!" the Signora cried.

Lincoln and the younger Hansum were already pulling the bed out of the other room, setting it on end against the other frame. Master della Cappa tried to squeeze through, but Hansum and Lincoln pulled him back.

"Leave me . . ." Agistino shouted. The pounding at the door now sounded like someone was battering at it with an ax.

"You must stay here and hold the barricade, Master," the younger Hansum said, squeezing himself past the upturned bed. He broke one of the slats from the base of a frame.

"No Hansum," Lincoln shouted, making a grab but missing him.

The door to the house burst open and there was Feltrino, standing menacingly, his clothes drenched in blood. He stepped in, his fierce look turning to a grin when he saw Hansum on the steps.

"A stick?" he commented, stepping forward. Right behind him was his captain, sword and knife in hand, equally bloody. "This time no talk . . ."

There was a crack in the air, a flash of blue, and then a quick guttural grunt of agony. Feltrino spun around as more blood spurted onto his face. It was his captain's, who now stood with a big red smile across his neck. The sword that had put it there was now pressing into Feltrino's chest. As the captain slumped dead to the floor, Feltrino slowly turned to see the man who had bested him.

"Apprentice!" he gasped, then flashed a gaze back to the stairs. The same face looked back at him from both places. "How?"

"Drop your weapons and lie down with your hands behind your back," commanded the Hansum with a sword. "I said . . ." he pressed the sword harder, causing Feltrino's skin to tear. Feltrino complied. "Tie his hands," he said to the other Hansum. As the younger Hansum came down the steps, he grabbed a coil of rope from a peg. As he approached

Feltrino, the older Hansum commanded, "Wait," and he placed the blade straight on top of Feltrino's spine, like he had seen him do when he murdered Lieutenant da Silva. "Part of me hopes you make a move, Gonzaga," Hansum said in a voice that told the prince this was not the same man who spared his life at the river. Feltrino strained his neck and looked up at both Hansums, and then went limp. The younger Hansum tied Feltrino's wrists together very tightly.

"Now tell me what's . . ." the younger Hansum began, but his other self talked over him.

"I saved her. Finally," the older Hansum said to himself in Earth Common. He exhaled deeply and smiled at his younger self. "We did it this time. Guilietta's safe." And a hot shiver went up Hansum's back. "We've saved her from more pain."

"Thank Cristo, he's bested him," the Master's voice shouted from up the stairs, and there was the sound of the barricade coming down.

"No, stay up there," the older Hansum shouted, but it was too late. The Master was already bulling his way around the barricade, pulling the older Shamira and Lincoln with him.

"Romero, you did it . . ." the Master stopped in his tracks as he saw twin sons-in-law.

"Get him back before the others see . . ." but that was too late as well. There was Guilietta, already standing on the steps, holding onto the railing, her eyes and mouth wide.

"What's going on?" another voice shouted behind Hansum, and in from the street ran the younger Lincoln and Shamira, horrified looks on their faces. The widening pool of the captain's blood and the trussed Feltrino, however, were not as surprising to them as seeing their other selves standing in front of them.

"Holy Cristo," the Master said crossing himself. There were three pairs of twins.

"Go to Guil," the older Hansum said to his younger self. "Take her back up."

"Tell me what is going on?" the younger Hansum insisted.

"All I can say is things are really screwed up and nobody knows why. But we're trying to fix it. The important thing is Guil is . . ." he looked at Guilietta and all his conditioning vanished. Tears streamed down his cheeks. ". . . safe."

The younger Lincoln and Shamira came and stood next to their older selves. They stared at each other.

"I'm lookin' good," the younger Lincoln chimed. "Hey, a bit a stubble," he said rubbing his other face with a thumb.

"We got back?" the younger Shamira asked herself.

"Yes," she answered.

"Mom and Dad okay?" the younger girl asked. A nod. Then, you could tell the younger one saw something in her older self's eyes. "We're in love." Of course, she would know.

The older Shamira smiled. "Oh yeah," she answered. "I guess it won't hurt now." She touched the communications node on her temple. "Kingsley," she said. "It's all clear here. You can come in." No answer. "Sweetie, there's someone here who wants to meet you. Kingsley. Kingsley?"

The older Shamira moved to the door. The older Hansum grabbed her arm.

"I'll go check," he said seriously, but Shamira tried to pull away. "Sham, you stay here," he ordered. "You two watch her," he said to the Lincolns.

"Kingsley," Shamira repeated, tapping her temple, panic in her voice.

"Who is . . ." started the younger Shamira, but her older self moved to bolt from the house.

"Hold her!" Hansum commanded, and both Lincolns and even the Master grabbed Shamira.

"What's going on?" shouted the Signora's voice from upstairs, adding to the confusion.

"What's wrong with my sister?" was the last thing the older Hansum heard Guilietta asking as he ran out of the house.

"Kingsley," he shouted as he passed the dead guards on the stoop, one's throat cut and the other lying in a pool of red, blood still oozing from his chest and mouth. "KINGSLEY!" he shouted as he jumped off the stoop and started running down the alley. "Kingsley! Answer me, Kingsley!"

"Kingsley," he heard Shamira's voice shriek from the house.

Hansum stopped momentarily at the body of a man in a deerskin jacket. "Kingsley!" Hansum shouted again. There. A figure on its knees, silhouetted in the dark. "Kingsley," Hansum said with relief in his voice.

He ran more easily now, touching his communications node. "He's in the alley. He's okay." The faces of the older Lincoln and Shamira came into his mind. They both looked relieved. Then, as Hansum neared the kneeling figure he scolded it. "Man, Kingsley, you had us all so worried. Why didn't you . . ." he stopped.

"The angel," came a voice from the kneeling figure. It wasn't Kingsley's voice, but a rasping croak. "The large angel appeared from thin air and saved me, Romero." Ugilino was speaking very quietly. He was kneeling beside Kingsley, who was on his back, his eyes staring up at the stars, his head surrounded by a dark halo. "He slew one and I ran away. And then he kept fighting. I guess, I guess he isn't an angel."

The others were running from the house now, the older Shamira in the lead.

"Kingsley, I was so afraid," she called from the dark.

"Stop her!" Hansum shouted. "STOP HER!" but the others couldn't catch up till she was only a few steps away. As the truth of the situation slammed into Shamira's mind, she jerked still, her arms convulsing backward. She gasped and froze, her skin instantly going white as blood drained from her face. The Master, both of the Lincolns and the other Shamira took hold of her, all standing with horror and confusion on their faces. Finally, the older Shamira was able to inhale. As she did, her face contorted in an agonized knot.

"KINGSLEY!" she shrieked, her wail echoing up the alley. She pulled her arm violently, almost getting away from one of the Lincolns, but the Master enveloped her in a massive bearhug.

A whirlwind came from the younger Lincoln's lirripipe and Pan appeared on the ground. Ugilino fell onto his backside and the Master looked on in astonishment. Pan peered at Kingsley closely, and then looked up at Hansum, shaking his head.

"Kingsley." This time the older Shamira said it very softly, and she slumped. The Master and both Lincolns helped her to the ground. Once there, she crawled over to her dead fiancé and lay over him.

A glow wrapped around the older Hansum's chest and Sideways appeared, returning from the 24th-century. His smiling face changed as he assessed the situation.

"I must go to my sister," they heard Guilietta's voice call, and she appeared hobbling along, holding the younger Hansum's arm. Her eyes took in everything, the two Lincolns, her one sister draped over a large dead man, the other standing, hands clasped over her mouth. Guilietta quivered as she looked into the face of the other Romero and her eyes bulged as she stared into the living face on his cloak. Her legs gave way. As she fell, her Romero caught her, helping her gently to the ground. But now she was eye to eye with a little man with hairy legs, goat feet and a gnarled, frowning face. Guilietta's eyes rolled up into her head and she fainted.

"We must go," Sideways said, and A.I. tendrils shot out from the cloak. They grabbed hold of each person from the future, including Kingsley, and disappeared. Pan snapped his fingers and winked out of sight.

Ugilino got to his knees. He looked at the remaining Shamira. "Were they angels or demons?" he asked. But Shamira didn't answer. She just stood there, staring at the spot where her other, terrified self had been screaming and crying over the body of a very beautiful man.

BOOK FOUR
Without Fear or Cost

Chapter 1

Hansum preferred being put to sleep during his DNA repair procedure, although it wasn't technically necessary. But it made his stomach queasy, something that just came with age the doctor told him. Then again, many things made his stomach queasy of late.

"If you just let Medeea do a deeper mind-delve, she could fix you up." Lincoln had been telling him this for years.

"No thanks, pal."

"I really don't know why you always refuse," Lincoln said, shaking the grey locks that now hung over his ears and collar.

Hansum had never allowed a deep mind-delve. He didn't want anybody to know what he was really thinking or, more to the point, feeling. He'd only allowed conversational delves, exchanging just what he wanted to say.

As he drifted asleep to receive his third and last allowable DNA repair, it wasn't long before the images came again. They were the Mists of Time recordings he hated reviewing during his monthly planning meeting with Lincoln, the ones they used while working on their ever-developing tactics for a next foray back to the 14th-century. The images came in waves, washing over him and causing high tides of emotion. He saw Kingsley lying dead as they appeared back in the medical facility, both the human and A.I. doctors rushing to save him. But he had been stabbed multiple times in the heart, lungs and liver, and his spine had been severed. He had also lain dead too long. It was almost twenty minutes before the older Hansum found him, and till Sideways returned to take him back to the 24th-century. The sights and sounds of Shamira's hysterical screams still plagued him. She pleaded that they go back immediately and change events so her fiancé wouldn't be killed. But that wasn't allowed. Shamira cried in Hansum's arms as Arimus explained how, when Kingsley's parents were informed about their son, they refused permission to change the event.

"His family loved him without reservation, my dear.
But of death and the concept of right and wrong,
people from the 26th-century think differently, I fear.
To think we are the same is a temptation,
but change comes with every generation.
This is among the hardest lessons to learn
and accept."

It was indeed a hard lesson to live with, but Shamira survived. She resigned from time travel and chose instead to marry herself completely to painting.

"My baby. My child," Hansum murmured in his dream sleep. He saw a new image, Charlene floating close by when Lincoln finally had time to tell him that Guilietta was pregnant. As the gravity of it hit Hansum, he collapsed. His vision morphed into him struggling to talk, his voice harsh and broken after hours of sobbing, confessing to his A.I. confidant, "When Guil died and burned in the fire, it was bad enough imagining her . . . there. But now I know there was . . . is a baby . . . my baby . . ."

"We have a baby somewhere in the universe," Charlene said softly. "Somewhere in time. We have to save it."

So, as hard as it was to imagine, the stakes were now even higher and Hansum could not let himself fall apart, no matter how much pressure he bore.

During the third day of his drug-induced coma, Hansum's memory re-watched an event that could be fixed. Arimus had simply sent Sideways back to tell the earlier Hansum hiding in the woods to go out of phase while reconnoitering the cannon testing. This forced Elder Parmatheon Olama to go out of phase to find him, so Chinza never saw anyone in the bush. That meant Lieutenant Raguso didn't order his men to scour the forests, Feltrino attacked and the battle ran as before. The timeline was restored, including the fact that Lieutenant Raguso and his brother, Chinza, as well as the other soldiers, weren't killed at the della Cappa home. But alas, Chinza was killed when Gina, the cannon, went back to exploding.

Maybe it was the molecules of every strand of his DNA being partly disassembled and repaired, but the next vision vexed the unconscious Hansum even more. It was the obsequious Parmatheon Olama smiling at him as if he were an old friend, acting like it was nothing he had done that initiated the stream of events resulting in Kingsley's death.

"I'm sure you will be pleased to know," Parmatheon's voice echoed in the mind, "I not only relinquished the chairmanship of the Council back to Elder Barnes, but I also started a new committee to organize all the resources you asked for."

It was true. When they got back, everyone, Arimus included, was again surprised how easily they were able to reverse the damage, while the other situation, saving Guilietta, seemed impossible. It gave more credence to the scientists' theory of temporal nexus points. That, along with the public's fascination with the ongoing Romero and Guilietta drama, triggered a stampede of demand for "the project." And the A.I.s fell in line too.

The dreaming Hansum watched the memory of himself bite his lip and start pragmatically cooperating with Parmatheon. He needed to get back to Guilietta as quickly as possible.

But then the memory of Arimus delivering more bad news showed itself. Hansum and Lincoln were in Cape Town at a meeting with the leading time travel scientists. Arimus asked the boys to come outside with him.

"I wanted you to hear this from my lips only, my sons.
Time has another blackout rendered.
Travel to the 14th-century has been suspended."

Hansum could once again feel the sweat dripping from every pore of his body. He didn't know if it was the memory of the tropical sun beating down on him or the fear dredged up from the depths of his soul. He lashed out.

"Arimus, you're from the future. Did you know this blackout was coming? Why didn't you tell me? We could have gone back sooner."

"You forget that things are happening differently
from what those of my time know as history.
Of this blackout you ask? You shout, you implore!
Yes, it's starting the same time as before.
So I am here to tell you, prepare, my son.
if it continues to happen the same,
it's going to be a very long one."

"It's going to be a very long one." The words echoed in his memory. Arimus then told Hansum the best thing to do was to relax, to keep his mind clear, for the good of himself and his family. Hansum became even more incensed.

"For the good of my family? For the good of my family? How about all my family? How about Guilietta and the baby?" Even in his dreams he felt the salty tears in his throat.

Arimus paused, gazing at his young protégé with his practiced look of compassion.

"Yes, that indeed is a further reason
to make sure your mind and body don't cause you a treason.
For if it's this rest of the family, you seek as your prize,
you cannot help them otherwise."

Once again, Hansum swallowed down the bile.

As the days of the body-repairing sleep passed, the weeks and months of Hansum's life during the new blackout streaked by. A long winter and a green spring that did not feel refreshing. The blackout's first-year anniversary came and went. Life went on for humanity. There were countless other times in history that people from the 24th-century could explore. History Camps continued to do the good work of helping educate youth about how it was each and every human's responsibility to keep humanity within the healthy confines of its place on the planet. Yes, the rest of the world was happy.

As a second year came and went. Hansum watched Lincoln and Medeea get married. A year after that they had their first child, a boy, Azure. As an A.I. mind-delver, he matured more quickly than humans. The next year Medeea and Lincoln had twins, Lima and Lami. All the kids loved their Aunt Shamira and Uncle Hansum and wanted them to visit often.

But there would be no children for either Hansum or Shamira. Both gave up their childbearing allotments and refused any and all advances from suitors. Instead, Hansum continued training, putting together his team and coordinating with the 24th-century scientists and Parmatheon's new logistics committee. Everything was in place for the time when travel to the 14th-century started again. But yet another year came and went and still nothing happened. Hansum didn't even ask Arimus for more information, for he knew he wouldn't get it. All the while, Hansum kept his vow to remain prepared, and that included not letting things he had no control over eat him up, body or soul.

To keep up his skills and accreditations, Hansum went on many missions to the other times humanity still could travel to, all with his delver partner, Lincoln. They had been given exemplary citations for each operation and were now senior journeymen in the History Camp Time Travel Corps. When he wasn't away, Hansum lectured at the History Camp Time Travel University, speaking about those missions. But he soon found the majority of people inevitably wanted him to talk about Verona and his quest to save Guilietta.

As time passed, Hansum became a prominent elder at the time travel school, training recruits and becoming an excellent mentor to the hard cases, just as Arimus had been to him. Eventually, while the blackout to the 14th-century continued, travel back to the 31st-century reopened and Arimus was able to go home. Arimus, now older than anyone knew, retired. Hansum heard little from him but seemed to be following in his footstep, gaining many interesting friends, both powerful and common, all throughout time.

Elder Parmatheon Olama passed away, and soon his special allocations committee disbanded, but that didn't stop Hansum and Lincoln from continuing to make their own plans to rescue Guilietta and her family.

Hansum rose within the History Camp structure and to all around him he seemed content. But deep down he lived for one thing, to rescue his wife, their unborn child and her family. Many more missions came and went and Hansum became a member of the Time Travel Council. A few years later, he was its chairperson. Now he was even retired from that.

"Well, looked what the cat dragged in," were the first words Hansum heard as he was awakened. "As I live and breathe, Elder Shamira," the voice said, "I believe this is Elder Hansum lying before us. Don't he look shiny and new?"

"Jerk," Hansum heard his scratchy voice say. As his eyes began to focus, Lincoln came into view.

"That's Elder Jerk to you," Lincoln responded. "What do you say, girls? Does he look a day over 70 now?"

Hansum turned his head and there were Shamira and Medeea. Medeea had allowed herself to age somewhat, only looking somewhere in the mid-forties, younger than the others. Shamira's green eyes were the same, except for some small crow's feet around them. And as an artist and lover of color, she had her hair follicles rejuvenated to keep her hair its original shade of light auburn, except for a few streaks. But Lincoln proudly wore his hair grey, letting it flow over his ears and collar, with severe bangs cutting across his brow. Medeea teased that he looked like a monk.

Hansum took a deep breath and sat up, swinging his feet over the levitation bed's energy field. He felt a familiar tingling on his chest and looked down to see that Sideways, now his permanent A.I. cloak, had transported around him.

"Hello boss," Sideways said. "Nice to have you back."

"And may I say, objectively," came a voice from Lincoln's cloak, "you do indeed look much younger than your years. Younger than the seventy years Elder Lincoln suggests in his usual jesting fashion."

Being a Time Travel Elder, Lincoln now had his own A.I. cloak. It was Zat, the A.I. who had been the tissue cloning minder so long ago. He, like some humans, had been a slow starter. But as he matured, he grew into a skilled and sought-after time traveling partner. Lincoln was lucky to have him.

"Thanks Zat. Oh, even my voice sounds younger to me," Hansum said. "Let me look in the mirror." He indeed did look younger than seventy. Probably closer to sixty, as well as he could remember what that was like.

"Okay, I'll admit it. Ya don't look bad for a hundred and four." Lincoln chimed in. He was an even one hundred and Shamira one hundred and two.

Hansum put a hand to his temple. He was getting a message on his implant. "Inter-temporal," he said, meaning that this could only be from a very few callers. "Yes? Oh, hello Talos."

"Elder Hansum," Talos's voice said. *"It's about Arimus."*

"Is there a problem?"

"*He's dying,*" Talos explained simply. "*He has already disengaged his support and is asking for you. Can you come right away? He has less than two hours.*"

"I'll be right there," Hansum said.

Chapter 2

"The loved and . . ."

Arimus whispered so low Hansum couldn't make out the words. The dying man smiled and leaned back into his pillow, summoning Hansum closer. Hansum came forward, feeling the stubble around his friend's lips pressing on his ear. The old man tried again.

"The loved and the lost
the brave pursue,
Compelled without fear or cost."

Hansum waited for more, but it didn't come. He pulled back to gain his mentor's eye.

"The loved and the lost," Hansum repeated, "the brave pursue, compelled without fear or cost. Is there more?" Arimus smiled faintly, closing his eyes momentarily and moving his head sideways once, to say no. "Okay then. Well, there are a few others who want to see you." Arimus raised his eyebrows, smiling agreement. Hansum motioned for them to enter.

Old man Lincoln popped his head into the doorway, making a goofy face.

"There's the guy who made my life miserable!" he joked.

Arimus laughed, but ended up coughing.

"Age really hasn't matured him," a woman's voice said and, as Shamira and Medeea entered the roo.m, Arimus's eyes went wide with delight. They came over and both kissed him on opposite cheeks. Arimus looked up at them, eyes twinkling.

"I've secretly watched you paint over the years,"
he whispered to Shamira.
"And here's the most beautiful and intelligent delver of any era in time.
Thank you all for coming."

"We're all glad we can be here for you," Hansum said.

"I'm so glad to see friends from the most trying of my adventures tall."
Arimus whispered,
"For I have something to confess to you all."

Just then, all three of the A.I.s made faces of astonishment.
"IT'S STARTED AGAIN!" they cried in unison.
Hansum and Lincoln's hands flew to their temples. The urgent message flashed into their minds too.
"TRAVEL TO THE 14th-CENTURY! IT'S RESUMED!" they shouted.
The looks of shock, surprise and exuberance beamed on every face. But just as quickly, Hansum and Lincoln's faces turned to those of men who now had a job to do. No matter they were on standby for eighty-six years, their training kicked in. Hansum looked over at Arimus.
"My friend, finally. Finally we can go back and try again. But what did you want to tell us?"
Arimus looked excited, and then serious.

"I wanted to confess . . .
in the history of my time it was deeded . . .
Hansum, you never succeeded."

This was shocking news.
"We never succeed?" Hansum said, his eyes troubled. Arimus struggled to explain.

"No, you, you never even got to go back and try.
But now in the time line there's a mutation.
A deviation where frustration can change to elation.
Time has opened up a chance, through it my friends, go, go dance."

"Well, how do you like those bananas?" Lincoln said, half joking, half in awe. "He knew we didn't succeed and yet this guy persisted throughout his whole life."

"Well, what's life mean,
without an impossible dream?"

Hansum felt a touch on his arm. It was Arimus's hand, moved with obviously much effort. The old man's eyes were dancing with hope, as if to say he was happy to have lived long enough to see this possibility. But he was tired, and when he spoke again, it was more like he mouthed the words.

"...compelled without fear or cost."

He moved his head toward Sideways.

"Take them!
Now!"

The trio of humans and three A.I.s fell through the tunnel of time.

"Thank you for coming, Shamira," Hansum said silently through a mind-delve.

"How could I say no?" she replied. *"I've had eighty-six years to get over what happened. But what's the plan?"*

"Plan seventeen?" Hansum thought, looking over at Lincoln.

Lincoln nodded. *"I agree this is the place to start. If it's not the nexus point, it would give us the other opportunities right after."*

"Medeea, would you share the whole plan and its contingencies with Shamira?" Hansum thought.

"With pleasure."

Shamira closed her eyes as the plan dumped into her memory. She shuddered as it integrated. *"Wow. You've got it down to the second,"* she said, opening her eyes.

"It has to be," Hansum replied.

"And we've had the time to work on it," Lincoln chuckled.

"Fifteen seconds to the 14th-century, location one," Zat said.

A storm was brewing, causing the shutters of Master della Cappa's shop to rattle noisily in the increasing wind. The storm had been one of the reasons Pan didn't perceive Ugilino peering through a crack in the shutters. The other was that Pan's brass lamp had been cracked, causing perception problems.

The out-of-phase humans and A.I.s were standing in the alley by the shuttered window.

"Time check," the older Hansum said to Sideways.

"Right on target, elder," Sideways announced. "Ugilino will be coming to tell Hansum that Guilietta is awake and asking for him. We have just under three minutes before he peers through the crack in the shutter and sees Pan."

"Okay, let's get into position. Shamira, you're with me. Lincoln . . ."

"I'll be right here by the shutter with Zat," Lincoln confirmed.

Hansum put out a hand to Shamira and led her right through the heavy wooden shop wall. As they emerged inside, they saw their younger selves. This was the original event when the younger Shamira was leaning over a piece of paper, writing the list of herbs Pan was dictating. Lincoln was carefully soldering a reinforcement around Pan's shell and Hansum was trying to help him.

"Ugilino just turned into the alley. He's coming," came Lincoln's voice.

"Get ready, Sideways," Hansum warned.

"All set," the A.I. cloak answered, closing his eyes and crunching up his face.

"Ugilino is about to lean against the building to relieve himself," Lincoln advised.

Pan was finishing dictating. "So, those are the ingredients I hope you'll find at Signora Baroni's house. If she's short anything, bring any and all dried bread mold, spider webs . . ."

"Now," the older Hansum ordered.

"Ugilino's outside!" Sideways broadcast in A.I. language, stripping off the code showing where the communications came from.

Pan's gruff satyr face froze, his eyes going wide. "Ugilino's outside," he repeated, and disappeared.

The younger Hansum, Shamira and Lincoln looked up.

"Ugilino's outside," Pan now said sub-sonically in each teen's ear.

The younger Lincoln ran and threw open the shop door.

"Hey, whaddaya doin' out there?" he yelled. Meanwhile, the young Shamira was stuffing both the notes she wrote and Pan's lamp into her apron pocket. A sheepish Ugilino walked into the shop, still tying up his braise.

"Why are you sneaking around?" the younger Hansum asked angrily.

"I was taking a piss," Ugilino answered, and then asked incredulously. "Romero, how did you know I was . . ."

"Never mind. What do you want?"

"Guilietta's awake. She's asking for . . ."

The younger Hansum was up and out the door, calling to the others, "Take the carriage to Signora Baroni's and get those herbs. Now!"

Lincoln and Shamira got up to leave.

"Maruccio, how did you know I was out there?" Ugilino asked again.

"Lock up the shop, meat head," Lincoln said as he and Shamira walked quickly by him. "And keep out of trouble!"

The older Shamira and Hansum joined Elder Lincoln outside. They watched their younger selves hustle up the alley through what was the start of a rainy night. They no doubt all had memories of making their way to the palace through it. But now it had changed.

"That was easy," Shamira mused. "I was expecting excitement but, just like that, crisis averted."

"No, you don't understand, Sham," Hansum said. "It was easy to change because we knew what was going to happen. We've been studying it for years."

"Exactly," she smiled.

"You still don't get it," Lincoln added. "Everything . . . everything is changed. Now we don't have a clue what's going to happen next."

Shamira's eyes went big as it sank in.

"Like things the other times," she said. "When everything went . . . bad."

"So now our job is to keep ahead of everything," Hansum pronounced. In a flash they site transported to the front of the house. The younger Hansum was just running inside and slamming the door, while the other Lincoln and Shamira were getting in the hired carriage, Lincoln shouting directions to Signora Baroni's to the driver.

"Let's go in the house," Elder Lincoln said.

As they passed through the door, they saw Bembo sitting on the steps, his head down, waiting to help in any way he could. The older

Hansum frowned as he saw Father Lurenzano sitting with Agistino, still plying him with wine.

"Bastardo," he growled, and they all site transported into Guilietta's room. She had fallen back asleep and young Hansum was kneeling by the bed, holding both her hands in his, the Signora and Nuca looking down at them.

"Wake my dove," the Signora cooed to her sleeping daughter. "Your best medicine is here."

"Good. Good," the out-of-phase older Hansum said. "We've avoided the fight in the shop, Pan is alive and Lincoln's arm isn't broken."

"And you're here with her instead of being locked up at the palace," the older Shamira added.

"If only I knew she was carrying our child at the time," the older Hansum said, a reverent look in his eye. "I just wish there was a way for you to help her more, Medeea."

"Me too. But my nano bits just won't work on people from the past. It's like the early programmers had this in mind. The most I can do is scan a person, boost their immune system and maybe put them in stasis."

"Will you get in her now and do what you can?" Hansum asked.

"Sure," Medeea and Lincoln thought at the same time.

Lincoln reached in his pocket and took out Medeea's tiny tear bottle. Pulling off the glass stopper, he held it over Guilietta's head.

"Won't they see the portal?" Shamira asked.

"We don't have to worry about that anymore," Lincoln smiled. With the bottle just over Guilietta's sweat-drenched hair, he tapped the air with his index finger and a tiny blue circle appeared. "The circle can only be seen from our side now," and he poured a single drop of Medeea's elixir onto Guilietta's head.

"My nano bits will travel through her scalp and . . . ah, I'm there," Medeea said. *"Oh my. She is low. I'll do what I can,"* and she closed her eyes and grimaced. *"The baby's okay for now and I can boost Guil's immune system, but she has very low reserves and the infection is set to start growing exponentially."*

Hansum clenched his fist with frustration. "Okay, you three. Get over to Signora Baroni's. The carriage should be there soon. Make sure they get everything." A split second later, Hansum was standing alone, out of phase with Sideways, watching the scene in front of him. Guilietta was still shivering and her breathing was labored. The younger

Hansum was alternately kissing her hands and whispering encouragingly to her.

"Hang on, Guil. Hang on. We're going to get you well," he said while the Signora and Nuca looked on.

Suddenly Guilietta's eyes popped open, her eyes focusing on young Hansum. Even her shivering stopped.

"Husband?" she whispered.

"Si, si, I'm here," the younger Hansum said joyfully, his laughter mixed with tears. "Look, she's going to be all right."

Nuca put her hand to Guilietta's forehead, and then the side of her neck.

"Fever broke," she pronounced in her scratchy voice.

"See, your best medicine worked," the mother said, crossing herself.

"Husband," Guilietta repeated, a wan though loving look in her eyes.

"You're going to be okay, Guilietta. You're going to be okay," the teen husband said embracing her.

But the older Hansum scowled. He knew what they were seeing was what Medeea explained. Guilietta's revival was because the A.I. delver had boosted Guilietta's immune system. When her reserves were gone, she would fail again, and fast. It was imperative they get the herbal antibiotics quickly.

"Good, good," Nuca said in a cracking voice, the result of a fierce fever that had burned out her hearing long ago. "Gui getting better."

"Oh my little chicken." The Signora laughed and cried while embracing both her daughter and son-in-law.

"Must clean up Guil. Dry clothes. Dry bed," Nuca said. "Omero. You go. We clean."

"No, I want my husband to stay."

"We clean first. Then I get food. He come back then," and Nuca pulled the younger Hansum to his feet. "Go soon, come back sooner."

"No, stay," Guilietta pleaded, but Nuca had him half out the door already.

"I'll be downstair . . ." and he was gone.

The older Hansum chuckled as he remembered how practical the 14th-century Nuca was.

"Oh, you sent him away." Guilietta complained as Nuca began undressing her.

"Come, Signora. Help dry Gui. Fever broke, thank Cristo, fever broke," Nuca said, and the older Hansum stopped chuckling. It wasn't over yet. He left the room to give the women privacy and check downstairs.

The older Hansum found his younger self on the lower floor, standing next to Bembo. The Master and Father Lurenzano were staring at him from the table.

"Her fever just broke," young Hansum said, a relieved smile on his face. "She's awake."

"Thank Cristo," was all that came from Agistino's mouth before he started crying with relief.

Bembo hugged Hansum and smiled.

"Bembo, you look tired."

"I haven't slept in two days, Romero." He scowled and motioned to the two drunk men at the table. "Watching over these two."

Young Hansum frowned as he looked to see Father Lurenzano in his cups, patting an equally drunk Agistino on the back.

"My prayers worked!" Father Lurenzano announced, lifting his glass and kissing his fingers. "A toast to God," and that's when the younger Hansum's training as a noble kicked in. He became very angry with the priest.

Chapter 4

The older Lincoln and Shamira were already in front of Signora Baroni's house when the carriage carrying the younger Lincoln, Shamira and Pan pulled up. The younger Lincoln was jumping from the carriage before it stopped and he landed hard on the cobblestones.

"I couldn't do that now," the senior Lincoln grumbled.

His younger self was already pounding on the door as his Shamira caught up to him. When there was no answer, he began shouting.

"Signora Baroni, it's Maruccio from Master della Cappa's. We need you. Please open up." Still no answer.

"Signora, it's Carmella," Shamira called. "Guilietta needs medicine."

"Maybe she thinks we've got the plague," Lincoln said. "Signora Baroni, please. We haven't got the sickness. Please." He took hold of the handle on the door and started shaking it, but it was well barred. He tried the shuttered windows. The same thing.

There was nobody on the street except for a few corpses. Some homes were wide open, but most were closed tight.

"What should we do?" Shamira asked.

Lincoln ground his teeth. "Maybe she's out helping. It's not like her to abandon people. Let's wait ten minutes and then leave a note."

"And knock on the neighbors' doors, to see if they know where she is."

"You," Lincoln called to the driver. "I don't want you running off. When we finish, there's a *florin* in it for you."

The old Lincoln couldn't help but sniff a laugh at his younger self's brashness. Then he bit his lower lip, thinking what he should do next.

"Let's check inside the house," and he, Medeea and the older Shamira walked right through the walls. It was dark inside, but someone was breathing in a corner.

"It's Elder Catherine," Medeea said, not needing light to discern shapes in the dark.

"Let's do it," Lincoln said, and all three of them came into phase. Medeea glowed.

"What the . . ." Elder Catherine started. "Whatever and whoever you are, turn off your light. They'll see us." Medeea dimmed. "Who the heck are you three? I don't recognize . . ." and then her eyes locked on Shamira. She peered at her recognizable green eyes. "You? You're supposed to be outside . . . When are you from?"

"About eighty years from now."

"But that's not how it happens in . . ." Elder Catherine's eyes went wide.

"Signora Baroni . . . I mean, Elder Catherine," Shamira began. "We've come back and changed the situation. Our younger selves are trying to save Guilietta. You know her. You like her. Please. She's very sick. Not with the plague, but . . ."

"Of course I know it's not the plague. It's a uterine infection. I know all about it."

"Then why won't you help?" Medeea asked. Nobody was surprised that the 31st-century Catherine could see the A.I. delver.

"So you're the infamous Medeea," Catherine said. "I never thought I'd meet you in person. I won't help because I'm not supposed to. And you three aren't either. Oh, this is bad."

"What are you talking about?" Lincoln asked.

"And who are you?" she asked the old man.

A pounding on the front door started again, followed by the voice of the younger Lincoln.

"Signora Baroni, please, we can hear you in there. Please, answer the door. We promise we aren't sick."

"I'm him," the older Lincoln said, pointing a thumb.

Now the 31st-century Elder looked downright panicked. "I've got to get out of here," and she quickly got up, no longer worried about keeping hidden. She snapped her fingers and two oil lamps lit, and then she grabbed what looked like an old valise and started shoving things into it.

"Elder Catherine," the older Lincoln pleaded, "tell us what's going on," but she didn't answer. She just kept shoving things into a bag that shouldn't be able to hold all she kept putting in. Lincoln tapped his node. "Hansum, we've got a problem. Elder Catherine won't cooperate and she's acting like something's very wrong," at which Catherine snorted scathingly.

"Oh, good Gia, he's here too."

Old Hansum watched proudly as his younger self took charge of the situation in his family's home. Father Lurenzano was getting Master della Cappa drunk and the strongbox with all of the family money was sitting open on the table, like it had previously.

"Master, why is the strongbox out?" the younger Hansum asked.

Agistino looked at his son-in-law through bleary eyes, his body swaying on the bench. Father Lurenzano looked up, his avarice showing.

"Are you saying Master della Cappa's money is not safe in front of a man of God?" he asked defensively.

Hansum ignored the question and walked over to the table, closing the chest with a bang. He picked it up, took it to the hearth and put it back in its hiding place. As he replaced the stone and firewood box, Agistino made excuses to the priest.

"Much of the money is Romero's, Father," Agistino explained.

"Still, he shouldn't accuse a priest . . ."

"Master, why are you drinking wine?" the young Hansum interrupted. "With the sickness about and all that is happening, the family needs you strong."

"Father Lurenzano gave me permission. After he gave Guilietta last rites, he said taking some wine was a good thing."

"Last rites?" Hansum looked at the priest with undisguised anger. "She's getting better."

Agistino smiled drunkenly and crossed himself.

"And praise to God for that," the priest answered, "but often people rally for a short time and relapse. In times like this, a bit of wine dulls the pain and lifts the spirit. It will also help ward off the sickness that is going around. I know these things," he said smiling and taking another few gulps. He motioned for Agistino to do the same. Agistino lifted his cup.

"Master, no!" Hansum ordered. "You mustn't. Father Lurenzano, I want you to stop giving wine to Master della Cappa."

"It will protect him from the pestilence!"

"No it won't. The sickness is caused by the flea bites of ship rats from the east, and from living in dirty cities and malnutrition."

"Rats and fleas? A bit of dirt? The illness is caused by bad humors in the air and punishments from God. And Jews are poisoning wells!"

The out-of-phase old Hansum was amazed how much of the conversation was similar to before, even though the circumstances had changed.

"Oh for Cristo's sake," Hansum scoffed.

"Don't take the Lord's name in vain!" Father Lurenzano demanded, shooting to his feet. "I am your Master's spiritual guide. And if you are his family, I am yours as well! You must heed me."

The younger Hansum had spent enough time around Podesta della Scalla to know how to push back. He stepped into Father Lurenzano's space and brought his face very close to the priest's.

"One thing you are not is my spiritual guide. And when the Master is not himself, I am the head of this house."

Lurenzano pounded his fist on the table and was about to yell back when the door opened. Ugilino walked in, followed by a tall military officer in full battle uniform.

"Romero, this general is looking for you," Ugilino announced.

"Lieutenant Raguso," Hansum said with surprise. "What's wrong?"

The officer stepped forward and bowed to young Hansum. The older Hansum couldn't help but remember the different ways he had known this man, as a feisty officer who had disagreed with the younger savant, only to then turn into an admirer, and as the older brother who looked out for his younger, bastard sibling. This was also the man who had his throat slit by Feltrino's men. Now here he was again, alive.

"Master Monticelli. Praise God I find you well."

"***Master*** Monticelli?" the priest said.

"I am well, thank you, Lieutenant. Why are you here?"

"I was ordered to bring my men to bolster the northern gate. The guard there told me of the sickness in your house. My admiration for you caused me to come and see if I could render assistance."

"*Grazzi, grazzi*," Hansum said. "This is Master della Cappa, my old Master. His daughter was ill, but not with the sickness. I'm pleased to say she is recovering."

"Master della Cappa," Raguso said, bowing. He then patted the leather case at his side, which contained his looker. "I use this most often."

This respect seemed to affect Agistino's demeanor. He sat straighter, nodding his head to the officer and then pushing his cup of wine away.

"And this is Father Lurenzano," Hansum said to Raguso. "He was just leaving."

"I protest. You cannot tell me what . . ."

Lieutenant Raguso took a step forward, placing his hand gently on the hilt of his sword and looking at Lurenzano with cool eyes.

"Della Cappa, are you going to stand for this?" the priest asked Agistino sternly. "This boy telling me what to do?"

"Father, I fear I have fallen back into bad habits," Agistino answered. "While I recover, for my family's sake, I must listen to my son-in-law."

This did not mollify Father Lurenzano. He straightened his robes and stood erect, his nose in the air.

"You'll see that no good comes to those who mock the church and its priests," and he strode to the door. As he passed Ugilino, Lurenzano motioned with his eyes a gesture that meant, 'I will be outside hiding. Come and find me.' When he got to the door, he looked back and gave Hansum a harsh look. But as he did, his eyes couldn't help but travel to the wood box by the fireplace and what lay hidden behind it. He closed the door hard behind him.

"Good," the older Hansum said to Sideways. "My younger self got rid of that wild card. I think things are safer now."

"I agree," Sideways said. "And when both Shamiras and Lincolns return with the herbs, that should take Guilietta out of danger."

Suddenly, a voice spoke in the senior Hansum's mind. *"Hansum, we've got a problem. Elder Catherine won't cooperate and she's acting like something's wrong."*

"I'll be right there," the older Hansum said. "Sideways, I think everything is stable here. Take me to Lincoln," and they were gone.

The younger Hansum turned to his father-in-law.

"Master, my apologies for ordering the Father away, but I do not think he had your best interests at heart, especially after you showed him our treasure."

"I was weak, my son. With the sickness out there and the Father giving Guilietta last rites, he said he needed means to have the church save Guilietta's soul and protect our house from illness."

"I don't think anything can assure that, Master. Tomorrow, when Guilietta is stable, we'll move the whole family to Master Calabreezi's estate. My new estate. We will quarantine it for a month, to be safe."

Just then Nuca came down the stairs. "How is my daughter?" Agistino asked, rushing to her.

"S'eeping. K'eaned up and s'eeping," the deaf woman squeaked. "Signora too. Me go make food."

Agistino grabbed Nuca's gnarled old hands and kissed them.

"Grazzi, Signora, grazzi."

"Gui like daughter. We all fam'ly."

Agistino was extremely emotional as he walked his neighbor to the door. As she left, he turned to Hansum. "Will Signora Baroni return with Carmella and Maruccio? Do you think her medicine will help further? Should we not get a physician?"

"If Signora Baroni is not available, I can go to the palace and bring a physician in the morning, Master."

"Oh no, signor," Lieutenant Raguso said. "I stopped there briefly on my way from the gate. All the physicians are preparing to flee the city. If you want, I will take you there now and," he patted his sword hilt again, "make sure one comes back with us."

Ugilino, who had been quietly watching the entire goings on, finally spoke. "I gotta piss," he said, and left.

The younger Hansum turned to his father-in-law.

"Master, I think your thoughts and the lieutenant's are good. Let us hope Maruccio and Carmella return with Signora Baroni and the herbs. But let us also fetch a physician for good measure. But to do that I must leave you here to guard our fragile women. Are you . . . sober enough?"

At first Agistino's eyes looked somewhat hurt, and then he blinked. "You are right to ask. Yes. Verjuice will once again be my only drink till I die. I vow this to you and God," and he crossed himself.

"Lieutenant, we must away," Hansum said, and they turned to the door. "Master, with the sickness out there, bar the door and let in only those you trust," Hansum said. "Only those you trust."

"Good Gia, now you?" Elder Catherine said as the older Hansum popped into her room. She shook her head and continued stuffing things into the bottomless valise.

"Elder Catherine, Guilietta needs your help," Hansum begged. "We've finally been able to get back here, but our modern medicines are programmed not to work on people from the past. We need your herbs."

"Where is that last . . ." Catherine questioned as she looked around frantically. "Ah, there," and she rushed over to her bed and reached under the mattress, pulling out a cracked, leather pouch. She removed a clear cube of crystal the size of a gambling die. It glowed bright yellow as she tossed it in the valise. "Done," she said.

"Will you help us?" Hansum asked, sounding desperate.

She looked at him, exasperation showing in her face. "You're from the 25th-century now, aren't you?" And then she laughed cynically. "You still know so little about time travel. A major deviation has happened! A mutation!" she said, like he was too stupid to see the obvious. Then her contempt turned to panic. "In my time we never thought you'd get this far in a trillion tries. We thought Arimus was crazy for taking on such an impossible project. A waste of time. But here you are. And if you're here . . . then a major deviation did happen. You must be close to a nexus point." Elder Catherine paused, staring wide-eyed at Hansum's old face. "And if you're close to a nexus point, the last place I want to be is anywhere around you. I've got family and grandchildren. I could get stuck here forever. I'm out of here." And with that she went to push an unseen node at the base of her neck.

"Wait," Lincoln shouted. "Our 25th-century medicines don't work on people from the past. How about your 31st-century medicines?"

She wrinkled her face one last time. "We don't need medicines," she derided, and pointed at the wall of shelves, full of herbs and various jars. "Help yourselves," and she was gone.

The older Hansum, Lincoln and Shamira looked at each other, desperation showing on their faces.

"What do we do now?" Lincoln said.

"Are you two still outside?" Hansum asked him.

Lincoln went and poked his head through the wall.

"Yeah, but we're just getting back into the carriage."

Hansum thought for a moment. "You guys disappear. Sideways, make me look like an older family member of Signora Baroni's," and in a blink Hansum appeared to be wearing homespun pants, a robe and sleeping cap." The others went out of phase and Hansum unbarred the door. "Wait!" he called as the carriage started to move. The younger Lincoln and Shamira poked their heads from the carriage window. "You are looking for Signora Baroni? She is away from Verona for some days now."

"We need her medicines," young Shamira called.

"It's an emergency," Lincoln added.

"If you know what you need, please come." Elder Hansum knew Pan would tell them what to take. They jumped from the carriage and ran to the house, Hansum limping ahead and then hiding in the back room. "Do not look upon me. I am sick and the humors may come out from my eyes and into you." He didn't want Pan scanning him. "Take what you want. They'll do me no good now."

"It's all here," Hansum heard Pan saying. "Everything we need." Within a minute they were gone from the house and speeding back toward the della Cappa home.

"Let's go back with them in the carriage," Hansum said, "in case something goes wrong on the way home," and they site transported away.

"Psst!" Ugilino peered into the night, looking to see where the sound came from. "Psst!" He turned and saw a black-silhouetted arm beckoning from down the road. Ugilino hopped off the stoop and trotted down the street, kicking a dog that snarled at him as it chewed on Signora Spagnolli's leg. She had been one of the first to succumb. A head popped out from the alley by the butcher's shop. It was Father Lurenzano.

"Quickly, before you're seen," Lurenzano hissed as he pulled Ugilino into the shadows.

"Romero's a big man now, eh Father? Even generals bow to him," Ugi said.

"He's too bold for an orphan. Telling me, a priest, what to do. And just when della Cappa was going to give such generous alms to the church. We must find a way to rescue the situation. Perhaps tomorrow ..."

"Romero's going to move the whole family to his big estate in the country tomorrow, Father. I heard he has over five hundred peasants and craftsman working for him."

"Five hundred? Then he really is rich. But tomorrow . . . that means della Cappa and his strong box will be gone."

"I wonder if I'll be able to be boss over some of those stupid peasants? Finally."

"What? You think he'll take you with him?"

"We're family," Ugilino said.

"Ha," Lurenzano replied. "They'll put you off with promises and delaying words, 'we'll sees' and then abandon you. No, Ugilino. The church and I are your only friends. You and I, we must not stand these insults."

Just then they heard the sound of a horse nickering and the clomping of hooves coming their way. They looked out the alley, being careful to stay in the shadow. A moment later, Lieutenant Raguso trotted by on his large horse with young Hansum sitting behind him.

"Romero's going to the palace to make a physician come back with him," Ugilino explained, "and Carmella and Maruccio took a hired carriage to get Signora Baroni. A carriage."

"The poor die and the rich always live. They have the means. Who's left in the house?"

"Nuca went home to make food. Only the Master's there. The Signora and Guilietta are sleepin' upstairs." Ugilino watched the priest thinking for some time, and then watched him reach into his robe's deep pockets, searching for something. He brought out a piece of paper, folded down into a small packet.

"What's that, Father?"

"A sleeping powder I brought for your Master. I give it to all my parishioners in time of sorrow, when they need a good night's sleep. I want you to go back and put it into your Master's drink."

"So he'll sleep? That's kind of you. When I tell him you sent it, maybe he'll like you again and . . ."

"No, you mustn't tell him. Just mix it in with his drink."

"His *vino*?"

"Whatever he's drinking!" Lurenzano spat with frustration. "Fool!"

"Who's there?"

"It's me, Master. Let me in."

"Is anyone with you?"

"No, Master. It's just me."

Ugilino heard the door's heavy wooden bar being lifted. The door opened a crack and Agistino's face stared at him.

"You're sure you're alone?"

"Si, Master."

Agistino opened the door just enough for Ugilino to squeeze past. No sooner was he in when Agistino re-barred the door.

"You're pissing a lot lately," Agistino said.

"What, Master?"

"I said you're pissing a lot lately. You said you were going out to piss. What, you've got piss for brains now?"

"Oh, yeah, yeah. It was all that good wine, Master. Grazzi."

"Poison. Poison is what it is to me." Agistino crossed himself. Then he looked at Ugilino and pointed a finger at him. "Beware the grape, Ugi. We are lucky to have Romero of our house, you and I," and then he went back to the table and sat on the bench. He picked up his goblet and took a sip, sitting and mulling over something.

"Master, I thought you vowed ..."

"Verjuice," and he picked up the bottle, offering him some. Ugi sat down and held out a cup, smiling. As the Master poured, Ugilino asked him a question.

"Master, do you think I can be a boss to some of the peasants?"

"What are you talking about?"

"On Romero's new estate. I heard Romero has over five hundred. Some of them have got to be really stupid. Do you think I ..."

"People are falling dead all over Christendom and you're worried about being boss over people stupider than yourself ..."

"Nuca, my chamberpot, per favore," came the Signora's voice from upstairs.

"But, Master, do you think that Romero will take me ..."

"Nuca ..." the Signora's voice pleaded again.

"I must help my wife," Agistino said standing. "I'm coming to help you, my dear," he called.

"Oh, Agistino, grazzi," came the Signora's happy voice.

"Master, will Romero take me to the ..."

Agistino stopped abruptly. "Romero is master of the estate. He'll take you if he takes you. I have no say. We'll see," and he turned away.

"But ..."

"We'll see!" and he disappeared up the stairs.

Ugilino stared at the empty stairs for some moments. His Master had said the exact words Father Lurenzano predicted, 'We'll see.'

'The Father was right. They'll abandon me,' he thought.

Ugilino took out the packet of powder Father Lurenzano had given him.

"She's asleep again. Both of them are," Agistino said as he sat down on the bench. Ugilino looked up at him with sullen and angry eyes. "What?" Agistino asked. Ugilino just stared. "What, you don't want to speak, don't speak. My ears thank you," and he picked up his mug of verjuice and took a large swig. He put it down and made a face. "It's bitter, like life. But it keeps you seeing the world as it is, not like wine. What, you don't like yours?" Agistino said, looking over into Ugilino's still-full mug. "Too bad," and he downed the rest of his drink." Ugi just stared at him.

"He's asleep, Father," Ugilino said with a voice that showed both fear and excitement.
"Where?"
"At the table."
"Alone?"
"Si. But Maruccio and Carmela should be back . . ."
"We must hurry."

The priest stood over the hulking form lying across the table. Agistino was snoring heavily, his head on his arm, his labored breath causing the flame of the oil lamp close to him to flutter. It was the brass lamp with the angel holding the lightning bolts, given to the Master by Hansum. Lurenzano moved the lamp and then pushed on Agistino's shoulder. The snoring continued. A sardonic smile crossed the clergyman's face and he looked over at Ugilino. Ugilino looked confused and Lurenzano's smile turned serious again.
"Watch the door," he ordered and went right to the fireplace, shoving the wood box away. Struggling, he pried the stone out and removed the strong box. "Ugilino. Come. Carry this."
As Ugilino picked up the gold and silver filled box he asked, "Are you sure it's okay . . ."

"Shut up," Lurenzano said, moving to the door. "It's for the church and they'll be gone without a care for you or I tomorrow." He carefully opened the door and looked up and down the street. "Now go. Straight to the church." Ugilino scuttled to the door, pausing only to look back at his unconscious master. "Move! Run!" the priest shouted and Ugilino was away. Lurenzano looked back. Agistino's care-worn face looked more so in the harsh lamplight. Father Lurenzano grimaced, walked over to the table and, without hesitation, knocked the lamp onto the straw floor. He watched as oil spilled and the dry straw caught fire. Nodding, he hurried back to the door, stepped into the night and, without another glance, closed the door behind him.

"And then I have Lincoln use the pestle and mortar to grind down the washed and dried bread mold to a fine powder, and then mix it with the rest of the recipe," young Shamira said. "We use the results to create a suspension with fifty parts boiled and cooled water. Guilietta and the Signora then receive a measure of it four times a day."

The young Lincoln and Shamira were sitting together on one of bench seats inside the carriage. Pan was standing between them, listening to the young Shamira recite the recipe for the antibiotic. The seat opposite was crowded with the older, invisible Hansum, Shamira and Lincoln, with Medeea on her husband's lap. The holographic image of Pan nodded and stroked his whiskers.

"Good. Very good," the satyr praised.

The young Lincoln blew out a big breath and leaned back in his seat. "Man oh man, I feel like I can finally relax a bit. We've got the stuff to save Guil."

"Thank Cristo," young Shamira said, and she crossed herself. The younger Lincoln looked at her wide eyed

"Maybe I'll do some Hail Marys," he added, and when Shamira realized what she did, they both laughed.

"I kind of agree with the little jerk," the older Lincoln added. "If this works, I'll thank Cristo too."

"Well, Elder Catherine did say we were near a nexus point," the Elder Hansum said, sounding hopeful, and he made a show of crossing himself.

"Hey, you almost poked me in the eye," Sideways complained jovially.

Now everyone on both sides of the carriage was laughing.

"I have a question," the older Shamira asked. "What happens if and when we can take someone out of phase? That person will freak out."

"At that point we won't care," Hansum replied, still smiling. "Then we take everyone out of phase and get them to the wall for the end game." They were finally feeling some hope.

The wagon, which had been going at a good clip, suddenly braked hard to a stop.

"Signor, quickly!" the driver shouted.

The younger Lincoln and older Hansum stuck their heads out of the window.

"What's wrong . . ." the younger Lincoln began, and then stopped. It was obvious to all in the carriage. His face was reflecting the hard flickering light of what could only be a large fire. Without another word he was out of the wagon and running.

"SIDEWAYS! NOW!" the older Hansum screamed.

Sideways and Zat transported everyone in front of the raging inferno of the della Cappa home. The heat was so intense that their younger selves couldn't get within fifty paces of the blaze. Lincoln ran up to Bembo, who was standing by Nuca and Bruno's home. Nuca was sobbing in her husband's arms.

"Bembo, is the Master and Romero . . . everyone?" The flames dancing off Bembo's expressionless eyes told it all. Lincoln went to bolt forward, but Bembo's strong hands grabbed him.

"Morto. Tutti morti," was all he said. They were all dead.

Shrieks came out of the younger Lincoln and Shamira's mouths, shrieks that rose above the roar and crack of the fire.

"GET IN THERE!" the older Hansum shouted at Sideways. He felt the older Lincoln's hand on his arm.

"YOU CHECK DOWNSTAIRS, BROTHER. I'LL CHECK UP," Lincoln told him.

Hansum frowned at the implication, nodded, and both winked away.

The blinding light in the heart of the fire turned objects into unreal, over-exposed lumps with silvery-white flames dancing off their undulating surfaces. While the fire could not hurt someone out of phase, it made it hard to see. Hansum had to get very close to the blackened lump lying across the table, a dark *thing* from which flames and charred flakes shot, rocketing upwards in the rising currents. It was apparent what the lump had been and no longer was. Hansum turned just in time to see the stairs disintegrate and fall, causing more circular currents to rise heavenward. He began to order Sideways to go upstairs when Lincoln appeared before him.

"No!" was all Lincoln said, catching his friend looking to the floor above. "Sideways. Outside," and they were gone.

As the senior Hansum and Lincoln appeared back in the street, the older Shamira was on her knees, watching her younger self screaming with terror and grief. The others were frozen in mute horror.

Hansum twisted his neck back to the house. By now his life had been conditioned by a career that included hundreds of sorties into the past. He was witness to countless deaths and had hundreds of close friends through the ages, all of whom were dead in his time. But this was different. He never got used to Guilietta dying, again and again.

His mind began to race. There was something else he had to consider. What had Lincoln and Zat seen upstairs? The prone figure lying on the bed, his Guilietta. Was the Signora with her? And . . . was the younger Hansum there? Was he, Hansum, dead in this reality? Could this be the type of irretrievably time-changing anomaly that caused Elder Catherine to flee?

He no sooner considered this when the shouts of men and the clomping of horses forced him to look up the road for his answer. Lieutenant Raguso was galloping on his horse in front of an open carriage with several men in it, his younger self included. His alternate self was already standing, screaming at the wagon driver and universe in general. When the wagon screeched to a halt, the younger Hansum was already in the air, leaping from the carriage and running toward the flames. Others went to drag him back, but the white-hot fire did its work and Hansum ended up shrieking and pulling his hair, running back and forth, left and right, in a useless effort that achieved nothing.

Then, Ugilino ran onto the scene. His fists were clenched and his mouth agape. He stood next to the weeping teens and neighbors, falling to his knees and dropping what was in his hands. A pathetic cache of silver coins spilled onto the cobblestones, some rolling in circles until, like the helpless onlookers, they exhausted their stored energy.

The old Hansum clenched his jaw, resolve and anger sharing their place on his wrinkled face.

*"Sideways. Zat. Take us back to **this** beginning,"* and the Sands of Time rose.

Chapter 4

The plan, if anything went wrong, was try to fix the situation and get back to the predetermined meeting place, up on the walkway of Verona's city wall.

Once again, like decades earlier, the fix had been frustratingly simple. They went back to when Ugilino was going to peer through the crack in the shutters and stood before the slightly earlier version of old Lincoln, just as he was to give the word about Ugilino to Sideways.

"It's not going to work. Abort," old Lincoln said to his counterpart.

The other old Lincoln looked at him incredulously, but said nothing. He knew the plan too.

"Everything is as it was," an exhausted Hansum whispered. He was leaning between two parapets, perhaps the same ones he and Guilietta had their first kiss between. "Time for Plan B." But, while he could make his mouth say the words, standing up straight was out of the realm of possibility right now.

It was dark on the wall and a low-lying fog almost obscured the moon. No amount of training could make the time travelers accept what they had just experienced with anything approximating philosophical detachment. Neither age nor experience offered an antidote for the kind of thing they had witnessed. But they knew one thing. The only chance they had for success was to push forward – now.

"Okay, let's go over what's next," the Elder Hansum finally said, forcing himself to stand straight. "Stopping the Master and Father Lurenzano from seeing Pan didn't work, so now we play on their belief in angels and demons, to legitimize Pan's presence. We'll intercede when our younger selves are being confronted in the shop." Hansum looked over to Shamira. She was standing stolidly, her eyes still glistening with emotion from the last situation. "Are you going to be okay? Do you need some time to collect yourself?"

She blinked hard and her face was almost normal again. "No. No, I'll be fine."

"It's important to feel the emotions, but that's later. Now it's time to work," Lincoln said.

"*Can you see Plan B, Sham?*" Medeea asked.

Shamira brought the exact details of the next part of the plan to her mind.

"Got it," Shamira said. "I'm ready."

"Costumes," Hansum called and, simultaneously, Sideways and Zat formed new clothing for the three humans, Zat hiving off a piece of himself and jumping to Shamira. The older Hansum was now wearing the vestments of a cardinal. With an under robe of cream-colored silk, the upper robe was the signature red for a prince of the church, full and flowing down to the ground, with the faces of angels embroidered onto the rich fabric. The faces had kind eyes and their mouths were opened, as if singing. The faces hid the fact that Sideways was looking out through those eyes, watching everything. To top it off, there was a matching red cap on Hansum's greying head. Lincoln and Shamira were wearing the dark robes of monks, the hoods hiding their faces. "Let's go!" and the Sands of Times rose.

Their timing had to be exact.

Once again, Agistino della Cappa and Father Lurenzano were annoyed at Ugilino when he dragged them out into the night, saying he saw the devil in the shop. But their drunken anger turned to shock when they spied through a crack in the shutter and saw a satyr standing on the worktable, the teens heads bent before him. Shamira was taking dictation and Lincoln and Hansum were reinforcing Pan's cracked shell. But to the superstitious 14th-century citizens, it appeared they were bowing to a satanic creature. The priest and the lens maker pulled away from wall.

"They revere him," Father Lurenzano said. "They pray to him." His eyes went wide with conviction as he pronounced, "They are servants of Lucifer!"

"Such evil in my own house!" Agistino gasped.

They were able to throw the shop door open and confront the situation before Pan could disappear, so the hologram had to make a decision on how to deal with the matter. He elected to transform his image into the handsome martyr, Saint Aurelius, patron saint of orphans, saying he was helping save Guilietta because the della Cappas had been so kind to the orphans in their care. But neither Father Lurenzano nor Ugilino were buying it. Not even though Ugilino had met Pan in what he thought was a dream.

"Didn't meeting me before make you a better person?" Pan as Saint Aurelius asked Ugilino?

"I'd rather be a murdering, filth-covered soldier in God's army, than a noble in the Devil's," Ugilino shouted as he hefted an ax and started for Pan. But before it could whoosh though Pan's image and break one of the new lathes, as previously happened, there was a man's voice at the door.

"What is this?" the voice asked. Everyone turned. They saw an older man in crimson clerical gowns. Behind him stood two monks in dark robes, their hoods hiding their faces. Immediately Father Lurenzano fell to one knee and bowed his head.

"Your Eminence," he crooned.

"What is going on?" Hansum as a cardinal asked. "I was told by a neighbor there was a priest here. One who could show me to the basilica. In the confusion of the pestilence, I've lost my way to an important meeting with the bishop."

"I am at your service, Eminence," Lurenzano fawned.

The whole room looked between the faux cardinal and the shimmering image of Aurelius, hovering by the ceiling.

"Ah, my friend, Saint Aurelius," the costumed Elder Hansum said, stepping forward and going to one knee. "Holy angel, it is good to see you again."

Shocked silence. The Signora, who had trundled in after her husband, was near fainting and standing only with the help of Agistino. Ugilino still held the ax over his head, Father Lurenzano looked puzzled, but the most confused had to be Pan and the teens. What could be happening? The image of Aurelius, Pan, wrinkled his nose, trying to figure it out. The cardinal was smiling at him, nodding slowly, like he was telling him to play along. This was the critical moment. The cardinal momentarily looked to his vestments. Pan as the saint, followed the gaze to the gold brocaded angels woven on the fabric and — one of the angels winked at him, oh so slightly. The Saint of Orphans smiled.

Ugilino saw the wink too, and blinked in surprise, but when he looked again, he saw just stitching.

"Cardinal Frey of Carinthia!" Saint Aurelius chimed, as if greeting an old friend. He alighted to the ground, walking silently past Ugilino, who was still tensed with the ax. Pan smiled at him and turned back to the kneeling cardinal, beckoning him rise.

"You know this man?" the younger Hansum asked the image of Aurelius.

"I know the cardinal's . . . *handsome* features well," Pan as Aurelius said, "although I don't know why he's here."

"Put down the ax, my son," Cardinal Frey said to Ugilino. "There's no wood here to chop." Ugi looked him hard in the eye.

"Don't be insolent to His Eminence! Do as you're told!" Lurenzano snapped, pushing Ugilino hard on the shoulder. Ugilino fell forward and bumped into one of the monks, coming nose to nose with the clergyman and getting a glimpse into the shadow of the cowl. The face was familiar. The monk pushed him back and repositioned the cowl over her eye.

"This monk looks like Carmella . . ."

"I told you to shut up!" Lurenzano said, now shouting. He cuffed Ugilino on the ear.

"But . . ." a harder cuff on the ear caused Ugi to shrink back in pain. He let the ax head fall to the ground, keeping hold of the handle.

"Eminence, you know this being?" Father Lurenzano asked, and the older Hansum began his rehearsed speech.

"Of course, Father . . .?"

"Lurenzano, of San Francesco al Corso"

"Just so. Father Lurenzano. I must now swear you to secrecy, for only cardinals and the Holy Father himself know of communing with Heaven's saints. For others to know of their true existence would cause a crisis of faith, and without faith, want evaporates. With certain knowledge of Heaven, people would end their miserable lives without hesitation, and then who would do God's work on Earth?"

Father Lurenzano stood there, transfixed, his eyes moving back and forth as he parsed the convoluted reasoning.

"But why then was the holy saint communing with these . . . orphans."

"On occasion, a holy spirit chooses to intercede with common folk. But why? The ways of the Lord are mysterious and not for us to question. And is it not your duty to . . . obey me?"

Pan sent the younger Hansum, Lincoln and Shamira a sub-sonic message.

"These people are from the future. Play up to the Master and Signora. Comfort them." The three teens went over to the kneeling Agistino and his wife.

"I'm sorry we couldn't tell you of the saint's help, Master," Hansum said.

"Mistress, please don't be frightened," Shamira said to the Signora.

"Yeah. Everything's going to be just zippy," Lincoln added, and he even smiled at Ugilino and Father Lurenzano. "Just zippy."

Lurenzano puffed out his chest, now one with special information about Heaven. "What must I do, Eminence?" the priest asked the cardinal.

Hansum as Cardinal Frey smiled. The plan was working. "Why, whatever the angel tells you, good priest," and he looked to Pan as the saint.

"Help the orphans," Pan pronounced. "They need herbs from Signora Baroni's. Go with them. Protect them. And rush to the palace and get a physician." Pan put one of his hands to his temple, like he was being psychic. "The last one is making ready to flee the city."

"I am most happy to serve," Father Lurenzano said, bowing obsequiously.

Ugilino was squinting at the Cardinal's gown again, staring at the brocaded eye he had seen wink. The eye was now just embroidered thread, but he felt the smile below was broadening a bit. Then he was sure of it.

"Father," Ugilino whispered urgently in his priest's ear. "The cardinal's clothes. It's smiling. It's a demon."

"Quiet, fool. Don't speak in front . . ."

"I'm telling you, Father," Ugi insisted, shaking the clergyman's sleeve. "It looked at me before and now it's smiling. It's alive?"

"Shut up and don't say another . . ."

But Ugilino would not be deterred this time. "Father, I think they're all demons. That monk looks like Carmella."

"Do you not hear me?" Lurenzano shouted, pulling his arm away. "What did I tell you? Now begone! Get out of here!" and Father Lurenzano shoved Ugilino hard toward the door. Shamira as the monk moved to get out of his way but, as Ugilino stumbled, he reached up and grabbed the gown's hood, pulling it off her face. Though older, her long red hair made it obvious that something was amiss.

Everyone, including the three teens, gasped.

"It's Carmella," the Signora cried.

"How?" asked the younger Shamira.

"Cardinal, what is the meaning of . . ." Father Lurenzano began, but Ugilino didn't wait for an answer. All his months of frustration at the orphans, his whole lifetime of frustrations, burst from his chest.

"LIARS!" he screamed, hefting the ax up with two hands.

"Think nothing of this," the older Hansum as cardinal was beginning to say, when Ugilino tensed his arms and screamed at the top of his lungs.

"DEVILS!" and he charged Shamira in the monk's robes. The ax came down right at her head and Zat momentarily took her out of phase. She disappeared and came back into view a few feet away. The ax embedded itself into the gravel shop floor.

"Satan's spawn!" Lurenzano cried.

"Cristo save us!" Agistino rejoined, "You're all the Devil's minions!" and he pushed the teens who were trying to comfort him away. Shamira took hold of the Signora's arm.

"Signora, we're not evil," Shamira pleaded, but what was happening was all too much for the medieval woman. She shrieked in Shamira's face, holding up her hands as if shielding herself from a blow.

"Master, please," the younger Hansum begged. "It's not how it looks. We're just trying to save Guilietta." But the big man twisted away from Hansum and grabbed his wife in a protective embrace.

Hansum as a cardinal turned to Father Lurenzano, "I can expl . . ." but the priest ran at him, his filthy hands and cracked nails curled into claws. He bounced off a force field that Sideways erected. Sparks flew and Lurenzano was thrown halfway across the room.

"Not my priest, you devil," Ugilino screamed, and he attacked the mock cardinal with the ax, but it too bounced off the force field.

"KILL THEM! KILL THEM ALL!" Lurenzano shouted from the floor.

Ugilino lifted his ax again and swung at the older Lincoln but, before the ax fell, Ugilino's eyes went wide when he saw Zat's cloak grow extra hands, coming to grab the ax handle.

"Ahieee," Ugilino screamed and ran to the other side of the shop.

"It's not as it seems," Pan as Aurelius cried, the bug-eyed Ugilino running right through him, swinging the ax. The sharp blade whooshed through the hologram and crashed down onto a lathe, smashing the spindle assembly.

"My lathes, my living!" Agistino cried, and Ugilino fell on the lathe, breaking it further.

"Pan, what should we do?" the younger Hansum shouted.

"The ax, get the ax!"

"Brother, stop," the younger Lincoln cried, running to Ugilino, "Let us explain . . ." but as Ugilino saw the boy he had lived with coming at him, he turned from his position on his knees and swung the ax backwards with all of his might, the butt of the blade catching Lincoln full force in the face. It exploded into a ball of red and Ugilino shot to his feet, the now-bloodied ax back in both hands.

"Lincoln!" both Hansums and Shamiras screamed. The older Lincoln threw off his cowl and stared in shock at his now prone younger self. He was lying on the floor without a face, his body twitching.

"Lincoln!" Medeea screamed, projecting herself toward the body. "The nano bits!" she shouted to the older Lincoln, who immediately ran to his body, fumbling in his pocket for the vessel of tears.

"Agistono!" the Signora cried, her pathetic face white with fear. "Save me!" and her husband dragged her bodily out the door as the melee continued.

"I'LL KILL YOU, UGILINO!" the younger Hansum screamed. Lunging, he ducked under the next ax blow and plowed his shoulder into Ugilino's gut, throwing him backwards and causing the ax to fly from his hand. As Ugilino crashed into the wall, the ax spun through the air and landed on the work table holding Pan's half-reinforced lamp. The table tipped and its contents crashed to the ground.

Pan's image broke into a million tiny cubes as his lamp bounced across the gravel, the image of Saint Aurelius turning back to a satyr.

"My lamp!" Pan shouted.

"It's his talisman!" Father Lurenzano shouted. "The beast lives in the talisman."

"I am undone, my children," Pan's disintegrating image cried.

The world began to move in slow motion for the older Shamira. She looked all around at the scene in front of her; at the old Lincoln pouring a few drops of nano bits onto the unrecognizable younger Lincoln.

"Medeea, can you help him?" the older Lincoln asked.

"We've got to save Guilietta!" the older Hansum shouted at the younger Hansum, who was still sitting on Ugi and beating him.

Shamira looked to Father Lurenzano, who was picking up the ax, his eyes fixed on Pan's lamp in the gravel. Then she looked at the younger version of herself. Their eyes locked.

"Save yourselves," Pan shouted, but the younger Shamira didn't heed him. She pulled her gaze away from her older self and ran toward Pan's lamp. But instead of racing Ugilino, as she had in the first reality, now she was racing the priest. Shamira lunged for the lamp. The older Shamira watched her younger self's hand reach out, expecting what happened before to be repeated, the ax would rip her sleeve and scrape her arm. Father Lurenzano's face turned into a snarl as he lifted the ax. It rose in an arch, still in slow motion, and began its descent. To the older Shamira, it was as if her younger self was half suspended in the air, her hand outstretched, her eyes locked on their target. The ax continued its descent and then the world snapped back into fast motion.

"NOT THE GIRL!" Pan screamed. The older Shamira's eyes sprung open in stark terror, and that's when the sharp blade sliced into the younger Shamira's spine, blood spraying up in a fan. Her body fell with a thump.

"NO!" the older Shamira shrieked.

Everybody turned as Lurenzano wrenched the ax out of the body and locked his eyes on the brass lamp. He didn't raise it high, but used the blood-drenched bludgeon to come straight down and pummel the tiny charm.

"PAN!" the younger Hansum shouted from atop Ugilino. He twisted around to disengage himself from his fight just as the ax met the lamp. An explosion of light and smoke rose around Pan. His beautiful and grotesque face contorted. He winked away without a word.

The older Shamira's head snapped back to the sound of the younger Hansum screaming while trying to twist away from Ugilino. But the strong oaf caught Hansum by the arms and stopped him for the briefest of moments. It was long enough.

"STOP!" Shamira heard herself screaming, finally trying to run to the young Hansum's aid. Something held her back. An energy field from Sideways. She looked on in horror as Father Lurenzano came toward Hansum with the ax already swinging, but the rising Sands of Time blocked her view.

"DEATH TO DEVILS," she heard Lurenzano cry.

"GUILIET . . ."

Chapter 5

Old Hansum sat bent over, his face in his hands, exhausted. This had been one of the few situations in time travel when there wasn't all the time in the universe to fix things. Their younger selves had been killed and they had to get back to repair the situation immediately. The new reality was racing through the folds of time and would soon catch up to the 24th and 25th centuries. Despite wearing their temporal protectors, this situation was unprecedented. They didn't know what would happen in the future if they were killed in the past.

So, despite their emotional exhaustion, they went back the few minutes and interceded with themselves *before* they entered the workshop as clergymen. Not a word was needed to be spoken this time. Not a single word. When their earlier selves saw their duplicates show up, dressed the same but covered in blood, they just shook their heads gravely, looked at each other and winked away.

Now back atop the wall, the older Lincoln smiled weakly at his oldest friend, Hansum. They were sitting together, backs leaning against the brick parapets.

"I guess we can now say with certainty there are not many things more off-putting than seeing yourself brutally killed in an alternate reality." He was trying to make light, but Hansum didn't smile. Neither did Shamira or the A.I.s.

Medeea, who was sitting next to Shamira on the other side of the walkway, looked over at her girlfriend. Shamira was staring straight ahead at nothing, her face like granite.

"Shamira, are you going to be okay? Do you want us to take you back?"

Shamira looked at her, eyebrows knit together.

"No. Let's get on with it." Shamira said, and she put a hand to her temple, calling up the details of the next linear point in the intervention. "This plan seems to be running out of timeline."

"I know," the older Hansum answered, his tired eyes drooping. He took a breath and stood, somewhat unsteadily. "Okay. I'll recap what's next. It's *after* the original fight at the shop this time. Pan is dead. Our younger selves have been barred from the house and we've gone to the palace to get soldiers and a carriage. But there are none to be had and the Podesta's going to show up in the morning. That's when we change things."

"Hansum, what happens if we don't find a nexus point there?" Shamira asked.

"Then I guess it's over."

Now Lincoln forced himself to his feet.

"It ain't over . . . till it's over."

Finally Hansum smiled. He rose, clapped his hands and began giving orders.

"Shamira, Lincoln, Medeea. You three go back a week, to when the market is still open. Buy the herbs and make Pan's antibiotic. Don't buy them from Elder Catherine. She could get suspicious. I'll meet Mastino at the northern gate, at the time we planned. Sideways. Zat. Costumes."

Everyone's appearance changed, and they were gone.

It was chaos at the northern gate. Few people were being let out and fewer in. Men and women were wailing and pleading with grim-faced soldiers who ignored them. Those not pleading either stood or sat silently, some scratching madly at their blackened buboes, the huge, swollen plague sores that would soon kill them. Against the wall, piled like so much cordwood, were the bodies of men, women and children who had already succumbed.

The older Hansum appeared in the shadow of a heavy cart laden with the wares of a merchant who had tried earlier to flee the city with his family. They were now lying under the cart, all dead.

"Time?" Hansum asked Sideways.

"The Podesta will be arriving in about a minute," Sideways reported. The gate to the city started to open, pushed and pulled by a phalanx of straining soldiers. The miserable souls inside became excited and converged on the gate, but were pushed back by other soldiers. Then in came half a dozen mounted knights, followed by an ornate carriage.

"Here we go," the older Hansum said, and Sideways's face disappeared into what looked like robes of a simple priest. Hansum stepped into the open and joined the throng of people pleading and gesturing up to the carriage's inhabitant. Hansum stood silently until he saw the Podesta Mastino della Scalla. The noble was peering through the window, ignoring the entreaties of the citizens, but looking out at what must be a first glimpse of his city since the plague hit.

"I have word of Romero Monticelli, Excellency," Hansum called and, as expected, Mastino locked eyes with him.. The noble called for the wagon to stop. Soldiers ran to block the carriage from the rabble, but Mastino beckoned Hansum forward.

"What?" the Podesta asked the old priest in front of him. "What about Romero? Is he ill?"

"No, Excellency. He is not ill, though he is in danger." Hansum looked around at the faces of the soldiers and citizens listening. He looked up at Mastino. "Excellency, there is much to tell. Vital, timely news. May I join you?"

After the soldiers checked Hansum for weapons, he was up in the carriage, sitting opposite della Scalla.

"Who are you?" Mastino asked.

"My name is Father Benjamin."

"What are you to Romero?"

"I . . . am his father," Hansum said.

"His confessor?"

"No. He has my blood in his veins." There was no need to explain further to a man with many bastards. "To my shame, I made him," Hansum continued his story, "but I have followed his life and am proud of his accomplishments. I had him raised by my brother and watched from afar. I never met him. Now that he is established, with your permission, I will reveal myself."

"To take advantage of his new wealth?" Mastino asked suspiciously.

"No. To protect him. And to do that, I must tell you, his benefactor, what I know."

"Tell me then."

"Well, first, he is already married."

A few minutes later, after hearing more fiction mixed with fact, Mastino got the attention of the driver.

"Take me to the della Cappa house before we go to the palace. Immediately."

Chapter 6

As in the original timeline, the younger Hansum, Shamira and Lincoln were together in one of the many comfortable bedrooms of the palace. Hansum was asleep on the floor and the young Lincoln was lying on top of the bed with his broken arm. Barred from their house, they had struggled through the rain and plague-infested Verona only to find the palace with no doctors, carriages or spare soldiers to retrieve Guilietta by force.

After a fitful night's sleep, the young Hansum awoke to someone shaking his shoulder. He looked up and saw the Podesta standing above him.

"The city has gone mad, Excellency," he said, jumping to his feet.

"The whole world," Mastino replied.

"There's dead in the streets," Hansum said, starting a speech designed to convince the Podesta to help him get Guilietta. "People are blaming evil spirits . . ." but Mastino was ignoring him and waved some people into the room. "Even my own has gone mad," the young Hansum went on. "Guilietta's father thinks I am to blame for his daughter's illness and that we are in league with the . . ."

"Put her on the bed," Mastino said to two men at opposite ends of a stretcher. "You boy, get off," he ordered Lincoln.

A nun and a monk were blocking Hansum's view of who was on the litter. The nun wore a full wimple and a veil covered her face. She pulled back the blankets and motioned for the soldiers to hold the litter close to the bed. Another woman followed, along with an elderly priest. Hansum was becoming flustered with all the activity deflecting attention away from what was most important to him.

"Please listen to me, Excellency," Hansum continued. "Master della Cappa has forbid me to come into his house and I cannot get in to rescue . . ." and then he saw who they were lifting onto the bed. ". . . Guilietta." Hansum stared in amazement. There she lay, eyes closed. The veiled nun was tucking in the covers and smoothing her hair over one of the plush pillows.

Hansum fell to his knees and leaned against the bed.

"Guilietta!" He fought back tears. "How?"

"I received word of your dilemma," Mastino said compassionately, "What else was I to do for my savant?"

Still on his knees, Hansum swung around to the Podesta and grabbed his hands.

"Grazzi, Excellency. Grazzi," he said kissing them.

"Also thank Father Benjamin. He is the one who found me at the gates and bid my help. And the one who arranged the monk physician, the silent sister and the medicine you were seeking."

The older Hansum, as Father Benjamin, stepped forward and smiled down at his younger self.

"Grazzi, Father. It was very . . ." and then it hit the younger Hansum. "You know about the medicine?"

Father Benjamin held up two fingers, as if to give a blessing, but then placed them at his temples, an unquestioningly familiar gesture.

"We're here to help," he said in Earth Common to the astounded teens, "but things have gotten complicated. Remain calm and play along. All of you."

Hansum's eyes bugged out. His jaw dropped. He turned to the younger Shamira and Lincoln, whose arm was in a sling. The three put their hands to their own necks and pressed the language nodes.

"Who are you? Why didn't you show up earlier . . ." Hansum began.

"All that later," Father Benjamin said. "Right now we must save Guilietta."

Hansum nodded dumbly and turned back to the other two teens, who were equally bereft of words. And then, as the consequences of what was happening began to compute, the younger Hansum smiled at his ailing Guilietta.

"Excuse the rudeness of talking in a foreign language before you, Excellency," the older Hansum said to Mastino della Scalla.

"Did you tell him who you are?"

"Not yet, Excellency. A bit at a time, under the circumstances."

The young Hansum's face was very close to Guilietta. He touched her cheek.

"Her skin feels normal," he said with wonder.

"Yes, the silent sister's medicine has already had its good effect," Hansum as Father Benjamin said. "Her color has come back."

"The medicine. You made the medicine we were trying to get?" young Shamira asked.

"We gave it to her an hour ago," the fake priest answered. "It was a good recipe you were given,"

"Yes, Pan knows what he's talking about . . ." and then the younger Hansum stopped. To him, Pan had been killed not a dozen hours earlier. He looked over at the veiled nun. She looked back at him with two very green eyes.

"Romero," a soft voice whispered. Both Hansums watched as Guilietta slowly opened her sleepy eyes. "Romero. Where?"

"You're at the palace, darling," young Hansum said tenderly. "You're going to get better, Guilietta. You're going to get better." Guilietta looked all around her; at the large, opulent room, at all the people standing about, then down at the beautiful sheets and blankets. "You're safe, Guilietta. You're going to get better."

"Father Benjamin tells me this medicine should most definitely stop any inner mortification," the Podesta said. "And, as he suggested, my men sent Father Lurenzano packing with orders not to associate with your family again. All the wine has been removed from the house. I will send a carriage for Master della Cappa and his wife tomorrow. When your wife is better, Romero, you can take them all to your estate for safe keeping."

"Thank you, Excellency," young Hansum said. "I very much appreciate . . ." and he stopped. The Podesta, the man who controlled every aspect of his life had referred to Guilietta as . . . his wife.

"That's right, Romero," Mastino said, his face serious. "I know. I know . . . everything." And then he laughed. "It would have been much better if you had told me earlier. Oh, how it would have simplified things. What you put me through."

"Excellency, I'm sorry. I never meant to . . ."

Mastino made a soft sound, blowing through his lips and waving his hand. "It's done, it's done. We all have reasons, and good and bad comes from what we do. Who's to know what will happen except God? Lucky for you, eh, you're my savant and have given me lookers and cannons, eh?"

"Ow," Guilietta said, wincing slightly.

The woman who had been standing silently in the corner came forward and put her hand on Guilietta's midriff.

"Does it hurt here, my dear?" the woman asked.

"Si. Si, a little."

"She should stay abed and not travel," the woman said.

"Who is this?" Hansum asked. "Another herbalist?" Given Guilietta's last experience with a woman the Podesta had provided, he was suspicious.

"I know of herbs for my trade, Signor," the woman said, "but I am not a herbalist."

"What trade are you then?" Hansum asked.

"A midwife, of course."

"A midwife?" Hansum asked. "Why?"

The woman looked astonished.

"Why? Why?" the Podesta laughed. "Oh, my savant, a midwife because your wife is with child."

The younger Shamira and Lincoln shrieked with laughter, bouncing up and down. Young Hansum on the other hand was stunned mute.

"With ch . . . child?" he stammered.

Mastino laughed uproariously again. "Was your head in the clouds when you did the deed, my savant? Another reason not to punish you. You no longer are just my vassal, but as the head of the house for a wife and child, you are in servitude to both for life! Ha. And I get to watch."

Hansum looked over to Guilietta. She looked back with apprehension.

"I'm going be . . . a father?" he asked.

"Si," she nodded.

A smile broke out on Hansum's face. "I'm going to be a father. We're going to have a baby," and he kissed his wife as everyone cheered.

"Quietly, quietly," the midwife warned, to little effect.

"Father Benjamin, I must go," the Podesta said. "While life is blooming here, thousands die all through my lands. Let us pray we survive to see all our dreams and schemes come to pass."

The older Hansum-as-priest looked back at this complicated man. For decades he had blamed him for so much. He was a tyrant, a man of war, but also a builder of buildings still admired a thousand years past his death. The della Scalla name still graced one of the most famous places where opera was sung, and Mastino's progeny went on to be some of the most influential kings, queens and statesmen across Europe for centuries.

"I shall add my prayers to the many," the older Hansum answered. "Perhaps things may pass for the better this time."

"This time?" Mastino enquired.

Oops. Hansum thought what to say. "Our Prince of Peace, Cristo, showed us the way over a thousand years past, and still we have not fulfilled his dream of a world where love and brotherhood rule. Many have tried, but still our world is . . . what it is."

The teens were giggling and laughing on the bed, all thrilled at their turn of fortune. Mastino put his hand on the shoulder of the man he knew as Father Benjamin and turned to walk to the door with him.

"Who knows, Father. Maybe with the cannons and ideas God gives my savant, perhaps I can be the man to tame this world. What do you think? Has God given the son of your seed such inspiration? Was this his plan, disguised in what you thought your sin?"

Now in the hall, the two men turned and looked at each other. The older Hansum chose his words carefully.

"Only God knows the future. At least we hope he does. But maybe it's up to us."

"You talk like no priest I've ever met, Father. Truly, tell me what you think. I like you and will not tell the bishop."

"Excellency. I think you will do what you will and others will do the same. It is in this clash where both inspiration and grief are forged. It has been over thirteen hundred years since the years of our Lord began, and I fear it will take the same number before his vision is fulfilled." Mastino could not know that he was hearing actual future history.

"You see things clearly, Father Benjamin. It is an ability few have." Hansum did not answer. A servant ran up the hall to them.

"Baron da Pontramoli needs you urgently, Excellency."

"I must go, Father. I'm glad I stopped for you this morning." He began to leave and turned. "You know, Father, when you hold your face like that, I can see you as you must have been in your youth. Much like our Romero."

"Grazzi, Excellency. You are most kind."

"When I can, Father. When I can," and he left.

The older Hansum returned to the bedroom. Happy sounds abounded from all the teens. The midwife was busy at a fireplace, heating up a cauldron of water. The older Shamira and Lincoln, in their disguises, were standing a few steps from the bed, watching their younger selves play. Medeea was over at the bed, looking at the youngsters.

"You guys were cute," she said.

"Lincoln, have you tried again?" the older Hansum thought. They had tried taking Guilietta out of phase in the carriage, but it didn't work then.

"I'll try now." He reached out and took Guilietta's wrist, like he was checking her pulse. The teens quieted and watched.

"What ya doin', old man?" young Lincoln asked. The older Lincoln didn't answer, put down Guilietta's hand and walked away.

"No. She wouldn't go out of phase," he thought.

"Okay, time to explain things to them." The older Hansum stepped toward the bed. There was his younger self, doing something the old Hansum never got to do. The teenage husband was lying on a luxurious featherbed with his bride, lying against an overstuffed pillow with Guilietta nestled in his arm.

"Back at Bella Flora," the younger Hansum was saying, "I dreamed of being in a bed like this with you, and here we are." Guilietta cooed and snuggled closer.

"Hey," the younger Lincoln joked. "You weren't always alone." Guilietta looked at him. "Yeah. I slept in the bed with him sometimes," and they all laughed.

"Nut," the younger Shamira chided.

"One could get used to a wonderful bed like this," Guilietta commented.

"Oh, wait till you see our new home, Guilietta," the young Hansum told her. "It's a huge estate with hundreds of workers and servants. And you will be mistress of it all."

"No, it can't be so," she said.

"Oh, you have no idea," Lincoln said. "You guys are rich."

"And having a bed like this is only the beginning," Shamira said.

"Yes, you'll have a whole house full of servants to boss around," Hansum added.

"But I will be busy with the baby, and Carmella and I must do housework," Guilietta answered.

"No more housework for me or you, Guil," Shamira said.

The older Hansum as Father Benjamin stepped forward.

"We must talk," he said, which got everyone's attention. It was like they all just remembered that he was from the future. "Let's go in the hallway."

"No," Guilietta protested. "I don't want my husband to leave."

"For a few moments, darling. I'll be back soon. We must talk with Father Benjamin about several things, including travel."

"Why can't you talk here?"

"It's best they leave, Signora," the midwife spoke up. "You must be bathed. Cleanliness is next to Cristo. All the men out."

"But I want to know about the travel," Guilietta protested.

"There will be no travel or bossing servants about till your spotting stops, Signora," the midwife bullied tenderly.

"Spotting? What's spotting?" young Hansum asked.

"Girl talk," the young Shamira said. "None of your business. Now get out of here."

"I would like you to come too . . . Shamira," the Father Benjamin figure added. Shamira blinked, surprised at being called that out loud.

"Why did he call you that?" Guilietta asked.

"It's a name from back home, Guil," young Shamira said, turning toward the door. As she passed the veiled nun, two sets of green eyes met for the first time. The nun looked away and stepped toward Guilietta.

"I'll explain in the hall," Father Benjamin whispered, seeing Shamira's surprise. They all left the room, leaving the nun and midwife with Guilietta. The young Hansum took a last look back at his wife and, just as the door was closing, saw the midwife removing the blankets.

"No good," the midwife said, and the door closed with a click.

Chapter 7

Elders Hansum and Lincoln looked at the three teens facing them.

"So, you finally got here," young Lincoln said. "Did you have to wait till I looked like this?" and he bared his teeth, showing the missing spot in front and pointing to his broken arm.

"My apologies," the older Hansum said. "There have been problems in getting you home. Time travel is more complicated than you could know."

"More complicated than we could know?" Lincoln continued complaining. "We didn't even know it existed."

"People from the 31st-century still have problems with time travel?" Shamira asked.

"Actually, we're from around your time. Time travel was announced to the public just after you three were brought here. People have been watching your adventures all over the planet. It's a new History Camp method to scare hard case teens into appreciating the easy time they live in."

"But when Arimus was killed . . ." Shamira began.

"The truth is . . . Arimus didn't die. It was all a ruse to make you three take things seriously. And if our changing the timeline hasn't altered things too much, he should show up to retrieve you soon."

The teens all looked at each other, confused. Lincoln especially wasn't seeing the bright side of things.

"You put me through all of this crap, just so I would appreciate . . ." The older Lincoln as monk reached out and took hold of his younger self's shoulder. The younger one batted him off. "Don't touch me, ferret face."

"Asshole," the older Lincoln retorted.

"Oh, finally this weird lookin' guy finds his tongue and all he can say is . . ."

"Cool it, Lincoln," the younger Hansum said, giving the kind of look a noble gives a servant. Lincoln quieted immediately. The young Hansum looked back to the man dressed as a priest.

"So, Arimus isn't dead, you've been trying to save us and Arimus should show up anytime now," Hansum summed up. "You'll excuse me for asking, but why don't you just take us back, and if you can't, how are you here? It doesn't make sense."

"Very little about time travel does, my boy," the elder Hansum agreed. "Listen, all of you. We've changed the timeline you and the Arimus you know lived before. But we're still hopeful he should show up to take you back, with one big difference. Before you went back by yourselves. This time, we hope Guilietta and her family can go with you. We've tried before, several times, but for some reason, we can't."

Silence.

"You're right," Lincoln lisped. "Time travel doesn't make sense? It's nuts!"

Young Hansum put up his hand again for silence. "What's this about Guilietta? You tried to do what before? Take her to the future?"

The old Hansum hesitated, looking at the older Lincoln, who nodded.

"Right now Guilietta is getting better, thank Gia, but in the last timeline . . . she didn't. We tried saving both you and her before, but failed. We're afraid she might be a person who can't move through time, except at certain points."

"We don't remember you trying before," the young Hansum countered.

The old Hansum became somewhat frustrated. "Of course you don't. We changed it all back. Hansum, we don't have time for me to get into the details. You've got to trust us."

"Just tell me what you mean, she didn't make it?"

"She and the baby. They died back at her parents' house." Silence. "But this time we manipulated the situation for the Podesta to go get her, and for you to have the antibiotic. Now she's here and alive." The old Hansum smiled. "Listen, please, we've never gotten this far and I think it can work this time. Be happy."

"Okay. Okay," the younger Hansum said, trying to take it all in. "What can we do to help?"

"Good. That's what I hoped you would say. There's not much to do right now," the older Hansum said. "Everything's been set up, the antibiotic is eliminating Guilietta's infection and the rest should play out by tomorrow."

"And what happens if Arimus doesn't show and you can't find a way to take us forward?" the young Hansum asked, "Or if we can go and Guilietta can't?"

"You choose then, my boy. You can stay here with her or go forward, whatever you like. This whole operation was to make you and her happy."

Young Hansum stood quietly, not saying what his face showed. Lincoln said it though.

"I can't believe Guilietta . . . died."

"None of you think about that," the older Hansum ordered, pointing at each teen. "Just be happy that things are going to work out now. Especially you, Hansum. You're going to be a father."

Hansum smiled at that. So did Shamira and Lincoln.

"Hey man, I'm sorry I was snarky at you," Lincoln said to his older self. "You look like an okay guy, for a ferret face."

There was a scream from the bedroom. "HUSBAND!"

"Guilietta," Hansum said, turning.

"No, Signora," the voice of the midwife cried. "No, you mustn't."

"I WANT MY HUSBAND!"

"She's being attacked!" Hansum said, banging open the door with his shoulder.

"No, Signor," the midwife cried. "Stay away," but it was too late.

There, standing by the bed, was Guilietta, her long nightdress soaked with blood from the waist down, a puddle dripping onto the marble floor.

"She's hemorrhaging," Zat said, his face appearing on Lincoln's chest.

"What's going . . ." young Hansum started.

"Lie her back down," Sideways called, his face appearing too.

"She will not listen," the midwife retorted. She saw the A.I. faces and fell to her knees, crossing herself. Gullietta slipped in the blood and crashed to the marble floor.

Both Hansums rushed to her side. "Husband," Guilietta moaned.

"Lincoln, put my sleeve on her belly," Zat ordered. "I'm a medical A.I. I'll scan her." The older Lincoln put his voluminous sleeve on Guilietta's blood-stained torso. "There's a hematoma in the uterus. It's caused an *abruptio placenta*. The placenta has separated from the wall of the womb."

"But the antibiotic?" the younger Hansum cried as he cradled Guilietta's head.

"That's taking care of the infection, but nothing we've got can stop this," said Zat.

"Romero," Guilietta's voice was now much weaker. "What is happening? Our baby? Romero? I'm afraid for our . . ." her voice trailed off.

"Hang on, Guilietta," Hansum pleaded. "Hang . . ." Her eyes unfocused. "CAN'T YOU DO SOMETHING?"

"Medicine brought from our time won't work here," the older Lincoln said, grimacing.

"Stay with us, Guil," the younger Shamira urged. "Stay with us," but Guilietta's eyes closed completely and her body started shaking in shock.

"Guilietta," both Hansums said at once, and then she convulsed, her whole torso seeming to ripple. A gush of new blood washed through her gown and poured across the marble.

"She's aborting," Zat called.

"The baby she comes. No good, no good," the midwife said getting up from her knees. She grabbed one of Guilietta's legs. "Sister," she said to the older Shamira. "Bend the other leg to free the way." As they did so, the sodden night gown hung like wet red drapes between Guilietta's knees. The midwife grabbed a knife and slit the cloth. "No good, no good."

"Guilietta . . ." Hansum pleaded in her ear, but she couldn't hear.

"*Madonna mia*, bless this mother and child," the midwife prayed as she worked.

"No, no, Cristo no!" the older Hansum said, almost praying.

"Oh man!" the younger Lincoln groaned, staring at the widening pool of red on the floor.

"What can I do?" the young Shamira begged. "What can I do?" She looked and found a hand holding her wrist. It was the silent sister with green eyes.

"Guilietta. Guilietta, don't leave me," the young Hansum pleaded to his wife's now pale face, her eyes two thin slits.

"Guilietta, I failed," the old Hansum wept. "Again I . . ."

Chapter 8

The roar of the vortex echoed in the hollow silence of the time travelers' souls. In all the other instances where death was imminent, the battle with the cannon and knights, the sword fights with Feltrino, the incident in the river, there was a chance of survival if you struggled hard and were lucky. But this, seeing the young woman they loved being drained of life, it ripped out their guts.

Now the only thing to do, once again, was to go back and stop the older Hansum from stepping out from behind the wagon and contacting Mastino della Scalla when he re-entered Verona. But for the first time in his career, Hansum couldn't do what was needed of him. Sideways went alone.

As Sideways rejoined the others in the vortex, he could tell that his Hansum was out of emotional fuel. Staring out into nowhere, the old time traveler didn't even acknowledge the A.I.'s reappearance. Looking at the others, Sideways saw they were all in a similar state, hanging listlessly in the vortex.

"Where to now, Elder Hansum?" Sideways asked telepathically. *"Back to the wall to regroup?"*

"Why?" Hansum responded. *"That was the last piece of our plan to find a nexus point."*

"We can't hang here forever, Master."

"Maybe it was never meant to be," Hansum thought back.

Nobody said anything for a long time. They just hung there, suspended in time.

"If that really was our last chance, can I ask a favor?" Shamira thought. The others looked over. *"Can we at least go back to when Guil passed away at home? We weren't there for her or her parents then, and I've always regretted it. I'd really like to be with her and the family one last time. To say goodbye."*

They all looked to Hansum, their leader. Tears were streaming from his eyes again. He needed to say goodbye too.

They returned to the della Cappa home. Guilietta was on her deathbed attended by her parents and Nuca. Bembo was out in the hallway, ready to do whatever he could. The women had been able to reduce Guilietta's fever for a while, but now it was returning with a vengeance.

After almost a hundred years of not giving up, it was time for Hansum to let go.

"*Medeea. Are you sure you can't do anything?*" he asked quietly.

"*Oh Hansum, I've been trying. But still, the most I can still do is monitor and stimulate her own immune system. And maybe, just maybe, put her into stasis when the time comes.*"

"*Please, do what you can to make her comfortable.*"

Lincoln opened up the smallest of openings in the air. He poured a drop of Medeea into a bowl of water Master della Cappa was using. The big man dipped the cloth in and put it to his daughter's mouth, squeezing the liquid between her parched lips.

"*I'm in,*" Medeea said. "*She's low, very low. I'll try to stimulate her immune system again but . . . . I'm sorry. It will only help for a little while. It won't be enough.*"

This pronouncement caused Hansum to fall to his knees. He looked at the young girl who had been his wife, was still his wife for a short while longer. Lincoln came and knelt by his friend, putting a hand on his shoulder.

"Goodbye, Guilietta. I'm sorry," Hansum whispered. "We tried. We really tried."

"Romero. My Romero," Guilietta murmured. "Where are you, my Romero?"

This stunned Hansum. It was as if she heard him.

"*No, she's not talking to you, Hansum,*" Medeea explained, "*Well, she is, but not you.*"

Hansum struggled to remember when he had heard Guilietta say those words before. Of course! It was when the younger Hansum was at the Podesta's palace, huddled in the corner of the room he was being detained in, out of his mind with worry for his wife. He thought it was a dream at the time, but here he was, at the other end of the conversation. It had been real.

"I hear your voice," Guilietta continued to mutter. "I see you in my mind, like a window to another place. Is this a dream? Is this Heaven?" The younger Hansum had opened his eyes, breaking the visual connection between the two, causing Guilietta to become agitated. "Where have you gone, my love?"

The young Hansum closed his eyes again and Medeea connected everybody to Guilietta and her Hansum's last conversation. Hansum said how the Podesta was keeping him at the palace, and Guilietta, even in her low state, gave him loving encouragement. She told how her father said Hansum and the others were devils. Hansum confessed he was from the future, trapped in the 14th-century, but he would find a way to prove he was not a devil and save her. And that's when Guilietta said those awful words.

"I fear not, husband. I fear not. I am dying." Hansum couldn't see what happened in the della Cappa bedroom before. Now he did. Guilietta's body started shivering uncontrollably and the Signora shrieked and collapsed. "Come to me, my darling," Guilietta's voice had said to the younger Hansum. "Hold me while I go to God."

"Can't we do something?" the older, out-of-phase Hansum pleaded.

"Medeea's trying," Lincoln said. "She's trying!"

The Elder Shamira was standing next to Hansum, staring down at the situation. The old Hansum and Lincoln were full of anguish. Even Medeea was gritting her teeth as she tried desperately to overcome her programmed inability to heal Guilietta. Shamira watched as the Signora became distraught and collapsed, and yet she remained calm. So calm. The Master called Bembo and, along with Nuca, moved the Signora to the other bedroom. All the while the older Hansum was on his knees, tears streaming from his aged, sunken eyes, his hands clasped almost in prayer. As the Signora was carried from the room, Shamira curiously decided to follow, walking out of phase through one bedroom door curtain and then the next. She watched as the despondent mother was placed gently on the other bed and passed out.

"Shall I go get more cool water from the well, Master?" Bembo asked quietly.

"No," the Master said, his hollow eyes looking at Bembo. Shamira knew her second father's face well enough to know he was making a very hard decision. "Tell Ugilino to run and fetch Father Lurenzano. It's time," the unspoken phrase being; "for last rites."

"Si, Master," Bembo said, hanging his head.

"I go get dry blanket at home," Nuca added, "Make Gui comfortable," and they all left the room with the Signora gently weeping in her sleep.

Shamira sat on the edge of the bed next to the Signora. This was the woman who "Shamira the hard case" thought of as just a crazy, old, fat person. How did she become such a cherished part of her heart?

"Goodbye, Signora. At least I get to say goodbye this time. Maybe we will see each other again," she whispered. "I'm pretty old myself and who knows, we could be sitting, holding hands together with your Archangel Michael one of these days. Wouldn't that be grand?" At that odd thought Shamira smiled and absentmindedly reached for the Signora's fat hand. She expected hers to go right through the old woman's, but felt plump flesh move under her fingers. The Signora's whole body began to shimmer blue and she awoke with a start.

The Signora looked up. Shamira's first response was to think the old woman was staring through her and up at the ceiling, like when she was talking to her hallucinatory angels. But then they blinked at the same time and realized they were looking into each other's eyes.

"Signora. You can see me."

"You, you look like Carmella, but you are not Carmella. Are you an angel?"

Shamira realized what had happened. "You've gone out of phase, Signora. Good Gia, you've gone out of phase," and she hugged the old woman and gave her a kiss. Then she looked her in the eye and smiled. The Signora looked back, not knowing how to react. "It's going to be all right now, Signora. It's going to be all right," and she let go of the old woman, who fell back onto her pillow, the glow disappearing from her with a pop. To her, Shamira would seem to have simply vanished.

"I must be dreaming," she said, crossing herself.

"No you're not, Signora," Shamira said, jumping to her feet. "Guys, the Signora. She's gone out of phase!" she shouted.

"Come to me, my darling," Guilietta's voice whispered desperately. "One last kiss before I meet Jesus. I am content that your voice is the last thing I'll hear."

Tears streaming down the old Hansum's face, he heard his likewise grief-stricken self back at the palace. "No, Guilietta. You're not dying. You mustn't die!"

"I am done, my love, but I am happy."

"You mustn't die, Guilietta. I love you. I need you. I've always loved you. Before we met, I loved the idea of you. I need more of you."

"We had the time on the wall, with the moon and cool breeze showing us we were alive," Guilietta murmured weakly.

"I want that time again," the younger Hansum wept. "You cannot go. I've not had enough."

"Who's to say what's enough? Not those who say it." That's when the communications had gone silent before, but not this time. Not by Guilietta's death bed. Death was not quiet.

Hansum looked on in horror as Guilietta went into convulsions, her breathing rasping as she fought to force air through her swelling larynx. Her body tensed and her beautiful hands grasped the sheets as her head jerked back and forth, battling to bring in enough oxygen to keep alive. Her father was alone with Guilietta. Unbridled panic and grief screamed from his eyes. He fell to his knees, collected his daughter in his arms and held her as she shook, desperately trying to hold in the life being torn away from her.

Guilietta's body bucked harder and harder as it was starved of oxygen. The bucking suddenly became less, then pathetic . . . and she went limp. The only thing moving was her father's massive chest. Slowly, Agistino released his grip and sat up, tentatively staring at her face. As reality seeped in, he closed his eyes and a stream of tears poured down his cheeks. He crossed himself and began to pray.

"Medeea, hurry! Can you put her in stasis?" the out-of-phase Hansum shouted.

"I've already done it," Medeea answered. *"But that can only last a few hours in these conditions. And the house fire is going to happen before then."*

That's when Shamira ran back into the room.

"Guys, the Signora. She's gone out of phase!" she said excitedly. "Maybe that means we can put them all out of phase and transport them to the future."

Lincoln reached out a finger and tentatively touched the back of the praying Agistino. His whole body glowed blue for a split second and, before the big man could open his eyes and see what the odd feeling was, Lincoln removed his finger and he went back to normal.

"Was that your sweet soul saying goodbye, my daughter?" Agistino said to the body. "Was that your sweet soul?" and he collapsed in tears beside her.

"We've found the nexus point," Lincoln said, astounded. "We found it."

Hansum, still on his knees, reached out his hand to touch Guilietta. "Then let's do it. Let's take them to the future."

"Wait," Lincoln said. He put a hand to his forehead, deep in thought. "We have to do it so nothing changes. So they just disappear from history."

"We have to do it now!" Hansum said. "She's dying!"

"No brother. Listen to me," Lincoln said softly. "She's already dead." That shocked Hansum. Lincoln held out Medeea's tear bottle. "Open your mouth brother."

"Lincoln, we have no time . . ."

"Trust me, brother." Hansum, still on his knees, opened his mouth and closed his eyes, like during communion in Verona. Lincoln put the bottle to his lips. "Med, make this a deep delve." A single drop of the liquid landed on Hansum's tongue. Then, as he opened his eyes, his world expanded. Within a second, Hansum could see a blue glow around his oldest friend, Lincoln. It was like an aura. "Now look at Guil."

When Hansum turned his head to see his poor Guilietta lying dead, her skin was no longer pallid. It too glowed a metallic blue. And there, at her head, kneeling alongside the weeping Agistino, was Medeea, her hand on Guilietta's brow.

"I don't understa . . ." Hansum began, but then he did understand. This was not a limited mind-delve like he had experienced in the past. This one joined him with Lincoln and Medeea in a way no technological mind link had ever allowed him to touch another being. Hansum now understood everything, including why Lincoln wanted to wait. "She *is* safe now," Hansum said. "If we can really move them through time, then, yes, we had better wait just a bit longer." He nodded at Lincoln. Then he reached out to take Lincoln and Shamira's hands and looked down to Sideways. "Take us to just before the fire," he said, closing his eyes. The Sands of Time rose around them.

When Hansum opened his eyes he was still kneeling by Guilietta's body, but it was now very dark. The Master was gone and, as Hansum's eyes adjusted, he could see a single linen sheet covering the form that was his beloved, a blue light glowing beneath.

This was the original time when Father Lurenzano got Agistino very drunk and stole the strong box with all the money. Right now the younger Hansum and Lincoln would be sneaking up to the house.

"Okay, this is the deal," the older Lincoln began. "We've got to wait till . . ." He stopped when they heard the sound of the door opening downstairs. "We're here. Our younger selves are here. Soon, my friend, soon," Lincoln said encouragingly. There was the creaking of footsteps coming up the stairs and shortly the light of an oil lamp glowed through the curtain door. A hand appeared and moved the fabric aside and then . . . in stepped eighteen-year-old Hansum. "This is the time . . ."

"I know," Hansum said. How could he forget? This was when Hansum had come and found his wife dead.

The young man took a tentative step into the room, the dim light from the lamp throwing confusing shadows. At first the poor youth thought the bed was empty, but then realized the cover was pulled over a still form.

"Guil," he said quietly, coming forward and falling to his knees. He touched the form's shoulder and his face morphed into a ghastly mask of pain. When he pulled the cover down, exposing Guilietta's hair and delicate face, the older Hansum remembered how he couldn't breathe, not until a rasping breath forced itself down into him and a wail of pain came back up. Now he was watching it, exactly as before.

"Guiiiiiil. Oh . . . my . . . Guil. I'm sorry, Guilietta. I'm sorry." And he broke completely.

A hand went onto the younger Hansum's shoulder. "I'm sorry, man," a young Lincoln said softly. "I'm really . . ." The sound of crashing furniture downstairs and the guttural sounds of a creature in mortal pain. "The Master," Lincoln said. "Hey, man, we've gotta go. We can't help here any . . ."

"ROBBERS!" the Master's hoarse voice shouted. "THIEVES!"

The older Hansum and Lincoln watched the young Lincoln run from the room. But the younger Hansum was frozen on the spot, afraid to betray his wife by leaving.

"DEVILS!" Agistino's voice boomed. "You ruin our lives and then steal what's left!"

"Master, we didn't steal," Lincoln's voice shouted back. "We just saw Ugilino and Father Lurenzano running down the street with the strong..."

"LIAR! I'll kill you. I'll kill..." and that's when the end began again. Agistino della Cappa collapsed from a heart attack, knocking the brass oil lamp and starting a fire.

"Hansum, help!" the younger Lincoln shouted and the young Hansum finally bolted from the room.

The older Hansum watched as the darkness in the hallway exploded into dancing flames. He heard the voices of the boys as they struggled to move the Master's body, and then saw the silhouette of the Signora stumbling from the other bedroom toward the steps.

"DEVILS," she began to scream from the stairs. "DEVILS! You've killed my whole family!" And she ran back up the stairs and right into the bedroom with the older Hansum and Lincoln. She fell to her knees over Guilietta's body and started to pray.

"Not yet," the old Lincoln said, and the tragic scene continued. The Signora cried for help from her angel. The butcher and his sons came and seized the boys. The flames started to eat their way through the floorboards.

"Help, Michael," the Signora cried. "Take me to Heaven to be with my beloved daughter and husband." Then she screamed. "They've killed my husband! Devils!"

As the noise of the fire began to dominate, what was happening on the floor below and outside became muffled. But this was the time when the younger Hansum and Lincoln begged the neighbors to save the Signora and Master. When they finally agreed, it was too late. The house was consumed with flames.

"Save me, Archangel Michael," the Signora prayed as the flames licked up from the floor and lit her gown. She cradled Guilietta's head in her arms and prayed. "Take me, take me to your bosom, Michael, so I may be with my beloved daughter and husband. Oh, Agistino, I'm coming," and she collapsed over her daughter.

"Now," the older Lincoln shouted, reaching out and touching the Signora. Immediately her body glowed blue and 'pop', she was out of phase.

Hansum touched Guilietta and she too moved between dimensions. They were all now safe, out of phase. Lincoln knelt down and grabbed the Signora's singed fabric, smothering the fire. He took out the tear vessel and poured a single drop onto the unconscious woman's burned calf.

"She'll be fine," Medeea said. "Poor soul . . . Oh good Gia," she exclaimed with a look of surprise. "My nano bits. They're not just boosting her immune system. They're actively healing her. I don't know why . . ." and then she realized, "Now that they're out of phase, the technology must see them as of our time."

"Then Guilietta," Hansum began.

"I'm already on it," Medeea said. Guilietta, pallid and still a moment earlier, convulsed alive. She shook for a second and then started breathing quickly. Hansum looked on, confusion and fear still apparent. Then Medeea's look of concern was replaced by a huge smile. "She'll be fine now. It will take a few minutes, but, I promise, she'll be fine."

Hansum wanted to cry again, this time from relief. But it wasn't over. They weren't back in the future yet. He steeled himself for anything that was yet to come.

The fire raged all around them, the voices of the arguing younger Hansum and butcher barely audible.

"I'll take the Signora with me," Lincoln said, pulling the unconscious woman to him. "Zat, take us to get the Master. Hansum. Take Guilietta to the end of your younger self's stay in the Arena. It's important we don't take her back till after that point." Hansum, now connected completely, understood why. "Collect your younger self and meet us on the wall." Zat winked an eye and they were gone.

Hansum watched the bedroom window blow out from the growing pressure of the fire. As the airflow increased, the light became even brighter. Then, as the wooden walls and floor exploded into total combustion, everything took on a polarized glow. Hansum looked over at Guilietta, safe among the flames, her breathing more regular and her skin closer to its natural, healthy hue. She was still unconscious, but her eyes were moving under their lids, as if she were dreaming. The old Hansum reached down and put his arms under Guilietta, picking her up and cradling her like a baby. Sideways's cloak grew around her, like a comforting blanket.

"All right, my friend," Hansum said to Sideways. "You know where to go," and the Sands of Time took them.

Chapter 9

From the blinding brightness of the fire to the dank dimness of the Arena prison, it took Hansum's eyes some moments to readjust. There was only a single lit torch, and it was held by the collector of the dead. Now Hansum knew it was Arimus and his rescue team in disguise, but back then it was four men heaving up dead bodies onto a cart.

The old Hansum stood there with Guilietta in his arms. She was breathing easy now, fast asleep as the nano bits worked to heal her. Hansum looked around as the scene before him played out.

The young Hansum was sitting on the floor of the dungeon, cradling the head of the almost dead Shamira, surrounded by a small mountain of bodies. The death cart was there to remove the corpses and take them to the fire pit.

"Make way then, move aside. The best man's here for the Devil's bride," Arimus as the collector of the dead chimed, and ordered his assistants to begin piling bodies on the cart. Women, men, old and young, children and babies.

"What's taking so long?" a jail guard shouted as he walked up waving a staff. "The live ones are getting hard to handle again. Begone quickly."

"A few moments more, Signor," the collector smiled.

"What about this one?" the guard asked, referring to Shamira.

"The young signor is tending to his friend. Not to worry. I'll no doubt take her in the morning."

"Take her now. I don't want her rotting corpse in here all night."

"She's not dead," the young Hansum wailed.

"I said out with it!" retorted the guard.

"NO!" Hansum screamed, pulling Shamira closer to him.

When the guard left, the collector looked down at Hansum with compassionate eyes.

"I'll take good care of your familiar, my friend. I won't bury her until she's at an end."

But Hansum didn't want her buried in the pit and gave up the last of his money, the gold florin Mastino originally tempted him with. The old Hansum still had that coin back home.

Hansum watched the scene end with the near-dead Shamira being placed on the cart with the cadavers. As the cart was pulled from the cell, the young Hansum sat down with his back against a wall, pulling his knees to his chest. The old Hansum, still out of phase, sat down opposite him. With Guilietta body's warming and her breathing now normal, she cuddled in his arms, reminding the old man of a sensation he hadn't thrilled to in the better part of a century.

"Soon, my love, soon," and he looked over at his younger self, cold and dirty against the wall. "Sideways. Please cover her face for a few moments," and the blanket gently grew, concealing the sleeping girl's face. The old Hansum reached forward and touched his younger self. There was a blue glow and the younger one sat up with a start.

"Who?"

"We've come to rescue you," the old Hansum said quietly. "I'm from the future."

He could tell his younger self wanted to smile, but couldn't.

"Now you come? Don't you know what's happened?"

"Yes. We're sorry it took so long."

"SORRY!" Hansum yelled, and then realized he might be heard by others in the cell.

"Don't worry. You are what's called out of phase. Nobody can hear you."

There were daggers in young Hansum's look. "Couldn't you come yesterday? Or last month? Shamira and Lincoln . . ."

"They're fine. Already home. It's just you now."

The young Hansum's eyes went wide as he tried to take it all in, tried to figure it out.

"But Guilietta and her family . . ." His face twisted in a knot.

"Shhhhh," the older Hansum soothed. "Look here, my boy. Look what I've got," and he smiled down at the blanket on his lap. "Sideways, if you please," and the blanket drew back off Guilietta's sleeping face.

"Guilietta!" the younger Hansum cried. He fell forward, his arm extended, almost afraid to touch her. "Is she . . ."

"She's sleeping. Healing." The young Hansum brushed his fingers along Guilietta's cheek and she smiled. "It's a long story," the elder continued, "but it's not quite over. We must leave here. Are you ready?"

"Yes, but how?"

"Leave it to me. Stand up then. Can you carry your wife?" Young Hansum picked Guilietta up in his strong arms and kissed her forehead. "Oh, to be young again," the old Hansum groaned as he struggled to his knees.

"What's your name, sir?" the young Hansum asked.

The older one laughed. "I guess I can tell. I . . . am an elder you."

"Elder Yu. I'm not familiar with that family name."

The elder chuckled. "I guess that can wait too," he said taking the other's arm. "Sideways. To the wall."

The full moon was barely visible through a heavy, churning fog. Wispy tendrils of the low-lying cloud wafted over the walkway of Verona's city wall. The Elder Lincoln was standing, a serious, worried look on his face, watching his time's Shamira, who was again hidden within a nun's habit and veil. She was kneeling over the Master and Signora. They were sitting next to each other, Medeea's nano bits helping them recover from smoke inhalation, burns and their other various maladies. Lincoln's serious look vanished as the older and younger Hansums appeared next to him with Guilietta.

"You made it! Good show," he laughed jovially. The younger Hansum, with Guilietta in his arms, looked around in astonishment.

"How? Who?" he began, looking to his older self.

"All in good time. And this fellow is . . . You know, I think it might be better not to say the rest of our names just now."

"Whatever you say, Elder Yu."

"Elder Yu?" Lincoln questioned. Hansum shook his head. Sideways shrank his blanket again, revealing Guilietta. "Oh, and look what we have here. Medeea, how is she?"

"Who's he talking to?" the younger Hansum asked. The older one waved his hand again, 'later'.

Medeea came and looked at the sleeping Guilietta, putting a hand to her own temple.

"Oh, she's much better. And we've caught the infection this time, before it hurt the fetus. The baby is fine."

Both the old Hansum and Lincoln laughed joyously.

"She's fine," Lincoln crowed. "She's going to be fine and so is the baby! Medeea, can you wake her up?"

"Absolutely," and she nodded.

"Baby?" the young Hansum began to ask, but stopped when Guilietta eyes fluttered. "Guilietta?"

"Romero," she said quietly. "Is it still a dream?" and she looked around.

"No dear. It's really me."

"Am I in Heaven? Are we in . . ."

"No darling. These people from my home saved us. And they made you better. Everything is going to be all right."

"I don't understand . . ." Guilietta began.

"All will be explained soon, young lady," the old Hansum said. "My boy, see if she can stand."

"But . . ."

"Modern medicine," the old Hansum reminded.

Guilietta was wobbly, but able.

"It's a miracle," Guilietta said.

"A MIRACLE! A MIRACLE!" came the cry of the Signora, waking up.

"What? Where?" Agistino's rough voice was heard as he bulled his way onto his feet, pulling his wife with him.

"Mama, Papa!" Guilietta cried, and she and young Hansum ran to them.

"Guilietta, my Guilietta, we're together in Heaven," the Signora cried as Guilietta fell between her parents in an excited embrace.

"Together in Heaven." Agistino cried joyously.

"Thank you, dear angels," the Signora said to the heavens, and then stopped when she saw the younger Hansum. "I suppose Cristo is kind and forgave you too."

"No Mama," Guilietta laughed kindly. "Apparently we're not . . ."

"Tell her later," the old Hansum advised. "Your journey is not over."

"We're not in Heaven yet?" the Signora asked. She put her hands to her temples. "My head. Voices and sounds don't echo anymore. I feel . . . different."

The old Hansum felt his Lincoln's touch.

"Let's confer," and the older Hansum, Lincoln, Shamira and Medeea stepped away. "I guess we did it," Lincoln said quietly, a smile on his face.

"Yes. Thank you. Thank you all," Elder Hansum laughed.

"Look at them. They look so happy," Shamira said.

"The nano bits have already balanced the Signora's brain," Medeea told them.

The younger Hansum had his arm around Guilietta, looking like he never wanted to let her go.

"I thought we were done," the older Hansum sighed, watching them. He looked back at his comrades. "I'm in this all the way. But are you sure you want to . . ." Shamira looked right at Hansum, her green eyes showing over the veil. They glistened more happily than Hansum had remembered seeing them since Kingsley's death.

"I'm all in too," Shamira assured him. "I have no regrets." She put a hand to the node on her neck and tapped it. "My temporal protection is off."

"And you two?" Hansum asked Lincoln and Medeea. "Once they go through the vortex . . ."

Lincoln looked at Medeea. It was a joint decision.

"Sweet heart?" Lincoln asked.

"This way, we get to do it all over again," she answered, *"and with all our good friends, including Guilietta."* They kissed.

"Thank you. Thank you all," Elder Hansum said, and he reached in his tunic and took off the necklace with his own temporal protector, dropping it to the ground. "Friends," he called out to the others. "It's time to go."

"Time to go to Heaven, kind angel?" the Signora asked.

The older Hansum smiled. "You could say that, dear woman. You truly could."

"Oh Agistino," the Signora said, taking her husband's arm. "Together," and the Master smiled and crossed himself.

"Friends, be not afraid of what you are about to see," Elder Hansum said. "It is but a doorway to another place. Sideways . . ."

And there, before them on the walkway, a vortex formed. But, instead of being vertical, it was horizontal, so they could all walk through it. A wind gusted and sucked in leaves and vapor from the clouds. The

Signora smiled broadly, gripping Agistino with one arm, her bonnet with the other.

"The stairway to Heaven," she chimed.

Guilietta was staring, almost trembling, at the sight of the whirl-wind. The older Hansum watched the light of it dance off her radiant features. Looking at her, he was almost frozen with awe, a softness in his eyes that bespoke a century of devotion.

"I'd almost forgotten . . ." the old Hansum began to say.

"Forgotten what, elder?" young Hansum asked.

"So beautiful. So . . ." Then he shook his head. "Please, enter now the Sands of Time."

"Come, my darling," Hansum said to Guilietta, gently pulling her by the hand. She held back, her lips slightly parted and worry in her eyes.

"It's safe. I wouldn't do anything to harm you," the older Hansum said, smiling.

As Guilietta passed him, she stopped.

"Signor, your eyes, they're so much like . . ." The old man leaned forward and whispered in Guilietta's ear.

"Hush. Tell me in fifty years. Now hurry."

"Aren't you leading the way?" the young Hansum asked.

"No, you go ahead. I'll be staying here for now. But first, let me look one more time upon the faces of my youth. The faces of all youth. Youth and courage. Youth and possibilities. Youth in a world where all is con-ceivable," and the older Hansum stepped back. "Farewell. Take care of each other."

The older Hansum watched his younger self step forward, smiling encouragement to Guilietta. As they stepped into the whirling vortex, one of Guilietta's hands was holding the younger Hansum's, the other was touching her belly, where the baby lay. The older Hansum beamed and was now truly content. The della Cappas followed into the vortex, walking happily to their own new futures, to the old Hansum's soon-to-be-extinguished past. But he didn't care.

"The meaning of life is to give your life meaning," the old man said to himself. "This I have done," and he smiled. Hansum turned to Lin-coln, Shamira and Medeea. "Good bye old friends. I guess we'll see each other on the other side of tomorrow."

The old Lincoln and Medeea stood in an embrace, both smiling at Hansum, and then they locked eyes with each other, making the other the last thing they would see. Shamira stood with her hands clutched in front of her, a smile of joy and awe on her face. With the roar of the vortex in his ears, Hansum's skin flushed with excitement and expectation, content in his submission to a successful sacrifice.

As the young Hansum's foot started to step out of the other side of the time portal, the elderly Hansum began to laugh with anticipation and felt his emotions peaking — his final emotions. He raised his hand to his cheek, in a gesture of awe, but as the two parts of his body came together, they passed through each other, as if vapor. Through fading eyes, he saw his younger self almost into the future. And as they became more solid there, he felt himself passing into nothingness, into a never-was-ness.

"Love has won," he whispered, "Love has . . ."

Coda

As countless generations of humans into the future watched this new scene play out on their Mists of Times Chronicles, it was like Hansum's parents' home was in a little snow globe setting. For thousands of years, what became known as *The Tragical Tale of Romero and Guilietta,* became one of the most watched History Camp stories. And at the end of it, Hansum always walked into his family's home with the beautiful young woman on his arm, presenting her to his parents.

"Mother, Father, Charlene, this is Guilietta. She is my wife," he said, his voice echoing in the cosmos.

Men and women, forward through the ages, watched as the two young people wed again in the 24th-century. It was not an elopement this time. Hansum's parents were present, as well as Guilietta's. Bringing the Signora and Master della Cappa forward in time, curing the Signora of her mental illness and giving them places in the future, seemed to work out. The History Camp Time Travel Council ruled it didn't change the time in between, so no harm was done. And Agistino was a huge help at the 14th-century Verona History Camp.

"Congratulations Guilietta," the sixteen-year-old Shamira said, as she embraced Guilietta at the crowded wedding reception. A proud Hansum of eighteen looked on, standing next to the fifteen-year-old best man, Lincoln.

"Thank you, sister," Guilietta replied, smiling radiantly.

"Oh, it's hard to hug you now," Shamira laughed, stepping back. "Can I touch?"

"Per favore, please," Guil answered. Shamira put her hand on Guilietta's beautiful large belly.

"It's harder than I thought. Oh, it kicked," and everyone laughed.

"How are you enjoying your art history courses, Sham?" Hansum asked, and a wicked smile came to Shamira's lips.

"Oh, it's been . . . very gratifying," she said waving someone over. Guilietta looked up as a shadow fell across them. "This is someone I met in class. He's a sculptor and from the 26th-century." A large hand extended to Guilietta and then Hansum. The other went tenderly onto Shamira's shoulder.

"Hello. I'm Kingsley."

> "Ah, there you are, Lincoln,"
> Arimus called.
> "I've found you at last."

"Oh darn, and I've been trying to hide from you, Arimus," Lincoln kidded. "You're the guy who put us through all that torture."

> "A student often calls the lessons of life a trial,
> But as you grow, there'll be no denial.
> Those same struggles are what makes one interesting."

"Arimus, did you find out who that Elder Yu was?" Hansum asked.

> "No, not yet. It still remains a mystery.
> I went back to retrieve you at the Arena
> and you were already gone . . . history."

"Strange. So strange," Hansum said. "Whoever he was," Hansum said looking to his Guilietta, "we have a lot to thank him for."

"Si, God bless Elder Yu," Guilietta said. "He seemed like a man of love. His eyes reminded me of yours, husband. Everything reminds me of you."

"The same here, Guilietta. I guess that's what love really is," and they kissed.

"Oh, there they go again," Lincoln complained. "You won't find me falling like that. Never. Ever. Okay, now that you found me, Arimus, what else ya got to make me even more interesting than this adventure already has?"

"Oh yes, of course, my young mind-delver,"
and Arimus reached into his robes and took out
a tiny glass tear vessel.
"Lincoln, please give your greetings to Medeea."

"Oh, zippy," Lincoln said, smiling at the bottle in his hand. "And yet another big adventure is about to begin."

-the end-

BONUS FEATURE
BACK STORY of the futuristic world
you'll find in *The Verona Trilogy*
by Lory Kaufman

Thank you for reading **The Verona Trilogy**. I truly hope you enjoyed it.

Most futuristic novels don't give you the back story of their civilizations. They just plop the reader into the middle of the characters' lives and start the story rolling. The writer lets readers infer much of how the civilization works from what happens around the characters. I do pretty much the same thing. After all, it's the characters and the story that is important, and the quality of its telling. But behind the scenes, writers of future fiction have to work out a general history for their world to rationalize why things are the way they are. But, I thought, why not share the backstory? Some readers might find it interesting. That's what follows here.

The Verona Trilogy takes place in three time periods; the 24th and 31st-centuries, when the characters are in the future, and 14th-century Verona, Italy, when they are in the past.

While writing the first book of the trilogy, **The Lens and the Looker**, I spent months researching 14th-century Verona, and even went to modern Verona, spending days taking in the many sights. What a difference that made to my vision of the tale's telling. Many of the buildings, streets and churches have been maintained much as they were in the past, so I felt I was wandering in and seeing the same things my characters did. I wanted details to be as realistic as they could and, for me, it's the details in the research that feed and inspire my writer's imagination.

Writing about the future also took lots of research, contemplation and then creative speculation. The research had to do with subjects that are very dear to me; ecology, green politics, population studies and futurism in general. All through my contemplation and speculation, I had one mantra: what hard decisions did my characters' ancestors have to make to ensure the existence of human civilization for another ten thousand years? This would inform me what the world my characters inhabited looked like.

Because of space constraints, I am only including the Back Story of my future worlds.

It is my hope that, after reading what follows, you may wish to re-read the series. If you do, you may see many more layers to the story.

Cheers,
Lory Kaufman,
Kingston, Ontario, Canada
January 2013

Population:

The Lens and the Looker starts in 2347, the 24th-century A.C.E. (After the Common Era). At that time, I have the population of the Earth at 300,000,000, or 300 million. Let's compare that with the population of humans alive as of this writing, November 2012. The population of "Spaceship Earth" has exceeded 7,000,000,000. That's seven billion or seven-thousand million, depending on what side of the Atlantic "pond" you're on.

I work into my fictional tale that the future population of 300 million is not just a number that happened by accident. It was a deliberate figure chosen by a planetary Council of Elders. Before I explain how I came to decide on that number, I think a short preamble comparing the population in my story to the actual number of humans in our present world could be interesting and informative. After all, there's a big difference in those quantities, and if you are anything like me, it's hard to conceive of and compare numbers that high. All I see is a heck of a lot of zeros and I think it's really important that we feel these numbers in our guts.

First, let's compare by just writing them out.

Three-hundred million, or 300,000,000
then
Seven billion, or 7,000,000,000

This doesn't really illuminate the difference in size for me.

How about doing it as a percentage?

300 million is only about 4.5% of **7 billion**. That means, for every 100 people alive today, only 4 or 5 people are alive in the History Camp world of 2347. Still not making very much of an impression?

How about drawing a mental picture this way . . .

If you take a package of common computer paper and agree that the thickness of one page is equal to one person, then stack up 300 million sheets, that pile of paper would be 100,000 feet high or over 18.9 miles. (30,400 metres or 30.4 km). Wow, that's high, you say. (I'm calculating an average computer paper at about 250 pages per inch or almost 1,000 sheets per 100 cm)

But what about the population of today, the planet we all live on, right now? If you piled one piece of paper on top of another for every human alive now, the pile you would get would be over 2,300,000 feet or an amazing 550 miles high. (701,040 meters or over 700 KM) The space shuttles orbited at less than half that altitude. Getting the picture?

Here's another thought that stretches my mind, not only with population numbers but also regarding time. Until as little as 10,000 years ago it is estimated that the natural population for humans planet-wide was only 1,000,000, when we lived as hunter gatherers. That's only one million. That puny paper stack would only be 333 feet high (101.5 meters), about the height of a 30 storey building. The space shuttle was higher than that standing on its launch pad. Ten millennium ago was also the time when humans invented rudimentary farming, and that's when populations started to grow.

Why 300,000,000 was chosen as a sustainable population number:

As mentioned above, I envisioned a planetary Council of Elders determining a target number of humans that could be sustained by the ecosystem of the planet for an indefinite number of millenia. I had them choose 300,000,000. I envisaged this happening in the last years of the 21st-century, with them choosing the early 24th-century as the target time for reaching the much lowered population goal. This is the time when the first book in the series, *The Lens and the Looker*, starts.

The impetus for the drastic lowering in numbers of people lay in the many cataclysmic events I envisioned happening in the latter half of the 21st-century; the rising of the oceans, droughts that starved millions, bacterial infections that wiped out billions and wars that caused diasporas of whole populations. Refugees, like hordes of locusts, limped from continent to continent, consuming, killing and dying. Wow, this short description brings to mind many of the great dystopian novels written since the early decades of the 20th-century, such as Olaf Stapledon's *Last and First Men: A Story of the Near and Far Future,* Yevgeny Zamyatin's *We*, and Aldous Huxley's *Brave New World*. This is all after World War One when there were initial glimpses of the possibility of world domination by one ideology or another. Then, after the first atomic bombs were dropped at the end of World War Two, visionaries started writing cautionary tales about humans now possessing the ability to really destroy the planet. Dystopian literature was born!

However, in the world that I created for *The Verona Trilogy*, I have the humans of the 24th-century already past these hard times and successfully rebuilding the world. I figured there's already enough dystopian literature out there. I'm calling my genre "post-dystopian." You see, this time, humans have retained enough knowledge and wisdom to not to repeat the mistakes of the past. There was no burning of the libraries of Alexandria, the world didn't fall into religious fundamentalism or create a fascist state. No. In this world humans rose from the ashes and prospered. Why and how this happens is described under several of the headings that follow, but let me mention a few of the "norms" that I have imbedded in the psyches of my characters, even when they're spoiled kids.

1) It was recognized that for humans to survive, we must allow other species to thrive. It became a common currency of thought that there is a complex underpinning to nature, a balanced and complex web of life, in which millions of various life forms and processes support and sustain each other. For this multitude of other species to survive, humans must share planetary resources. To share planetary resources, our numbers must be lowered. The people of the future I've imagined recognize that the world their ancestors (us) lived in was literally a house of cards, one where, if too many cards were removed, the whole structure would collapse.

2) It was accepted that humankind had outstripped its biology, that is, nature could no longer keep population numbers in check. For millions of years, before we developed agriculture and medicine, a very high reproduction rate was needed for any species to survive. As I mentioned earlier, it is estimated that, as little as 10,000 years ago, there were only about 1,000,000 homo sapiens on the planet. That's when humans invented agricultural skills. Because of this, and because of other unique, adaptive qualities of our human brain, infant mortality rate steadily decreased and the average human lifespan increased. Within the blink of a galactic eye, ten-thousand years, the population of our specie's shot up to where it is as of this writing, over seven billion. That's where my imagination fast-forwards to sometime in the late 21st-century when humans finally collectively decide that, since nature can no longer control population size, if we want to survive, it will be our responsibility to control it ourselves.

3) Besides agriculture and medicine, it was recognized that every invention humans created allowed its population to grow. I include in the definition of "invention," not just technology, but also human organizations: governments, businesses, corporations, economic systems, traditional and non-traditional families, etc. It became another ingrained concept that, throughout history, and to ill effect, both technology and societal systems were progressively tweaked by the people in power to concentrate control over resources and the way people thought into fewer and fewer hands.

Some logical future thinker then determined the following: the whole of human society must turn this thinking on its head. Humankind must burn into the front of its consciousness that the purpose of inventions must be to allow populations to remain low while helping to keep the individual's quality of life high. This would not only allow the demands humans make on the planet to remain small, but also allow them to expand the ability to express themselves creatively or to just live in peace. (How they achieved this is described in the section called "Artificial Intelligences, A.I.s.")

None of these ideas are expressed explicitly in the narrative of my story. After all, it is supposed to be an exciting action adventure. However, this is an example of all the machinations a writer has to go through when world-building a future society.

"All right already, Lory," you're saying. "Get to the part where you tell us why you had your Council of Elders pick 300 million as the number of people that should be on the planet." Okay. Fair enough. Here's how I came to that very specific number . . . I made it up.

The 300 million figure in some ways seems high in relation to historical human numbers on the planet (as compared to the one million figure for before agriculture), and low compared to historical human memory, (seven billion in only 10,000 years and growing . . . and growing). However, suffice it to say that the fictitious late 21st-century elders considered that if humans could use technology to keep quality of life high, but also have as the criteria for technology that it must be designed to make a small footprint on the Earth's ecology, then a much higher number of humans could survive. The reality is that, the number could be five hundred million or it could be two hundred million, two million, five or ten million. I suppose it would all be dependent on the technology at the time. And after all, this is just fiction. But hey, I'd love to hear what readers think our human numbers should be - and why.

Artifical Intelligences (A.I.):

Some readers have asked, "Why did you give every human on the planet a companion artificial intelligence from birth?"

For me, the A.I.'s are a symbol of the fact that humans seem not to be able to work together without some faction undermining things.

"What does this have to do with artificial intelligences?" you ask. Well, as I already mentioned, by the end of the 21st-century I have humans on the brink of extinction. Plagues and bacterial infections are threatening calamity and some population centers are already collapsing. But, at the same time, human technology is also successfully creating synthetic intellects, superior to humans in many ways. (Given where we are with computer technology now, I don't think this is out of the realm of possibility.)

So, as opposed to some dystopian literature, where A.I.s rebel and dominate humans, I have chosen another road. I have artificial intelligences become the saviors of humans, though not as benignly as one might think.

I've done it like this. Each person's A.I. is with them from before birth. At first the A.I. acts as nanny to the baby and toddler, and a helper to the parents. Then the artificial intelligence takes on the role of tutor when the person becomes a youth, then an adolescent, watching out for that individual and monitoring his or her progress. This role changes as the human grows into adulthood. Like a loving aunt or uncle today, the A.I. changes into a life-long friend and confidant. By constant and gentle vigilance, A.I.s allow humans to find their own path in life, as long as their actions don't put at risk the long-term safety of society or that of the other life forms on the planet.

So, humans have ceded ultimate control to their A.I.s, which have become both the "philosopher kings" and the "protector class" of humankind. They are a benevolent police force, making sure that small factions of people can't sabotage society's long-term survival for personal or tribal purposes, which, when I think of it, seems to be among the most repeated themes in human history.

Another very important fact to understand is that the A.I.s do very little of the actual work for humans. It's not like "The Jetsons" or like some cheesy science fiction movie where people walk around in identical plastic suits and use mass-produced, computer-made products. In the world where History Camps exist, individual craftsmanship and self-sufficiency is the new way of things and the norm. Clothing is made by individuals and small, local shops, not by large corporations. The purpose for A.I.s is not to provide for humans, but to protect, love and nourish them — and the protection is mostly from ourselves and our own natures.

After finishing the first drafts of **The Lens and the Looker**, I realized mine was not such a new idea in science fiction. While watching a rerun of the 1951 movie **The Day the Earth Stood Still**, I saw how the race of aliens, represented by the character "Platu," had recognized their inability to control themselves as a culture and given control of their long-term wellbeing to a race of "robots," such as the one in the movie named "Gort." I can't honestly say whether I reinvented the idea or subconsciously adopted (stole) the concept from watching the movie as a child. I suspect the latter, but it really doesn't matter. Orson Scott Card does a similar thing in his new series **Pathfinder**, Robert J. Sawyer in his **W.W.W.** series, but both in very different ways.

As humans, we shouldn't be too hard on ourselves for being aggressive and individually greedy. Any creature that had to fight its way out of the primeval ooze and survive by consuming others and protecting its offspring by destroying and consuming the family units of other creatures over billions of years cannot be expected to change its instincts quickly, if ever. Was it a mistake of nature to give us an intelligence that would cause us to outstrip our biology and not be regulated by the immediate environment? Was it a divine plan (or joke on the creator's part) to give humans the ability to destroy ourselves and much of the planet's life forms much more quickly than the evolutionary forces that usually bring down a species? At this point, we can't know. (Hey, that just gave me an idea for another story.)

One last thing on this topic. I have in my little brain the idea that, in some future story, I'm going to show that in the 31st-century, humans are gaining the ability to control themselves and thus the one-to-one necessity of A.I.s to humans is being lowered. I don't know if I'll do that because people have changed culturally or because they'll have actually have bred out of themselves this need to dominate others to an extreme. We shall see.

Time Travel:

At the beginning of **The Lens and the Looker,** humans in the 24th-century can't time travel. They can in the 31st-century and a History Camp counselor from that future, Arimus, comes back and kidnaps three spoiled hard cases: Hansum, Shamira and Lincoln. He takes them back to a time when there is no social safety net and he abandons them. That's when the fun and adventure starts.

So, as a writer whose stories depend on time travel, do I actually believe it's possible? Not in the way it's used by me or most speculative fiction authors. Am I suggesting that in the foreseeable future it's possible? I used to believe it, but now I'm not sure. It's impossible to be certain about things like that.

Then why do I use time travel? Well, it's a great literary device that allows characters from different times to be thrown into the same arena of life to compare notes and knock heads - and the more outrageous the situation the better. You see, for me the art of writing (and the fun) is to make the impossible seem real and truly plausible; to craft words in a way that the reader will want to suspend disbelief. Also, time travel works especially well for me since my interest in doing these stories is to be part of a discussion about what type of world the human race will plan for the future. Time travel allows me to compare the past, as well as the future, and then I hope some readers will decide to live the changes they want to see happen in the world. Hey, like Arimus said, ". . . what's life mean, without an impossible dream?"

One last thought about time travel and the one thing I am certain about. We shouldn't hold our breath about it coming soon enough to help fix and save the world. The older I get, the more obvious it becomes that we're on our own for that.

The Steady-State Economy:

This is a bit of a catch-all section. Because of space constraints, I have included a few brief thoughts that could each have their own sections. I'm hoping these thoughts will be expanded in a longer version of a "Back Story" to my books, or on my website, in the future.

In the 24th-century of **The Verona Trilogy**, I created something called a steady-state economy. In our present economic system there must be continual growth and expansion, which leads to the continual consumption of natural resources and, as a repercussion, the continual growth of populations. At the present time we cannot have one without the other.

In a steady-state economy, I envisage scientists having determined (and the A.I.s confirming unbiasedly) the amount of calories of energy that would be safe for three hundred million people to extract from the planet without interfering with the delicate and very long-term balance of nature.

These units of energy are then converted into "money" (like gold and silver was used as a standard in the past) and divided among the population as a guaranteed income.

I retain "money" in this future because I see it as probably the greatest of human inventions. It has allowed humans to engage in complex bartering and include knowledge and service to be part of economies. So, where do the phrase, "Money is the root of all evil," and other related clichés come from? While money has the potential to distribute the wealth of a community in some kind of equitable fashion, it also has the potential to centralize power into fewer and fewer hands over time. That's where our world is at now.

However, in my future world, after individuals use what resources they need for food, clothing, shelter, transportation and their other general needs, they can invest the rest of their share of the world's bounty with people who have the talent and ambition to create technologies, goods and services that other people want. If these technologies are innovative and use smaller amounts of resources than previously, then the surplus energy (which is money) is their profit, allowing them to have more latitude to be more creative and innovative.

So, this is not a nanny state. It has recognized that it is vital to allow people to have outlets for their creative energies and ambitions, whatever they are, (business, entrepreneurial, technological, scientific, artistic) But it has also recognized that the natural world is finite and the rest of the ecosystem of the planet has to be taken into account on society's balance sheet. This is the one line the ultra-ambitious can't overstep. That's where the A.I.s come in.

Finally, I did an online search on a phrase I thought I invented, "steady-state economy." What popped up was a group of professors, economists and environmentalists who have already started an association on this topic. So, it's started. We shall see where it goes. Look it up if you want.

Elders as opposed to super consumers:

There's a clichéd phrase in our culture, "Those with the most toys when they die, win." Of course, the originator of the phrase is definitely saying this ironically, but so many people in our world live like this. As a baby boomer, I was part of the Yuppie (Young, Upwardly-mobile Professional) generation in the 1970's and 80s. As boomers age, we all now aspire to be Woopies. (Well Off Old People).

But seriously, so many people today have lost hope in the future, or more dishearteningly, they don't even know we're supposed to be having a discussion about it. In my 24th-century future, as opposed to wanting to be rich and decadent, people aspire to be elders. These are experienced leaders in the community who accept the responsibility and are given the authority to keep society strong and steady. After all, who wouldn't want to be an elder when along with that role comes the respect and admiration for helping keep the world in a shape that will allow humans to continue existing on planet Earth for thousands of years?

Education in the future:

As everyone has a guaranteed income in the future I envisage, schools are no longer factories to train industry's workers at society's cost. Everyone receives a classical education, including sciences, maths, technology basics, history, arts, crafts, food production, etc. As people get older, the ambitious ones will specialize in their interests. And, as mentioned a bit earlier, regional craftsmanship reemerges for clothing, household goods, building, food, etc. Most people will be happy to lead healthy lives, able to express themselves through their talents, raise their children and be part of a community. Progress is measured very differently in this world.

Why the planet's average community has sixty people:

One of the fun things I have happening in this future world is people living in small communities of 30 to 60 people. Anthropologists have determined that this was the size of the majority of human settlements up to around 10,000 BCE. It's a natural number then, one that allows survival of a group. It gives enough variety of personalities and talents to fulfill the group's needs: hunters, gatherers, artisans, men, women, leaders and followers. I envisioned a good portion of people in the future choosing to go back to living in these smaller communities. However, in my future model of modernity, because we've been able to retain a very high level of technology, people don't live lives of subsistence. They don't live lives of opulence either, but ones in which they are comfortable, produce most of their own food, and are able to communicate with and contribute to the rest of the world. This goes hand in hand with the steady-state economy, where growth is not necessary or seen to be good. Progress is now the development of ideas and the ability to continually do more with less.

Why New York City in the 24th-century only has thirty thousand people in it, and why it isn't on Manhattan Island anymore?

Large cities were necessary, in part, so people could be safe from "others"; *other* tribes, then *other* city states, and then *other* civilizations. As they grew, their leaders harnessed the populations in different ways to grow further. Cities were also the engines of economic growth and growth was seen as desirable. They centralized resources and production, allowing surpluses, which eventually became known as profit. And the natural world? Up until recently, it was treated as an inexhaustible storehouse of materials, just waiting for humans to put it to *good use*. In the new economy of the early 24th-century, where the physical size of a city doesn't matter and the planetary population has diminished to a thirtieth of that of early 21st century Earth, cities were no longer necessary or desirable.

I gave New York City the arbitrary size of 30,000. That was to show that what we now think of a small city in the early 21st century could once again be seen as a large center. But it's a large center not for industry or commerce, but for culture and education. It also acts as a meeting place, when online conferencing just won't do. Even in the future, some things are best done face to face.

I have Manhattan Island underwater. Why? With our glaciers and icepacks melting and our planet going into a warming cycle, (arguably sooner than it would have because of humans burning fossil fuels) the oceans are rising. In this future world, the coastlines of the continents have changed again, just like they've always done over long stretches of time. I thought it would be engaging to show one of the liveliest cities of our civilization now resting with the ancient ports of Alexandria under water.

It could be interesting to note here that, at the height of the last ice age, about 18,000 years ago, ice sheets many **miles** thick extended south of Seattle, Washington, Chicago, Illinois and even New York City in North America. In Europe and Asia, ice sheets covered all of Greenland, most of Great Britain and the Irelands, all the Scandinavian countries, the northern part of Germany, Poland, Belarus, and much of what is now northwest Russia. Because so much of the world's water was locked in the ice, sea levels were as much as 400 feet lower than they are today. So, the world as we know it is not as permanent and perpetual as most people in our modern cultures think. If we are to survive, we must understand the cycles of our environment.

Why I chose the Haudenosaunee, or the Iroquois Confederation, as a positive 24th century example in *The Loved and the Lost*:

When constructing a world for **The Verona Trilogy**, I wanted to show that a future civilization in harmony with the planet doesn't necessarily have to be monolithic, or a single type of culture. There is variety, experimentation and growth, although the philosophy and laws for society's long term survival still prevail. So, while you'll find people who live in micro-communities of around sixty and in cities in the low thousands, you also will find regions like Haudenosaunee.

I chose this society because I was so impressed when I studied how it had been organized. Anthropology and oral histories are at odds about when the League of Six Nations, or The Iroquois Confederation was formed, somewhere between the mid 12th and 15th century. But what is not in dispute is that there did exist an advanced, egalitarian democracy, where individual and group rights were balanced and heavily entrenched in the culture. Five and then six native nations, including the Mohawk, Oneida, Onondaga, Cayuga, the Seneca nations and, then in 1722, the Tuscarora, banded together under the vision of a man named Deganawida. He was known as the Great Peace Maker, a Christ or Buddha-like figure who convinced warring tribes to come together in peace. The region of what is now New York State, Ohio and the Saint Lawrence Valley of Southern Ontario and Quebec held millions of this native population. Although still a culture that had not progressed far technologically, it transformed millions of acres of land into a sophisticated balance of field crops, hunting grounds and areas of trees selected for food and housing materials. It also developed trade routes and built large settlements of long houses.

But what I wanted to showcase was the political system. It was one where the leaders followed their populations, where the clan mothers picked the leaders, and everyone contributed to the general welfare of the group. Individuals in this culture had a measure of personal freedom that caused many of the newly-arrived, indentured European settlers to run away from their masters and join the natives. It is said that the American constitution was partly inspired by the Haudenosaunee civilization, although the American Founding Fathers didn't quite get it right with their highly centralized government.

History Camps:

I won't speak much about History Camps here, because I think their operations are pretty well described within the stories. The one example I use in **The Verona Trilogy** is "History Camp, Verona 1347." It's a very close approximation of Verona in medieval times.

What I do want to enlarge upon here is that, with a steady state economy, people could dedicate their whole careers to building places like this. With no corporate, short-term profit motive, many men and women could find it interesting and challenging to recreate the skills of masons, carpenters, weavers, millers, butchers and the other hundreds of other trades in other times, keeping alive these skills of the various ages. And because they would have to interact with young people who came, not as visitors, but to "live" the lives of young people from the past, everyone working in History Camps would also require the skills to work effectively with their charges. It would be incumbent upon them to help instill in each young person the benefits of modernity by showing them what humans had to endure in the past.

Although it's not stated anywhere in *The Verona Trilogy*, my future books will reveal that there are more than fifty History Camps around the 24th-century planet, reflecting many major cultures from every epoch in time.

The Mists of Time Machine

One of my inspirations for writing this series was the old saying, "Those who do not learn from history are condemned to repeat it," and time travel was a way that I could have my characters see and experience many historical events. However, when I came up with the idea that people would naturally send cameras back in time to watch past events as well, it was a short leap to having whole populations watch them. It would be like us watching video programs on a television or computer screen. Along with History Camps, Mists of Times programs became a way of reinforcing the future population's understanding of history and helping them avoid the mistakes of the past. Of course, I imagined a three-dimensional holographic projection and that's just a lot of fun. But wouldn't it be amazing if something like this could someday be real?

Why some people in the future speak in verse:

I'm told that English is the language of business, French of diplomacy and Italian of love. The point being, speaking and thinking a particular languages produces a bias in the way we understand the world.

I have some people from the future speaking in verse to show how, in a world where there is a steady-state way of life, although progress happens, it's not at the expense of everything that makes life worth living. People's greatest concerns then are about quality of life, philosophy, family, love, self-awareness and self-improvement. My intention in having someone from the far future speaking in verse is then to show that it's ideas and emotions, the more esoteric things that life, that are important to them.

As well, writing the Arimus character in verse was an enjoyable challenge. I'm thinking that in the next series an elder from the future will speak in blank verse instead of rhyme. I actually planned to have Arimus speak in blank verse, but for some reason he didn't want to. As much as I tried, his speech insisted on coming out as rhyming couplets for the most part. Hey, I'm only the writer and must do what the muse comands.

More post-dystopian futuristic stories from different eras are coming down the pipe in the future. In the meantime, now that you've read this BACK STORY, you may wish to reread *The Verona Trilogy* in full or part. You may see things differently, now that you understand a bit more of the world the characters inhabit.

Next in the series is a book that is tentatively entitled *The Olive Tree*. It is an adventure that involves a boy, Tammond, from the 24th century A.C.E. (After the Common Era) and a girl, Enheduanna, (Eanna) born almost 5,000 years earlier in the 24th century B.C.E. (Before the Common Era) The girl's father is King Sargon the Great, the first man to rule what could be called an empire. And the mother of the girl? She is a time traveler from the 31st-century A.C.E. Talk about dual citizenship for the girl. Tammond and Eanna also find they have more in common than ties to the future. And who knows. You may even see some of your favorite characters from previous stories making an appearance.

To keep up to date on what's happening with any future stories, updates to the BACK STORY, blogs from myself and comments from readers, you are invited to visit my website at www.lorykaufman.com. See you there.

About the Author

Lory Kaufman lives and works in Kingston, Ontario, Canada. His post-dystopian novels and their positive bent come from his interest in environmentalism, sustainability, population studies, history, and wanting to have a serious discussion about the future. Plus, he likes to have a good time.